The Dressmaker

BENITA BROWN

headline

First published in 2007 by
HEADLINE PUBLISHING GROUP

First published in paperback in 2008 by
HEADLINE PUBLISHING GROUP

2

Cataloguing in Publication Data is available from the British Library

ISBN 978 0 7553 3474 2

Typeset in Centaur by Avon DataSet Ltd,
Bidford-on-Avon, Warwickshire

Printed and bound in Great Britain by Clays Ltd, St Ives plc

Headline's ... and
recyclable pr... forests.
The logging ... rm to
the e...

To Norman,
my children and their spouses,
and all my grandchildren,
especially the new arrival, Maria Aurelia

Part One

A Mother's Dreams

Chapter One

December 1888

Melissa pulled the eiderdown up and tried to get back to sleep. She didn't know what had awakened her but something was different. She raised her head and peered over the edge of the bedclothes. An eerie light filled the room, almost as bright as daylight. But it could not be morning. Surely she had come to bed no more than an hour or two ago?

Now thoroughly awake, Melissa reached for the shawl lying on the bed and pulled it towards her. She sat up and drew it round her shoulders as quickly as she could. Then, with her arms wrapped around her body, she kept very still and listened. Nothing. After a moment or two she pushed the bedclothes aside and swung her legs over the edge of the bed. Spurred on by curiosity and a vague sense of dread, she rose and hurried across to the window. She pulled the curtain aside to gaze out on a world of cold beauty.

A light fall of snow covered the road and the gardens of the small but respectable terrace houses in West Jesmond. The rooftops sparkled under a frosty moon. Melissa smiled with delight. If the snow lasted just a few days there would be a white Christmas, and the streets and brightly lit shops would look as cheery as the pictures on the greetings cards.

She wondered if the snow was deep enough to allow sledging in the nearby park. But her smile faded a little when she realised that she would probably be considered too old for such games. She didn't even look like a child. She was tall, taller than her mother. She had been fourteen the previous February, and her body was already taking on the graceful appearance of young womanhood. She knew she appeared to be older than her years, which was something she regretted.

She gazed out for a while longer and then the cold drove her back to bed. But even though she had solved the mystery of the strange light, she still could not settle. She lay listening to the silence. Then she sat up. That was what was wrong. The silence. Any noise in the street would be muffled by the snow, but that was not what Melissa was listening for.

Her mother slept in the room next to hers. Emmeline Dornay was a poor sleeper and Melissa's sleep was more often than not punctuated by her mother's restless movements and her coughing. Tonight she had heard nothing and yet she must have been awake for half an hour at least. The only explanation was that her mother wasn't there. Unless . . . no, Melissa pushed the fearsome thought into the well of dread that lay deep inside her.

Melissa got out of bed again and this time reached for her robe and her slippers. Her mother had been working late to finish the ball gowns for two of her regular clients, Mrs Winterton and her daughter, Gwendolyn. The order had come with little time to spare but Lilian Winterton, so rich, so gay and so charming, had persuaded the dressmaker to take on the task, reminding her that the Wintertons, mother and daughter, were good customers and promising that there would be plenty of work in the future.

Melissa had wanted to stay up and help, but just before midnight Emmeline had insisted that her daughter go to bed.

'Off you go, Cinderella,' she'd said, 'or you might find you've turned into a pumpkin when the clock strikes twelve!'

'Oh, Mama, that's not what happened,' Melissa said, but she looked up from her work to find her mother laughing.

'I know, I know,' Emmeline Dornay had told her, 'but there's not much more to do and I want you to get your beauty sleep.'

'You need your sleep too.'

'I promise I won't be long.'

But now Melissa could only suppose that her mother had not yet come up to bed and was still working quietly in the front parlour that served as their sewing room – their 'salon', as her mother liked to call it. At least she hoped that was the explanation. She decided she would go and help – no matter how much her mother might object.

After opening her bedroom door she paused, trying to remember exactly which floorboard it was that creaked. She didn't want to awaken Miss Bullock. Their landlady slept in the back bedroom. She was deaf as a post when it suited her and yet she claimed that the slightest noise after bedtime disturbed her sleep. When Melissa and her mother came upstairs they had to say good night in whispers otherwise the old lady would complain the next day and hint that it was time she found less bothersome tenants.

It would not do to annoy Miss Bullock. The rent was reasonable and the rooms were perfect for them. There was room for Emmeline Dornay's established dressmaking business and, as the old lady hardly ever used the dining room, preferring to eat by the cosy warmth of the range in the kitchen, Melissa and her mother had that room to themselves also. They could take their meals away from the workroom for an hour and gossip without Miss Bullock glaring at them or cupping her ear and telling them to speak up.

They had to share the bathroom and the kitchen with Miss Bullock, but long ago Emmeline had offered to cook for the landlady when they were making their own meals. The old lady appreciated the offer; especially as she never contributed to the cost of the food.

Melissa managed to avoid the loose floorboard and she opened the door of her mother's bedroom as quietly as she could. The room was filled with the same cool blue-white light of the reflected snow. In fact it was even brighter as the curtains had not been closed. As she had suspected, her mother's bed was empty. She felt the small knot of anxiety begin to unravel and she closed the door.

The landing was cold with the draught coming up from the passageway, and Melissa shivered as she crept downstairs. The cold struck up even through the soles of her slippers. She was chilled to the bone by the time she reached the door of the front parlour.

At least the room was warm. A small fire burned in the grate, its glow providing most of the light. The gas lamp overhead had been turned low. Melissa shut the door quietly and looked at the day bed where her mother lay sleeping with her head on the cushions that Melissa had embroidered with pansies when she was only ten years old.

The rug, which had been covering Emmeline Dornay, had slipped to the floor and Melissa picked it up. Then she realised that she had been holding her breath until she saw the soft rise and fall that told her that her mother was breathing easily. But, even in sleep, her mother looked exhausted.

The light from the fire cast rosy hues into the room and yet her mother's complexion was as pale as parchment. Her long chestnut hair had lost its lustrous shine. Emmeline had always been small-boned and dainty, but of late she looked more and more fragile; like a china doll that could easily be broken if care was not taken. But her constant fatigue had not stopped her from working as hard as ever, and as Melissa arranged the rug carefully over her mother's slender form she was overcome by a fierce surge of love.

Blinking back hot tears, she turned to look at the two dressmaking dummies, standing by the worktable. One of them wore the evening gown her mother had made for Lilian Winterton. The Parma violet silk shone in the flickering light; the moiré pattern glimmering as if it were already moving and swaying to the rhythms of a waltz.

Mrs Winterton had pored over the fashion magazines that Emmeline kept and had chosen a gown with a fitted bodice and scooped neckline – 'To show my diamonds to their best advantage!' she had exclaimed.

She had insisted on the exaggerated puffed sleeves but, thankfully, had decided against a bustle. Emmeline was sorry that bustles had come back into fashion. She'd told Melissa that in her opinion the earlier version, all deep frills and flounces, which had been fashionable when she had been a child, made society women look like elaborately draped pieces of upholstery.

This second version of the bustle, introduced in Paris – where else? – was altogether more uncompromising. With fewer frills and furbelows it jutted straight out like a table top and, in Emmeline's opinion, made the women who wore them look ungainly. 'They look like the back end of a pantomime horse!' she'd said, and she and Melissa had shared a moment of laughter.

Mrs Winterton had at first been attracted to this latest fashion but Melissa's clever mother had drawn the talk round to the music and the dancing, and soon had her client thinking it was her own idea that the bustle would restrict her movements on the dance floor. So Mrs Winterton had settled for a flowing gored skirt, but she had won the battle over the deep purple lace and, much against her inclination, Emmeline had added rows of fussy flounces to the front of the dress. That was what had kept her up so late. That and the alterations she had agreed to make to Gwendolyn's gown.

When Melissa had gone reluctantly to bed the younger woman's gown had been on the other body form. Now it lay on the worktable. She went to examine it. Cut in the same style as that of her mother, Gwendolyn Winterton's ball gown was made from creamy white satin and, apart from the exaggerated puff sleeves, it was unembellished. There were no frills, no lace, no flounces, and this was the way Mrs Winterton had wanted it.

Gwendolyn had complained. She'd wanted something fancier, but her mother had been adamant. 'You are young and beautiful but as yet you are unsophisticated – no, darling, don't frown, that is not a criticism. That is your strength. I want you to look fresh and . . . innocent.'

'I'm eighteen.' Gwendolyn's frown deepened to a scowl, her peaches-and-cream complexion flushing a dull red. 'You want me to look plain in comparison to you,' she'd said. 'You want to be belle of the ball, as usual.'

'Gwendolyn, how could I ever be the belle of the ball when you are there?' Mrs Winterton's smile was genuinely affectionate.

Her daughter's sulky expression softened a little. 'But that dress is just like my school party frock.'

Her mother looked at the dress critically. 'Well, maybe you are right,' she said. 'Perhaps the gown is a little too young for you. I tend to forget that you are no longer my darling schoolgirl. Maybe our dear, clever Emmeline can think of something to liven it up a little. A little passementerie, perhaps?'

Emmeline Dornay had promised to do her best although any trimmings on such a classic gown would have to be applied with a light hand. The Winterton women had left with peace restored between them.

Melissa examined Gwendolyn's ball gown now. At first she thought nothing had been done but, when she looked closer, she saw that her mother had begun to sew a delicate pattern of seed pearls and gold bugle beads around the neckline, and here and there were tiny rosebuds made from curls of white satin. This was exhausting work. No doubt Emmeline Dornay had decided to have an hour or two's rest and then start early in the morning in order to have the work finished before the Wintertons returned for the final fitting.

Melissa glanced at her mother and saw that she was still deeply asleep. She moved quietly to the fireplace and added coals to the fire. She arranged them carefully; she did not want it to blaze up noisily. Back at the worktable she lit the oil lamp, then sat down and examined the pattern on Gwendolyn's ball gown. It only took a minute for her to work out exactly what her mother had in mind. She took up the needle and thread.

Her concentration was so intense that she did not notice the hours passing. The window was draped with rich burgundy brocade trimmed with gold. Emmeline liked the room to look stylish in order to impress her customers. But the expensive, lined curtains, as well as being fashionable, were heavy enough to help keep the room warm and to exclude all light. So Melissa didn't realise that morning had come until she heard the rattle of the churns on the milk cart and the crunch of its wheels on the snow as it made its way to the dairy at the bottom of the street.

By the time the work was finished Melissa's shoulders were aching and her eyes were stinging. She rose from the worktable and went quietly to the window, pulling the curtain aside a little. She sighed with disappointment. The snow was already melting and treading into slush as grey hunched forms made their way to work. She let the curtain fall and, looking round, she saw that her mother was still sleeping.

Melissa moved silently to the fireplace and lifted the kettle from the side of the hearth, judged that it had enough water in it and put it on the trivet. Then she left the room and hurried along the passage to the kitchen at the back of the house. When she opened the door she was met by a sudden blast of cold air. Mrs Sibbet had just arrived and was in the act of closing the door that led to the back yard.

'Hello, hinny, you're up sharp,' Martha Sibbet said as she placed a jug of milk on the table. It was her job to call at the dairy each morning and buy the milk for the day. 'Couldn't you sleep?' she asked.

She removed her shabby coat and hung it on the back of the kitchen door. Martha Sibbet was Miss Bullock's daily maid of all work. She came in early to clean the range and get the fire going before scrubbing floors, sweeping, dusting, preparing the vegetables, or whatever was needed.

Mrs Sibbet looked much older than her thirty-six years and had her own large family to look after so she was always in a hurry to get through her assigned tasks and go home. But she did her best because she was grateful for the money and could not afford to lose her job.

She was pleased that Mrs Dornay had told her not to bother with the front parlour as she and Melissa would prefer to clean and tidy their workroom themselves. This was partly due to consideration but mostly because Emmeline did not want anyone interfering with the swathes of material or her paper patterns; especially as Martha's hands, even after she had just washed them, seemed to be permanently ingrained with grime.

Mrs Sibbet sat down on a chair at the kitchen table to remove her boots. Long ago Miss Bullock had told her that she must not wear her dirty, clumsy footwear in the house, and the poor woman had actually been working in a pair of holey old socks with her toes pushing through until Melissa's mother gave her some of her own cast-off and neatly darned stockings and a pair of cloth-lined, embroidered carpet slippers.

'Eeh, what a treat!' Mrs Sibbet had said when she'd first put the slippers on and performed a comic pirouette. 'It's like walking on velvet – not that I've ever had that pleasure!' And she'd laughed out loud.

'Well, then, pet,' she said now as she stood up and tied her pinafore around her angular body, 'what's got you up this early?' Then she answered her own question: 'The cold, I'll be bound. It's perishing out there although it's not quite cold enough for the snow to lie long. I'll get the fire going straight off and you can make your breakfast.'

'It's all right. I'll boil a kettle on the fire in the parlour and make a pot of tea in there. I've just come for the bread and butter,' Melissa told her.

'That's a good lass. You look after your mam, divven't you? She's lucky to hev you.'

'And I'm lucky to have her.'

'Yes, pet, you are.' The kindly woman looked solemn for a moment. Then she shrugged and made an effort to smile. 'But, hawway,' she said, 'this won't buy the bairn a new bonnet. I'll give you a hand. What do you want? Bread? Butter? That nice little jar of honey? Shall I slice the loaf for you?'

'No, that's all right.'

She took what was left of yesterday's loaf from the stone crock in the pantry and cut several slices. The baker would call soon with a fresh loaf but this one would do for toast.

While she was occupied, Mrs Sibbet took the tray from its place beside the dresser and put it on the table. She poured some of the milk into a small jug and placed it next to Emmeline's rose-patterned teapot while Melissa took what she wanted from the larder. By the time Melissa left the kitchen Martha Sibbet was on her knees cleaning out the grate.

'Best hev things shipshape before the old termagant comes down,' she said with an anxious glance at the clock on the mantel shelf. Then she turned to look at Melissa and covered her lips with a sooty chilblained hand. 'Eeh, divven't tell Miss Bullock I called her that, will you, pet?'

Melissa smiled and shook her head. 'Of course not.'

She balanced the tray on one hip as she shut the door behind her.

Martha Sibbet paused from her labours for a moment and thought about her life.

Her husband had never earned enough to keep their growing brood of bairns and that was why she was here, charring for Miss Bullock, who never seemed to be pleased with anything. Thank goodness for gentle little Mrs Dornay, who had shown her kindness in so many ways: giving her leftovers from their table and even making up clothes for the bairns with remnants of material. Working for Miss Bullock wouldn't be anywhere near so agreeable when Mrs Dornay had . . .

The good woman shook her head in an attempt to rid herself of unwelcome thoughts. She began to rake the ashes out vigorously. She mustn't think like that. Mrs Dornay was frail, it was true, but sometimes femmer little bodies like that could hold out for years if they just took care of themselves and didn't put too much strain on their hearts. She hoped that would prove the case; not just for her own sake but for that poor little lass, Melissa, who loved her mother dearly and despite being almost grown up and clever with it, was still too young to be left an orphan.

When Emmeline Dornay opened her eyes she felt disorientated. Was she in bed? She didn't remember coming upstairs. After a second or two, she realised she was fully clothed and her limbs were stiff. She turned over and a cushion fell on to the floor. She looked down at it and frowned as she tried to marshal her exhausted wits.

A cushion not a pillow . . . I'm on the day bed . . . I'm still downstairs . . .why?

Emmeline raised her head and caught the flicker of a movement near the fireplace. She squeezed her eyes tight shut to clear them of sleep and opened them to see Melissa kneeling by the fire, her long dark hair hanging down her back; her beautiful face was illumined by the soft glow of the flames. Her profile is like that of a Grecian lady on an antique vase, Emmeline thought as she puzzled over what her daughter could be doing.

As if aware that she was being observed, Melissa sat back on her heels, turned her head and smiled. 'Good morning,' she said.

Emmeline now saw that Melissa was toasting bread with the long toasting fork held over but not too close to the flames. Behind Melissa the tray was resting on the ottoman and on the tray were cups and saucers, milk, a dish of butter, a jar of honey, and a rack already filled with slices of toast.

'I thought we'd have breakfast by the fire,' Melissa said as she put the last slice of toast in the rack. Then she opened the caddy and spooned tea into the teapot.

'Be careful, darling,' Emmeline said when Melissa took the quilted pot holder from its hook at the end of the mantel shelf and reached for the kettle.

'Really, Mama,' Melissa said as she poured boiling water into the teapot, 'I'm not a child.'

'Yes, you are,' Emmeline said so quietly that her daughter did not hear her. You are my darling only child, she thought, and the fact that one day soon you may have to fend for yourself haunts all my waking hours.

Emmeline's eyes filled with tears and she blinked them away, wiping her cheeks surreptitiously with her lawn handkerchief. Then the significance of what Melissa had said came home to her.

'Breakfast!' she said, and she sat upright, causing the rug to fall to the floor in her haste. 'For goodness' sake, Melissa, what time is it?' Her glance flew to the clock on the mantel shelf. 'Nearly seven o'clock. Oh, no!'

Her heart started to pound and she began to rise from the day bed, but Melissa put the kettle back on the trivet and hurried towards her.

'It's all right. Sit down. We'll have our breakfast and a lovely gossip over tea and toast.'

'But you don't understand. I only meant to rest a little while. Instead I've slept for hours and there's so much more to do.'

'No, there's not.' Melissa crossed to the window and looped the curtains back with the corded tassels she had helped her mother to make. Despite Melissa's order to sit and wait, Emmeline got up and followed her. Daylight fell across the gown lying on the worktable and the reluctant winter sun glinted on the completed pattern of beads and pearls. Emmeline was mystified.

'I don't understand,' she said. 'Did I wake up, finish the work and then go back to sleep?'

She looked up to find Melissa smiling at her and she understood. '*You* did this!' she exclaimed, and she lifted the bodice of the gown to examine it carefully. 'But this work is excellent, Melissa! It must have taken you all night. You must be exhausted.'

'Not quite all night, and I'm not tired so much as hungry. Do let's sit down and make a start on the toast.'

Melissa loved moments like this. Just her mother and herself, gossiping cosily. They would talk about the latest fashions, the fabrics, the practical styles and some of their impractical customers. Some were only too pleased to be guided by Emmeline Dornay, who had a reputation for good taste, but others would insist that they have exactly whatever latest fad had caught their fancy.

Emmeline was always uneasy about giving in to such demands. It went without saying that she would do her very best and that the garment could not have been better made, but if the lady in question looked ridiculous she worried that it would reflect on her skills.

But she could not afford to turn work away. Not since she had become a widow with a child to support. Melissa's French father had been a sailor. He had been tall and broad-shouldered, and Melissa could remember him sweeping her up into his arms each time he came home. And she owed her ability to speak French to her father. For although he spoke English very well he wanted his daughter to speak and understand the languages of both her parents, a wish her mother had honoured and was now paying for Melissa to have French lessons lest she forget.

Bertrand Dornay had run away from his family home in Marseilles and become a cabin boy as soon as he could pass himself off for the age of fourteen. He had never told his wife why he had run away, only that he would never go back there. She assumed it was because of some family matter, for he remained proud to be a Frenchman.

Emmeline herself spoke reasonably good French. Even before she had met Bertrand, while she was still working in the sewing room of the department store, she had paid for private lessons so that she could read the French fashion magazines. Working for long hours at the cloth-covered tables with the other girls, she had formed the ambition to have her own dressmaking business one day. And it wouldn't be the usual little corner shop where mending and alterations were the main part of the business.

She would find rooms in a respectable house and her clientele would feel they were visiting a friend. She would provide tea or coffee, and her customers would be able to select a dress design from the latest magazines from Paris. Then Emmeline would run it up on her very own sewing machine, although the finishing touches would still be hand sewn. She had worked hard and saved as much as she could but she knew it would be years until she could achieve her ambition. But then she had met Bertrand and he had helped her realise her dream.

'Come and sit by the fire,' Melissa told her now. 'I'll pour the tea.'

Her mother took the armchair while Melissa sat on a small padded stool and insisted on doing everything for Emmeline as if their roles of mother and child had been reversed.

'It snowed during the night,' Melissa said as she buttered them each a second piece of toast. 'But it looks as though it's melting already. What a pity.'

'Why is it a pity?'

'Because the streets look so pretty in the snow. The dirt and grime are covered up – everything looks clean and new.'

They were both silent as Melissa stared into the fire.

'Are you looking for pictures?' her mother asked. 'Pictures in the flames.'

'Yes.' They often played this game when they had time to sit and dream.

'What do you see?'

'A sailing ship tossed on a stormy sea,' Melissa said, and immediately wished she hadn't. 'I'm sorry.'

'No, sweetheart, no need to say sorry,' her mother said, but Melissa could see the tears glistening in her eyes. 'Your father was lost at sea, and I wish with all my heart that was not so. And yet I will be ever grateful for the happy time we had together and the greatest gift he could give me . . . you, Melissa, my own darling daughter.'

Chapter Two

Lilian Winterton sat forward in her bed while Ena arranged the pillows behind her. The maid had lit the lamps and the fire had been made up by one of the housemaids while she was still sleeping. The luxurious bedroom was both comfortable and warm. When Lilian announced herself satisfied with the arrangement of the pillows Ena took the breakfast tray from the bedside table and put it across her mistress's knees.

'Will there be anything else, Mrs Winterton?' she asked.

'Yes, would you bring me my correspondence?'

'The post has not been delivered yet, madam.'

'I know that. I mean those letters over there – look – on my escritoire.'

Ena knew this was a posh word for the daft little writing desk by the window. It wasn't half the size of the desk in the morning room but Mrs Winterton preferred to keep her more personal correspondence in her bedroom. 'Yes, madam,' the lady's maid said.

'No, don't open the curtains yet,' Lilian told her, and gave an exaggerated shudder. 'I'm not yet ready to face the gloom of a winter morning.'

Ena brought the letters over and asked when she should return to help Mrs Winterton bathe and dress.

'I'll ring for you. Just go. Oh, wait a moment – is Miss Gwendolyn awake yet?'

'I don't believe so, Mrs Winterton. She hasn't rung for her morning tea.'

'Dear girl, no doubt she's tired after the late night we had. My guests simply didn't want to go home! But in any case, I want you to take her breakfast tray and awaken her as gently as possible.'

Ena's lips tightened. She dropped her gaze to hide her scowl. 'Yes, madam,' she said unenthusiastically and she left the room, closing the door without making a sound, as was required.

Lilian had seen the sulky grimace and she wondered if she ought to have reprimanded the girl. After all these years as the wife of a rich man, Lilian was still sometimes at a loss as to how to deal with subtly recalcitrant servants. But Lilian Frost, as she had been before her marriage to the successful property developer Austin Winterton, had been the daughter of two dancing teachers to whose studio Austin had gone to learn how to acquit himself in fashionable ballrooms.

Trained by her parents in deportment and elocution, Lilian was both vivacious and enchantingly pretty. She had partnered Austin in his dancing lessons and had won his heart. Although she had already given her own young heart to Dermot, a handsome but impecunious musician, there was no way she could have refused Austin's offer of marriage. As his wife she would not only be wealthy but would move in a much grander social circle than that of her parents.

Once she became Mrs Winterton she had worked tirelessly to make the right sort of friends. Austin approved of this. His own background was 'trade'; his father had been a builder, and it pleased him that he and his wife were now on speaking terms with those he regarded as his betters. He knew very well that his money made him both respected and despised. So he encouraged Lilian to play the society hostess, although he was often aghast at how much this cost him.

Lilian read all the ladies' magazines to seek advice on the table, the flowers, and the menus, and had several books on household management. She was satisfied that last night's dinner party had been successful and imagined that every single guest would have been impressed by her ability to arrange such things so tastefully.

Now she spooned apricot preserve on to a freshly baked bread roll and took dainty bites from it while she sipped her coffee. Thank goodness Austin had not 'bothered' her last night. He had stayed up even later than she and Gwendolyn in order to discuss business with two of the guests he was hoping to interest in a new development. Those two gentlemen had sent their wives and daughters home and had talked into the small hours.

Lilian had decided to feign sleep if Austin came to the bedroom but, thank goodness, he must have gone straight to his dressing room where there was a bed kept ready for him.

She poured herself another cup of coffee and topped it up with warm milk. Then she settled back more comfortably against the pillows. All in all life was good, she thought, and tolerating Austin's attentions was not too high a price to pay.

She hoped Gwendolyn would not be in one of her moods this morning. Honestly, she didn't know how to deal with her grown daughter sometimes. Gwendolyn, at eighteen, was the same age as Lilian had been when she had married Austin. Lilian set her coffee cup down and gazed into the near distance. She sighed and, in a moment of honesty, she admitted to herself that that was the problem. Gwendolyn was a grown woman and certainly old enough to marry although, pretty as she was, her petulant manner was not attractive to any of the suitable young men who might have come courting.

Holding on to her breakfast tray with one hand, Lilian reached for the hand mirror she kept in a drawer in her bedside table. She stared at her own reflection thoughtfully. With her blue eyes, and her pale blonde hair loose about her shoulders, she liked to think that she didn't look old enough to be the mother of a grown girl. In fact she believed that the virginal white linen nightgowns that Austin preferred made her look almost the same age as Gwendolyn.

She frowned. She would much rather have had nightwear made from China silk that would flatter her shapely figure but Austin disapproved of such frivolities. Or so he implied. Lilian sometimes wondered if some dark need in her husband required him to see her as a very young girl rather than a fully formed woman.

Lilian put the mirror aside. She wondered if there had been any truth in her daughter's accusation that she always wanted to be the belle of the ball. She did like to be the centre of attention – why not? And perhaps she was finding it difficult to watch her own child become a beautiful young woman. That was why she had unconsciously chosen the simple design for Gwendolyn's ball gown.

Thought of the ball gowns that were to be collected today prompted her to pick up one of the envelopes that Ena had handed her. She had opened it some time ago and now she took out the single sheet of paper and looked at it again. She frowned as she examined the dressmaker's bill. Emmeline Dornay had been good to let it run on so long and she really ought to settle it before Christmas but she wasn't sure how she was going to manage that.

Instead of being pleased with her because she had found a dressmaker who could run up gowns that looked as though they had come straight from a London salon, and at a fraction of the price, Austin was continually telling her that she had too many clothes and she was being extravagant. It was very tiresome of him. After all, he was very rich and he could easily afford to indulge her. Lilian thought that it must be his puritan upbringing in a God-fearing home that made him disapprove of her frivolity, as he put it. Which made his behaviour in her bed all the more strange . . .

Suppressing an involuntary shudder, Lilian brought her mind back to the vexed question of the dressmaker's account. She knew she didn't have enough of her allowance left to settle with Emmeline before Christmas and she felt guilty. Emmeline was such a sweet person and she had always been prepared to put other work aside in order to please Lilian. And then there was the favour she had done her some years ago . . .

And now she had taken on the ball gowns with only weeks to spare and that had added more to an account that Lilian would already have struggled to pay. Austin had told her that she and her daughter between them had more pretty frocks than they needed but he simply didn't understand how the minds of women worked and how the other guests would have gossiped if she and Gwendolyn had appeared at Lady Bowater's ball in gowns they had worn before.

Then the very thought of the ball made her smile. It was such an achievement to have been invited to the ball in the Assembly Rooms, even if the invitations had come at the last respectable moment, which had made Lilian suspect that the Winterton family had been invited to take the place of other, more important, people who had had to refuse the invitation for some reason. It was because the invitation had been so tardy that she had been driven to beg poor dear Emmeline to work so hard and have the gowns ready in time.

She had reminded Emmeline Dornay what good customers she and Gwendolyn were . . . and that was true. She always settled her account eventually and the dressmaker had never complained. But this time it was Christmas. What if

Emmeline had planned to spend the money on treats for herself and her daughter?

This thought reminded her that she had another problem and she frowned. With only days to go she had not yet bought any of the presents she intended to give to her husband and her daughter, and also to some of her fashionable friends. Just a few days ago she had seen the most delightful little corsage watches in Fenwick's. There was a choice of red, green, black or blue enamel, all set with pearls. You could buy the watch only or also get the brooch to match. She had already worked out which of her society friends would be given the watch only and which would receive the brooch as well.

And then her brow cleared as a solution presented itself. There was no problem at all really. She would do all the shopping she needed and put everything on her account. And that also solved the problem of what to do about Emmeline. Well, it didn't exactly solve it but it would alleviate the situation a little.

Lilian pushed the tray aside, not noticing or caring that the dish of apricot preserve tumbled on to the rose silk eiderdown, and sprang out of bed. First she rang for Ena and then she hurried over to the escritoire and, sitting down, took pen and paper and began to write. When Ena arrived Lilian was already putting the paper into the envelope.

'Miss Gwendolyn is having her breakfast, madam,' the maid said.

'Good. But now get one of the housemaids – Joan, perhaps – to take this note to Fenwick's; the name of the gentleman who will deal with it is on the envelope. Tell her to hurry. I suppose I'd better give her the money for a cab.' Lilian took some small change from her purse and handed it to Ena, who looked at it doubtfully.

'That's all right,' Lilian said. 'She can walk back.'

'And what does she have to say at the shop, madam?'

'Nothing, it's all explained in the note. Just tell her to hurry. Then come back and help me get dressed.'

'You go up first,' Melissa told her mother. 'You'll feel much better if you have a proper wash and change your clothes.'

'But I should tidy the room.'

'I'll do that. What time is Mrs Winterton coming?'

'She said about eleven thirty.' Emmeline smiled. 'But you know what she's like. She's never been less than an hour late.'

'There you are, then. I'll have the bathroom when you've finished and we should still have time for coffee before they arrive.'

When her mother had gone upstairs Melissa tidied the worktable and swept the scraps of material from the floor. Any bits of cloth that were big enough she stored in the chest where they kept their remnants. When she had been a small child she had loved to go through the scraps of material, especially the velvets, the silks and the satins. Her mother had taught her to sew almost before she could read and write, and as soon as she had mastered the stitches, Emmeline made the lessons more interesting by making outfits for the French doll Bertrand had brought for Melissa when he returned from one of his voyages.

Ninette had a porcelain head with beautiful blue glass eyes and extravagant silky, gold ringlets. Her body was made of jointed kid and her pretty party frock was in the latest fashion. She had arrived with one change of clothes; the second outfit had been a dress and smock more suitable for a peasant girl. But over the years Melissa and her mother had made her so many new dresses and coats and items of underwear that there surely had never been a better dressed *poupée* in the entire world.

Melissa still had the doll. She kept her in a cardboard box

with all her clothes and, even now she was fourteen, she sometimes amused herself by choosing some of her mother's remnants and making up a gown in the latest style – although Ninette's sturdy kid body was not quite the right shape for more grown-up fashions.

Just when she thought she had finished tidying, Melissa noticed a scatter of beads under the table. She kneeled down to pick them up and returned them to their glass-fronted box. Then she straightened up and looked at the two ball gowns. Mrs Winterton was an exceptionally pretty woman and she would look attractive in the Parma violet, but Melissa's favourite was the white satin gown made for Gwendolyn. The gown itself was as beautiful as her mother could have made it, and the exquisite detail of beads and satin flowers around the neckline and on the upper bodice made it as good as any garment sewn in a London salon.

Melissa stared at the shimmering satin, which seemed to have some inner glow in the diffused winter light filtering through the lace curtains. She wondered what it would be like to lead the sort of life that Gwendolyn did; to have more clothes than she could possibly wear even though convention called for her to change them two, three and maybe four times a day.

She opened the chest again and took out a large remnant of the white satin cloth. Then she slipped off her dressing gown and draped the material around her body. She closed her eyes and imagined she was in a gilded ballroom. The floor was polished ready for the dancing to begin, and around the room were set huge jardinières filled with masses of white blooms. She could smell their fragrance and as she stood with her eyes tight shut she could hear the musicians tuning their instruments.

With a tap of the conductor's baton the orchestra began to play and Melissa began to sway to the imaginary music.

'Of course,' she murmured when a tall handsome young man bowed before her and asked her to dance. 'Just let me consult my card – oh, yes, this dance is free.'

She was clutching the draped material about her body with one hand and the other was raised as if resting on her dancing partner's shoulder when Emmeline came back into the room. She paused in the doorway and smiled fondly as she watched her daughter. Melissa was so beautiful, so graceful, that many a time Emmeline had been tempted to design and make up dresses that would do justice to her looks and her figure. But what was the point when they did not lead the sort of life where these dresses could be worn?

Instead she had made sure that her daughter had good, modestly tasteful clothes; made from the best quality cloth that she could afford and of styles suitable for a dressmaker's daughter without being at all pretentious or showy. She knew Melissa dreamed of wearing some of the more luxurious dresses they made, and Emmeline remembered her own girlhood dreams.

She had been born into a poor but respectable family who managed well enough on the money her father made working as a jobbing gardener at several big houses. Perhaps it had been his love of natural beauty that had inspired her own artistic dreams. The flowers he had brought home whenever he could would be received by her practical mother with barely a smile. She told her husband that some tatties and a cabbage or two would be more use to her. Of course he brought them too when he could.

Although bright and hard-working, Emmeline had had to leave school when she was thirteen because her mother said they could not afford to keep her there any longer. And, in any case, book-learning was not meant for girls. But at least Emmeline, or Emma Johns, as she had been then, had won the battle over what she was to do next.

Her mother had wanted her to go into service in a big house, for there she would have room and board, and there would be one less mouth to feed at home. But Emmeline had seen a notice in a corner shop dressmaker's advertising for an apprentice. If she was taken on her board and lodging would be provided, but the first drawback had been that there was no pay, and the second and more serious was that Emma would have to pay a fee for her apprenticeship.

Her mother had been outraged. 'What, pay for you to go to work?' she'd said. 'Not likely. We need money coming in, not money going out!'

Emmeline's father, usually happy to let his wife rule the roost for the sake of peace and quiet, had intervened on his daughter's behalf. It was probably the only time he had done so. 'Let the lass go,' he'd said. 'We can afford it. And anyways, our Janet is bringing a wage home from the pickling factory.'

Hannah Johns, amazed that her husband had stood up to her for once, and seeing that he was determined, had given way ungraciously and Emmeline had got her apprenticeship. She had never lived at home again.

Now she watched her daughter's game of make-believe and reflected with pain that, whatever became of Melissa, she herself might not be here to see it. Her cough had led her to believe that she had consumption but the doctor had told her that she had a weak heart and that she mustn't put too much strain upon it. Rest whenever you can, he'd said.

Oh, how she'd wanted to take his advice. And she did try. But she still had a living to earn and Melissa must be provided for. She had taught her daughter everything she knew about dressmaking and she now believed that Melissa had much more talent and flair than she had ever had.

If I can survive a few more years, Emmeline thought, Melissa will be able to make a good living for herself. But at the moment she is still too young. I'll have to think of some way of safeguarding her future. Her gaze moved beyond her daughter to the two evening gowns waiting for the Wintertons. Perhaps there is a way, she thought.

'Oh!' Melissa opened her eyes and saw her mother standing there. 'I was just . . . I was just . . .'

'Dreaming. I know. Don't look so guilty, there's no harm in a game of let's pretend. But now you'd better go and get ready. I want you to slip along to the baker's shop before Mrs Winterton arrives. Get some mince pies and a box of fancy cakes. I think we'll offer our best customers a little Christmas treat.'

Melissa had no sooner left the room than there was a knock at the door. 'Mrs Dornay, pet, you've a visitor,' Martha Sibbet said as she put her head around the door.

'Visitor?' Emmeline said anxiously. 'Surely Mrs Winterton has not arrived so soon?'

'No, pet, it's not that posh wife. It's Mrs Cook.'

Emmeline was relieved but not exactly pleased. 'You'd better show her in.'

'Right oh. And if you want me to make you a cup of tea I divven't mind.'

'No, thank you, that won't be necessary. My sister won't be staying long.'

Emmeline prepared herself for her elder sister's censorious expression. Janet had never forgiven her for persuading their father to pay for her apprenticeship. Janet had seen it as a prideful attempt to rise above her station. She believed that Emma, as she still thought of her, should have been content to join her at the pickling factory and marry an ordinary decent working man instead of that fancy French sailor.

She had even disapproved of Bertrand calling his wife Emmeline because that was a French name. Janet thought her sister should have been content with the name her parents had given her. And when the baby came she had asked what sort of fancy name Melissa was.

'I can see you'll bring your daughter up with even more far-fetched ideas than you have,' she'd said.

Furthermore she had never forgiven Emmeline for finding so much happiness in her brief marriage. It was only when Bertrand was lost at sea that she could even bring herself to try to restore sisterly relations, such as they had been.

Emmeline watched as Janet unbuttoned her coat and then stooped to rub her hands together in front of the fire.

'By, it's cold outside,' she said.

'Yes.' Emmeline never knew how to respond to Janet's attempts at conversation.

'You've got it nice and warm in here, though.' The words, harmless enough, somehow managed to suggest disapproval. Before Emmeline could think of some sort of reply Janet continued, 'But I suppose you have to allow a little luxury when you're as ill as you are.'

'It's not a luxury to keep warm,' Emmeline responded.

'It is for some folk.'

'I know that.' Emmeline tried her best to keep her voice from betraying her exasperation. 'I work hard and I can afford to provide the basic comforts for Melissa and myself.'

'Aye, but you've still managed to become mortally ill, haven't you?'

'I haven't "managed" to become ill. The doctor says that this trouble of mine is a consequence of when I had rheumatic fever as a child.'

Janet didn't like to be contradicted. 'Whatever the cause,' she said sourly, 'what is going to happen to that precious daughter of yours?'

'Please keep your voice down. Melissa doesn't know . . . she doesn't know how . . .'

'How little time you've got left? Then it's time you told her.'

'But I don't know exactly. Even the doctor doesn't know. If I'm careful I could live to see my daughter settled.'

'What do you mean by settled? Married?'

'Perhaps. But what I want more than that is to see her being able to take over from me.'

'A dressmaker.' Janet's tone was disdainful. 'Like yourself.'

'Yes, like myself, and I don't see anything wrong in wanting my daughter to follow a respectable trade and be able to support herself even if it happened that she doesn't get married.'

'Respectable? I've heard it's more like sweated labour.'

'Stop this, Janet. We've been over this before. It's true that some young women work long hours in backstreet workshops for very little, but Melissa will never have to live like that. I have my own business with established customers and one day it will be Melissa's.'

'Well, let's hope you live long enough to make sure that happens.'

Emmeline gasped at the brutality of her sister's words. 'Why are you doing this?' she asked. 'Why are you being so cruel?'

Janet took off her coat and placed it over the back of the armchair. Then she took her time sitting down before she replied, 'I don't mean to be cruel. Or rather I'm being cruel to be kind.'

Emmeline sank on to the sofa. She sighed. 'I don't know what you're talking about.'

'Yes, you do. You ought to be providing for your daughter.'

'I thought that was what I was doing.'

'Stop fooling yourself. Melissa couldn't take over your business now or even in a year or two.'

'She's clever. I've taught her everything I know. She's a

better needlewoman than I am already, and she has a real flair for design.'

'But she's only a girl. Your grand customers aren't going to come to her.'

'I don't see why not.' Emmeline felt the familiar cough starting and she clutched at her chest.

'For goodness' sake, Emma, get the lass a proper job before it's too late.'

'And by a proper job you mean in a factory or a shop, or in service in a big house?'

'There's nothing wrong with any of those.' Janet glared at her.

'I know. I didn't mean to imply that there was. But Melissa is capable of so much more.'

'Look, I believe you if you say the lass is good with the needle. So why not get her a job in the sewing room of a department store? After all, that's what you did after you'd served your apprenticeship.'

'Melissa is already more accomplished than I was then. Her talent would be wasted.'

'But I keep telling you, she's not much more than a bairn.'

'I know – I know, but will you please stop haranguing me like this!' Emmeline looked at her sister bleakly, her eyes filled with tears, which she brushed away hastily.

'Look,' Janet said, and her voice softened a little, 'I didn't mean to make you cry but I have Melissa's interests at heart.'

'Do you?'

'Of course. She's my niece. I'll do the best I can for her when you . . . when the time comes.'

'I'm sure you intend to. But what you consider is "the best" might not be the best at all.'

'You're talking in riddles.' Janet looked and sounded exasperated.

Emmeline looked at her elder sister searchingly. 'I'd like to believe you but I can't help feeling that you've never quite forgiven me because our father gave me the chance to better myself, and that it would give you the greatest satisfaction to thwart my plans for Melissa in the guise of doing the best for her.'

Janet's lips thinned with displeasure. 'Well, if that's what you believe, I can see I'm wasting my time here.' She stood up. 'So I'll take what I came for. It is ready, isn't it?'

'Yes, it's in the cupboard over there. You can try it on if you like.'

Janet opened the tall cupboard and took out the three-quarter-length jacket that Emmeline had altered for her. The jacket had been passed on to Emmeline by one of her customers who had put on weight. Too small for Mrs Cunningham, it was a little large for Janet, so Emmeline had taken it in.

One or two of Emmeline's dressmaking customers let her have good quality clothes they had finished with, knowing that she could alter them and sell them second-hand. Some of them expected a little discount on their bill for this favour. Some of them didn't care.

Whenever she could she would put something aside for her sister, and Janet kept up the pretence of paying her for them. Pretence because she would ask Emmeline how much she owed her and Emmeline would say it didn't matter. This had developed into a ritual.

'No, I must insist,' Janet would say, and when Emmeline refused payment yet again she would add, 'Well, here's something for the bairn,' meaning Melissa. Then she would make a show of putting some coins in Melissa's money box; this was never more than a penny or two, but Janet thought she had done her duty.

'Very nice,' she said now as she tried the jacket on. 'How much do you want for the work?'

'Nothing. You know that.'

'Very well.'

Janet took off the jacket and put on her coat. This time she didn't ask for Melissa's money box. Emmeline got up wearily and took a sheet of brown paper from the cupboard.

'Sit yourself down again, I'll wrap it up,' Janet said. 'Where's the string?'

Emmeline indicated one of the shelves in the cupboard. She sat in the armchair by the fire as her sister, pin thin and angular, made up the parcel. Janet had always been neat and precise, and ever since the day she had married Albert Cook she had boasted that her floors were clean enough to eat off. Heaven help Albert or their lanky only son Bert Junior if they forgot to take their shoes off at the door. The Cook menfolk might be big and strong but it was Janet who wore the trousers, like her mother before her, as their father used to say. Emmeline relaxed back into her chair a little and remembered their father with affection.

If he had been alive he would have understood her ambitions for Melissa even though their mother wouldn't. Poor Ma, Emmeline thought; she used to be the domestic tyrant and now she's forced to live with Janet and obey her daughter's orders meekly. Try as she might Melissa could not feel sorry for her. As you sow so shall you reap, she thought.

'Why are you smiling?' Janet asked as she put her coat on and buttoned it up.

'Was I?'

'Humph,' Janet snorted. 'You always were a strange one.'

She picked up her parcel and walked to the door. Then she paused and turned. She looked uncharacteristically awkward.

'What is it, Janet?' Emmeline asked.

'Christmas. What are you doing for Christmas?'

'Melissa and I will enjoy ourselves together as usual.'

'Well . . . yes . . . I know you've never wanted to come home . . .'

'Home?'

'To my house. To your family.'

'I've never been invited.'

For a moment Emmeline thought that Janet was going to walk out but, visibly controlling her temper, she said, 'Perhaps I didn't think you'd accept my invitation but let's not quarrel about it.'

'I agree.'

Her elder sister pursed her lips and, after a pause, she continued, 'Ma thinks you ought to come along.'

'Whatever for?'

Janet didn't reply. She looked uncomfortable.

'Oh, I see. You all think it might be my last Christmas, don't you?'

'Perhaps.'

'And you actually want to spend time with me?'

'Maybe.'

Suddenly Emmeline couldn't help laughing at Janet's mulish expression. 'Don't worry, Janet. I'll make sure that anyone who might care knows that I was invited – that my family did the right thing. But, if you don't mind, I won't accept your invitation.'

'Please yourself.' Janet placed her hand on the doorknob and turned to deliver one more barb. 'And on a cold day like this you might have offered me a cup of tea.'

She left before there was time to reply and Emmeline didn't know whether to laugh or to cry. In the past she had always offered a cup of tea to Janet, and her sister had refused. Her words were always the same: 'No, don't bother, thank you. I won't be staying long.'

And she never had stayed long. Not until this time. Emmeline thought over everything Janet had said. Her elder sister was quite right in suggesting that she ought to be thinking of what would happen to Melissa if – she forced herself to think the words – if she died. Lord help the poor girl if she was to rely on Janet, who would probably have her working in the pickling factory as soon as possible. No, it was unthinkable. But she hoped there was a better way to deal with this heartbreak. Emmeline had already decided what she was going to do.

Chapter Three

No matter how grand the landau looked there was no denying the windows were small and therefore, inside, it was always dim. And on days like today it was also cold and draughty. Lilian Winterton huddled inside her black sealskin coat, glad of the shoulder cape with its lining of grey and white squirrel. The cape also had a standing fur collar, which was just as well because her almost brimless hat, perched forward on her upswept hair, gave no protection at all against the weather.

She tried to sit comfortably as they swayed and lurched over the slush-covered cobbles. Gwendolyn, sitting opposite her, was glowering to compete with the dark winter sky. Gwendolyn Winterton's coat was also made of sealskin but did not have a shoulder cape. Instead there was a neat silver fox collar and a matching muff. She wore a fur hat, also silver fox, which Lilian thought made her look romantic – like a fairytale princess. But a princess who must learn not to scowl like that; for no reason at all as far as Lilian could see.

Gwendolyn was gazing out of the window and Lilian studied her daughter surreptitiously. There was no doubt she was good-looking, but in a more robust way than Lilian herself. Gwendolyn was tall and, so far, slender enough, but there was already a hint at her waist of the corpulence that lay in wait for her if she did not control her desire for cakes and confectionery – especially cream buns.

As they made their way through the busy streets Lilian began to rehearse in her mind what she would say to Emmeline Dornay. She could hardly plead poverty, for everyone knew that Austin Winterton was enormously rich. And it would be embarrassing to admit that her husband had refused to make her allowance more generous because he believed her to be excessively extravagant. And what if I am extravagant? she thought rebelliously. Austin likes me to dress fashionably; he likes people to see how beautiful I am because he is so ugly.

She shuddered at the thought of her husband's long raw-boned face and his lanky, awkward frame. And then she tried to suppress the disloyal thoughts by reminding herself that she had willingly married the man because of the life he could offer her. He had taken her away from the dismal little lodging house where she lived with her parents and installed her in one of the largest and most luxurious houses in Newcastle. And now there was to be a country house too, where she could play at being lady of the manor and queen it over the unsophisticated country gentry whom she considered to be 'bumpkins'.

She sighed. If only he didn't sometimes exhibit this mean streak Austin would be all that she required of a husband. That is, if you didn't expect love to be part of the relationship. She had been in love with Dermot, very much in love, but even at the height of her passion she had known that she could not bear to be the wife of an impoverished musician. She had only to consider her parents' life, always working for long hours at the dance studio they leased from the Assembly Rooms and never earning quite enough to buy their own house so that they had to live in a succession of shabby lodgings. No, she couldn't have faced that sort of existence.

How lucky Gwendolyn was, she thought; brought up in luxury, having been a pupil at the most fashionable school in the North of England; never having had to lift a finger to fend for herself. So it was all the more vexing that the girl was always so dissatisfied with life.

For a moment Lilian considered her dressmaker's daughter, Melissa Dornay. As far as she could see the child never complained and assisted her mother as much as she was able; even helping to prepare the meals and then working late into the night with her mother at her dressmaking.

Emmeline had also told her how happy she had been with her French sailor husband. How she had met him at church and how her mother and sister had disapproved of him. Simply for being foreign as far as Lilian could make out. They had not even come round when he had used his savings to help Emmeline set up her own little business. Indeed, that seemed to offend them even more. Emmeline had hinted that her sister had believed she was 'getting above herself'.

Her dressmaker had told her all this, woman to woman, during some of their cosy chats, and Lilian had responded with confidences about her own life. Well, it was so intimate, somehow, stripping down to your petticoats and letting another woman take your measurements. In Lilian's opinion you had to like that woman otherwise the whole process would be distasteful. She stirred uncomfortably. For if Emmeline had confided in her then so had she confided in Emmeline. And her confessions had not been so innocent.

Oh dear, now she felt all the more guilty about not being able to pay Emmeline what was owing to her. And by the time the carriage drew up outside the decently modest house where the Dornays lived, Lilian Winterton had not even the faintest glimmering of an idea of how she was going to explain the fact that she could not settle her account.

The coachman, William, leaped down from the box seat and opened the door; he let down the folding steps and helped them out, first Mrs Winterton and then Gwendolyn. Then he preceded them up the short path and rang the bell before returning to see to the horses. It was Melissa who opened the door and greeted them.

Lilian and Gwendolyn entered, bringing a draught of cold air in with them. Melissa had helped her mother put the dressmakers' body forms in the bay window and a ray of winter sunshine struck through the lace curtains like a spotlight on the stage. Melissa thought the gowns looked perfect and she was rewarded with smiles of delight from both the Winterton women. Mrs Winterton was lavish with her praise and even Gwendolyn was smiling, although it appeared to Melissa that the smile was a trifle grudging. It was as if she had not expected to be pleased and, finding that she was, she didn't want to admit it.

'My dear Emmeline,' Lilian said, 'you have excelled yourself. Now shall we have a final fitting?'

'No, I don't think that's necessary,' Emmeline told her. 'You were both satisfied with the fit yesterday. It was simply the frills and furbelows that had to be adjusted.'

'Emmeline, please don't look at me like that.'

'Like what?'

'So reproachfully. You know how I like my frills and flounces.'

Emmeline laughed. 'Yes, I do, and I don't really mind. I forget sometimes that the customer should have what she wants even if it wouldn't be my idea of what's right.'

'Oh dear, you don't think the gown is ruined, do you?'

'No, of course not. I wouldn't have done it if I thought it

would ruin the gown. I would have talked you out of it somehow.'

'Well, I'm glad you didn't because I think the result is simply perfect. And, as for Gwendolyn's gown, it is divine!'

Melissa and her mother exchanged smiles. They were used to Mrs Winterton's extravagant way of expressing herself and it amused them.

'I've brought a small trunk,' Mrs Winterton went on. 'I'll get the coachman to bring it in, if you will do your usual magic with the tissue paper and pack the gowns carefully for me. Perhaps you would get your maid to go out and tell William?'

Melissa had to suppress a laugh at the idea of Martha Sibbet being their maid. 'It's all right,' she said, 'Mrs Sibbet will be busy. I'll go and tell the coachman.'

A sleety rain had begun to fall through the soot-stained air and Melissa, who had pulled a cloak over her shoulders, wondered if the Wintertons' coachman minded sitting out in the bitter weather. But he seemed well wrapped up in waterproofs and he gave her a cheerful grin. The carriage horses were steaming gently and Melissa thought how good they were to stand there so patiently in the dismal weather.

The coachman unloaded a small trunk from underneath his seat and carried it into the house, turning into the front parlour as Melissa instructed him.

'Thank you, William,' Mrs Winterton said. 'Please wait in the hallway. I don't want you dripping over Mrs Dornay's carpet.'

Melissa thought she detected a long-suffering look on the coachman's face but he waited, as patient as his horses, until the gowns were packed and, when called, he took the trunk back to the coach.

'That's all for the moment, William, but I shall send for the – that other thing in a moment,' Mrs Winterton said mysteriously. Then her expression changed. Melissa thought she looked nervous – or perhaps embarrassed was a better word. 'Now, Emmeline,' she said, 'I'm afraid I have to tell you that—'

But whatever she was going to say was curtailed when Emmeline Dornay, equally ill at ease, it seemed to her puzzled daughter, said, 'Do you have time to stay and take a cup of tea with us?'

'Oh . . . I don't know.'

Emmeline persisted. 'Please do. I planned a small treat – for Christmas, you know.'

'Treat?'

'Yes. Some mince pies and fancy cakes and, if you prefer, instead of tea the girls can have blackcurrant cordial with a dash of hot water, and you and I will have a glass of sherry.'

Melissa stared at her mother. Why, despite her smile, did she suddenly look so anxious? And Mrs Winterton too – why had she lost her usual air of confidence?

While Mrs Winterton hesitated Emmeline Dornay hurried from the room. 'I won't be long,' she said, and they were all left staring at each other.

'I don't see why we can't stay for mince pies and cakes,' Gwendolyn said. She was scowling again.

Her mother glanced at her daughter's mutinous expression and sighed. 'Oh, very well then.'

Emmeline returned. 'I've asked Mrs Sibbet to take a tray to the dining room. We'll sit properly at the table. Melissa, take Gwendolyn along; I'll just have a word with Mrs Winterton before we join you.'

When Melissa and Gwendolyn had left the room Lilian faced her dressmaker apprehensively. She was certain that Emmeline was going to ask her to settle her account.

'Mrs Winterton . . . Lilian . . . I have something to ask you,' Emmeline began.

'Yes?'

'But please sit down; here by the fire.'

Lilian sat down and watched nervously while Emmeline took the chair at the other side of the hearth. There was a small silence broken only by the crackling of the burning coal. Emmeline is worried because she doesn't like having to ask me for money, Lilian thought. She thinks I've forgotten and she feels awkward. Should I speak first?

She had decided to pretend that she had left her purse at home and that she would send the money along later. She wouldn't say exactly how much later this would be. This was feeble, she knew, but it was all she could think of. However, before she had opened her lips, Emmeline forestalled her.

'We have known each other for some time now, have we not?'

'We have.'

'I hope I am more to you than just your dressmaker?'

'Yes, of course you are!' Lilian injected sincerity into her affirmation. She wondered where this conversation was leading. 'And . . . and I haven't forgotten the – the favour – you did for me.'

Emmeline shook her head slightly as if she would never have mentioned that favour. She paused and then, looking solemn, she said, 'Now I am going to ask you to do something for me.'

'Anything!' Lilian exclaimed. 'Just ask.'

Then Emmeline looked so grave that Lilian was frightened. 'What is it?' she asked.

'It's Melissa . . .' Emmeline paused and Lilian thought she saw tears glistening in her eyes.

'Melissa? Is she in trouble of some sort?'

Emmeline shook her head.

'Is she ill? Do you need a good doctor? I have a very fine physician. I will send him to see you. And don't worry about the cost of his visits. My husband will be pleased to pay for whatever is needed.' Austin likes to be thought of as a philanthropist, Lilian thought, so he won't object to that.

'No. That's kind of you, but I have a good doctor and I can afford to pay him. But it isn't Melissa who is ill. It's me.'

Emmeline told her how grave the situation was and when she explained that she might not have long to live, easy tears came to Lilian's eyes.

'My dear,' she said, 'what do you want me to do?'

'I want you to look after her.'

'Look after Melissa? Do you have no family?'

'Yes, as you know, I have a sister but I don't trust her to do the best for my daughter. Melissa has the makings of a fine dressmaker, better than I could ever be. I don't want her ending up in the pickle factory.'

'Melissa work in a pickle factory?' Lilian was startled by this patently absurd suggestion. 'Why should she?'

'Because that's where my sister, Janet, would send her if she goes to live with her.'

'Oh, no.' Lilian was genuinely aghast. 'Why couldn't she stay here and carry on with your business? I'm sure none of your customers would desert her.'

'I know she has the appearance of a young woman and, indeed, she is very sensible, but she is only fourteen.'

'But surely you don't expect to die just yet?' She saw Emmeline flinch at the baldness of the words and hurried on, 'I mean – you look so well.'

Emmeline smiled sadly. 'Do I? Do you honestly think so?'

'Well, a little tired perhaps, but I'm sure you're not going to – I mean – I'm sure you'll be with us until Melissa is old enough to be independent.'

'Obviously I hope so. But if I'm not then I want you to be – well, a sort of guardian. Make sure that she can go on making her living with the needle. Miss Bullock would let her stay as long as she can afford to pay the rent. But I am worried that my sister would take her to live with her.'

'Could she do that?'

'Until Melissa comes of age my sister would be considered to be her guardian. She could insist.' Emmeline stared at Lilian Winterton bleakly. 'I know this is a great deal to ask of you but . . . but . . . if you could . . .'

'Yes – of course I will. If the need arises I shall act as her guardian. I'm sure nobody could object to that. Melissa will not have to stay here on her own and risk being taken by your sister. She must come to my house. I insist. I shall find a place for her.'

'Are you sure?'

'Of course I am. And I will see that she has everything that she needs until, as you say, she can be independent.'

Lilian saw Emmeline's taut shoulders relax a little but her eyes were still troubled.

'One day she must have her own business, a salon of her own. That is my ambition for her.'

'Of course. I promise you.'

'Thank you. And now, just give me a little time to compose myself and we'll go and join our daughters.'

It was not long past noon but outside the sky was dark and indoors the lamps had been lit by Mrs Sibbet when she built up the fire. The dining room was cosy and, thanks to Emmeline, had an air of modest elegance. But Melissa had to acknowledge that no matter how much lavender polish was applied by Martha Sibbet, it couldn't disguise the musty smell of age emanating from Miss Bullock's ancient sideboard.

Gwendolyn, already starting to eat her second cream cake, watched as Melissa poured hot water from the jug into the glass beakers of blackcurrant cordial.

'Do you do that yourself ?' she asked.

'Do what?'

'Pour the drinks. Shouldn't your maid do that for you?'

Melissa, understanding even if Gwendolyn did not, what a difference there was in the way they lived, decided not to confuse their guest. 'I'm sure Mrs Sibbet would have poured the water into the cordial if I'd asked her, but I prefer to do it myself.'

'Do you?' Gwendolyn was clearly puzzled. 'And I didn't mean that rough-looking woman who brought the tray, I meant your chambermaid.'

'We don't have a chambermaid.'

'No? It's so difficult to find reliable staff, isn't it? But I'm sure you will find someone soon.'

Melissa simply nodded. It would be no use trying to explain to Gwendolyn Winterton that they had never had a chambermaid and were never likely to have one. Gwendolyn lived in a different sort of world. A world where she had never had to lift a finger to do anything for herself; a world where she never even had to pour herself a cup of tea.

'I say, these cream fancies are delicious,' Gwendolyn said. 'At least you seem to have found a very good pastry cook.'

Melissa stared at Gwendolyn as the older girl dabbed daintily at her mouth with a napkin. This was more than ignorance of the way other people lived, it was sheer stupidity. Gwendolyn and her mother had been coming to this house for years now. Had she never noticed that it was far too small to have a large contingent of household staff ? Quite apart from the fact that Melissa's mother was a dress-maker, and only the dressmakers who owned the fashionable salons in London were likely to be able to live in such a way.

And why did Gwendolyn always look so discontented, Melissa wondered. She lived in a fine house. She had all the clothes a girl could ever wish for and a mother who was both kind and charming. Didn't she know how lucky she was?

Suddenly Melissa was reminded of Hetty Barras, one of the girls in her class at school. She was always neat and well-fed-looking and she was pretty, with blonde ringlets and deep blue eyes. But she was never happy. Most of the girls avoided her but Melissa had once come across her sobbing in a corner of the playground.

'Whatever is the matter?' Melissa had asked.

'Go away,' was all the reply she got before Hetty sprang up and ran across the playground to the other side.

'Let her go.' Melissa turned round to find Miss Robson standing behind her. 'Poor Hetty,' the class teacher said.

Startled to find the teacher talking to her almost as if she were an equal, Melissa was emboldened to ask, 'Why do you say that?'

'Because Hetty is a nice child – or could be if only her parents wouldn't expect so much of her.'

Melissa frowned. 'But I know her mother and father; they live in our street, they're very kind, very . . .' she searched for a word that would best describe Hetty's parents, '. . . cheery.'

'You are right, Melissa, and that can be exhausting to live with. Mrs Barras is always bright and gay and makes friends easily. She is proud of her pretty daughter and she is forever thrusting her into the limelight. She would like the poor child to be more like herself whereas Hetty hasn't the wit to make sparkling conversation and she knows it. She's not very bright, you know. Each day is a puzzle to her. She feels too much is expected of her and that is why she is so cross all the time.'

'Oh.' Melissa could think of nothing to say.

'But I have said far too much to you,' Miss Robson said. 'I trust that you will not repeat a word of this.'

'Of course not.'

Miss Robson studied her for a moment and then said,

'Good. And now we must arrange those French lessons your mother has enquired about. That's why I came to seek you. I am prepared to take you on but it will have to be after school and at my own house, I'm afraid. My mother doesn't like me to arrive home too late.'

Now, studying Gwendolyn as she sipped her cordial, Melissa wondered if she had the same problem as Hetty Barras. Mrs Winterton was so beautiful and bright and gay; perhaps she expected too much of Gwendolyn and perhaps Gwendolyn felt overshadowed by her glamorous mother.

Just then the door opened and her own mother came into the room followed by Mrs Winterton. Soon they were sipping sherry and chatting over their mince pies. Gwendolyn had eaten four of the half-dozen cream cakes even before they arrived and now she said, 'Oh, look, Melissa, two cream cakes left. We can have one each.'

The talk was of Christmas and the various parties and dances the Wintertons would be going to, and how Lilian Winterton was sure that she and Gwendolyn would be the envy of all the ladies at Lady Bowater's ball when they saw their magnificent gowns.

When it was time to go Mrs Winterton put a hand to her mouth and said, 'Oh, I nearly forgot! Melissa, be a dear and go to the door and tell William he can bring it in now.'

'It?' Melissa asked.

'He'll know what I mean. Just wait and see.'

Melissa thought that Mrs Winterton looked as excited as a child. She opened the front door and saw that the weather had worsened. The streetlamps had been lit already and damp flakes of sleety snow were illumined briefly as they fell through the pools of light, then landed on the pavements and melted almost immediately.

William leaped down from the coach as if he was expecting her.

'You can bring it in now,' Melissa said, and hoped that he really did know what was meant. He did and she watched as he pulled a wicker hamper from under his seat and lifted it down.

'Where to this time?' he asked.

'The dining room, I suppose.'

'Just lead the way.'

'William! Your nose is red – almost purple! You haven't been drinking, have you?' was Mrs Winterton's greeting to her coachman. 'I know all about that flask that you keep in your pocket.'

'It's the cold, ma'am,' he replied in that long-suffering way of his, and Melissa would not have thought less of him if he had indeed taken comfort with a nip or two of something warming.

'Well, put the hamper down. Here on the table?' The last was directed to Melissa's mother, who nodded. 'We won't keep you waiting much longer.'

'Perhaps your coachman would like a hot drink?' Emmeline Dornay asked. 'It would be quite in order for him to sit in the kitchen where Mrs Sibbet will make him a cup of tea.'

Melissa thought she saw a hopeful gleam in the coachman's eyes but it died away when Mrs Winterton said dismissively, 'Oh, no, we really must be going now. Wait outside, William. Now,' she said when the poor man had gone, 'this hamper was made up at Fenwick's this morning and it is a little gift from me in appreciation of all your hard work. Oh, go on, open it!'

Emmeline Dornay opened the hamper as she was bid, and she and Melissa stared at the provisions inside. There were slices of cold roast meats in glass containers, dishes of pâté, two whole game pies, cheeses wrapped in cloth, a Christmas cake, a Christmas pudding, boxes of sugared almonds and

Turkish delight, and various packets of biscuits such as shortbread and Bath Olivers. And a bottle of port wine.

'It's ten years old,' Mrs Winterton said, pointing to the bottle of dark red liquid. From her enthusiastic tone Melissa realised that must mean it was a good one.

'How very kind you are,' Emmeline said. 'There is so much here.'

Melissa thought that Lilian Winterton's smile was like that of a pleased child who has just been praised. Gwendolyn looked bored and restive.

'I thought of ordering a plucked goose for you,' Mrs Winterton said, 'but then I realised that you would probably already have ordered something for your Christmas meal.'

'Yes, I have,' Emmeline said, 'but this is quite luxurious. Thank you.'

'Well, then, I must go. But let me wish you and Melissa a very happy Christmas.'

The Wintertons took their leave and it was only when William had placed travelling rugs across their knees and was folding up the steps that Lilian remembered that she had not even mentioned her unpaid account.

'Wait!' she said, and William, who was just about to close the carriage door, paused and looked at her questioningly.

'Yes, madam?'

Lilian pushed her rug aside a little and began to rise. 'I should . . .' She did not see her coachman's resigned smile as he began to unfold the steps again and, after a moment of hesitation, she sank back down on to her seat. 'No, it's all right,' she said. 'Take us home now.'

As the coach pulled away Lilian was overwhelmed by an uncharacteristic feeling of shame. This morning, while she was still in bed, she had come up with the idea of presenting Emmeline with a Christmas hamper in order to soften the blow of not settling her account. But she had not been able to think of a satisfactory excuse and, in the end, she had forgotten all about it. Really, she had. Or rather she had put it at the back of her mind until the last moment and then the excitement of giving Emmeline the hamper and watching her open it had driven all thoughts of her dressmaking bill clean out of her mind altogether. She would settle the bill after Christmas. Or rather make it the first of her debts to be paid in the New Year.

Having made up her mind she sat back and began to think about which of her necklaces and earrings would look best with her new ball gown. Well, there was no question, really. She had requested this neckline because it would show her diamonds to the best advantage, and Gwendolyn must wear the purest, softest ivory-tinted pearls. Anything else would not go with the delicate passementerie on the bodice of her frock.

At the thought of the pearls her happy mood of anticipation faded. Before she had married Austin she had had only one pretty necklace and that was the single strand of pink-tinted pearls that Dermot had given her for her seventeenth birthday. She still had it, along with the matching drop earrings. She kept them in a little drawer – almost a secret drawer – in the base of one of her jewellery boxes.

Every now and then, if a sentimental mood came over her, she would take them out and look at them. She ought to have thrown them away or given them to one of the maids; especially as, over the years, the lustre had faded and the surface thinned until she could see the glass beads that they really were. Dermot's pearls had been false. But his love had been true. And after she had married Austin and experienced his notions of lovemaking, she realised more fully what she had done.

Thought of the pearls led her on to the episode she would rather forget for all kinds of bittersweet reasons, and the memory of it made her feel guilty all over again about the way she had treated Emmeline. At that marvellous but unhappy time in her life her dressmaker had been a compassionate and understanding friend.

Was Emmeline really going to die? Now true unease took hold of Lilian's soul. I must not leave it too long before I visit her, she thought. If she should die and someone else began to tidy her affairs, they might find Dermot's letters. That must not happen. I don't know why I've kept them, really. It's time I asked her to destroy them.

'What are we going to do with all this food?' Melissa asked her mother. 'There are only two of us. We won't be able to eat half of it even in a month of Sundays!'

Emmeline smiled at her. 'Martha Sibbet has five mouths to feed – as well as herself and her husband, so that makes seven. I wonder what the Sibbet family are having on Christmas Day.'

Melissa, guessing what her mother intended, asked, 'Shall I go and ask her to come here?'

'Yes, catch her before she goes home. And tell her to bring the old shopping basket from the pantry.'

Martha Sibbet was in the kitchen and so was Miss Bullock, the Dornays' landlady. These days the old lady liked to sit in an ancient rocking chair pulled close to the range, with her feet up on a cracket, a little wooden stool. Mrs Sibbet was spreading a clean cloth on the scrubbed tabletop. She looked up when Emmeline entered, grinned and put a finger to her lips, at the same time nodding sideways to indicate that Miss Bullock was sleeping. She came over to the door where they held a whispered conversation.

'I'm just setting the table up for her tea. There's bread and cheese, jam and the currant cake that your ma made yesterday. Is that right?'

Melissa nodded.

'And will you see to her if she doesn't wake up before it's time for me to go?'

'Of course. But first my mother wants you to come to the dining room. Oh – and bring that old shopping basket from the pantry.'

When Martha Sibbet saw the hamper and took in the fact that she was being asked to help herself to anything she fancied, her eyes opened wide.

'Eeh, no, Mrs Dornay, hinny,' she said. 'I can't take any of that.'

'Why ever not?' Emmeline asked her.

'Because the lady meant it for Melissa and you for Christmas.'

'There's far too much here for the two of us.'

'But you'll be providing for Miss Bullock as well, won't you?'

'Yes, we'll be having dinner together. So that's me, Melissa and one old lady. Most of this food will go to waste if you don't help us out.'

'Help you out? That's a nice way of putting it,' Mrs Sibbet smiled.

'But it's true,' Emmeline said.

'Then how can I refuse?'

After that Melissa watched as her mother and Miss Bullock's daily maid of all work argued about every item of food that was being offered.

'We cannot possibly eat two game pies,' Emmeline said. So one of them, wrapped in a clean tea towel, went into the old basket, followed by one of the cheeses, the Christmas pudding and the Christmas cake. Martha Sibbet argued long and hard about those two festive items but Emmeline reminded her that Melissa had helped her to make a pudding and a cake some weeks ago. The former, wrapped in a pudding cloth, was in the pantry ready to be taken out and steamed, and the latter was being stored in a large biscuit tin.

Martha also accepted some sliced roast beef and a jar of piccalilli to go with it. But she spurned the pâté. 'It's just like meat paste, isn't it?' she said. 'And, if you don't mind me saying so, Mrs Dornay, the bairns get enough of that and they wouldn't think it special on Christmas Day.'

While they were arranging everything in the shopping basket they suddenly heard Miss Bullock shouting something. Mrs Sibbet opened the dining-room door and they all held their breath and listened.

'Sibbet!' the old lady yelled. 'Where the dickens are you? The kettle's steaming its head off !'

'Just listen to her,' Martha Sibbet said. 'She might be deaf as a post but there's nowt wrong with her squealy box. I'd better gan and see to her.'

'No, wait a moment; there's something else I want to give you. Would you come along to the sewing room?'

'But what about her ladyship? She'll hev a proper fit if I don't go and make her pot of tea.'

'Melissa can do that.'

'Eeh, but . .' She looked doubtful.

Emmeline smiled at her. 'Melissa doesn't mind, do you?'

'Of course not.'

'Well, if you say so.' Mrs Sibbet shook her head. 'Like Daniel to the lions' den,' she said as Melissa set off along the passage.

Once in the sewing room Emmeline opened the cupboard and took out five little red and green woollen stockings, one for each of the Sibbet children.

'Christmas stockings!' Martha exclaimed. 'Eeh, they're lovely. Green and red are real Christmas colours, aren't they – the evergreens and the holly berries. Did you knit them yourself ?'

'No, Melissa made them.'

'Well, she's done a good job. They look so grand that it's a pity that all I'll be able to put inside them is the usual – an apple and an orange and mebbes a few nuts.'

'But that's what they expect!' Emmeline said. 'It wouldn't be the same if those simple gifts were not there.'

'You're right, hinny. And I'm very grateful to you – and Melissa, an' all. And now, I'd better gan along to the kitchen and rescue the bairn from the old termagant.'

'Wait – there is something else to go into each stocking – Melissa made them with pegs and pipe cleaners. One each. She dressed them too with scraps of material. Three pretty ladies for the girls and two handsome sailors for the boys.'

Emmeline took the little figures from the cupboard and laid them on the table. Mrs Sibbet's homely face shone with pleasure.

'Eeh, they're lovely. Little dresses and pinafores, and look at the sailors' hats!'

'At first the plan was to make soldiers for the two boys but we decided the caps would be too difficult.'

'Well, she's done a grand job. And now, if I can trouble you for a bit brown paper, I'll wrap everything up to keep them clean.'

She made her parcel up and put it in the basket, and she was about to go when Emmeline said, 'Mrs Sibbet, if you don't mind there's something I want you to do for me.'

'Anything! If it's within my power I'll do anything you ask.'

Emmeline looked grave. 'If anything should happen to me—'

'Don't talk like that, Mrs Dornay!'

'No, I must. If anything should happen to me I want you to go and tell my sister.'

'Of course I will.'

'And there's someone else who should know. One of my clients, Mrs Winterton.'

Martha Sibbet looked puzzled but she nodded and said, 'All right, pet. But . . . but what am I to say to the grand lady?'

'You won't have to say anything. I'll write her a letter. I'll put it under the lining paper in the top drawer of the chest in my bedroom. The address will be on the envelope.' Martha Sibbet looked uncomfortable. 'Please say you will; it's very important.'

'Yes, pet. Of course I will.'

'You mustn't let anyone else find it.'

'Anyone else in particular?'

'My sister.'

'I won't. I promise. But for pity's sake don't say any more. I don't know if I can stop meself from crying.'

Then, despite her brave intentions, she did start crying.

Emmeline Dornay put her arms round the good woman's shoulders and comforted her.

Chapter Four

On Christmas Day Melissa and her mother came back from church to find Miss Bullock dozing in her rocking chair by the kitchen range. She was dressed in her best, and the old-fashioned clothes made her look like a relic of a previous age. The old lady was wreathed in the steam coming from the pan boiling on the range. She could have moved her chair back but she did very little for herself these days. As it was, the translucent swirls of steam gave her a ghostly appearance. She looked as though she might fade away with the dissipating vapour.

The pan contained the plum pudding. Tied up ready in muslin, it had been set to boil in the large pan before they had even got dressed that morning. Now a sweet spicy aroma mingled with the tantalising smell of roasting beef coming from the oven.

Emmeline put a finger to her lips. 'Hush,' she whispered. 'We'll let Miss Bullock sleep until the meal is ready. We don't want her telling us how to do things properly like they did in the days gone by, do we?'

Miss Bullock, convinced that the world was going to the dogs, loved to tell them how things were done in the 'old days' when she was a girl. If she was in the kitchen when Emmeline or Melissa was preparing a meal – and she was very rarely anywhere else – she would constantly interrupt what they were doing although she would never actually offer to do anything herself. And she had never complained about the food they set before her either, always managing to have a second helping.

'Just a spoonful,' she would say. 'I have the appetite of a bird; a poor little sparrow.'

'Of course,' Emmeline would reply, while making sure that the spoon in question was heaped generously and, if another spoonful was added, Miss Bullock still managed to clear her plate.

While her mother put on her apron and added the finishing touches to their meal, Melissa was sent to the dining room to set the table and make sure it looked suitably festive with the best tableware set out on a damask cloth and evergreen decorations around the candle holders. Only when everything was ready and the food waiting on the table in the fancy serving dishes was Miss Bullock awakened gently and led through to the dining room.

The old lady was uncharacteristically quiet. She smiled and thanked Emmeline politely. But despite the 'appetite of a sparrow' she managed to eat every generous portion that was set before her – and more.

When they had finished the Christmas pudding Melissa's mother asked Miss Bullock if she would like a cup of coffee.

'No, thank you,' she said. 'No coffee. I'd rather have a sip of port wine and perhaps a cracker or two and a nibble of cheese to go with it.'

'Cheese?' Emmeline asked.

'Yes, cheese. Some of that nice cheese you've got in the hamper along with that bottle of port wine.'

'Ah, yes. As for the cheese, do you have any preference?'

Miss Bullock missed Emmeline's slightly acerbic tone and the look that passed between mother and daughter. 'No, you choose,' she said. As Emmeline left the room Miss Bullock called out, 'Don't forget the port wine.'

While her mother was absent Melissa glared at Miss Bullock indignantly. It was obvious that the old lady had been looking in their room, probably while they were at church, but it also seemed that her mother didn't want to make a fuss.

Melissa was allowed a small glass of port and, over the cheese and oatmeal biscuits also taken from the hamper, Miss Bullock raised her glass as if to make a toast.

'I drink to you, Mrs Dornay,' she said. 'I am glad we have had this Christmas together. I shall miss you.'

Melissa saw her mother's eyes widen and heard her gasp. 'What is it, Mama? What does Miss Bullock mean? We're not leaving, are we?'

'No, of course we're not,' her mother said, but she had caught her breath. 'Miss Bullock is confused,' she said quietly. 'It sometimes happens when you get old.'

'What are you saying?' their landlady demanded. 'Don't you know it's rude to whisper? Are you talking about me?'

Emmeline lowered her gaze and shook her head.

Miss Bullock glared at her suspiciously and then said, 'I need to have a little rest now. A proper rest in my bed. The girl can help me upstairs.'

'Of course.'

Melissa guided their landlady up the stairs and into her bedroom at the back of the house. She wanted very much to ask Miss Bullock what she had meant just now but she was frightened of what the answer might be so she simply helped the old lady take her shoes off and lie down on the bed, covering her with the counterpane.

Miss Bullock's eyes closed as soon as her head touched the pillow and she began to breathe evenly. Melissa tiptoed to the door and was just about to close it behind her when Miss

Bullock said quite clearly, 'Wake me up in time for tea. I want some mince pies and Christmas cake.'

When she got downstairs again Melissa asked her mother, 'Why didn't you say anything?'

'Say anything?'

'About the hamper.'

'What would have been the point? She's old and she's becoming more and more eccentric. If I said anything to annoy her she might give us notice and that would be a terrible upheaval. I don't think I would be able to cope with that just now.'

Their mood was subdued as they cleared the table and washed the dishes. Melissa noticed that her mother was reluctant to meet her eyes.

When they had finished Emmeline said, 'Shall we have coffee by the fire in the front parlour? I think we should open one of the boxes of fancy biscuits. Oh, and the Turkish delight – I noticed it's the sort that has pistachio nuts in. Your father used to bring me that from Istanbul. He said it was Napoleon's favourite.'

The front room was warm and peaceful, and although it was dark enough for them to light the lamps they preferred to sit in the firelight. They sat each side of the hearth and drank their coffee while they nibbled shortbread biscuits and discussed quietly what they would do with some of the food in the hamper, for they knew they would never be able to eat it all themselves.

'I'd like to take something round for Miss Robson and her mother,' Melissa said. 'They seem to be . . . well, I believe they live quite modestly.'

'I'm sure they do if a teacher's salary is all they have to live on. It's a scandal, isn't it, that women teachers earn far less than men do? Especially as they do the same work. But don't get me started!'

They smiled at each other. They had often talked about women's place in the world and how it was beginning to change, thank goodness, but the changes were progressing far too slowly for Emmeline's liking.

Suddenly serious, Emmeline said, 'Just think what my life would have been like if I had not had this dressmaking business. When we lost your father I wouldn't have been able to get my old job in the sewing room back because they don't take married women. I might have ended up doing piecework at home; sewing men's shirts or ladies' blouses for a few pence a garment. I don't think it would have been possible to make more than ten shillings a week, and with that I would have had to pay the rent and clothe and feed us both.'

Suddenly she leaned across the space between them and took Melissa's hand. 'I have taught you all I know,' she said. 'And you have reached a stage where you are beginning to teach me. If anything should happen to me I want you to carry on with your dressmaking and perhaps, one day, you will own not just a parlour dressmaker's establishment like this, but a fashionable salon. Who knows what you could achieve?'

'But we will own that salon together, Mama, if we work hard together, won't we?'

'I would like to think so, Melissa. I would like to think so.'

Melissa looked into her mother's kind face. There were so many questions she wanted to ask but, at that moment, the quiet of the afternoon was broken by the sound of a brass band.

Emmeline's face lit up. 'The Sally Army!' she said. 'Oh, do let us put our coats on and go out and listen to them. But we must wrap up warmly.'

Before they left the house Emmeline took the old tin tea

caddy from its place on the top shelf of the sewing cupboard. The caddy was decorated with pictures of tea clippers, the fast sailing ships that raced to bring their precious cargoes of tea from China to London. Melissa remembered her father telling her that the two clippers on the tin were the fastest of all, the *Cutty Sark* and the *Thermopylae*.

Emmeline kept her day-to-day expenses in this tin and anything she had managed to save. She took out a handful of small coins. 'For the collection,' she said. Then, instead of putting the tea caddy back on its shelf in the cupboard she held it out towards Melissa.

'I'd like you to keep this in your bedroom,' she said.

Melissa was astonished. 'Why?'

'Well, if Miss Bullock has started poking around in our belongings . . .'

'Yes, but she wouldn't steal anything, would she?'

'No, I'm sure she wouldn't. However, I prefer to keep to ourselves our business and how much money we have. Go along, put it in the cupboard in the corner, on the top shelf with your old schoolbooks and pencil case. I don't think anyone would think anything there was worth looking at.'

Melissa was puzzled by this request but she could see that her mother was determined. 'All right,' she said, and took the tea caddy.

She hurried upstairs and, reaching up, put it exactly where her mother had told her, on the top shelf of the cupboard. It only occurred to her at that moment that Miss Bullock, smaller than anyone they knew, would not have been able to reach the tea caddy where it had rested originally. But, not wanting to upset her mother, who had seemed anxious about the matter, she decided not to say anything and hurried downstairs.

Then mother and daughter left the house and walked to the end of the street. It was still trying to snow but the flakes were too wet to lie for long. Smoke rose from all the chimneys and, with very little wind to blow it away, it hung like a pall over the city and the smell of coal dust mingled with the sharp winter air. Any snow that did manage to lie for a while, hard up against the garden walls, was a sooty grey.

The bandsmen and women of the Salvation Army were standing in a circle playing Christmas carols. Many of the neighbours had come out and they accepted the tracts they were handed good-naturedly. When a young woman Salvationist came round with the collection tin everyone gave what they could afford.

Melissa did not consider herself too grown up to hold her mother's hand and when they joined in and sang the old carols together she was almost overwhelmed by her feelings of pure happiness.

After they had sung 'O Little Town of Bethlehem', which was Melissa's favourite, she noticed that her mother's voice, usually so sweet and clear, had grown husky. She looked up into Emmeline's face and saw that, although she looked happy, she also looked tired.

'We'd better go now,' Melissa said. 'I promised Miss Bullock that I would wake her up for Christmas cake and mince pies.'

The old lady had woken herself up and was sitting in her usual place by the range in the kitchen. 'Couldn't sleep with that dratted noise!' she told them. 'Ought to be a law against it. Brass bands on a Christmas Day afternoon, indeed. They're playing fit to wake the dead!' Miss Bullock saw Melissa and her mother looking at her in astonishment. 'I'm not that deaf, you know. It's only when folk mumble at me that I don't catch the drift of things. I can't abide mumblers!'

Settled once more at the table in the dining room, Miss Bullock tucked in to the mince pies with relish. When her sparrow's appetite had allowed her to consume two mince pies with brandy butter, a piece of Christmas cake and a generous slice of white, crumbly Lancashire cheese, washed down by strong sweet tea, their landlady said she was tired and was going to go up to bed for an early night.

'See me up the stairs, if you don't mind,' she told Melissa, 'and if you two are going to sit and talk I'd oblige you to keep your voices down.'

Downstairs again Melissa found her mother was determined to be cheerful.

'Shall we sit by the fire in the parlour and tell each other stories?' she asked. 'That's what we're supposed to do on Christmas Day, isn't it?'

'Yes,' Melissa agreed. 'I love making up stories.'

'Well, let us have cheerful stories. You may have dashing heroes and beautiful princesses but whatever befalls them I want happy endings, is that understood?'

'Perfectly. But first, may we open our presents?'

They had purposely delayed opening their presents until this moment when they knew they would be without interruption. 'Oh, goodness, how could I forget?' Emmeline said. She reached down and opened the lid of the padded velvet-topped box that acted as a footstool. Two small gaily wrapped parcels were in there. Both she and Melissa had agreed that neither of them would even look at them until the time they had both agreed on.

'Who shall go first?' Emmeline asked.

'You!'

'Very well.'

Emmeline undid the red satin ribbon and opened up the wrapping paper, which was decorated with sprigs of holly. She lifted up the cream linen handkerchief case she found inside.

'Melissa, this is beautiful!'

The handkerchief case was shaped like an envelope with

embroidery on the flap. The motif was oriental. Two Chinese lanterns hung from a branch bearing delicate pink flowers.

'You made it, of course?'

'Yes.'

'I had no idea. How clever of you to keep it secret.'

'I worked on it whenever you took an afternoon nap, but as that doesn't happen very often, mostly I took it to bed with me.'

'And did this exquisite embroidery by candlelight?'

'Mm.' Melissa nodded.

'But your eyesight! Don't worry, I'm not going to scold you.'

Emmeline looked down at the handkerchief case and she was silent for a while. The only sound was the comforting crackling of the coals. Then she looked up and smiled.

'You must open your present now,' she said.

When Melissa undid the ribbons and opened up the paper she found herself staring at two exquisite faux tortoiseshell hair combs. Each comb had six prongs and each of the ridges at the top was decorated with a row of tiny crystal flowers.

'They're beautiful,' Melissa said. 'I've never seen anything like them.'

'They're French. Your father brought them home from one of his voyages.'

'But then they belong to you.'

'No, I have mine – look, I'm wearing them.'

Emmeline bent her head so that Melissa could see the combs holding up her hair.

'But you wear those every day – and they are not as grand as these combs.'

'I have finer hair than you. These combs are more delicate and less heavy without the crystal flowers. They are just as dear to me, believe me. But even when you were a small child your hair was luxuriantly abundant and your father and I agreed that this pair should be kept until the time came for you to put it up.'

'Put my hair up? But I'm too young to do that, aren't I?'

'Yes, you are, my dear.'

'So why are you giving me the combs now?'

'You needn't wait until you're old enough to put your hair up. You can use them to hold it back. I want to see you wearing them. I want to see the combs shining in your bonny dark hair.'

There was a disturbing intensity in her mother's tone and Melissa stirred uneasily. Emmeline must have seen her discomfort for she seemed to make an effort to relax.

She smiled and said, 'Tomorrow I will brush and comb your hair just like I did when you were a little girl and I'll show you how to use the combs to best effect, but now why don't you go to the kitchen and warm a small pan of milk? We'll have a cup of cocoa while you tell your stories.'

It didn't take Melissa long to make the cocoa and, soon, settled by the fire with a box of fancy biscuits open beside them, she began to lose herself in the imaginary worlds she found it so easy to create. Her mother looked peaceful and happy, and she interrupted and asked questions about the stories just as a child would have done.

The memory of their closeness and contentment that day would live with Melissa for the rest of her life.

No matter that it was Boxing Day; Martha Sibbet was expected to report for work at Miss Bullock's house first thing in the morning as usual. She could have caught two trams, one into town and another out in the other direction, but she saved money by walking from her home in Byker to Miss Bullock's neat terrace house in West Jesmond, not far from the Town Moor.

I wish the weather would make its mind up, she thought as, head down, she made her way through wind-driven rain. One moment it looks as though it's snowing and the bairns get all excited and get the old tin trays out, then the next it's turned to rain and the streets are a mess of melting slush.

But despite this she was cheerful, carried on her way by memories of the good time they had had yesterday and the fact that her man, Billy, was at home to mind the bairns instead of having to trust them to the old woman next door.

When Martha arrived at Miss Bullock's house the kitchen was still filled with the delicious smells of the Christmas dinner that had been cooked there the day before. But she imagined it would be only a little more delicious than the feast the Sibbet family had enjoyed with the little extras provided by Mrs Dornay.

Melissa was sitting at the table drinking a cup of tea. Martha was surprised to see her up so early on a day when she and her ma probably wouldn't be receiving customers, but even more surprising was the fact that she had her coat and hat on.

'Am I late or are you up early again?' Martha asked.

Melissa looked at her over her teacup. 'I'm up early.'

Martha took off her thick woollen gloves and stuffed them in her pockets before unwinding her long scarf. 'Going somewhere?'

'I am but I waited to see you before I go out.'

'Now why's that, hinny? And where exactly are you off to on Boxing Day morning?'

'I'm going to visit my old teacher, Miss Robson.'

'Not for a French lesson? Not today?'

'No, I just want to take her a present.'

'Why so early?'

'Because my mother has some new fashion magazines; she gets them sent from Paris. So I'd like to go and visit Miss

Robson and come back in time to spend a whole lovely day looking at the new season's fashions and planning how we can adapt them to suit our clientele.'

'Clientele? What's that when it's got its socks on?'

Melissa smiled at her. 'Our customers. You know that.'

Martha Sibbet chuckled. 'Aye, hinny, I do. I just like to tease you a little when you put that la-di-da voice on.'

'Put it on? Oh, I don't, do I?'

The lass looked upset and Martha, who had just hung her coat on the back of the door, came over to the table and looked down at her.

'No, pet, you don't. That was a silly thing to say. You talk the way you do because that's how your mother's brought you up. And I wouldn't hev you any different. Now why did you wait to see me?'

'My mother isn't awake yet. I would have taken her a cup of tea and told her myself that I was going out but when I looked in she was sleeping peacefully. It seemed a shame to disturb her.'

'Divven't fret. I'll tell her where you are the minute she comes down. Or better still, why don't I leave it a little while longer and then take her a cup of tea meself ? She deserves a treat.'

'Would you?'

'No bother at all. Now get yourself off to see that school teacher.'

It was an easy walk to Miss Robson's house in South Gosforth. Melissa set off carrying a large basket with a waterproof cover stretched over the top. The rain, which had pattered against her windowpane earlier that morning, had stopped and the drenched streets began to look more cheerful as a pale sun broke through the clouds.

Here and there in the neat respectable streets children

were out with their new toys – tops and whips, hoops and skipping ropes – and Melissa smiled sympathetically when she came across two little boys with a tin tray. They were looking for snow, she guessed, but the little there had been had melted away and there would be no sledging today.

Miss Robson was surprised to see her. She showed her into the front parlour, which was the room she used in the evenings to receive the pupils she took for French lessons.

But almost as soon as they had entered, the tall, thin woman gave an exaggerated shiver and exclaimed, 'Ooh, but it's chilly in here! I would have lit the fire if I'd known you were coming but, as it is, if I light it now it will take too long to get going. Would you mind coming through to our little living room?'

'Not at all,' Melissa said, and she followed Miss Robson curiously. She had never been invited to the domestic rooms in the house.

The living room was not much warmer than the front parlour. The fire was part of a small range. There was just enough coal to keep it going and grey wisps of smoke rose from the coals rather than flames. An old lady sat beside it, wrapped up in so many shawls that she looked like a swaddled baby.

'This is my mother,' Miss Robson said, and the old woman looked up and smiled.

'Is this one of your pupils, Harriet? I didn't realise that you were teaching today.'

'Mother, this is Melissa Dornay, and she is one of my pupils. But today she is making a social call.'

'Melissa? The dressmaker's daughter? How very good of her,' Miss Robson's mother said and, although her smile was welcoming, her surprise was evident.

Melissa guessed that the Robsons, mother and daughter, did not have many visitors.

But now the old lady was frowning as she eyed the basket Melissa was carrying.

'Oh, but perhaps this is not a social call after all.'

'What do you mean?' her daughter asked.

'Melissa has brought our mending back, hasn't she? That is what is in the basket.'

Miss Robson looked helplessly at Melissa, who realised straight away that this had not occurred to her teacher, and that she too was disappointed.

'I have brought your mending,' Melissa told them, 'but I would not have come out on Boxing Day just for that.'

'That's true, Mother,' Miss Robson said with relief, and Melissa saw that the kindly teacher had not wanted her mother to be disappointed. 'Melissa, will you take off your coat and sit down at the table there?'

'Oh . . . but . . .'

'You will not feel the benefit when you go out again if you don't take it off.'

'Oh, of course.'

Melissa took her coat off and sat down as she was told. She had not wanted to stay too long but she could not bear to disappoint them. As Miss Robson took her coat out into the hall to hang it up Melissa looked around her. There was a chair at each side of the fireplace, a large dark oak sideboard against one wall and the chenille-covered table at which she was sitting now. She guessed that the other door led to the kitchen. The room was too small for all this furniture but Melissa guessed that they lived here most of the time so that they would only have to light one fire.

Miss Robson didn't ask Melissa if she wanted tea; she simply assumed that she did. She hurried through to the kitchen and Melissa heard the tap running and the kettle being filled. Miss Robson brought it through and placed it on the hotplate of the range, which served as both fire and cooker. She took an exquisite but faded embroidered tablecloth from a drawer in the sideboard and placed it over the dark green chenille on the table. Then she busied herself setting the teapot, milk and sugar and cups and saucers on the table.

The tea, served in rose-patterned bone china, was weak and the biscuits were a little stale. Miss Robson and her mother, dressed in dull black bombazine, looked like characters from a novel by Mr Dickens. Melissa, lowering her head to sip her tea, suffered an ache of sympathy for the two women. She suspected that they had known better times and that, now, their lives were harder.

Emmeline Dornay was happy to pay whatever Miss Robson charged for Melissa's French lessons, but every now and then Miss Robson would ask Melissa if she could do some mending for her and her mother and then she would refuse to take payment for the lessons.

The undergarments, always perfectly clean, would need new tapes, or ribbons, the stockings would need darning, and the blouses Miss Robson wore at school might need their cuffs and collars turning or a button or two replaced. Although she would have been astonished to have been told so, with her slimness and height Miss Robson had a certain air of elegance. Melissa would have loved to have altered her teacher's sensible and outdated clothes and made them discreetly fashionable, but she had never dared suggest it in case she caused offence.

As soon as they had finished the tea and biscuits Melissa got the brown paper parcel of mended clothes from her basket. Miss Robson thanked her and put the parcel on the sideboard.

'I needn't check them over,' she said. 'I know everything will be satisfactory.' And then she puzzled Melissa by saying, 'I suppose you did the right thing.'

'I beg your pardon?'

'By leaving school as soon as you had your fourteenth birthday. I would have liked you to stay on, you know, become a pupil teacher – you have the intelligence.' She paused and smiled. 'But why on earth should you want to be an impoverished teacher when your talent with the needle will surely lead to a most successful career as a dressmaker?'

Miss Robson's mother had fallen asleep with her cup and saucer in her hands. Now the saucer had slipped to the floor and the cup was about to follow when her daughter saw what was happening and hurried forward to retrieve them. The way she smiled at her sleeping mother was revealing. Perhaps they were struggling to get by but it was obvious that Miss Robson loved her mother and did not resent having to look after her.

Melissa rose to her feet. 'I'm sorry but I had better go home now,' she said. 'My mother will wonder what is keeping me.'

'Of course she will. I have been selfish to keep you here. I'll get your coat.'

'Miss Robson, wait, I brought you something.' Aware that her teacher might be offended, Melissa had been worrying about what she should say. 'One of my mother's clients gave us a hamper for Christmas. There was far too much in it for my mother and myself. We hoped that you would accept these.' She took one of the little pots of pâté from the basket along with a box of Bath Olivers and a generous-sized dish containing some of the sliced cold meats.

'Oh, but, my dear, I can't accept—'

'Please do. It would be so dreadful to waste anything – a sin.'

'Yes, it would, wouldn't it? Well . . . if you're sure . . .'

'Yes, I am. And I hope you will accept these as well.' Melissa added a paper confectionery bag to the things already on the table.

Miss Robson opened the twist of paper and exclaimed, 'Sugared almonds. My favourites!'

'Yes, I know.'

'What are you smiling at?'

'I'm remembering the day in the school yard when you pulled a handkerchief from your pocket and a packet of sweets came out as well. The packet dropped and the sweets – sugared almonds – rolled all over the place. You looked dismayed.'

'Dismayed? I was positively heartbroken!'

'Now, thank you for having me but I ought to go home. My mother and I are going to have a lovely quiet day together.'

'I'll tell Mother that you said goodbye.'

Miss Robson saw Melissa to the door and reminded her that her French lessons would begin again the following week. When they said goodbye both of them were smiling.

Melissa was halfway home when the sky clouded over and it started to rain again. But she was happy and she didn't mind the rain. She lifted her face up towards it, heedless of the fact that her skin would be speckled with soot long before she got home.

Did I forget to draw back the curtains? she thought as she approached the house where she lived. She frowned as she tried to remember. It was very early so perhaps I did. But she was sure she could recall opening the curtains and seeing to the fire so that the room would be comfortable when her mother came down.

Melissa opened the gate and walked up the short path. She was just about to take her door key from her pocket when the door opened. Martha Sibbet stood there and her eyes were red as if she had been weeping.

'Come in, pet,' she said, and it seemed to Melissa that she was choking back tears.

'What is it?' Melissa asked.

Mrs Sibbet shook her head and motioned for her to come in but Melissa, full of an unnamed dread, remained on the doorstep. She became aware of a cold wind blowing at her back and rain spattering across the black and red tiles of the porch.

'Mrs Cook is here,' Martha said.

'Aunt Janet? Why?' Melissa was suddenly afraid.

'I went to get her – like your ma said.'

'My mother told you to go and get Aunt Janet?'

The fear receded a little. Her mother had sent Mrs Sibbet to fetch her aunt so she couldn't be . . . couldn't be . . .

But then she saw Martha Sibbet's tears flowing freely and heard the anguish in her voice. 'Come in, Melissa pet, divven't let the cold in. It's miserable enough in this house this morning. That's right – let me shut the door behind you – now give us your coat and hat and gan in to see your Aunt Janet.'

Her aunt was standing by the sewing cupboard. The doors were open and Melissa wondered why. Aunt Janet turned quickly to face Melissa and said, 'About time. Where have you been?'

'To see Miss Robson – my teacher – I left a message for my mother.'

'Well, she never got it.'

'Why? Didn't Mrs Sibbet tell her? She said she would.'

'Aye, well, no doubt she intended to. But when she went upstairs it was too late for messages. Your mother's dead.'

Chapter Five

Melissa swayed forward and clung to the back of the armchair. It wasn't just for support. She wanted to put something solid between herself and her aunt, who was staring at her stone-faced, and saying such hateful things.

'My mother is dead?' she whispered.

'Aye, dead. The doctor's still upstairs with her. He said she must have passed over in her sleep and that he'd been expecting it.' Aunt Janet paused and narrowed her eyes before saying, 'You wicked child!'

The words were like a slap across the face. Melissa wondered if she'd heard aright. 'Wicked? What do you mean?'

'Gallivanting off in the morning to see your la-di-da friends and not having the decency to look in on your ma. You knew how poorly she was. How near to death's door.'

'No – I didn't know!'

But as soon as the words were out of her mouth Melissa knew that she should have known. That she *had* known and that her mother had surely tried to warn her. But she hadn't listened properly because she hadn't wanted to believe anything so dreadful could happen.

'No more to say for yourself ?' her aunt asked.

'No – I mean, yes. I did look in on my mother this

morning. She was sleeping and I didn't want to wake her up. I asked Mrs Sibbet to tell her where I was and she offered to take up a cup of tea.'

'Well, the poor woman did as you asked and it was her that found her. Ice cold, your mother was. Dr Liddell says she probably died not long after she went to bed last night. And you know what that means, don't you? It means she was already dead when you said you went to her room.'

Her aunt stressed the word 'said', making it plain that she thought Melissa was lying.

'I did go in – I didn't want to disturb her – she looked so peaceful.' Suddenly Melissa whirled round and made for the door.

'Stop! Where are you going?'

'Upstairs to see my mother.'

'You can't. Not right now.'

'Why not?'

'Mrs Hewitt is there. She's come to lay her out proper. All ready to go in her coffin.'

'Please don't!'

Her aunt looked affronted. 'Don't what?'

'Please don't keep saying such terrible things.'

'I only tell the truth.'

'I know. I'm sorry. But please go home now and leave me alone.'

'Go home? The very idea! I've come to see to things just as your ma wanted me to. Not that I don't have enough to do. When Martha Sibbet turned up on my doorstep this morning I knew at once why . . .'

The hateful voice mercifully began to fade away. Melissa felt her eyes mist over . . . everything in the room became blurred. Someone was calling her name – telling her to stand up properly . . . I am standing up, she thought, but the very next moment she slumped sideways to the floor.

*

Dr Liddell had just gone and Martha Sibbet was standing at the table in the kitchen. Mrs Hewitt had come down for a moment before going back to carry out her sad task.

Bessie Hewitt was a woman who acted as a midwife; bringing most of the local bairns into the world, and when someone's life came to an end she would lay the body out and prepare it for the funeral. Martha thought it strange that Mrs Hewitt should be there at the beginning and the end of folk's lives. The woman was both cheerful and practical, going about her business without fuss, sharing the joys and worries a new bairn brought and showing a proper respect for the dead.

She was small and round, with a pink and white complexion and fine white hair that rose around her head like a halo. She sat at the table and Martha was pouring her a cup of tea when a bell rang. Martha looked up in fright and almost dropped the teapot.

'What is it?' Mrs Hewitt asked. 'You look scared out of your wits.'

Martha was staring at Miss Bullock, who was sitting in her usual place. The old lady was rocking to and fro with her eyes closed. Her prayer book rested on her lap. 'It wasn't her,' Martha Sibbet said, 'because she's right here in the kitchen.'

Mrs Hewitt turned to look at Miss Bullock, then said, 'Well, that's obvious.'

'Did you hear the bell just now?'

'Of course I did.'

'Like I said, Miss Bullock is right here so it can't have been her ringing from her bedroom.'

'You're talking nonsense.'

'And there's no one else upstairs who could hev rung, is there?'

'No, the doctor's gone home.'

'So . . . who . . . ?'

'Take hold of yourself, you daft woman,' Mrs Hewitt said kindly. 'I've dealt with the dead for many a long year and I can tell you that poor lady upstairs has passed away, no question about it. And furthermore, there's no such thing as ghosts.'

At that moment the bell jangled again and both Martha and Mrs Hewitt glanced at the row of bells on the wall above the door that led to the passage.

'It's the front parlour,' Martha said.

'Why didn't you think of that in the first place?'

'Because if Mrs Dornay is downstairs she never rings the bell, she's too considerate. She always comes through herself or sends the bairn.'

'Well, she won't be doing either in future, will she, Martha, hinny?'

They looked at each other solemnly and while they did the bell rang again, furiously. The coiled spring connected to the bell danced up and down, jangling Martha's nerves.

'So who's in the parlour right now?' Mrs Hewitt asked.

Martha's lips thinned.

'Mrs Dornay's sister, Mrs Cook. You'll know her when you see her. She gans about looking as if she's just supped a bottle of vinegar.'

'Oh, aye. Her.'

'I suppose I'd better get in there.' Martha was reluctant.

'And I'll drink this tea, then go upstairs and see to the poor lady. I'll do my very best for her.'

Martha paused outside the parlour door, wondering whether she ought to knock. She decided she wouldn't and walked straight in.

'You took your time,' Janet Cook said angrily. 'Didn't you hear me ringing?'

The usually good-natured maid of all work was just

about to tell Mrs Cook that she didn't expect to be at her beck and call when she noticed Melissa lying on the floor.

'What on earth has happened here?'

'She fainted. Can't you see for yourself ?'

Martha kneeled down beside Melissa and lifted one of the bairn's hands. It was icy cold. Martha's heart skipped a beat. No, it couldn't be, she couldn't have died of shock, could she? But then she saw Melissa's chest rising and falling gently. The lass was breathing.

'And you just left her here?' She glared up at Mrs Cook, who glared back.

'That's why I rang for you!' she snapped. 'To help me get her on to the sofa.'

'Couldn't you at least hev put a cushion under her head?'

'I wouldn't have needed to if you had come straight away.'

There was no time to argue so Martha nodded tersely and, without waiting for help from Janet Cook, she lifted Melissa in her arms as if she were a little bairn and laid her on the sofa.

'Pass me that rug,' she said over her shoulder, 'the one on the chair. The lass is as cold as death.'

Realising what she had said, she covered her face with her hands for a moment and then pulled herself together.

Janet Cook stood back while Martha eased a large cushion under Melissa's head and then covered her gently with the rug.

'Poor little lass,' Martha said as she straightened up. 'It's the shock that's making her cold. I'll build up the fire, shall I?'

'No, that won't be necessary. I'll take her home with me once she comes round.'

'I don't think so,' Martha said. 'She's best off here.'

'How dare you? I'm her aunt and it's what her mother would have wanted.'

'Her mother wouldn't hev wanted her to be torn away from the only home she's ever known; not today of all days.'

'I quite agree.' A voice came from the doorway.

Martha and Janet Cook both turned to see Miss Bullock standing there. The old lady held herself erect and she appeared determined.

She didn't look as though she could be argued with but Janet tried. 'This may be Melissa's home,' she said, 'but it's her family she needs at a time like this.'

'A family she hardly knows,' Miss Bullock replied. 'There will be time enough to sort out what's going to happen after the funeral, but until then I would be obliged if you will leave Melissa here with me.'

For a moment it looked as though Janet was going to protest but she must have decided it wasn't worth the bother, not for now.

'Well, speaking of the funeral,' she said, 'there must be an insurance book somewhere. I've looked in the cupboard.'

'So you hev,' Martha said, eyeing the open door, 'but I don't suppose you found it.'

'No, I didn't.'

'Well, divven't fret, you won't hev to bear the cost of your sister's funeral yourself. Here's the book.'

Emmeline Dornay's sister took the funeral club book from Martha Sibbet and eyed her suspiciously. 'What were you doing with it?'

'I found it this morning.'

'Where?'

'Where I was told to look.'

'And was there anything else there?'

'No, at least nothing that need concern you. So you can get along home now. I'll see to things here.'

Janet Cook took her coat from where it had been lying over the back of a chair, put it on and buttoned it up with quick angry movements. 'I'm surprised you let your servants talk to their betters like this,' she said to Miss Bullock.

To Martha's surprise the old lady gave a wry smile. 'Firstly I've only got one servant, and secondly, if it wasn't for the fact that your sister has just died and I must assume you are grieving, I would have spoken to you in much the same way myself. Now is not the time to upset Melissa any further. So if you don't mind, I'd like you to go home now. You are welcome to come back here to deal with the undertaker and also to hold the funeral tea in this house.'

'But Melissa . . .' Janet Cook gave one last try.

'Don't worry about Emmeline's daughter. I will sit with her tonight. She will not be alone.'

Martha watched in amazement as Miss Bullock took charge of the situation. Emmeline Dornay's death seemed to have brought the old lady back to life – or at least back from the half-world that she had inhabited for many years. Janet Cook could see that she had been bested and allowed Martha to show her out but with ill grace. When she had gone Martha returned to the front parlour to find Miss Bullock seated in the armchair.

'I think Melissa is stirring,' she said. 'I'd be grateful if you could see to her. My old bones need a rest.'

Martha assumed that Miss Bullock wanted her to comfort the lass and she went over to the sofa and kneeled down. Melissa's eyes were open but full of tears. She turned her head to look at Martha.

'Is my aunt still here?' she whispered, and looked fearfully over Janet's shoulder.

'Divven't fret, lass. She's gone.'

'And it's true? What my aunt said. It's really true?'

'Aye, it is, pet. I'm sorry.'

'But she never showed me how to do my hair,' Melissa said.

Martha frowned. Had the poor bairn's head been addled with grief ? 'You know how to do your hair, Melissa. Your ma taught you a long time ago.'

'No . . . the combs . . . the pretty combs she gave me for Christmas. She was going to show me this morning how to put them in my hair. She was going to brush my hair for me like she did when I was a child. But I went without even saying good morning to her. My aunt is right. I'm a wicked person.'

'No you're not,' Martha said angrily. 'And if your aunt told you that, it's her who's wicked!'

'But I shouldn't have gone out.'

'You did no wrong. You thought your ma was sleeping and you didn't want to disturb her.'

'But she wasn't sleeping, was she?'

'No, hinny, she wasn't, and there was nothing you could hev done to bring her back.'

'Nothing at all,' Miss Bullock echoed. 'And now, Melissa, I think you should try to eat something. Martha has managed to make a pan of broth. Do you think you could take a little?'

Melissa shook her head.

'Just to please me?'

All the years Martha had worked for Miss Bullock she had never seen her behave in anything but a selfish manner. It was a pity that it had taken a tragedy like this to bring out the old besom's human side.

Martha brought a tray with a bowl of broth for Melissa and then another for Miss Bullock. She made sure the old woman had a footstool and, seeing she seemed determined to sit there all night, she brought her a blanket as well. Miss Bullock had decided it was better for the lass not to go upstairs that night, but when Mrs Hewitt came down and told them that 'everything was tidy', it was hard to deny the girl the chance to go up and say goodbye to her mother.

Martha went up with her, worried that Melissa would pass out again. But although tearful, the lass was as brave as a soldier. She kissed her mother's brow, kneeled down to say a prayer, and then allowed Martha to lead her downstairs to the parlour again where she lay on the sofa wordlessly until misery eased her into a fitful sleep.

For the rest of the day, as Martha went about her duties, she tried not to think about the moment she had set the cup of tea down on Mrs Dornay's bedside table and then turned to discover that the poor lady had no need of it. She had been shocked but had retained the presence of mind to look for the letter Mrs Dornay had told her about before going down to tell Miss Bullock.

It had seemed wrong, somehow, to be opening the drawer and looking through her personal things when the poor woman was lying there behind her. But Mrs Dornay had begged her to make sure that no one else found the letter she had written to Mrs Winterton. Martha had found the letter but it wasn't the only one. There was one for Martha herself. She opened that straight away and the tears streamed down her face as she read Mrs Dornay's last words to her.

My dear friend,

If you are reading this I ask you to remember your promise to take the letter to Mrs Winterton. I think you should know that she has promised to take Melissa for me. I do not want my daughter to go to my sister's house. But, of course, my sister must be told what has happened and I ask you to go there first and give her the little book you will find under my stocking case. It's my funeral club payment book. Janet will need it if she is to arrange my burial, which she has agreed to do, no doubt because, as family, it will be expected of her.

When she read those words Martha Sibbet almost choked on her tears but she wiped her face with the back of her hand and continued to read.

I wish I had been brave enough to prepare Melissa more thoroughly for this event. If I live long enough I will say something. I must pray to the Lord to advise me. Whatever the circumstance she will need comforting and I hope that you will do that until my dear friend Mrs Winterton will take my place, as she has promised to do.

There is one last favour I must ask of you. In the cabinet beside my bed there is a rosewood sewing box. It is not very practical for a working dressmaker but it is very beautiful and, more importantly, it is the first gift that Bertrand gave me. I want Melissa to have it. No one else. No doubt my sister would offer to look after it so, rather than offend her, it is better that she should not know of its existence.

Martha paused again and this time lifted her pinafore to wipe her eyes more thoroughly. *Look after it, indeed!* She sniffed. Her nose was itching. Probably with indignation, she thought. She knew very well that poor Mrs Dornay simply didn't want her sister to get her hands on it for, if she did, no doubt Melissa would never see her mother's workbox again.

If it is not convenient for you to give the workbox to my daughter straight away then would you ask Miss Bullock to keep it safe for her? I'm sure she will oblige. But try to make sure that Melissa gets the workbox before the day is over. There is a letter inside for her.

The poor lady had ended her letter by thanking Martha for all her kindnesses over the years. And asking her to remember her with affection.

'Of course I'll remember you, Mrs Dornay, hinny,' Martha had said and then felt awkward to have spoken out loud.

She looked down at Mrs Dornay's still form. Lying in her bed as peaceful and as beautiful as an angel. As for thanking me for my kindnesses, she told her silently, it's me who will be ever grateful to you, and not just for the clothes you gave me for me and the bairns but for the sweet way you talked to me as if I was just as good as you were. Divven't worry, pet. You can rest quiet. I won't let you down now.

Martha had stuffed the letters and the insurance book in the pocket of her pinafore and found the workbox. Then she had gone to tell the old lady what had happened.

Miss Bullock had just got herself downstairs and was sitting at the table in the kitchen pouring tea from the pot Martha had made and left there. At first Martha thought the old lady hadn't taken in what she had told her. She had two or three sips of tea and then had placed her cup carefully back in her saucer before saying, 'I suppose you'd better go for Mrs Dornay's sister first. And then go for Dr Liddell. And Mrs Hewitt too.'

Martha waited for Miss Bullock to say something else and after a long pause the old lady sighed and dabbed at her eyes with one of her little Swiss handkerchiefs. It was the first time Martha had seen her employer show anything approaching human emotion. Miss Bullock told her to give the workbox to her.

'I'll keep it by me under my chair here until it is safe to give it to her,' she said.

It seemed Martha wasn't the only one who didn't trust Mrs Dornay's sister.

Then, 'Run along,' Miss Bullock said. 'I'll go upstairs and sit with Mrs Dornay. This is my house and I must show a proper respect.'

Martha was surprised that the old woman was prepared to stir herself. Not that it would do any good – it was too late for words of hope and comfort. But perhaps Miss Bullock was going to say a prayer. Martha saw that she had guessed right when the old lady rose from the table and took an old leather-bound prayer book from the drawer in the sideboard. Miss Bullock held herself upright but her gait was slightly unsteady as she made for the door.

It was late by the time Martha got away. Even before she'd gone to tell Mrs Cook, she had drawn the curtains in every room of the house. Later she had remembered to cover all the mirrors, as was the custom. Now Miss Bullock reminded her that before she went home she must make sure that the window in Mrs Dornay's bedroom was closed again.

Mrs Hewitt had opened the window when she had arrived, as was proper. This was to allow the spirit of the dead woman to fly away. But now the window must be closed so that the poor soul did not try to get in again. Martha had always thought this a cruel thing to do until Billy had explained to her that the souls of the dead must find their way to heaven and not wander the earth and bother the living.

Thinking about these things made Martha pull her collar up around her neck before glancing up at the evening sky. Smoke from the many chimneys swirled up to join the black clouds, but here and there she glimpsed a star shining faintly through the gloom. She felt her thoughts taking a morbid turn and she shook her head as if the physical action would chase those thoughts away. She thought instead about Billy and the bairns and the warmth that was awaiting her.

She was later than usual and Billy would be worrying about her. And she was worried about him. He would have hardly any rest before he went to work on the night shift at the goods yard. Reassured that Miss Bullock seemed to be coping with Melissa, she decided to leave the delivery of the letter to Mrs Winterton until the next morning. She would just have to get up even earlier than she usually did.

A cold wind seemed to be blowing her home, plastering her coat to the back of her legs and grabbing at her hat every time she turned a corner. What a miserable day for the poor woman to die, she thought. And what a miserable time of year for a funeral. She was saddened and tired, and too weary to think beyond that and to wonder what would become of Melissa now that she was alone in the world.

Melissa didn't know whether she had been asleep or not. When she had closed her eyes Miss Bullock had been nodding off in the armchair at the other side of the fireplace and now when she opened them again the old lady was still there drowsing in the firelight. Nothing seemed to have changed.

But something was different about the room. Melissa watched the flickering shadows on the ceiling and realised the fire had burned low and the oil lamps had been turned down. She could hear the steady tick-tock of the clock on the mantel but it was too shadowy to see the time. A sudden gust of wind blew rain down the chimney and the coals sizzled as a puff of smoke curled outwards into the room.

Melissa closed her eyes and tried to escape the misery that flooded in and threatened to drown her. Her mother was dead. Her life would never be the same again. At this moment she had no idea how she was going to manage . . . what she was going to do.

She became aware of a sharp pain in her shoulders and her neck. She realised she had been lying in an awkward hunched-up way and she moved, trying to make herself more comfortable. The rug that was covering her slipped to the floor. When she reached down to retrieve it she noticed that the cracket, the little wooden stool that her grandfather had made for them, had been placed within reach, and resting on top of it was a wooden box. The polished wood, reflecting the light of the fire, seemed to glow with an inner life.

Melissa almost stopped breathing when she realised what the box was. Her mother's sewing box. What could it mean? Had her mother not died after all? Had everything that had happened until this moment been a terrible dream? Perhaps she was ill and that was why she was sleeping on the sofa in the parlour. And her mother was here somewhere, waiting for her to wake up. She looked around the room wildly, searching the shadows.

But no one was there. There was no one in the room save for Miss Bullock and Melissa herself. At least no living person . . .

Melissa sobbed when she realised where her thoughts were leading her. She closed her eyes and concentrated on a wisp of a memory. She had been lying here stunned with grief, drifting in and out of sleep, when she had heard Mrs Sibbet taking her leave of Miss Bullock. Mrs Sibbet had asked a question and Miss Bullock had answered her.

What had she said?

'Don't disturb her now. Just leave it there beside her.'

Melissa sat up and reached down for the workbox, lifting it on to her knee. Her mother had told her that it was the first present her father had given her. He had brought it home from one of his voyages. It was made of rosewood with inlaid decorations of mother-of-pearl. Melissa remembered how she had loved to open it and look inside it as a child. Inside there was a tray lined with pink silk, and little boxes and compartments to hold needles, thimbles, threads and buttons. Under the tray there was a large cavity for larger objects such as scissors and bits and pieces of fabric or half-done embroidery.

Wonderingly she opened the box. Lying on top of everything else there was a letter and a photograph. She picked up the photograph and saw her parents. They were young and smartly dressed and looking at each other as if there was no one else in the world. The image was faded, browns merging into browns, but she could see that they were standing before a painted backdrop representing a garden. Her mother was holding a posy of flowers. The photograph had been taken on their wedding day.

Melissa laid the photograph back on to the tray of the sewing box and picked up the letter. Opening it with trembling fingers she began to read.

> My darling Melissa,
>
> This letter must be practical. I had hoped that I would live long enough to see you at least established in my place as a dressmaker with all my customers happy to come to you. But of late I have realised that this is not going to be so. I know I should have talked to you about this – please forgive me. I wanted to delay things until after Christmas, but if you are reading this I have left it too late.
>
> Please don't worry, my darling. My friend Lilian Winterton has promised that she will look after you. You will live with her and she will guide you until you are old enough to have your own establishment. All

the money in the old tea caddy is for you. Keep it and save it. Also, and I am loath to talk of such practical matters, you must sell all the fabrics and sewing materials that are in our store cupboard, also the two sewing machines. Invest the money against the day you want to set up your own dressmaking business. Mrs Winterton will advise you, I'm sure of that.

I feel as if I am being mean-spirited to say this, but although your aunt Janet has promised to take charge of my funeral arrangements, you must not go to live with her. She will offer to take you. She may even insist; but she does not have your best interests at heart.

I wish we'd had more time together but every day with you has been a joy.

God bless you.

With love from your mother.

By the time Melissa had finished reading the letter she felt hollow; as though there was nothing left of her that mattered. She folded the letter and put it back in the sewing box along with the photograph of her parents on their wedding day. Then clutching the sewing box in her arms she fell into an exhausted sleep.

Martha Sibbet had arrived at the Wintertons' town house while it was still dark. She had got up extra early and as soon as Billy arrived home from the night shift she set off to deliver the letter. Now she stood on the pavement wondering what to do. Should she go down the area steps to the servants' entrance or up the grand steps to the porticoed entrance, which stood one storey above street level?

Normally she would never have dreamed of going to the front door but this was an exceptional circumstance, wasn't it? Mrs Winterton was a friend of Mrs Dornay and she wouldn't want a message from a friend – especially such an important message – to be taken to the servants' entrance, would she?

So, clutching the letter in her hand, she mounted the steps and, reaching for the brass bell pull, gave it a vigorous tug. She heard the resulting sound echo through the house and stepped back nervously. What a clatter to make so early in the morning. She hoped she hadn't annoyed anyone.

A tall smartly dressed young man opened the door. Martha glanced beyond him and saw a lofty hall with rich oriental rugs on a marble floor. She glimpsed huge arrangements of hothouse flowers in vases bigger than any one of her bairns. Their scent mingled with that of furniture polish and something else, something she couldn't name, but she supposed it to be the smell of a house where rich people lived. The sort of house she would never enter no matter how long she lived.

Her gaze travelled back to the fellow who had opened the door and who was looking down his nose at her with a mixture of surprise and disdain.

'I believe you've come to the wrong door, my good woman,' he said.

She looked back at him and saw that despite his bonny looks, fancy uniform and his superior manner, he was even younger than she had first thought.

'I'm not your good woman, you cheeky young monkey, and I've come with a message for your mistress.'

'You still ought to have gone down those steps to the servants' entrance.'

He began to shut the door and Martha stepped forward and pushed it open again.

'Lissen,' she said, 'I haven't time to argue with a young lad who's still got his mother's milk on his chin. A good friend of your mistress has passed away and I can assure you that Mrs Winterton will want to know about it. Now are you going to let me come in and give her this letter or aren't you?'

The young footman looked genuinely horrified. 'Come in?' he said. 'I can't possibly let you come in. And please don't make a fuss here on the doorstep.'

Without warning Martha felt tears well up and she began to cry.

'Oh, goodness,' the young man said and his haughty expression vanished. 'Please don't cry.' He sounded genuinely concerned, which made Martha cry all the harder. 'Look, give the letter to me. I promise you I'll give it to Mrs Winterton as soon as she's awake.'

'Will you?'

'Yes, that's part of my job – to see that everyone gets any letter or cards sent to them.'

While Martha stood there uncertain what to do, the young chap walked over to a table standing in the hall and came back carrying a silver tray. 'Look,' he said, 'the first delivery of letters has already arrived.'

Martha looked at several letters resting on the tray.

'Put your letter on top of them – go on, put it there yourself. Then you can be sure that Mrs Winterton will get it.'

'All right,' Martha said. 'I'll trust you. But please mind how important it is.'

She put the letter with the others and turned to go. She didn't know what else she could have done. The door closed behind her and she could imagine the young footman's relief at having got rid of such an unsuitable visitor. She hurried away, intent on getting to Miss Bullock's to see how Melissa was.

And then a thought struck her, which raised her spirits a little. Melissa was going to be taken in by Mrs Winterton.

She was going to live in that lovely big house with all the comforts that riches could provide.

It went without saying that nothing would ever make up for the fact that she had lost her mother; but at least the poor bairn would not want for anything. And she was certainly going up in the world.

Chapter Six

The young footman shut the door, placed the tray with the letters on the hall table and went straight down to the kitchen in the semi-basement to cadge a cup of tea and a slice or two of bread and jam from Mrs Barton, the cook. He knew he'd be all right because Mrs Barton had a soft spot for him – as did most of the female servants in the Winterton household.

He had been chosen for the job of footman because he was tall and good-looking; apparently these were prerequisites of the job. At least that's what his mother had said. She also told him that despite his physical advantages he would never have got the job if she hadn't taught him good manners and how to speak properly.

His mother had worked in a grand house in London before she had come back to Newcastle to marry her childhood sweetheart who worked in a gentlemen's outfitters, so he supposed she knew what she was talking about.

'Who was at the door, Douglas?' Mrs Barton asked as she poured him a cup of tea and cut him a generous slice of a new-baked loaf.

He sat down at the scrubbed kitchen table and reached for the butter. 'A woman with a message for the mistress.'

'At this time of the morning? And in this bitter weather?

Why didn't you invite the poor soul to step inside?'

'Because she ought not to have been there. She ought to have gone to the servants' entrance.'

Mrs Barton looked at him enquiringly. 'Why's that?'

Douglas frowned as he finished a mouthful of bread and butter and then said, 'She looked . . . well . . . poor.'

The cook shook her head. 'She didn't know her place.'

Douglas wiped a crumb from his lip with his tongue and nodded sagely. 'If any of the neighbours had seen her I don't know what they'd think.'

'What was the message?'

'I don't know. She handed me a letter. Said it was from a friend of Mrs Winterton's.'

Mrs Barton cut him another slice of bread, then poured herself a cup of tea and sat opposite to him at the table. 'Well, whatever you do, don't bother the mistress with it this morning. They didn't come back from the ball until the early hours and she's left orders that she and Miss Gwendolyn must not be disturbed.'

'I know very well what time they came back,' Douglas said as he spooned a generous helping of plum jam on to his bread. 'Mr Winterton excused Mr Beckett his duties and sent him to bed early so I had to wait up for them, didn't I? And so did Ena. She was yawning her head off, but it seems Mrs Winterton and Miss Gwendolyn couldn't get themselves ready for bed.'

'Well, of course not. Getting dressed and undressed is a full-time occupation for those two. But how did you get on with Mr Winterton?'

'All right. He doesn't ask for much. I think he could manage without a valet, if he had to, but he doesn't like to pay old Charlie off.'

'Cheeky young beggar. Old Charlie, indeed. It's Mr Beckett to you, and he's been a great help to Mr Winterton over the years; showing him the way to dress and behave like – well, like . . .'

'A gentleman.'

'Mr Winterton wasn't brought up to it but he tries his best.' Mrs Barton looked uneasy. 'But we shouldn't be talking about them like this and you know it. Now shouldn't you be setting the table for breakfast?'

'For the family, you mean? I thought you said they weren't coming down until later.'

'The ladies aren't but Mr Winterton will go to the office as usual. And as you probably won't be required for carriage duties today, you can take this opportunity to clean the cutlery – all of it. No shoving the things that aren't often used to the back of the drawers, mind. Now off you go, I've got Mr Winterton's breakfast to prepare.'

Douglas sighed, gulped down the rest of his tea and got up a trifle wearily. He found himself yawning and remembered to cover his mouth as his mother had taught him. It wasn't just the late night that had made him tired. When Mr Winterton was settled and Douglas had got to bed at last, thoughts of Gwendolyn Winterton in her beautiful ball gown, and the way she had looked back over her shoulder at him as she went up the stairs, had made sleep impossible.

The master was as alert and keen-eyed as ever. Not bad for a fellow of his age, Douglas thought as he poured Mr Winterton's second cup of coffee and then watched him going through a sheaf of business papers, something he wouldn't have done at the breakfast table if his wife and daughter had joined him.

Douglas struggled to stay awake and decided that when Mr Winterton had left for his office he would clear the table and then find somewhere to hide and have forty winks before starting on the cutlery.

Mr Winterton drained his cup, dabbed at his lips with his

napkin, then rose from the table and stuffed all the papers into a small travelling case. 'Any letters?' he asked.

'Yes, sir, I'll get them.'

Now, feeling more tired by the minute, Douglas brought the tray from the hall and Mr Winterton picked up the letters without looking at them and put them in the case along with his business papers.

Mr Winterton strode out of the room and Douglas followed him, hurrying to get his overcoat.

'A cold morning, sir,' he said as he handed his master his hat and his walking stick. 'Do you want me to run along and get a cab?'

Mr Winterton never took the carriage to work; he left it for his wife and daughter to use at their convenience.

'No, that's all right, Douglas. I'll walk. The cold air will clear my head. Please see that Mrs Winterton is informed that I shall be home at about seven o'clock this evening but if I'm late she and Miss Gwendolyn are to leave for the theatre without me. I'll catch up with them there.'

Douglas opened the door and Austin Winterton's tall, soberly clad figure soon merged into the morning mist as he set off to walk just over a mile to his offices down by the river in Dene Street.

Only when his master had been gone for at least ten minutes did Douglas remember that one of the letters on the tray had been for Mrs Winterton.

He wondered if he should go after the master but realised that he would be nearly halfway there and might not like to be stopped in a city street by one of his household staff. No, Douglas thought, best to face a ticking off and let him bring it home with him.

At six o'clock that evening Austin Winterton looked up from his desk and realised that he had better bathe and change at the office and meet his wife at the theatre as he had suggested. He kept a suite of rooms on the top floor of the building, which included a sitting room, bathroom, bedroom and dressing room. He also kept a good supply of clean shirts and a spare suit of evening clothes.

That way he could work late and still fulfil any social obligations such as dinners and concerts and visits to the theatre. Lilian did not seem to mind as long as he turned up on time. For that he was grateful. He knew that many a wife would have scolded and complained that her husband was not spending enough time with her – that he was neglecting her.

But not Lilian. She was easy-going and even-tempered. He suppressed the thought that perhaps she did not care that she saw little of him, and that as long as his business was successful and he could provide her with the luxuries she thought were her due then she would never complain about how hard he worked. He sometimes had cause to take her to task about her extravagance, but he liked to indulge her when he could and he was quite prepared to sit through yet another light-hearted musical entertainment at the Palace Theatre in the Haymarket.

In his rush to prepare for the theatre and get there in time to join her in their box he quite forgot that one of the letters he had brought from home that morning was for her. It would be another full day before he took the letter home and by that time his wife had retired to bed early to recover from the hectic time she had had during the Christmas festivities.

Three days after Boxing Day Emmeline Dornay was laid to rest. Her sister, Janet Cook, had not spared any expense for the funeral. After all, Emmeline herself had paid for it and not just for the interment but also for the funeral tea to be catered for by the corner bakery.

Janet grieved over the extravagance but, nevertheless, managed to imply by a word here and a hint there that she had opened her own purse in order to pay proper tribute to her beloved sister.

She had made the announcement in the local paper, as was expected, and she was surprised by the number of people – mostly women – who turned up at the church. She looked around at the respectable matrons and young women who had been Emmeline's customers and hoped fervently that they would not all come back to Miss Bullock's house for the tea.

She also hoped that Bert Junior, left in charge of the arrangements at the house, would manage to have everything done before they got back. And she wasn't thinking of the catering; two women hired by the bakery were seeing to that.

She walked beside Melissa at the head of the solemn mourners who followed the coffin to the open grave. Janet's husband, Albert, uneasy in his best suit and celluloid collar, walked behind them and mumbled incoherently whenever anyone spoke to him. Janet was annoyed and she resolved to tell him later that he had shown himself up in front of Emmeline's fancy friends.

Melissa had hardly spoken although she had smiled tearfully whenever one of her mother's clients offered words of condolence. Janet Cook glanced at her out of the corner of her eye as they wound their way past ancient gravestones and across the dripping grass. She noticed with displeasure that her niece's pale-faced grief only made her look more beautiful.

Melissa was wearing black. Janet's keen eye took in the fact that the hem of the coat had been let down. The coat must have belonged to Emmeline, and Melissa, taller than her mother had been, had altered it to fit. She just hoped Melissa didn't have her eye on many more of her mother's clothes; she'd already earmarked them for herself. She frowned with exasperation. If only she'd thought to tell Bert Junior to empty Emmeline's wardrobe as well as clearing out the sewing room.

When Melissa stepped forward to throw the first clod of earth on to her mother's coffin, she stumbled. Martha Sibbet moved quickly to steady her and kept her arm round the girl as they stepped back again. Miss Bullock's maid of all work didn't say anything but she turned an angry face towards Janet and glared as if to imply that it should have been Melissa's aunt who was supporting her.

To Janet's annoyance quite a few of the mourners came back with them. She heard Miss Bullock inviting them and she would have liked to tell the old woman that it wasn't her place to do so but she had to admit it was Miss Bullock's house. They walked through the streets, a sad procession in mourning black, and gentlemen passers-by removed their hats and bowed their heads in respect.

Janet held back impatiently as Miss Bullock fumbled with her front door key but then managed to get herself in ahead of anyone else. Bert Junior was waiting in the doorway of the sewing room. He closed it quickly behind himself and gave a nod and a wink to his mother to signify that her orders had been carried out. He drew his mother aside.

'All done?' she asked. 'The sewing room?'

He nodded.

'Anything else?'

'Nothing very much. There was a fancy tin in a cupboard in what looked like the lass's room.'

'And?'

'There was some cash in it.'

'What did you do?'

'I left the tin in the cupboard. The cash is in my pocket.'

'Good lad.'

After their whispered conversation Bert Junior, more socially adept than his father, began to help any of the ladies who wished to remove their coats. Most of them didn't. Janet hoped this meant that they didn't intend to stay very long.

Albert looked more uncomfortable than ever and Janet told him to excuse himself, go home and see if Mother was all right. Janet and Emmeline's mother had said she was too ill to go to the funeral of the daughter she had never forgiven for bettering herself. Janet suspected that it was no more than a heavy cold but she had agreed that, considering her age, the cold and the damp could turn it into something much worse and then who would have to nurse the old woman?

She allowed herself a moment of pride as she watched her son guiding the guests to the dining room. Unlike his father, Bert Junior knows what's what, she thought. Martha Sibbet hurried away to the kitchen to make the tea, after which she made herself available to help the two black-clad waitresses. Janet noticed with annoyance that Mrs Sibbet was wearing a black dress that she could have sworn belonged to Emmeline. Melissa must have given it to her. She just hoped that she hadn't given much more stuff away.

Miss Bullock seemed to be more than usually weary and, having removed her coat, she sank down gratefully into her rocking chair. Everyone else stood round uneasily, not knowing what to say or do.

Then, after looking at Janet questioningly, a tall, well-spoken but bossy-looking woman took charge of the proceedings, exhorting the guests to take a sandwich or a fancy cake from the proffered plates and to have a cup of tea. Again Janet had been made to feel that her behaviour was wanting.

She watched the proceedings sourly and noted how the plates of ham and pease pudding sandwiches and iced fancies were emptying. She had already told the women from the bakery that anything left over must be packed up carefully and given to Bert Junior to take home.

Thankfully, very soon the guests began to take their leave. She heard one or two of them saying to Melissa that they hoped she would find some way to carry on with her dressmaking. Janet would have liked to have told them, not if she could help it. She had no intention of turning her house into a dressmaker's shop and she was going to see to it that the girl had a proper job bringing a regular pay packet home.

The last person to leave was the tall, bossy woman who turned out to be Miss Robson, a teacher from Melissa's old school. As the two waitresses began to clear the dishes from the table Miss Robson took Melissa aside.

'I hope that whatever happens, my dear, you will continue with your French lessons,' she said. 'I shall not require payment if you'd like to do our mending as before, and perhaps a little dressmaking.'

'I should like to,' Melissa replied. 'But I'm not sure where I will be living.'

'With me, of course,' Janet interjected. 'Where else would you live?'

'I thought – I mean, my mother said her friend Mrs Winterton would take care of me. She said she had promised.'

'Where is she, then?'

'I don't know.'

'Has she been here since your mother died?'

'No. But perhaps she doesn't know what's happened.'

'Were you supposed to tell her?'

'No.' Melissa looked bewildered.

'There, then,' Janet said, and looked around as if that explained everything. 'Your mother can't have arranged things properly.'

'Yes she did!' Martha Sibbet spoke up indignantly. 'Mrs Dornay left a letter for me to take to Mrs Winterton.'

'And did you take it to her?'

'Yes . . .' Martha looked uncomfortable. 'I took it along the very next day.'

Janet Cook's tight-lipped smile was smug. 'Well, Melissa, I think you can forget about going to live with Mrs Winterton. If she intended to keep her promise she would have come to the funeral, wouldn't she?'

'But I don't see why Melissa should be uprooted from her home, at all,' Miss Robson said, and earned herself an irate glare from Janet Cook.

'Are you suggesting that she should stay here on her own? She's only a child.'

'She's nearly fifteen and she is sensible and mature, and furthermore she wouldn't be on her own. Miss Bullock is here and Mrs Sibbet comes in every day, even Sunday. Melissa would have good friends to guide her. And she knows she can always come to me if she needs advice.'

Janet was saved from answering when Miss Bullock gave a gentle cough and said, 'No, I'm afraid that won't be possible.'

Everyone had assumed she was dozing and they turned to look at her enquiringly.

'And why is that?' Miss Robson said gently.

'I'm selling up – moving. I'm too old to keep this house going by myself and my married niece wants me to go and live with her in Whitley-by-the-Sea. She thinks the sea air would be good for me. I'm not so sure about that – it can be cold at the coast even on a summer's day and the sea mist won't help my bronchitis – but I've decided it's better that I go and live out the rest of my days with family.'

'Selling up? Moving?' Martha Sibbet exclaimed, and it was evident that she was shocked and dismayed.

'Don't worry, Martha. I'll give you a glowing reference and also a little something to tide you over until you find a new position. An honest, hard-working woman like yourself won't be out of work for very long.'

'But I like it here!' Martha exclaimed. 'You might be a bit – well – hard to please at times, but you and Mrs Dornay and Melissa . . . well, you're like my own family.'

There was silence for a moment and then Miss Bullock replied, 'But Mrs Dornay has gone before us, Martha; let us hope to a better place. And I am old and I don't want to die here away from any family I have left. I'm truly sorry, but Melissa will have to go to her aunt.'

'No!' It was the first time Melissa had spoken with any passion. 'That's not what my mother wanted. She wanted me to go to Mrs Winterton's.'

'Maybe she did,' Janet Cook said. 'And more fool her.'

'Why do you say that?' Miss Robson enquired.

'My sister didn't think her own family was good enough for her or her daughter.'

'Have you forgotten what we have just done today?' Martha Sibbet exclaimed angrily. 'We've just laid your poor sister to rest and already you're speaking ill of her.'

'Oh, please stop!' Melissa cried suddenly.

Martha looked shocked. 'I'm sorry if I've spoken out of turn. I'm really sorry.'

'No, it's not you. It's just . . . just everything!'

She turned and ran from the room and those left looked at each other guiltily, even Janet Cook.

'Should I go after her?' Martha asked.

'No, perhaps I'd better go,' Miss Robson said.

But before anyone could leave the room Melissa returned and burst into the room, eyes bright with shock and fury.

'Everything's gone!' she cried. 'Everything my mother left me. The sewing machines, all the threads, the scissors, the dress patterns, the needles, the pins – all the fine fabrics and even the magazines. The cupboard is empty!'

*

Lilian Winterton thanked Ena for bringing in her breakfast tray and allowed the girl to pour her coffee. When her maid left her bedside and started to tidy the room, Lilian yawned discreetly behind her hand. She did not like anyone to see how tired she was. She wondered if she was getting old.

She was still some years off forty and she certainly didn't look her age, but it was getting harder and harder to rouse herself in the morning after a late night, and the last few days had been hectic. She would have to take care of herself. Austin had been attracted to her youthful looks as well as her beauty and if she was to keep him in thrall she mustn't allow her complexion to dull into premature middle age. Why, she knew some women of forty who grew disgustingly stout or who took to the *chaise-longue* and hardly ever stirred themselves again.

Today she would rest, she decided. Perhaps get up mid-morning, have a soak in scented water and, after dressing, not do much more than go over the programme of hospitality she had arranged for New Year's Eve, which was in two days' time.

She and Austin were entertaining some rather grand people – the city fathers, Austin liked to call them – as well as at least one important landowner. Lilian had hired a small orchestra to play a selection of light classical music as well as tunes from the latest musical shows.

And she had engaged a caterer to provide a buffet meal, much to the disgust of Mrs Barton. She admitted to herself that Mrs Barton was an excellent cook and could have provided an equally grand repast but it wasn't the food that was important so much as the cachet. She wanted it to be known – she would drop a hint or two – that she and Austin could afford Marcel Lecompte, the fashionable French chef who had recently settled in Newcastle.

Ena had just finished hanging Lilian's clothes away and laying out clean underwear. 'Do you want your mail now, madam?' she asked.

Lilian suppressed another yawn. 'I suppose so.'

She didn't really want it for there would probably be an unpaid bill or two – for example, from the haberdasher – but she supposed she should at least open the envelopes before filing them away to be dealt with later.

Ena handed her three envelopes. Two of them were bills, just as she had suspected: one from the haberdasher for the three hats she had bought in November and one from the furrier from whom she had bought that delicious little fox-fur scarf complete with brush and paws. She put them on the bedside table. Then she looked at the third envelope. No postage stamp. The letter had been delivered by hand.

Lilian frowned as she studied it. She thought she recognised the handwriting and she stirred uncomfortably. She knew that she owed her dressmaker money but she had given her that most generous hamper and, besides, it was not like Emmeline to be importunate. She opened the envelope and her eyes widened with shock.

'When was this letter delivered?' she asked Ena.

'I'm not sure, madam. Mr Winterton left it with me this morning. He said he had taken it to his office with him by mistake.'

'When? Did he say when?'

'No, madam, he didn't.'

'Will the newspapers still be in the house? I mean the papers of the last few days?'

'I think so, madam. They're used to lay the fires.'

'Well, go and get them – just the local newspapers for the last three or four days. Hurry.'

She could see how puzzled the girl was but she was too worried to care. She pushed her breakfast tray aside roughly so that the coffee slopped over the embroidered tray cloth. She'd lost all interest in the hot buttered toast and the freshly brewed coffee. When Ena came back with the newspapers she told her to take the tray away. She saw the maid raise her eyebrows as she looked askance at the mess she'd made.

'Come straight back,' she told Ena. 'I may be going out.'

When the girl had gone Lilian turned the pages to look at the funeral announcements in each newspaper. 'Today . . .' she breathed. 'The funeral is today.'

When Ena returned to the room Lilian was already out of bed.

'You can help me dress,' she said. 'And – erm – I'd better wear black.'

'Black, madam? Are you going to a funeral?'

'Yes, if I'm in time.'

She saw the girl's growing perplexity but there wasn't a moment to explain. Not that she could explain to anyone the real reason for the urgency.

A minute or so later, wearing a black satin dress, she sat at her dressing table and picked up her brush and combs. 'I'll do my hair myself,' she said. 'Go and tell the footman to order the carriage and to be ready to accompany me.'

As the landau carried her through the city streets she hardly had thought for the sweet-natured dressmaker who had just died, nor for the girl she had promised to look after. Her concern was solely for the letters that Emmeline had been keeping for her. They must not fall into anyone else's hands.

In Miss Bullock's house Melissa had returned to the front parlour along with Martha Sibbet, Miss Robson and Miss Bullock. Janet Cook and her son had followed reluctantly. Janet knew she would have to explain things to these busybodies and she marshalled her thoughts carefully.

Melissa gestured wildly to indicate the bare table and the empty cupboard. 'Look,' she said to everyone who had assembled. Then she faced her aunt. 'What have you done with my belongings?'

'I did what your mother wanted me to do,' Janet said.

Melissa's eyes widened. 'What do you mean? My mother left everything to me.'

'Yes, that's right. She wanted you to benefit from them.'

'She wanted me to sell them and save the money so that I would be able to start my own dressmaking business one day.'

'Exactly. She wanted you to sell them. And that's what I'm doing.'

'*You* are doing?'

'Listen, Melissa, you're just a child. You wouldn't know how to go about these things.'

'I would have advised her,' Miss Robson said.

Janet shot her a look of fury. 'Well, I didn't know that, did I? And it's no use talking about it now, anyway. I arranged for Mr Grainger to come along and collect everything while we were at the church. That's why Bert Junior stayed here. I thought . . . thought it would cause less heartache that way.'

'Mr Grainger?' Miss Robson asked.

'From the auction rooms. He'll, er, he'll see to it that we get a good price.'

'Do you mean Melissa will get a good price?' Miss Robson enquired mildly.

'Yes. Well . . .' Janet rallied her spirits. She was not going to allow herself to be browbeaten by this skinny stick of a schoolmarm. 'Obviously my sister would have wanted some of it to come to me.'

'Rubbish!' Martha Sibbet exclaimed.

Miss Robson spoke more quietly but, nevertheless her tone was ominous. 'I'm not sure why,' she said. 'Can you explain?'

'Emmeline wouldn't have expected me to be out of pocket.'

Martha was red in the face with anger. 'What do you mean?' she asked. 'Are you trying to say that you paid for the funeral? I know you didn't. I gave you Mrs Dornay's club book, remember? And I know for a fact that there was plenty there to pay for everything.'

Janet began to feel persecuted but her resolve hardened. 'No, I don't mean that. I mean, if I am to look after her. Melissa will need feeding and clothing.'

'I see,' Miss Robson said. 'You are making sure that you won't, as you say, be out of pocket.'

'There's nothing wrong with that.'

Janet never found out what would have been said next for at that moment the sound of the doorbell echoed through the house. Bert Junior edged out of the room. He looked as though he was relieved to escape. They all waited for his return.

There was a murmur of voices and then he came back followed by an elegant woman dressed in black. A filmy black veil attached to her hat gave a glimpse of a beautiful but anxious face.

'This is Mrs—' Bert started to explain but the lady hurried forward.

'I'm Lilian Winterton,' she said. 'I've come for Melissa.'

Chapter Seven

Lilian knew at once that she had interrupted something. She had not expected to see happy faces in the circumstances but perhaps she had hoped at the very least for a friendly greeting. However, the people surrounding her looked distracted rather than pleased to see her. The hostility in the room was palpable.

Was the enmity directed at her? Were they annoyed because she had not come to the funeral? No, she didn't think so. Judging by the suppressed anger in some of their faces she guessed that she had walked into the middle of an argument.

She was at a loss; uncertain what to say, when a tall, threadbare, but rather elegant woman said with an air of authority, 'Mrs Winterton, I'm glad you're here.'

'And you are?' she asked.

'Forgive me. I am Harriet Robson. I am a teacher at the school Melissa used to attend. I am, I hope, a friend of hers.'

Lilian's relief at this courteous greeting was short-lived. An incongruous-looking woman, who was vaguely familiar and whose rough-hewn face was completely at odds with the elegant black gown she was wearing, stepped forward and addressed her in a brusque and disrespectful manner.

'What kept you?' she asked.

'I beg your pardon?'

'Poor Mrs Dornay thought you were a friend of hers yet you couldn't even be bothered to turn up for her funeral.'

'Martha Sibbet!' a little old woman who nevertheless had an air of authority addressed the presumptuous creature. 'You will not be rude to guests in my house. Mrs Winterton does not have to explain herself to you.'

'But all the same I will,' Lilian said. She could not bear to be disliked or disapproved of. 'Someone delivered a letter to my house. I think it must have been the day after Boxing Day.'

'It was me, and it was,' the woman called Martha said cryptically.

'Then I must thank you.' Lilian smiled disarmingly, injecting gratitude into her voice. 'But the sad thing is that I did not receive the letter until this morning.'

'And why's that?' Martha Sibbet asked. Her tight-lipped expression revealed that she had not been won over.

'Because our footman—'

'That lanky piece of good-looking impertinence?'

'If he was rude to you I'm sorry. Especially since you came from Emmeline. But, anyway, there was a muddle. The letter went astray.'

Martha Sibbet nodded. 'I can believe that. I shouldn't hev trusted him.'

'But it was given to me this morning and the minute I read it I checked in the newspapers and I set off for the church. Of course the service was over so I came here.'

'Well, you shouldn't have bothered.' Another woman spoke and Lilian turned in her direction.

She saw a middle-aged woman, angry and sour-faced, and yet who must once have been beautiful. Perhaps her evident spleen had spoiled her beauty. Lilian frowned. The woman reminded her of someone . . . of course, Emmeline, but a coarser more ill-defined version of Emmeline. This must be the dead woman's sister, the woman who intended Melissa should work in a pickle factory.

'And why is that?' Lilian asked pleasantly. 'Why should I not bother to come when I had promised Emmeline that I would take care of her daughter?'

The woman's tight-lipped and determined reaction suggested that this was not news to her.

'There's no need for that,' she said. 'I'm the girl's aunt.'

For all Lilian's easy-going appearance she was as tough as bell metal when it was a matter of getting her own way. And in this instance there was more than one reason why she wanted Melissa to come home with her.

'I know,' she said, 'and it's good of you to be concerned, but if Emmeline had wanted Melissa to come to you, she wouldn't have asked me.'

'That's true.'

It was Miss Robson who had spoken and Lilian shot her a grateful glance. The schoolteacher would make a redoubtable ally.

Then the old lady, whom Lilian realised must be Miss Bullock, the landlady she had never met, spoke up. 'Why don't we ask Melissa what she wants to do?' she said. 'She's old enough to make up her own mind.' She smiled at Melissa. 'Well, child? Do you want to live with your aunt or Mrs Winterton?'

Melissa had been standing in the midst of it all and yet she had appeared isolated and totally disorientated. She was dressed in a black grosgrain dress that was surely too old for her. Her mother's, Lilian guessed. She had altered it to fit. My goodness, how beautiful she is, Lilian thought, those fine bones, that shining fall of dark hair.

Melissa said, 'My mother wanted me to go to Mrs Winterton.'

Lilian wasn't altogether sure that this was a positive

enough answer but everyone else in the room took it as such.

'That's right,' Miss Bullock's maid said. 'You'll be much better off there.'

'Good.' Judging by the tone of her voice the old landlady seemed to agree. 'That's settled then.' She turned to face Emmeline's sister. 'Mrs Cook, I'd be obliged if you and your son would go now. I don't think there's anything else in this house that will interest you.'

Janet Cook bridled at Miss Bullock's manner. 'I shall go as soon as I've sorted out my sister's clothes.'

'You've already cleared this room out,' Martha Sibbet exclaimed. 'What more do you want?'

'It's my duty to—' Janet Cook began but Lilian Winterton interrupted her.

'I beg your pardon,' she said. 'What do you mean that Mrs Cook has cleared out this room?'

'Look around – everything has gone from the table. The doors of the cupboard are open and the shelves are bare. While we were burying poor Mrs Dornay this morning that young fellow-me-lad who is cowering by the door sent everything off to the auction rooms.'

'Everything?'

'The sewing machines, the fabrics, the papers. There's nothing left.'

Lilian suppressed a surge of panic. 'What do you mean by the papers? Do you mean Mrs Dornay's personal documents? Her letters?'

'No, not those, they're all upstairs. I mean the paper patterns and the fashion magazines,' Martha Sibbet said. 'All gone to Grainger's.'

'But Mrs Dornay's personal papers are still here?' Lilian needed to be reassured.

'Yes, and I don't think Mrs Cook should have anything to

do with those,' Martha Sibbet said. 'It's up to Melissa to sort them out.'

Feeling more comfortable now that she knew her letters had almost certainly not gone off to the auction rooms, Lilian asked, 'But why have you done this, Mrs Cook? Surely Melissa alone should have decided what was to be done with her mother's belongings?'

'My mother left everything to me,' Melissa said. 'She said I could sell whatever I pleased and save the money for when I am old enough to set up on my own. She left me a letter.'

Lilian tried to sound reassuring. 'Well, I shouldn't imagine there'll be an auction held until after the New Year. That gives us a few days and I can see to it that Mr Grainger knows the proceeds are to come to you, Melissa. Shall I do that?'

Melissa's eyes glittered with unshod tears. She nodded speechlessly.

Her aunt's sharp features grew even sharper, her voice hard. 'Now wait a minute, Mrs Winterton. I'd like a word with you, if you don't mind. In private.'

Her stare was obdurate. She was obviously not going to budge.

Miss Robson took charge of the situation. 'Miss Bullock,' she said, 'would you allow us to return to the dining room? Perhaps Mrs Sibbet would make a fresh pot of tea. Mrs Winterton and Mrs Cook can talk in here in private.'

Miss Bullock nodded wearily. It was clear that the day's events had taken their toll. She led the way out of the room.

'Melissa, I think it's best if you come with us,' Miss Robson said. Melissa, who was looking more and more distraught, responded to her old teacher's firm tone, perhaps out of habit, and left the room.

'You too, young fellow,' Martha Sibbet said to Bert Junior, who was lurking by the door, not knowing what he was supposed to do. His mother nodded and he followed the others.

Lilian found herself alone with Mrs Cook who asked, 'Why are you so keen to take the girl?'

'I made a promise.'

'Were you really such good friends? You and our Emma?'

'Why do you doubt it?'

'You are a very rich woman. My sister was only a dressmaker.'

'You should not say *only* a dressmaker. She was a very good one.'

'That still doesn't explain things.'

'We liked each other. We got on very well.'

Janet Cook looked at her long and hard and then shrugged. 'Well, I suppose you're foolish enough to agree to take on someone else's bairn but Melissa is my niece. She's family. She should come to me.'

'You don't really want her.'

'What makes you say that?'

'I believe you and your sister were not exactly on the best of terms; I can only guess why, but Emmeline was worried that you would force the child to work in some pickling factory rather than encourage her to go on with her dressmaking.'

'And what's wrong with that?'

'It would be a sin.'

'And if she came to you, would you encourage her?'

'Of course.'

'Very well. If I allow Melissa to go with you—'

'Allow?'

'She's only fourteen. I'm her next of kin. I could insist. I could accuse you of taking her away from her family like many a poor bonny little lass is 'ticed from the streets in this city.' She paused and her expression became sly. 'For goodness knows what purpose.'

Lilian was both sickened and angered by the insinuation. 'You wouldn't suggest anything so wicked!'

Janet Cook's smile was humourless. 'Mebbes I won't. So long as you leave things be at the auction rooms. Do you understand what I mean?'

Lilian wondered how such a sweet woman as Emmeline could have a sister like this. 'I understand. You're selling Melissa to me.'

'I wouldn't put it like that.'

'Well, I would. But if I agree that must be all that you take.'

'What do you mean?'

'Go now, as Miss Bullock requested. Be satisfied with what you have removed from the house today and leave everything else for Melissa.'

'What would the girl do with her mother's clothes?'

'What would you do with them? They're very good quality. Would you sell them?'

Janet glared at her angrily. 'And what if I did?'

'For goodness' sake. You don't really want to give your niece a home. Just be satisfied that I'm going to allow you to keep the proceeds of the auction.'

'And, of course I'll be taking home what is left of the funeral tea.'

Lilian shrugged. She didn't care what happened to the food that was left over. 'Of course.'

'I think I'll put everything in that nice hamper along with what's left in there.'

'Hamper? But that was my Christmas gift to Emmeline and Melissa.'

'My sister has no need of it where she's gone and if Melissa is going home with you she doesn't need such treats either.'

Lilian was weary of dealing with this odious woman and beginning to wish that she had never made that promise to Emmeline. 'Very well,' she said. 'I think that's all we have to discuss. I don't suppose you and I will ever see each other again.'

Janet knew she was being dismissed and it rankled. She drew herself up. 'Albert and I will go now. But I warn you, if things ever go wrong for Melissa – if you should tire of keeping her – that's just too bad. Tell her not to come to me!'

'I wouldn't want to!'

Lilian turned to see that Melissa had come into the room and was standing behind her. Janet Cook must have known she was there.

As soon as Mrs Cook and her son had gone Lilian sought out Martha Sibbet. 'Go out to my carriage,' she told her; then she smiled. 'You'll find a friend of yours there.'

'A friend of mine?'

'Douglas, my footman.'

Martha sniffed. 'Oh, him!'

'He will be sitting with the coachman. Tell them to bring the trunk in now.'

'And what trunk is that?'

'I brought a trunk for Melissa. For her clothes – her books – whatever she wants to bring.'

'So you're taking her away today?'

'I think it's best. Don't you?'

'Aye, I suppose so. She's had a miserable time of it. She's due a bit of comfort.'

'Comfort?'

'Well . . . you to take care of her – in that lovely house of yours.'

'Oh, yes, of course.'

When Douglas and the coachman brought the trunk in Lilian asked them to take it upstairs and then told them that they could wait outside until it was packed and ready to go out again.

'Excuse me, Mrs Winterton,' Martha Sibbet said, 'have you any objection if the two of them wait in the kitchen? It's mortal cold out there and I think they deserve a hot cup of tea and mebbes a sandwich or two.'

'Oh, of course.'

'Right. I'll settle them and go upstairs and help Melissa.'

But Lilian Winterton didn't wait for Martha Sibbet to help. She went upstairs herself where she found Melissa simply sitting on the bed in one of the rooms.

'Is this your bedroom?' Lilian asked. She looked around at the simple furnishings. It reminded her of the room she had had as a girl in her parents' house.

'No, my mother's.' Melissa didn't look at her. She was staring down at her hands clasped in her lap. Her face was so pale that she looked otherworldly; her complexion translucent like an alabaster angel.

'Shall I help you?'

The girl looked up at her. 'Help me?'

'Yes, my dear. I've chased your aunt away and now you can pack whatever you want and bring it to my house.'

Martha Sibbet arrived a moment later and made it obvious that it was her place to help Melissa. Lilian noticed that the girl gave the woman a lot of Emmeline's clothes and she was pleased about that. No matter how clever the child was with the needle Lilian thought it would have been mawkish and somewhat unhealthy if Melissa had wanted to alter them and wear them herself. And, besides, some of them were almost as good as her own clothes, and that wouldn't do at all.

Lilian knew she was getting in the way but she looked in every drawer and on every shelf – pretending to be helping but, in reality searching for Dermot's letters. She began to panic when she couldn't find them. What if they had been in the cupboard downstairs after all and had gone to Grainger's, mixed in with the dress patterns? What if someone bought the patterns and found the letters?

Lilian's heart began to pound. Some unscrupulous person might follow the trail and find her and try to blackmail her. She would have to pay them because she could not risk any scandal.

At last she could be silent no longer and said, 'Mrs Sibbet, I thought you said Mrs Dornay's personal papers were up here?'

'They are. They're inside this old nightdress case. It was in the drawer along with Mrs Dornay's undergarments.'

'Let me see.'

There was a hint of lavender in the air when Martha Sibbet took the pretty embroidered case from the drawer and handed it over. Lilian held her breath as she looked inside. She tried to appear casual as she rifled through the papers. When her fingers found the small bundle of letters tied up with a pink satin bow she felt a surge of relief.

'I'll put that in the trunk, shall I?' Martha Sibbet said.

'No, perhaps I should keep this – just until Melissa is settled in.'

'And why is that?'

'Well, as her guardian I must go through the papers and see if there is anything important. You know, certificates, papers to do with her father, whatever.'

Martha Sibbet frowned as if trying to make sense of it but then she said, 'I suppose so.'

As soon as the room was cleared they went into Melissa's room and Lilian followed, not really knowing what to do. She watched as the child's simple bedroom was cleared of her possessions. Melissa had lived for most of her life in this small respectable house with a loving mother. There was no doubting how close mother and daughter had been.

She and Gwendolyn had never enjoyed such a happy

relationship, nor had Lilian with her own mother. She wondered if Melissa had any idea of how lucky she had been and how much she had lost.

When the trunk was packed Douglas and the coachman were summoned to take it back to the coach. Melissa, dressed in a warm coat that looked almost as good as a coat Lilian would have chosen for Gwendolyn, went into the dining room to say goodbye. Miss Robson told the child that she must keep in touch and Martha Sibbet wept as she said that she hoped and prayed their paths would cross again someday. Only Miss Bullock remained quiet. But before they left she beckoned the child over and pointed to her papery cheek. She wanted Melissa to kiss her.

'I wish I had been more pleasant to you and your mother,' Miss Bullock said. 'I could not have asked for better tenants.' Her rheumy eyes filled with sadness. 'Goodbye, child,' she said, 'I shall miss you, but at least I know you are going to a good home.'

After that the leave-taking was subdued. Martha Sibbet insisted on coming out and seeing them settled into the carriage.

'My,' she said, trying her best to smile, 'you look a proper lady sitting there.'

'Mrs Sibbet,' Lilian said, 'it's cold with the door open.'

'Oh, sorry, I'm sure.'

Melissa managed a weak smile before the footman closed the door and then they set off. She took one last glance from the window and then averted her eyes so that she could not see the street where she had lived all her life and the old familiar houses disappear from view.

Chapter Eight

Melissa sat opposite Mrs Winterton. Neither of them spoke. Whenever their eyes met Mrs Winterton gave her a sympathetic smile but Melissa thought her mother's friend had a distant air. She looked surreptitiously at the fur scarf Mrs Winterton had draped around her shoulders. It had the head of a fox with a sharp nose and glass eyes. Melissa dropped her head to hide her unease. She knew such scarves were fashionable but she could never have brought herself to wear one.

Mrs Winterton was carrying a large muff made from the same reddish brown fur as the scarf. She had thrust the embroidered nightdress case inside, along with her purse, and she was holding the muff close to her body; perhaps because of the cold.

Melissa had never ridden in a carriage before. Not even in a hansom cab. If she went into town with her mother they would walk or catch one of the horse-drawn omnibuses or trams. Often when they saw a grand carriage coming up the street Melissa would pretend that it was coming for her and that she and her mother would be taken home in style to one of the grand houses in one of the squares or terraces where the rich people lived.

Now she was going to such a house; a house where Mrs

Sibbet had told her she would live in luxury, but she would have given anything if the clock could strike midnight as it did in *Cinderella* and the carriage would transform itself not into a pumpkin but into a simple omnibus to take her home to her mother.

The carriage entered a large square with a formal garden in the centre. The garden was bound by iron railings, no doubt to keep out anyone who didn't live in the square. They came to a halt before a tall double-fronted terraced house. The footman opened the door for them and then went swiftly up the grand entrance steps to the front door, which was flanked by two pillars. He tugged the bell pull and the door was already open before Mrs Winterton and Melissa had arrived on the top step.

The footman hurried back to the carriage and Melissa was concerned to see him climb nimbly up into his seat beside the coachman. Mrs Winterton saw her concern and guessed its cause.

'Don't worry,' she said. 'William will take the carriage round to the stables. Then he and Douglas will carry the trunk into the house.'

Melissa remembered from Sunday walks through the town that behind these grand houses there were stable blocks, and she watched the carriage set off again. She realised it would go right round and on to the main road again before entering the lane at the back of the houses.

'Come along, dear.' Prompted by Mrs Winterton, Melissa then stepped into a world the like of which she had seen only in illustrations in ladies' journals.

There were black and white marble tiles on the floor, covered here and there by oriental rugs of rich red and blue. The stair carpet on the grand, sweeping staircase was of the same design. Fixed to the oak-panelled walls there were gas lamps in ornate globes. They had already been lit and Melissa supposed this was because it was a dark winter's day. They made the hall a place of light and warmth. The whole was reflected in tall gilt-framed mirrors, which deceived the eye into thinking this was a much larger place.

The door was shut behind them and a young woman stepped forward. She was dressed in a grey twill gown and a white frilled pinafore that was surely meant for show rather than work. The maid, for that's what Melissa realised she was, waited in respectful silence for Mrs Winterton's orders.

'Ah, Ena. This is Melissa Dornay, the little seamstress. Will you take her upstairs to her room? I ordered it to be made ready before I left this morning. Go with Ena, Melissa. I'll probably see you later.'

Mrs Winterton swept up the stairs and, disconcerted by her seemingly abrupt withdrawal of amity, Melissa hesitated before stepping forward to follow her.

'No,' Ena took hold of her arm. And then, emphasising the first word, she said, 'You come this way.'

She led the way down a passage and then pushed open a door that opened on to a dark and gloomy vestibule. Melissa paused and blinked. Gradually some stairs became visible ahead of them. She saw that the staircase went both up and down.

'Hurry up,' Ena said as she bustled ahead. 'Don't you think I have plenty to do?'

There were no gas lamps to light the way up, only a pale wintry beam filtering down through dust-filled air from a roof light high above them. The stairs were uncarpeted and the narrow landings were covered with brown linoleum, which gave off a faintly oily smell. Ena hurried ahead of her without speaking and Melissa, who had not slept properly since the day her mother had died, began to feel faint. She found herself clinging on to the handrail as they climbed higher and higher.

She became aware of noises behind her. Bumps and thuds and curses in the sort of language she had sometimes heard in the streets before her mother told her to cover her ears. Curiouser and curiouser, she thought to herself, remembering a favourite childhood storybook. But this thought was immediately followed by the reflection that this was not Wonderland and she was not Alice.

I am light-headed, she thought. I really must rest but what would Mrs Winterton's maid say if I simply sat down on the stairs? I cannot imagine that she would be pleased. Melissa blinked, trying to clear the gritty tiredness that was impairing her vision. Thankfully the higher they climbed the stronger the illumination from the roof light became. Nevertheless she found it difficult to concentrate on each step ahead of her.

At last the maid stopped at a door and waited impatiently for Melissa to catch up. She didn't say anything. She simply pushed the door open and they stepped out into what Melissa took to be a passage on the fourth floor of the house. From the road she had glimpsed that there was an attic floor at the very top. A little way along the passage Ena opened another door.

'Here you are,' she said, and she led the way in.

The lady's maid looked round the room, her eyes rested on the small fire burning in the hearth and she sniffed audibly as if she disapproved of something.

'Very nice,' she said, but there was no pleasure in her tone. Then she said abruptly, 'Well, I can't waste any more time on you. I'll send Reenie to help you unpack.'

Ena left briskly and closed the door behind her.

Melissa looked around her. The room was small and clean, with a bright patchwork quilt on the bed and flower-patterned curtains at the window. There was an old but decent-looking rug covering most of the linoleum, a chest of drawers on which stood a mirror, and a washstand with a jug and washbasin. When Melissa opened a door set into the wall opposite the window she discovered a cupboard with one shelf at the top. Below the shelf there was a rail with empty clothes hangers.

What was she supposed to do? How could she unpack? There was no sign of the trunk that contained all she had left in the world. But almost immediately there was a knock and the door opened.

'There you are,' Douglas the footman said. 'We've brought your things up.'

So this explained the noises on the stairs Melissa thought as she watched the two men manoeuvre the trunk into the room. Both of them smiled at her before they departed.

They were the first smiles she had received since she had entered the house and they completely overwhelmed her. She sat down on the bed and dropped her head into her hands. She had never felt so alone. She began to cry.

She didn't hear the door opening and the voice startled her.

'Eeh, divven't take on like that, hinny. I know it must be upsetting, starting somewhere new but it's not so bad here, you know.'

Melissa looked up to see a child looking at her with an expression of concern. She rubbed her eyes, looked closer and realised that child she may be but the skinny little scrap who stood before her was dressed as a servant; but not a superior servant like Ena.

'Are you Reenie?' Melissa asked.

'Aye, that's right. I've come to help you.'

She pushed some strands of wispy hair back up into her mobcap and looked around the room. She grinned.

'Eeh, isn't this grand?' she said. 'You're a lucky one, aren't you?'

'Am I?'

'Are you joking? A bonny bedspread and curtains; a rug to cover the cold floor and a fire in the grate! Some folks is lucky!'

Melissa wondered why she shouldn't have a fire in her room. 'Don't you have one?' she asked.

Reenie raised her eyebrows, obviously wondering whether she should take this question seriously and when she realised that she should she laughed and shook her head. 'Why, no,' she said, 'but this won't buy the baby a new bonnet. Let's get your things unpacked.'

Her words reminded Melissa of one of Mrs Sibbet's favourite sayings and she almost began crying again but, fearful of upsetting this friendly girl, she controlled herself.

'If we're quick about it we can get down first for tea,' she said.

'Tea?'

'Aye, Mrs Barton sets a good spread.'

Reenie was quick and efficient, and she even began directing Melissa where to put her clothes. Which drawer would be best for the underwear, which for her stockings, which for her blouses and so on. She had already commented on the fine quality of the petticoats, drawers and chemises, but when she began to hang up the dresses her eyes grew round with wonder.

'My, you've got some bonny fine frocks here,' she said. 'Did your last missus give them to you?'

Melissa shook her head. She didn't know what to say. It was obvious that Reenie thought she was a maidservant of some kind rather than the daughter of a friend of Mrs Winterton.

'Divven't tell me you've pinched them and the lady doesn't know yet?' the girl said with mock horror. 'Hey – divven't take on so. I was teasing.'

In spite of Melissa's pain and confusion she had to smile. 'No,' she said. 'Don't worry. I haven't pinched them. My mother and I made them.' As she saw Reenie's eyes widen even further than before she added, 'My mother was a dressmaker.'

'*Was?*' the girl asked perceptively.

'She's dead.'

'Eeh, I'm sorry, hinny. That's why you were crying.'

For a moment Reenie looked awkwardly at Melissa and then she rallied. 'Well, I can tell you one thing: if your ma was a dressmaker she was a bonny fine one. Now, hawway, we're nearly done and me belly thinks me throat's cut.'

Reenie returned briskly to her task. 'We can put the books on the top shelf in the cupboard,' she said. 'But what about this?'

She held up the carved rosewood box.

'That's my mother's sewing box,' Melissa said.

'Cupboard?'

'Yes, please.'

'Now for this shoebox,' Reenie said. They had already placed Melissa's shoes and boots on a rack in the bottom of the cupboard. 'Are these your best ones? Must be boots by the size of the box.'

'No – not shoes. It's just . . . wait don't . . .'

But Reenie had already opened the box.

'My goodness,' she said as she stared at the contents. 'Isn't that the bonniest thing I've ever seen?' She took a few steps backwards and sat down on the bed. 'Can I get it out of the box?' she asked, and when Melissa nodded she put the box down on the counterpane and lifted the doll out reverently.

'Just look at its pink and white complexion,' she said. 'And the silky ringlets – almost as dark as your hair.' She fingered the plum-coloured frock. 'Is this silk?'

'Yes. It was some my mother had left over from a ball gown she made.'

'Has the doll got a name?'

'Ninette.'

'What sort of fancy name is that when it's at home?'

'It's French. My father was French. He was a sailor. He brought the doll home for me when I was small.'

Reenie looked up at Melissa. 'So you're an orphan.'

Melissa didn't answer.

'You said your father *was* French.'

'He was lost at sea.'

'I'm sorry. But that makes us sort of sisters.' She smiled engagingly. 'Except I can't even remember my mam and dad. I was dragged up in the workhouse. The matron there said me mam's name was Irene and that's how I got Reenie, but nobody knew me da's name.'

The two girls looked at each other. The skies beyond the small window grew darker. Then Melissa said, 'I'm sorry.'

Reenie looked back at Ninette and then, laying her down gently on the bed, she began to lift out the clothes that had been lying underneath the doll.

'Did your mam make these?' she asked.

'No, I did.'

Reenie looked at her with dawning respect. 'I wish I could do something like this,' she said. 'I wish I could do anything at all but, to tell the truth, I even have trouble with my letters. I don't think I've ever read a whole book from beginning to end.'

She put the doll's clothes back into the box carefully and then she laid the doll on top of them and replaced the lid.

'Now all that's left is this empty tin with the sailing ships on. Tea caddy, was it?'

Melissa was taken aback. 'Empty?'

Reenie shook it. 'Aye, by the sound of it.'

'Let me see.' Melissa took the tin and opened it. Reenie was right, it was empty. The money that her mother had kept there, her day-to-day expenses and her savings, had gone. Now Melissa understood why her mother had asked her to take the tin up to her own bedroom. She had been worried that if she should die someone – and Melissa could guess who that someone was – might take the money that was meant to help Melissa plan a future for herself.

Now she remembered the whispered conversation between her aunt and her cousin Albert when they had returned from the funeral. Her aunt had managed to take the money after all, though Melissa didn't suppose that there was any way she could prove it.

Reenie, completely unaware that anything was wrong, smiled cheerfully and reached for the tin. 'Shall I put it in the cupboard?' she asked.

Wordlessly Melissa handed the old tea caddy over. 'Yes,' she said.

'Well, that's it,' Reenie said as she closed the cupboard door. 'Now your jerry's in the cupboard in the washstand,' she said briskly, 'and there's a bathroom at the end of the passage. But it'll be more comfortable to nip along and fill your jug and wash yourself in here by the fire. Eeh, you are lucky to hev a fire,' she said again. 'Now, let's gan down for wor tea.'

Lilian Winterton decided to take afternoon tea in her own small sitting room. Gwendolyn had been invited to visit Serena Charlesworth, an old school friend. She had set off as soon as Lilian had returned with Melissa and she had told her mother that she did not need the carriage. She would take a cab but it would be better if the footman accompanied her. He would be able to wait in the Charlesworths' kitchen.

After giving her orders Lilian removed her outdoor clothes and gave them to Ena to put away.

'Oh, leave that with me,' she said when her maid picked up the nightdress case that had fallen out of the muff.

Ena brought the tray with the tea and a selection of dainty sandwiches and cakes. She placed the tray on a small table already waiting by the fireside chair. Lilian told her to build up the fire and light the lamps.

'Oh, and you might as well draw the curtains,' she said. 'It's too, too gloomy out there.'

When all this was done Lilian dismissed her maid and settled in the chair by the fire to enjoy her repast. No matter how delicious the tiny sandwiches and dainty cakes Lilian was careful not to eat too many. Austin had promised to come home in time to dine with her tonight so she must leave room for the substantial meal that Mrs Barton would undoubtedly prepare.

When she laid aside her plate she took up her teacup and as she drank her tea she gazed contentedly into the fire. The events this morning had been much more exhausting than she had anticipated but, all in all, she thought she had acquitted herself well. She had retrieved Dermot's letters without too much bother. Goodness knows, she had been foolish to ask him to send them to Emmeline's house but, at the time, she had not known what else to do. She could not have had them arriving here. Nor dare she risk keeping them.

The truth of it was that when she had met him by accident in the park that day she should have refused to renew their acquaintance. She ought not to have given him any hope or encouraged him to write to her. And yet... Lilian sighed when she remembered how much in love with the handsome musician she had once been. And how unwise it would have been to marry him. Her conscience stirred – but not too much. She had not been unfaithful to Austin – not in the physical sense – but she knew he would have been just as angry if he had discovered that she was carrying on a romantic flirtation with her former admirer.

Lilian rose from the chair and went to fetch the letters

from where they still were inside the embroidered nightdress case. She went back to the fireplace and, for a moment, she held the ribbon-bound bundle over the fire. Her hand trembled. Should she burn the evidence of her romantic foolishness?

No, she couldn't do it. The dreams of love she had been too mercenary to fulfil were still part of her. A forlorn bittersweet part but, nevertheless, a part she could not bring herself to consign to the flames. She would keep Dermot's letters; find a hiding place for them.

Lilian Winterton sank down on to her chair, temporarily thrusting the letters behind the cushion at her back. She sighed. That was that. Now she must honour her promise to Emmeline and provide a home for Melissa. Austin would approve of her charitable action especially when she told him that she would no longer have to pay a dressmaker for now she had her very own seamstress living under their roof. She smiled. She would be able to follow the fashions more avidly than before without extra expense. For she had realised at once that Melissa was now as good a needlewoman as her mother, if not even better.

And then a troublesome memory surfaced. She had not settled Emmeline's final account. She thought about it for a moment and then she relaxed. The debt was to her mother and the child would hardly expect to be paid when she had been taken into the Wintertons' home rather than being left to the mercy of her incredibly unpleasant aunt. Of course she wouldn't. No doubt right at this moment she would be feeling intensely grateful for her good fortune.

Melissa sat next to Reenie at the table in the servants' dining room. There was plenty of food on the table: bread and butter, hardboiled eggs, cold cuts and jars of homemade chutney. There were also scones and dishes of jam, and a plate piled high with slices of raisin cake. Good order prevailed and it was hardly 'first come, first served', as Reenie had suggested. But Melissa watched her new companion fill her plate time and time again and wolf down more food than looked possible for the needs of such a tiny frame.

Reenie looked up at one stage and saw that Melissa was watching her. She looked abashed. 'You think I'm greedy,' she said quietly so that no one else could hear.

'No . . . not greedy . . . Just . . . just hungry.'

'I am. I'm always hungry. I think I'm making up for all those years that there was never enough on the table.'

'In the workhouse?'

'Yes – whisht – don't let anyone hear you say that word.'

'Why? Don't they know?'

'Oh, aye, they know all right, and they take every opportunity to bring it into the conversation. To mock me and make me feel small.'

Melissa suddenly had a glimpse of misery as acute as her own and she felt herself drawn to this strange child who looked no more than twelve years old and yet was probably working from dawn to dusk for very little pay.

Suddenly she wanted to know more about Reenie. 'Have you been here long?' she asked.

Reenie wiped some crumbs from her lips and grinned. 'Aye. Ever since me twelfth birthday. That was four years ago.'

Melissa's surprise must have shown.

'I know,' Reenie said. 'I divven't look me age, do I?'

'No. You're older than I am.'

'Am I?' Now it was Reenie's turn to look surprised. 'I was thinking that mebbes we would be about the same age.'

At this point the imposing lady at the head of the table, whom Melissa had learned was Mrs Barton, the cook, frowned and shushed them audibly.

'She doesn't like chatter at the table,' Reenie whispered. 'Just the usual is allowed. "Would you mind passing the bread and butter?" or the likes. And "Please" and "Thank you". But she's all right – so long as you do as you're told and work hard.'

Melissa was puzzled. Did Reenie think that she had come here as a servant? But that wasn't the case. She had come to be part of Mrs Winterton's family, hadn't she? Melissa tried to remember exactly what her mother had said in the letter she had left her.

My friend Lilian Winterton has promised that she will look after you. You will live with her and she will guide you until you are old enough to have your own establishment . . .

Now Melissa realised that didn't necessarily mean she was going to be one of the family. It could mean that Mrs Winterton was simply going to be her guardian. To allow her to live here. But surely it wasn't intended that she should be a servant, was it? Her mother would not have wished that . . .

Melissa glanced around at the other people sitting at the table. She recognised Ena, Mrs Winterton's maid. Douglas, the footman, wasn't there, and nor was William but she supposed that the coachman would be in his own quarters in the rooms above the stable. The others at the table were women apart from one older, important-looking man. 'Mr Beckett,' Reenie had whispered. 'Mr Winterton's valet.'

Apart from Mrs Barton's brief welcoming smile and Rennie's cheerful and genuine friendliness, Melissa felt that the others were not exactly pleased at her presence.

Perhaps it is a mistake that I am here, she thought. Perhaps Reenie was supposed to take me to Mrs Winterton. She watched as the others rose to leave the table. Reenie immediately began to clear the dishes away. It seemed she was going to do all the work. No one else came forward.

'Shall I help you?' Melissa asked.

'Don't be daft. That's my job. And then I'll hev to start the washing up.'

'But what am I supposed to do now?'

Reenie stopped what she was doing. She tucked a wisp of hair back into her cap, something she seemed to do all the time. It crossed Melissa's mind that she could easily tighten the ribbons for Reenie and make the cap fit properly. She decided to offer to do that when the girl stopped whirling around.

Reenie paused, clutching a loaded tray. She said, 'I don't know what you're supposed to do. I was sent to help you and bring you down for tea. You'd better ask Ena – quick, catch her before she leaves the room.'

Melissa hurried to the door. 'Ena,' she said.

The young woman turned and looked at her with displeasure. 'It's Miss Watson to you.'

'I'm sorry.'

'What do you want?'

'What am I supposed to do – I mean, am I to go and see Mrs Winterton now?'

'Goodness, no. Mrs Winterton is resting before she gets ready for dinner.'

'And am I supposed to see her then? At dinner?'

'Of course not. You'll get a light supper here with the rest of us. Just go to your room until it's time to eat. Reenie will come and get you. I'm sure Mrs Winterton will send for you in the morning.'

Melissa found the door that led to the dismal staircase and climbed wearily to her room. She supposed it really was her room. Ena had brought her here as Mrs Winterton had ordered. But why was it on the servants' floor?

Once inside she noticed that the fire had burned low. She stooped and added some coal from the scuttle. There wasn't much left. She judged the amount critically. There was just about enough to last the night if she banked it low.

She didn't bother to light the oil lamp that stood on the

small bedside cabinet; instead she sat by the fire, watching the flames crackle and remembered the games she used to play with her mother, seeking pictures in the burning coals.

'Good gracious, what are you doing sitting in the dark like this?'

Melissa hadn't heard the door open and she rose in fright as the sharp voice rang out behind her. It was Ena.

'Mrs Winterton has been kind enough to provide you with an oil lamp. Why not use it?'

'Yes, I will. Does Mrs Winterton want to see me now?'

'For goodness' sake, don't keep asking me that. Just wait until she sends for you. Here you are. I was told to give you this.'

Ena threw something on the bed and left as abruptly as she had come.

Melissa went over and picked up the nightdress case that Mrs Winterton had insisted on looking after, saying there might be something important inside. Melissa supposed that she had decided there wasn't, but this was another puzzling incident in a sad and confusing day.

She held the embroidered nightdress case close to her face and breathed in the comforting smell of lavender. She remembered Mrs Sibbet taking it out of her mother's chest of drawers and handing it over to Mrs Winterton somewhat reluctantly.

Martha had believed Melissa was going to find comfort in the Wintertons' house, and that was true if you believed that a clean, warm bedroom and plenty to eat was all you meant by comfort. Martha had said it was a lovely house Melissa was going to. And that also was true – except that she had already discovered that she might not be welcome in the loveliest parts of it.

What had her mother believed would happen to her when she came here? Did she think that Melissa was to become part of the family? Perhaps not. But at least she might have supposed that her daughter would be a guest here – even if not an important one.

No, I am not a guest in this house, Melissa thought, and now there was no doubt in her mind. She stared around the room bleakly. I believe I have been brought here to be a servant.

Part Two

Forgotten Dreams

Chapter Nine

During the lonely and confusing days that followed, Reenie, the little skivvy, often sought Melissa out. She never stayed long – she couldn't, she had far too much work to do – but a friendship grew between them. And each of them, it seemed, was in need of a friend.

One snowy day in January Melissa, alone and still grief-stricken over the death of her mother, found herself wandering aimlessly round the house. The snow had deadened all noise from the street and, in the hour when Mrs Winterton usually took her afternoon nap, the house was kept quiet. Curiosity took Melissa up to the attic floor where the maidservants slept. An open door gave her a glimpse of a narrow iron bedstead and a bare linoleum floor. She wondered whose room it was.

Reenie had told her that four people slept in the attics: Reenie herself; Peggy, the kitchen maid; Joan, the in-between maid; and Sarah, the parlour maid. Ena, Mrs Winterton's personal maid, had a room on the fourth floor where Melissa's room was. Reenie said that Ena was not too pleased when she discovered that Melissa was to be her neighbour.

Mrs Barton had a bedroom and a comfortable sitting room of her own in the semi-basement and Mr Beckett also had a room there. Douglas sometimes had to stay up late in order to open the door if the family had been out or if Mr Winterton came back very late from his office, as he often did, so he also had to sleep downstairs, and he often complained that his room was no better than a broom cupboard.

Apparently he coveted Mr Beckett's cosy room, with its table, armchair and fireplace, and dreamed of the day when it would be his. Reenie had enjoyed telling Melissa all this and Melissa was grateful to learn the particulars of the household that was so different from the modest home in which she had spent her happy childhood.

After exploring the attic floor Melissa returned to the servants' staircase. The skylight above was covered with a thick layer of snow and Melissa descended into the gloom. She went beyond the door that opened on to the fourth floor and went down one flight further. She pushed open the green baize-covered door and looked out on to a different world.

This was the floor where the family had their bedrooms and dressing rooms. The floors were richly carpeted; there were oil paintings on the walls spaced evenly between the gas lamps. And here and there, there were large ornate pottery jardinières supporting bowls of leafy green plants.

Melissa would have loved to have opened one of the doors but good manners overcame her curiosity. Emboldened by the silence in the house, she walked to the head of the grand staircase and looked down. She wondered if she dared descend one floor further. Then she heard a door close somewhere behind her and turned, startled, to find a very tall gentleman looking down at her curiously.

He frowned and as the skin rearranged itself around his bony features Melissa was reminded of a picture of a troll in one of her childhood fairytale books.

'Who the devil are you?' he said.

'Melissa Dornay.'

He pondered her reply for a moment then his frown

cleared. 'Ah, yes, the dressmaker's daughter. You have come to help with the sewing and mending.'

'Have I?'

To Melissa's dismay Mr Winterton began to frown again. 'That's what my wife tells me.'

'Oh . . . yes. That's right.'

So far Mrs Winterton had not told Melissa anything about her role in the house. She had not even seen her since they had arrived here on the day of the funeral. But this was the answer that Mr Winterton was expecting so it must be so.

'Are you looking for Mrs Winterton?' he asked.

'Er . . . no . . . I was wondering what to do.'

This was clearly a problem for Mr Winterton. 'Mrs Winterton is resting,' he said at last. 'She will no doubt send for you when she wakes up. So,' he began to look more cheerful as the problem resolved itself in his mind, 'I should go back to your room, if I were you, and wait.'

His duty clearly done, he nodded to her and went downstairs. Melissa fled back to the service door and hurried up to her room. Once there she flung herself down on her bed and wept anew.

After a while she sat up, wiped her eyes and tried to convince herself that Mrs Winterton did not mean to be unkind to her. She must honestly believe that she was doing all that was required of her by providing a home. It probably had not crossed her mind that Melissa, who had been used to a close and loving relationship with her mother, would be lonely.

Over the days and weeks that followed Mrs Winterton, although thoughtless, never scolded her; never spoke harshly to her. Instead she provided everything she thought might be needed for the sewing room. Melissa was shy at first but Mrs Winterton urged her to tell her what was required – and whatever she provided, whether it was the latest sewing machine or an adjustable body form, it was the best money could buy.

When Melissa asked her if she could go to her French conversation lessons with Miss Robson, Mrs Winterton said, 'Of course you may. I understand that many of the terms used in the world of fashion are French. But you must not stay out too late. As long as you keep up with your needle-work, you do not have to ask before visiting your teacher. Oh, and you had better use the servants' entrance when you come and go. After all, you are not one of the family.'

Even this, said so thoughtlessly, was not meant to hurt, and Melissa began to settle into her isolated place in the house as neither servant nor member of the family. Her friendship with Reenie grew more important.

Melissa learned that she could also go to church, take a walk in the park and even go into town to do a little window shopping. She wondered if Mrs Winterton had been artful when she had used the word 'needlework' instead of 'work'. For Melissa, who must only use the servants' entrance, was indeed going to earn her keep.

'Come along, sleepyhead.'

Melissa roused herself one morning in February to find that Reenie had crept into her room and was bending over her. 'What is it? Have I overslept?'

'No, I just wanted to remind you that it's my half-day today.'

'Oh, yes, I remember.' Melissa yawned and turned over.

'No! Divven't gan back to sleep. If you get up now you can get on with whatever sewing you're doing nice and early and then, by the time I've finished we can go out.'

'Mm.'

Melissa yawned and stretched her arms above her head.

Her long dark hair fell around her face as she raised her head from the pillow.

'Sit up,' Reenie commanded. 'Look – I've brought you a cup of tea and a biscuit. No – open your eyes!'

'All right,' Melissa said sleepily. 'Don't worry. I'll do everything I have to do and we'll go out as soon as you're free.'

Reenie smiled brightly. 'Where shall we go?'

Melissa yawned and stretched again and looked out of the window. The rooftops were sparkling with frost but the sky was cloudless.

'It looks as though it's going to be a lovely day,' Melissa said. 'Let's go to the park.'

If it had been allowed Reenie would have sung as she went about her duties. She had never had a friend until Melissa came to live at the Wintertons' house and, apart from Mrs Barton, who was all right so long as you did your job properly, no one spoke to her unless they had to, and even then they made it clear that they thought themselves much better than she was.

Melissa never looked down on her. It was as if she had no idea how different they were. She treated her like a normal person, not the lowliest servant in the house. Hard to believe though it was, they were real friends. And already Reenie loved Melissa so much that she would do anything for her, even die for her.

Now as she cleaned the grates and set the fires, Reenie thought about their friendship. Even though Melissa was much taller than she, she was two years younger and was still a child. At least that's how Reenie liked to think of her. She was someone who needed looking after. And that someone was going to be Reenie.

As soon as lunch was over they went to Leazes Park.

Even though the sky was a bright clear blue, the air was

bitterly cold. Reenie and Melissa watched as some boys played on a slide they had made on a frosty path. The little lads shouted with enjoyment, their cheeks red and their breath condensing in the chilly air. Then a boy smaller than the others fell over. His friends ran off laughing, and he howled more with indignation than hurt.

Reenie and Melissa hurried towards him and, stepping carefully on the glasslike surface of the slide, Reenie helped him up and led him on to the grass.

'Whisht now,' she said, but he didn't stop crying.

He rubbed his face with his hands and left a smear of dirty particles of ice across his rosy cheeks. Reenie kneeled down.

'Hev you got a handkerchief ?' she asked the boy.

He nodded.

'Well, where is it? Up your sleeve?'

He shook his head.

'In your pocket?'

He sniffed and nodded.

'All right . . . stand still . . . let me get it. Here you are, pet.' She dabbed at his cheeks, then said, 'Now can you blow your nose?'

The child was just about to do so when an angry woman rushed up to them.

'Leave my son alone!' she said.

Reenie got up, looking puzzled. 'I was only trying to help,' she said.

Another woman joined the little group. 'What is it, Mildred?' she asked the first woman.

'I found this ragamuffin talking to Arthur. And look – that's his handkerchief she's got in her hand.'

'I know it is,' Reenie protested. 'I didn't intend to steal it. I was trying to mop his tears up.'

'And no wonder he was crying,' the boy's mother said. 'Just look at you.'

Reenie bristled. 'What do you mean by that?'

The child was now crying harder than ever. His mother snatched the handkerchief from Reenie's hand.

'Do you want me to call the park keeper?' her friend asked.

'Yes. Tell him he shouldn't allow that sort of person in the park.'

'No!' Melissa stepped forward. 'My friend has done nothing wrong. Your son fell down and she tried to help him.'

'Your *friend*?' the boy's mother said. 'This grubby creature is your friend?'

'I'm not grubby!' Reenie said.

'Hush,' Melissa told her, then spoke to the woman. 'She isn't grubby. That's an insult. And she came to the park with me.'

Both women raised their eyebrows and then the boy's mother shook her head. 'Well,' she said, 'I hope your mother knows the sort of company you're keeping.'

By now the boy's sobs had subsided into gulps and sniffs. He tugged at his mother's hand.

'What is it?' she asked.

'It's true. She was helping me. I fell down. You were talking to Aunt Ada. You didn't see.'

His mother looked vexed. 'Very well, but you've played here long enough. We'll go home now.'

The two women and the boy walked away.

Reenie glared at their retreating forms. 'I'm not grubby,' she said again.

'Of course you're not,' Melissa assured her.

Reenie turned to face Melissa. 'I wash meself every day even when I can't get any warm water.'

'I know you do.'

Suddenly Reenie sighed. 'But you can see why they said that.'

'No, I can't.'

'Oh, hawway, Melissa. Look at me. Look at the way I'm dressed. This coat is old and threadbare and the sleeves and the hem's all frayed. Me boots are battered and past repair – look,' she lifted one foot up, 'the sole's hanging off this one – and me hat looks as if I've pinched it from a scarecrow.

'And look at you. Neat and clean and pretty as a picture in that good woollen coat, red tartan scarf and mittens, and those shiny button-up boots. No wonder those women didn't believe that we'd come to the park together. And as a matter of fact I don't think we should go out together again.'

'Stop this!' Melissa said. 'I don't care what your clothes are like; it's the person who's wearing them that's important.'

'Is it?'

'Of course it is, and of course we'll go out together again on your next day off. Just wait and see.'

Reenie did not know what Melissa meant by the 'wait and see' bit, but on her very next day off she found out. She went to the sewing room with every intention of telling Melissa that she hadn't changed her mind but Melissa greeted her smiling broadly.

'Here you are,' she said. 'Try them on. There's a skirt and a blouse and a coat, even a pair of shoes.'

Reenie was astounded. 'You've bought new clothes for me? You shouldn't hev done. I can't accept them.'

'I haven't bought them. These were all mine. Things that I've outgrown. I hope you don't mind.'

'Mind what?'

'Taking cast-off clothes.'

Reenie laughed. 'Eeh, Melissa,' she said, 'when hev I ever had anything but cast-off clothes? Even me work clothes used to belong to the last poor lass that worked here, and as for what I wear on me days off, the only clothes I can afford are things from Paddy's Market on the Quayside. And most of them don't even fit properly.'

'Well, I hope these will fit,' Melissa said. 'I had to guess at your size because I wanted this to be a surprise.'

'Well, it is a surprise, but I still can't take them.'

'Why ever not?'

'Because I can't afford them.'

'I'm not *selling* them to you. I'm giving them to you.'

'Are you sure? They're too good for Paddy's Market and you could get a fair old sum for them at a second-hand shop.'

'Maybe so but I don't want to sell them. And you would be doing me a favour if you would accept them.'

'How's that?'

'Because you threatened never to come out with me again in your old clothes and I don't like going out by myself. Now go on, for goodness' sake, try them on!'

The clothes fitted Reenie perfectly, even the shoes, which Melissa had also outgrown. 'That was a stroke of luck,' Melissa said when Reenie walked up and down to see if they were comfortable. 'I can make and alter clothes but there would have been nothing I could do about the shoes.'

After that Melissa took charge of Reenie's wardrobe, as she called it, even her underpinnings. Every now and then Reenie would protest half-heartedly but Melissa told her that altering the clothes was good practice for her. And, besides, Melissa was accepting cast-off clothes too. At first only those of Miss Gwendolyn, but later some of Mrs Winterton's more sober garments. And that antagonised Ena who, as Mrs Winterton's personal maid, felt she was entitled to all her cast-offs.

In order to prevent the other maids from becoming jealous of Reenie's growing wardrobe they decided that she would keep everything in Melissa's room. Over the years it became part of the fun to get dressed up together before going out.

Then, not wanting to be seen in their finery, they would hurry down the service stairs, along the passage, to the door that led to the back door and across the stable yard; stifling their giggles until they had reached the safety of the road at the back of the house.

Away from the house they were no longer the skivvy and the seamstress. They could pretend to be anyone they liked. Their favourite game was to imagine that they were the daughters of the house going for a stroll, or going into town to do some window shopping. But they never took it further than a game between themselves.

'You could pass for a lady, any day,' Reenie told Melissa. 'But the minute I opened me mouth and spoke to anyone, we'd be rumbled.'

They both laughed but that remark sparked Reenie's sense of fun and, after that, rather than being the daughter of the house, she would pretend to be Melissa's maid. Sitting in the window table at Tilley's, wandering around the grand department stores where Melissa never tired of looking at the new fashions and the fabrics, or simply sitting in the park on a sunny day, they invented new lives for themselves.

Melissa became Miss Melody Fotheringham and Reenie was Clarabelle Potts. Reenie had found the names in a serial story in one of the tuppenny weeklies that Mrs Barton subscribed to. When she had read them the cook-housekeeper would pass them on to the maidservants. Eventually Reenie would get her hands on them and read them in her draughty cubicle of an attic room by spluttering candlelight when her long day's work was done.

'What are you going to buy today, Miss Melody?' Reenie would ask as they gazed at gloves, lace collars or embroidered handkerchiefs in the window of the haberdasher's shop at one end of the large indoor Grainger Market where they usually ended up on a rainy day.

Melissa would purse her lips then shake her head. 'There's nothing that takes my fancy, I'm afraid,' she would say. 'Come along, Clarabelle, let's go up and have tea and cream buns in the mezzanine café.'

And so they would. Sitting at one of the gingham-covered tables on the balcony that overlooked the main hall of the market, they would sip their tea and make their cream buns last as long as possible; defying the glares of the busy waitresses who wanted to clear their table and set it up for the next lot of customers.

On summer days in the park Reenie would carry the pretence one stage further. She would insist that Melissa should sit and wait at one of the tables set out around the pavilion café while she queued up at the counter for lemonade and currant buns. She would bring the tray to the table and give a little curtsey before sitting down.

Often these games collapsed into fits of giggling. And more often than not it was Melissa who would bring the make-believe to an end, saying, 'Please can you just be my friend, now, Reenie?'

Sometimes they would stroll up and down the paths, looking at the floral displays, or watch the children playing on the swings, and Reenie never told Melissa how keenly she was looking out for the little lad she had tried to help. How she wished she could see him and his mother again. And that his mother would see her in her fine new clothes. She still smarted when she remembered that the woman had called her 'grubby'.

Well, thanks to Melissa she wasn't grubby now and she would daydream that the obnoxious woman would see her, stop and stare, and then apologise profusely for having insulted her. But the years passed and they never saw them again.

As Melissa grew older she grew more and more beautiful. At least that was Reenie's opinion. She noticed that her friend would attract admiring glances from young men but Melissa herself never seemed to notice.

Often there would be a band concert in the park and, rather than sit on the uncomfortable slatted seats, Reenie and Melissa would sit a little distance away on a grassy bank. They both loved the music, especially the songs from the musical shows, and for a while all the cares and worries of their everyday lives would vanish.

Then one day Reenie noticed a very handsome young man sitting not far away from them and watching them intently. She was just about to say something to Melissa when she saw what he was doing. He had a large pad of paper on his knee and he was drawing.

He looked up, realised that Reenie was watching him and, curiously, he put one finger to his lips as if to say 'shush'. She frowned, not knowing what he meant. Then the tune the band was playing came to an end and the audience began to clap loudly. Reenie turned to see the bandsmen, in their bright uniforms with shiny buttons, taking their bow and when she looked back the young man had gone.

On the way home she told Melissa about him and they wondered what he had been sketching and whether he was a student from the art school. They decided that he probably was and after that they didn't think much more about it.

The next time they went to the park he was there again. Melissa took her place at one of the café tables and Reenie, as she always insisted that she did, went to join the queue at the counter. When she turned to go back with the tray she saw that the young man had taken a seat not far away from their table and he was drawing again. She paid for the two fruit sundaes, placed them on the tray, and then walked as quietly as she could towards where he was sitting.

The normal noises of conversation from the other tables, plus the sound of children playing nearby, meant that he did not hear her footsteps and she was able to stand immediately behind him and look down at his page without him being aware that she was there.

What she saw astounded her. He had been drawing Melissa. It must have been barely ten minutes since he had begun and yet the quick sure strokes had already captured the way Melissa sat so lightly on her chair, the graceful folds of her white lawn dress, her fine profile and the way her dark hair, caught up behind her ears with her bonny combs, tumbled down her back.

Reenie caught her breath and, for a moment, she forgot about the tray she was carrying. The fruit sundae glasses wobbled and slid into each other. The artist turned, startled by the noise, and half rose from his chair. Reenie stepped backwards quickly but not before the young man's shoulder had caught the corner of the tray, tipping it up and causing the fruit sundae glasses to slide towards the edge.

He grabbed at the tray but it was too late. The tall, fluted glasses crashed on to the ground behind his chair. The glass was thick and didn't break, but the contents were emptied across the paved area around the tables.

A woman at the next table saw what was happening and stood up quickly, holding her skirt out of harm's way. The man with her moved her chair further away from the spreading puddle of red jelly and melting ice cream and tutted crossly.

'Really, some people,' he said, and shook his head in disapproval.

Reenie and the young artist looked at each other and

burst out laughing, which attracted further disapproval from nearby tables.

'Eeh, I'm sorry,' Reenie said.

'No, I'm sorry,' he replied. 'I knocked the tray out of your hands.'

'But I shouldn't hev been standing so close behind you. Serves me right for being so nebby. Nosy,' she corrected herself when she saw his look of bemusement.

The staff behind the counter had seen what had happened and an unsmiling waitress came towards them. She picked up the almost empty sundae glasses and stared at the mess on the ground with displeasure.

Reenie flushed. 'I'm sorry, get us a bucket of water and a broom and I'll wash it all away,' she said.

The waitress compressed her lips and looked Reenie up and down. Reenie thought she was on the point of accepting the offer when the artist spoke.

'Of course you won't,' he said. 'You are a customer here and, besides, it was as much my fault as yours. Please go and join your mistress and I will pay for any damage and buy some more fruit sundaes.'

Reenie saw money changing hands and heard him say, 'I'll be joining the ladies. Would you be so good as to bring the replacements to their table? Oh, and perhaps you will bring one for me.'

He turned to busy himself gathering up his sketchbook and pencils, and put everything into a sort of canvas bag something like a bairn's school satchel. Embarrassed, Reenie hurried over to join Melissa, who had been watching the incident in disbelief.

'What on earth did you do?' she asked.

'Tell you later. But, whisht! He's coming over.'

She had only time to settle herself at the table when the young man came up to them. 'Hello,' he said to Melissa.

'Let me introduce myself. James Pennington.' He smiled. 'And please don't be angry with your maid, it was entirely my fault.'

'My maid?' Melissa said. 'Oh, but . . . ouch!' She shot a look of pained surprise at Reenie, who had kicked her under the table.

James Pennington frowned at her odd response but as no explanation seemed to be forthcoming he decided to ignore it. 'And you are . . .'

'Oh . . . yes . . . sorry. My name is Melissa Dornay. And this is my fr—'

Another kick.

'This is Reenie.'

Suddenly every one of them seemed to be feeling awkward but the mood was broken when the waitress approached with the tray.

'You don't mind if I join you?' James Pennington asked.

'Oh, please do.'

Reenie noticed that Melissa had flushed a delicate pink. She had never seen her friend disconcerted before and wondered if it had something to do with James Pennington's clear grey-eyed gaze. As for James, he seemed equally taken with Melissa's eyes, which were a deep dark brown.

They talked hesitantly at first but that James certainly had a way with him. He knew how to draw a girl out without being in the least flirtatious. During the conversation that developed, Reenie thought she might as well not have been there. They had not even been deliberately playacting and yet from the minute she had opened her mouth James had taken her to be Melissa's maid.

Well, it had not bothered her. Not in the slightest. But Melissa had been bothered. 'It's all right when it's just the two of us playing our game,' she told Reenie later. 'But involving other people doesn't seem honest somehow.'

'There's been no harm done,' Reenie said. 'I mean, we might never even see him again.'

But they did, of course. Each time they went to the park James was already there as if he had been waiting for them. One day Reenie had pretended to be feeling poorly and she had urged Melissa to go to the park without her. James had taken her to the art gallery and she had been surprised and pleased by the easy way they had been able to talk to each other.

Another time Reenie said she had to take her shoes to the cobbler's and she told Melissa to go ahead to the café in the park and get a nice table in the shade of the trees.

'You've never bothered about the shade before,' Melissa said.

'Oh, for goodness' sake, can't you do as you're told for once!'

Reenie seemed genuinely cross so Melissa, puzzled, agreed and set off for the park on her own. But she had guessed even before she had reached the gates of the park what Reenie was up to and she knew she was right the moment she saw James Pennington waiting at a table under the trees. She hesitated, almost deciding to walk away, but James saw her and stood up. He was smiling.

Melissa knew it would be rude to refuse his invitation to sit with him but she could not help saying, 'When did you and Reenie arrange this?'

His eyes widened and he stared at her.

She felt hot with embarrassment. Oh, no, she thought, I was wrong. This has not been prearranged. What must he think of me?

But then he laughed. 'I can see we haven't fooled you,' he said. 'I hope you won't scold your maid. It is entirely my fault.'

Although she was relieved that she had not made a

complete fool of herself, she felt even more uneasy. James still thought Reenie was her maid. She must tell him the truth. But first, and more pressingly, she wanted to know how he and Reenie had managed this.

As if he had read her mind he said, 'I spoke to Reenie last week when I dropped my satchel and all my papers fell out. I asked her to help me gather them up, remember?'

Melissa frowned. 'I do.' In fact she had been a little puzzled at the time as the papers – his drawings – had not exactly scattered far and wide.

'And Reenie agreed to this – to this . . . ?' She was genuinely lost for words.

'Impertinence? Is that the word you're looking for? Oh, Melissa, please don't be angry. I just wanted a few moments alone with you, that's all.' He reached across the small wrought-iron table and took her hand. 'And my attentions are quite honourable, I promise you.'

Her white lace gloves were no protection against the touch of his hand on her skin. The chatter and laughter of the people at the other tables seemed to recede and leave them cocooned in a world of their own. Melissa looked at him and smiled at the way his ever unruly lock of hair fell down across his forehead and she wondered how a pair of clear grey eyes could seem so warm.

'Shall we walk?' he asked.

Melissa nodded. She seemed to have lost the power of speech. James was still holding her hand and she allowed him to draw it through the crook of his arm. They turned to walk towards the lake.

Behind them Melissa could hear the clink of teacups and the cheerful chatter of the café; ahead of them were the cries of children as they sailed their wooden boats, and the splash of oars as adventurous souls set out across the water in hired craft. But here, under the cool shade of the trees, all was silent. It was as if the world was holding its breath.

Melissa wondered at how strange and yet how right it felt to be walking here with James. She sensed that although neither of them spoke out loud, some deeper kind of communication was at work. Strangers though they still were, it was as if they had known each other for ever.

A slight breeze blew up and set the leaves rustling; their shadows moved restlessly across the ground. James stopped walking and turned towards Melissa.

'We're in a sylvan grove,' he said. 'Our own sylvan grove right here in Newcastle.'

'Rather than in Arcady?' Melissa said.

James's eyes widened in pleased surprise and with one arm he made a wide gesture that took in the trees around them and then the ground at their feet.

'Beechen green and shadows numberless,' he said. He looked up. 'And a whispering roof of leaves and trembled blossoms.'

Then he looked at Melissa, his smile infectious, and she laughed.

'I think we have mixed up at least three of Mr Keats' poems,' she said.

'You like poetry?'

'I do. When I was at school some of the others used to groan when our teacher, Miss Robson, handed round the poetry books. I didn't. I loved those lessons.'

'Me too.'

Somehow the atmosphere had eased. Some of the highly charged tension that had puzzled her had dissipated but, paradoxically, she sensed that the bond between them was even stronger. James took hold of both her hands. A bright ray of sunshine penetrated the shifting cover of leaves and momentarily dazzled her. When she could see again she found that he was looking at her intently.

He held her gaze. She didn't know how long the silence between them lasted; how many heartbeats there were before he spoke again and his words brought the world flooding back.

'I know we haven't known each other very long,' he said, 'but I would like to call on your parents.'

'My parents? Why?' Melissa was shocked to the core. She knew what he meant but she had to hear him say the words.

James smiled. 'Because a proper gentleman should always seek the approval of the parents of the lady in question before he comes courting.'

Melissa withdrew her hand. The game could not go on any longer. The moment had come when she must tell him that, not only did she have no parents but that she was not the person he assumed her to be. What will happen if I tell him now? she thought. He might never want to see me again. Nevertheless I must tell him the truth.

'Have I spoken too soon?' he asked. 'Have I shocked you? Do you want time to think about it? Oh, Melissa, take – oh – a week but, for heaven's sake put me out of my misery and tell me that you at least feel some of the emotions that I do.' His words were dramatic but his eyes were smiling as if he were surprised but not dismayed by his own feelings.

'I do,' Melissa said, 'but—'

'Don't say any more. If there is a "but" I think I'd better wait until you have considered the things. And next week you must tell me whether I can come calling or not.'

'James, I . . .' she began, but stopped in puzzlement when she saw that he was looking beyond her.

'I believe that's Reenie,' he said. 'She's looking for us. We'd better go and join her.'

They left their sylvan grove regretfully. The spell was broken.

Reenie smiled when she saw them. 'My, it's warm,' she

said. 'I could do with a glass of iced lemonade. I'll go and fetch some, shall I?'

'I'll come with you,' James said. 'I think Melissa needs a moment or two to herself.'

Reenie looked at him questioningly but he shook his head. He won't tell her what we've been talking about, Melissa thought. He's too much of a gentleman to talk about something which should remain confidential. She watched them making their way through the other tables to join the queue at the pavilion counter.

She had not had the courage to speak but suddenly she knew what she must do. She reached for the canvas satchel that James had placed on one of the chairs. Hastily she fumbled with the leather straps and opened it. She took a pencil and a plain piece of paper and, as simply as she could, she told James the truth. She folded the paper and pushed it back into the satchel before fastening it again. She completed her task just as Reenie and James started back to the table with the tray.

She tried to sip her lemonade as though nothing untoward had happened but James noticed her agitation.

'Perhaps you had better take your mistress home,' he said to Reenie. 'I think she is a little perturbed. It's my fault but I make no apology.'

As soon as they had finished their drinks Melissa rose to go. James insisted on seeing them to the gates of the park and took Melissa's hand before they parted. He raised it to his lips. He didn't speak but the look in his eyes almost broke Melissa's heart.

Reenie looked at her keenly. 'What's happened?' she asked.

Melissa told her what she'd done.

'So you've written it all down and left it for him to find?'

'Yes. I couldn't face his anger.'

'Why would he be angry?' Reenie asked her.

'Because our friendship would have been based on a lie. He might think that I had deliberately set out to deceive him.'

'But you didn't! Set out to do that, I mean. We were just playing a game.'

'I've explained that. But even if he believes me, he still might not be interested in someone he would consider to be a servant.'

'Don't talk about yourself like that. You're a real lady as far as I'm concerned.'

Melissa, warmed by the other girl's sincere feelings, managed a wan smile. 'Maybe so,' she said, 'but you know what I mean. In the eyes of the world I am merely a seamstress.'

Chapter Ten

May 1893

The trees in the square were drenched and the leaves dripped rain on to the beds of scarlet dwarf tulips and creamy miniature narcissi. Melissa sat on the window seat of the room that was next door to her bedroom. It was the sewing room and it had been Melissa's domain for more than four years.

Now she had taken a break from work and was gazing through the rain-spattered windowpanes. She was lucky that the room was at the front of the house rather than the back where the windows looked out on the yard and the stable block.

Here, on the fourth floor of the tall house, she could enjoy the view. In summer she saw the nursemaids unlock the gates and take their little charges into the garden to play. Sometimes their mothers would stroll about in twos or threes, exchanging gossip. And the occasional gentleman, forbidden to smoke in the house, would go there to enjoy his cigar.

In the winter, when the branches of the trees were bare, the houses opposite could be seen more clearly. Each house looked identical to its neighbour, displaying elegant but anonymous façades. In the evening as the sun sank below the horizon and the streetlamps became disembodied globes of light in the gathering dusk, the garden became a place of mysterious shadows. Then one by one the windows of the houses opposite would come to life as the lamps were lit.

Melissa liked to imagine what life was like for the people who lived in those houses. She would make up stories for herself and contemplate how her mother would have loved to share the make-believe world with her.

Today, despite the rain, a warm sun did its best to break through the clouds, and steam had begun to rise from the soaked roads and pavements. Melissa rubbed the back of her neck and rotated her shoulders to ease them. She would have to return to work. She had promised Gwendolyn that she would have the repairs to her gown done before the evening meal and it was already past three o'clock. She went back to her sewing table and was just about to take up her needle when there was a knock at the door.

'Come in,' Melissa called, knowing who it would be.

The door opened and a small figure slid in sideways and closed the door softly behind her. 'I shouldn't be here,' she said with the air of a conspirator.

'You always say that,' Melissa said. She smiled.

'But it's true. I'm not supposed to distract you.'

'You don't. I like having you here, and if you talk too much all I have to do is tell you to be quiet.'

'And so you do,' Reenie said. 'Like a proper schoolmarm you are. I divven't know why I put up with you!'

'Nor I you!'

The two of them smiled fondly at each other and then burst out laughing. But not for long. Reenie covered her mouth with her hand and, withdrawing it again, she said, 'Whisht, or we'll hev that tartar Ena in here, and then I'll be for it!'

'Where are you supposed to be?' Melissa enquired mildly.

'Nowhere, as far as I can tell. I've finished all me chores for the moment and I want to stay out of sight in case someone finds something else for me to do. That Mrs Barton can't abide to see any poor soul taking her ease.'

'Well, why don't you make us a pot of tea?'

'I hoped you would say that.'

Melissa examined the small round holes near the bottom of Gwendolyn's gown while Reenie went over to the fireplace, lifted the kettle from the trivet, shook it to make sure there was sufficient water inside and put it back again. She took up the poker and pushed the hotplate further towards the burning coals. She stood and watched it for a moment and then, when the kettle began to build up steam and rattle its lid, she wiped her hands on her pinafore and went to the small table at the side of the fireplace where the cups and saucers and teapot waited.

Melissa looked up. 'There's plenty tea in the caddy but I forgot to bring a jug of milk up.'

'What about sugar?'

'There's plenty.'

'Then we'll do without milk. I daresn't gan down to the kitchen. Mrs Barton's resting in her room but there's bound to be someone who'd catch me and find a job for me to do.'

The kettle boiled and Reenie made the tea.

'Let it brew for a moment,' Melissa said without looking up from her work. 'And then pour the tea but don't bring it over to the worktable.'

'Yes, madam, of course, madam, three bags full, madam. Eeh, Melissa, I sometimes wonder what your last servant died of.' She said all this with a smile.

Melissa looked up. 'Have I been imperious?'

'If that means bossy, aye, you hev.'

'I'm sorry. I don't mean to be. You know I don't think of

you as a servant. You are my friend, and friends can talk to each other how they will, can't they?'

'Hmm.'

'What's the matter?'

'Are we proper friends, Melissa? I mean, can we be? I am a servant in this house. Even though I'm a proper kitchen maid now, I'm not treated much better than the skivvy I used to be. And you . . .'

Melissa smiled sadly. 'What am I exactly? I'm not one of the family, am I?'

'No.'

'So where do I fit in the scheme of things?'

'Well . . . you're a . . . sort of guest.'

'Guests are not kept prisoner in the sewing room.'

'You're not a prisoner!'

'You know what I mean. I make and mend the family's clothes. I am lodged and fed and I receive a small amount of money that Mrs Winterton calls an allowance but, in truth, it is a wage. In my eyes that makes me a servant.'

'Well, the others don't think you're a servant, do they?'

Melissa looked troubled. 'No, they don't. At least they make no effort to include me. I sit at the table with them and no one talks or makes conversation.'

'Mrs Barton doesn't like too much chatter at the table.'

'I know, but it's more than that. They even avoid looking me in the eye.'

'You know what I think?'

'Tell me.'

'It's because they're not sure of you. Mrs Winterton doesn't talk to you the same way she talks to the rest of us, even to Ena. She doesn't give you orders. She asks you most politely. In their eyes that makes you neither fish nor fowl nor good red herring. You know what I mean.'

Melissa sighed. 'I do. And I can't understand Mrs

Winterton's attitude. Every now and then she will talk to me about my mother. About how sweet-natured she was and how she regarded her as a dear friend. And yet I am not treated like the daughter of a friend. I am not invited to their table nor asked to spend any time with them. Sometimes I feel that I shall be here in this sewing room for the rest of my days, making and mending and designing gowns for Mrs Winterton and Gwendolyn so that they can go to the ball!'

'You mean like in one of them fairy stories you tell me?'

'I suppose I do. But I'm not poor little Cinderella, I'm like Rapunzel in her tower. But I despair of any handsome prince coming along and asking me to let down my hair so that he can climb up and rescue me.'

Her tone was light-hearted but she kept her head lowered over her work rather than let Reenie see her expression and perhaps guess at the anguish she still felt. For even if a fairytale prince did come to rescue her she knew that she would always be comparing him to James Pennington. James, the first and only man she had fallen in love with, and the man whom she had believed loved her.

'Melissa . . .' Reenie's concerned voice brought her back from her reverie, 'is anything the matter?'

Melissa carefully tied off the stitching of the piece she was working on and cut the thread. She looked up and smiled.

'Of course not. Shall we have that cup of tea before it gets cold?'

Sitting each side of the fireplace they drank their tea in companionable silence, then, regretfully it seemed to Melissa, Reenie got up and put the cups and saucers on the tray.

'I'll see to these,' she said, 'and when I bring the tray back I'll bring a small jug of milk so you can have another cup of tea later if you want to.'

'Thank you,' Melissa said. She went back to the worktable

and sat down. She looked up to find Reenie still standing there. 'What is it?' she asked.

'That's Miss Gwendolyn's new gown, isn't it? The one I saw you making just a week or two ago?'

'Yes, it is.'

'Then what's she done to it?' Reenie walked over to have a look at the pale blue georgette fabric marred by brown-ringed holes at the bottom. 'What are those? They look like burn marks.'

'They are.'

'Has she stood too near the fire? Have the coals popped a few sparks out?'

'No, these are caused by hot ash dropping from a cigarette.'

'The little monkey!'

'Gwendolyn is twenty-two years old. I suppose she can smoke if she wants to.'

'But she hasn't told her mother?'

Melissa shook her head. 'Mrs Winterton believes that smoking is bad for the complexion and will give you wrinkles. And, in any case, Mr Winterton has forbidden smoking in this house.'

'Yes, I know,' Reenie said. 'That's why Douglas goes out into the back yard – in all weathers. But where does Miss Gwendolyn smoke?'

'When she visits her friends, I suppose.'

'And how are you going to mend those holes, then?'

'There's plenty material in the hem. I'll manage somehow. But as she wants to wear this dress to the theatre this evening I shall have to get on with it.' Melissa began work on the gown again but Reenie still lingered. 'What now?' Melissa asked without looking up.

'Do you ever wonder why Miss Gwendolyn hasn't got married?'

'She hasn't found anyone who suits her.'

'She's had plenty chances. She's bonny enough even if she is getting a bit elderly.'

'Elderly at twenty-two!'

'You know what I mean. Girls from families like the Wintertons should be married long before they reach the age of twenty-two. And we all know her mother would like to have her settled. And even if the young gentlemen who come courting aren't attracted by her bonny looks, her da's money is a mighty powerful reason to pop the question.'

'I had no idea you were so cynical.'

'And what does that mean?'

'So suspicious of people's motives – of their reason for doing things.'

'Well, I am. But in any case she doesn't encourage any of them. And the reason Miss Gwendolyn won't countenance any one of those fine young fellows is because she's already given her heart to someone else. At least that's my opinion.'

Melissa was astonished. 'How would you know something like that?'

'Servants know a good deal of what goes on in any household and what their so-called betters get up to. Especially when another servant is involved.'

'You're talking in riddles.'

'Honestly, Melissa. You sit here in the sewing room day in, day out, and you don't know what's going on all round you.'

Melissa laughed. 'But you're going to tell me, aren't you?'

'Aye, I am. The reason Miss Gwendolyn won't hev anything to do with those fine young gentlemen is because in her eyes there's no one finer than a certain footman. And there's only one of them in this house.'

*

Two floors below the sewing room was the library, a grand book-lined room, which had a small balcony overlooking the square. The doors that led on to the balcony were ajar and a fine rain blew in and made wet trails across the Turkey carpet. But Gwendolyn was oblivious to this. Her father was at his office and her mother was visiting a friend. She was alone in the house. The servants didn't count. At least all but one of them, and he stood with her, not quite out on the balcony but hidden from the room and anyone who might enter it by the floor-length velvet curtains.

They blew the smoke from their cigarettes out into the rain-washed air. When they had finished them Douglas leaned forward and stubbed them out on the balustrade. Then he put them in one of his pockets to be disposed of later.

Gwendolyn noticed for the first time that the linings of the curtains were wet. 'We should close the windows now,' she said.

Douglas didn't answer. He simply drew her into his arms and kissed her.

Very early the next morning, even before the birds in the garden in the square had started to sing, Melissa got up and left the house. She was going to visit an old friend.

'I can't thank you enough for coming to help me.'

Miss Robson stood in the front parlour of the rented house she had lived in with her mother. She was surrounded by suitcases and tea chests. They contained all her worldly goods; at least those worldly goods she had decided to take with her to France. The rest she had sold.

Very soon the removal men would arrive to take the boxes to the station, where they would be loaded up in the carrier's own railway wagons. From thence they would be transported to London and on to Dover. Miss Robson, carrying only a handbag and a large travelling case, would go to the station in a hansom cab.

She looked at Melissa and smiled helplessly. 'I don't think there's anything left to do,' she said, 'except to sit on the packing cases until the cab arrives.' She glanced at the cold hearth. 'We can't even have a cup of tea.'

'I'll come with you to the station. We'll have a cup of tea in the refreshment room.'

Miss Robson smiled. 'What a good idea. And we'll order buttered toast too.' Suddenly her smile vanished. 'I'm going to miss you, Melissa.'

'And I shall miss you.'

'I shan't ever come back, you know. There would be nowhere to come to. But perhaps one day you will come to Pau to visit me.'

'I would like that.' Melissa saw that Miss Robson was close to tears. 'Are you sure there's nothing else I can do?' she asked.

Miss Robson sat down on one of the packing cases. Her shoulders drooped wearily. 'No. Everything has gone. Mr Grainger came last night and took away the furniture and all the things I won't need any more. I believe he gave me a good price.'

'But where did you sleep?' Melissa sat facing her on another packing case.

'I haven't slept. Even if there had been a bed available I wouldn't have been able to settle. I have lived here so long . . . so many memories . . . and now I am leaving. But you know once Mother had died and I had retired schoolteaching there wasn't very much to keep me here, was there?'

'Especially when your girlhood friend had begged you to go and live with her in France,' Melissa said encouragingly. 'You told me how close you used to be.'

This brought a smile. 'Amelia . . . yes, we were close.

Neither of us had siblings so she and I were like sisters. When she married and went to live in South-West France I thought we might never see each other again. We've corresponded, of course.'

'And now you *are* going to see her again.' Melissa encouraged Miss Robson to talk. She sensed how emotional she was becoming.

'She's widowed. She is happy in her English-style villa overlooking the Pyrenees, the mild climate is conducive to good health and she could never contemplate returning to England. But she yearns for contact with the world and the people she used to know. She doesn't put it as strongly as to say she is homesick – after all, France has been Amelia's home for so many years now. And yet . . . and yet . . .'

'She thinks it would be wonderful if her old friend would come and live with her and gossip about old times,' Melissa finished the sentence for her.

'Yes, my dear. And I confess that when I think about it, it will be wonderful for me too. Just think – a new life at my age! Amelia wants me to talk to her small grandchildren in English – she says that she herself speaks French as a matter of course these days. I find that amusing – she was always bottom of the class at French in school, you know.'

Miss Robson's eyes were beginning to shine and her drooping shoulders had straightened. She sounded happy and enthusiastic. Suddenly she reached across the small space between them and took Melissa's hand. 'You are kind and clever. You saw that my spirits had plummeted and you made me talk to cheer me up.'

'I've enjoyed listening to you. And I hope you will write to me and tell me more.'

'I shall write constantly. And I hope you will answer my letters.'

'Of course.'

Miss Robson suddenly looked grave. 'But how selfish I've been. Worrying about my own future and not considering yours.'

'There's nothing to worry about.'

'Isn't there? What about your mother's hopes for you? She wanted you to have a dressmaking salon of your own one day. You are certainly talented enough.'

Melissa shook her head. In the years that she had been living with the Wintertons she had never quite forgotten her mother's dreams. But she did not know how to make them come true. She would need more money than she had saved from her modest allowance in order to start her own business and Mrs Winterton seemed to have forgotten that she had promised Emmeline Dornay that she would help and encourage her daughter to open her own salon.

'I have made you sad,' Miss Robson said. 'Forgive me.'

Before Melissa could answer the sound of the front doorbell echoed through the house. Miss Robson rose quickly. 'That will be the carrier,' she said.

It didn't take long to load Miss Robson's belongings and Melissa stood at the front door with her and they watched while the schoolteacher's worldly goods set out on the journey before her.

The cab arrived almost as soon as the carrier's wagon had turned the corner. Miss Robson and Melissa buttoned up their coats. Miss Robson locked the door behind them and slipped the keys through the letter box as the landlord had instructed. She closed her eyes for a moment and then opened them and smiled.

'Come along, Melissa,' she said. 'I'm so pleased you are coming to the station with me!'

They had tea and toast at the station as they had planned, but neither of them did more than nibble at the toast and sip the tea. Melissa saw her old teacher on to the London train and then stood on the platform and watched as it steamed its way out of the station on the curved track that led to the High Level Bridge, then on across the River Tyne. Melissa turned and walked away.

It was still very early but the streets were already busy. The tram Melissa caught was crowded with both men and women, going to work in the offices and shops. There were one or two girls not so smartly dressed as the others, and Melissa supposed them to be domestic servants on their way to work in one of the big houses such as the Wintertons'.

By the time they reached the stop nearest to the square where the Wintertons lived the tram was nearly empty, and when Melissa got off she was followed by one of the girls she had assumed was a domestic servant. She watched as the girl hurried away ahead of her. When she'd passed her, her expression had been anxious and Melissa guessed that she was late for work.

Well, at least there is no one to scold me, she thought as she descended the stone steps that led to the yard of the semi-basement and the servants' entrance. I may not be one of the family, but I can come and go as I please during respectable hours so long as I do all that is required of me.

It is not what my mother wanted for me. With a pang Melissa remembered how dismayed she had been when she discovered the old tea caddy had been emptied of the money her mother meant for her – and how her aunt had taken and sold everything her mother had left her.

But at least I love most of the work I do for Mrs Winterton and Gwendolyn. They trust me entirely to copy the latest fashions for them and they even allow me to draw up designs of my own. Melissa tried to convince herself that she had nothing to complain about. She was even looking forward to her day's work.

Mrs Winterton had ordered some of the latest fabrics

from Wilkinson's Drapery Store and they were to be delivered today. Melissa had been trusted to go and choose the fabrics herself and to put them on Mrs Winterton's account.

'I don't trust myself, my dear,' Mrs Winterton had said. 'If I get anywhere near those gorgeous silks and satins I know I shall be foolishly extravagant, whereas you have an eye for a bargain without ending up with something cheap-looking.'

Melissa had thoroughly enjoyed herself looking at and handling the satins, the silk crepes and the voiles, as well as the lace trimmings and the various velvet ribbons, silk cords, beads and tiny satin flowers that she would use in the passementerie.

Soon she must be looking ahead to designing and making mother and daughter clothes for autumn and winter, but Mrs Winterton had suddenly decided that she and Gwendolyn must have some fancy gowns to take with them when they decamped to the house in the country for the whole of August.

She was cross that her husband had decreed they were not going to London for 'the Season'. They had a house in the capital, but they hardly ever inhabited it unless Austin Winterton had some business matter to attend to and could be persuaded to take his wife and daughter with him.

The London Summer Season lasted three months and there were fashionable places to visit and a round of parties and balls. Lilian Winterton would dearly have loved to go to London for the entire Season but usually her husband told her that a month was more than enough and that he was not prepared to spend any more time away from his business concerns in the North.

But this year they were not going at all. Her husband had just had a large extension built on to their country house and he told his wife he wanted to enjoy it. Lilian Winterton had sulked for a while so, in a spirit of compromise, her husband had told her that, once there, she could arrange as many dinner parties and balls as she wanted. Hence the sudden need for new gowns.

'White, silver, gold,' she had told Melissa. 'And some of those delicious sugar almond tints. And perhaps something transparent for the sleeves of the evening gowns. Melissa, dear, I trust your taste entirely. I want to give those worthy countrywomen a vision of high fashion. Just because we live in the North doesn't mean that we have to dress like provincials, does it?'

The staff's breakfast had been over for some time. The housemaids had already set about their daily duties and Melissa could hear the clash of pots and pans coming from the scullery where, no doubt, the new little skivvy had started to wash them. Melissa hurried along the stone-flagged passage towards the door that opened on to the staircase to the upper floors. But before she reached it an imposing figure came out of the large kitchen where the staff took their meals. Mrs Barton.

'So there you are,' she said. Her voice dripped displeasure. 'It's too late for breakfast.'

'I know.'

'I suppose I could get the girl to make you a slice or two of toast.' By the girl she meant Reenie. 'She can make you a pot of tea as well, but you'll be eating alone.'

'That's kind of you.' Melissa didn't really want any toast but it would be a chance to talk to her friend.

'Have you been out?'

As Melissa was wearing her coat and had come from the direction of the door the question was hardly necessary but she could see that Mrs Barton had been struggling with her curiosity.

'Yes, I saw a friend off at the station,' Melissa said.

The cook-housekeeper's raised eyebrows formed the question.

Melissa answered it. 'My old schoolteacher – she's going to France.'

She didn't know why she felt obliged to divulge this information. Perhaps it was Mrs Barton's air of authority.

'I would be obliged if you would let me know when you do not require breakfast. Now, as I said, Reenie will make you tea and toast. Tell her that I said she should. And now forgive me, Miss Dornay, but I have my accounts to do.' Mrs Barton, the keys at her waist jangling, swept along the passage to her own little sitting room.

Melissa was left feeling awkward and disorientated. No matter that she had been addressed as 'Miss Dornay', there was no doubt that Mrs Barton had just reprimanded her. She was relieved that the large kitchen was, for the moment, empty. Polly, the skivvy, had gone to fill the coal scuttles and the rest of the staff would be about their duties. Melissa crossed to the door that led to the scullery and stood there for a moment, watching Reenie working.

Her friend had not grown much since Melissa had first come to live at this house and now the little maid stood on a slatted wooden platform in order to be able to bend over the large sink. She had started peeling the huge mound of potatoes that would be needed for the day's meals.

Reenie's hair was escaping from her cap as usual. No matter how many times I slot new ribbons through for her, Melissa thought, in no time at all they have worked loose and the cap begins its journey down to her nose.

Almost as if Reenie could hear Melissa's thoughts, she raised one reddened hand and used the back of it to push the frill of her mobcap up her forehead. Melissa laughed softly and Reenie jumped in alarm. The potato she had been peeling fell into the dirty water with a splosh. She turned indignantly to face Melissa.

'You!' she said. 'You fair frightened the life out of me!'

'I'm sorry,' Melissa said.

'So you should be.' Reenie's expression softened when she saw Melissa's contrite expression. 'But what are you doing here?'

'Mrs Barton says you are to make me some tea and toast. But it doesn't matter. I can see how busy you are and, in any case, I'm not hungry.'

'Well, mebbes you're not hungry, but I am! Look, I'm nearly finished here. I'll just tip this lot into some pans of cold water and get Polly to do the rest. Take your coat off and gan and sit down and I'll get the kettle on. Then I propose to sit at the table with you and take the weight off me feet for a while.'

'Can I help you?'

'Aye, you can.' Reenie hurried through to the kitchen and crossed to the pantry where she took the remains of a loaf from the stone crock. She began to slice it at the table. 'I divven't want to light that gas oven. It scares me silly, so I'll stick the kettle on the range and give you the toasting fork. You can begin to toast this lot the proper old-fashioned way – over the fire. Now divven't sit too close or the heat will mottle that bonny face of yours.'

As Melissa sat toasting the slices of bread one by one, she remembered all the times she and her mother had sat gazing into the fire, looking for pictures formed by the burning coals. She didn't look for fire pictures today because her eyes had filled with tears.

'Now, then,' Reenie's voice rang out cheerfully behind her. 'We've got butter and marmalade. Bring that plate of toast over to the table and I'll pour the tea.'

Sitting with Reenie and watching her eat with such enjoyment, Melissa found that she was hungry after all and she began to enjoy the slices of toast that Reenie had cut like doorsteps.

'Where have you been?' Reenie asked her. 'When you didn't come down for breakfast Mrs Barton sent me up to your room to find out why. She thought you might be poorly and might welcome a cup of tea.'

'Did she?'

'Aye, divven't look so surprised. She might be a tyrant but she does hev a heart in there somewhere. And besides, I think she quite likes you.'

'Well, she certainly doesn't show it.'

'No, she wouldn't. The only person here that gets a smile from her is that stuck-up so-and-so Douglas. Which just goes to show that no matter how old a woman is, she can hev a soft spot for a good-looking nowt. But where were you, anyway?'

'I went to help Miss Robson pack her things up – although she'd already done most of it. Then I went with her to the station.'

'Oh, aye, she's off to France, isn't she?'

Melissa nodded.

'You'll miss her.'

'Yes.'

'So what will you do for your French lessons now? I mean, you've been going all these years for – what do you call it? Conversation?'

'That's right. But these last few years I have been going out of friendship more than as a pupil.'

'Well, you still need your French so's you can read all those fancy fashion magazines you buy.'

Melissa smiled. 'I think I'll be able to manage. I was brought up speaking French, you know.'

'Oh, aye, your da was French, wasn't he?' Reenie paused and said, 'That's one of the reasons the others resent you, you know.'

Melissa was startled. 'Because my father was French?'

'No, don't be daft. I mean because you can go out if you want to. Nobody else here can do that.'

'I know, but there's nothing I can do about that, is there?'

'No, I suppose not.'

As soon as they had finished their tea and toast Reenie sprang to her feet and carried the dishes through to the scullery. 'Now, off you go,' she said, 'afore anyone catches us gossiping.'

Reenie vanished into the scullery but as Melissa picked up her coat from the chair where she'd left it, her friend appeared again in the doorway. 'And don't forget it's my day off tomorrow and I've decided you and me's going to the park.'

'I won't forget.'

Melissa climbed the stairs to the fourth floor, put her coat away in her room and went to the sewing room. Reenie's enthusiasm had lightened her mood and she smiled as she remembered the happy times they'd had on Reenie's days off.

Sometimes they simply strolled about the city, looking in the shop windows, and then Melissa would treat Reenie to a cream tea in Tilley's. Sometimes they ventured as far as the river and would watch as passengers embarked for places such as Hamburg and Rotterdam, or Antwerp and Malmo.

Some paid for berths on the colliers taking coal to London. Others were going much further afield; they were off to start new lives in the 'Land of Promise': America. Reenie would look yearningly at these families and she often asked Melissa what she thought it would be like to live in such a wonderful place.

Sometimes Reenie's questions sparked a game of make-believe as the two friends imagined they were about to set sail themselves. Once in America Melissa would open a fashionable dressmaking salon in New York and Reenie would keep house for her.

On their days by the river Melissa and Reenie would have

coffee and pastries in Olsen's, the Norwegian café on the quayside. They would order cardamom coffee cakes or their favourite, *lefse,* a sort of scone made from potatoes, flour, butter and cream. The only trouble with the latter was that they found them addictive! Occasionally Melissa would persuade Reenie to come with her to an art gallery or a museum. It was some months since they had been to Leazes Park, but Reenie said it was time they went back there. She thought there might be a band concert tomorrow.

Melissa walked to the window and stood looking down at the trees in the square. The leaves were trembling in a light breeze just as the leaves in the park had trembled on the last day she had seen James Pennington. He had kissed her hand and smiled and promised he would be there to hear her answer the very next week. But after the note she had left him she had never seen him again.

She wondered what would have happened if she had never written that letter; never slipped it in his satchel for him to find. They might have had more golden summer days together just walking and talking in the park. For a moment she allowed herself to dream about what might have been, but all too soon the dreams slipped away. James had wanted to see her parents. Sooner or later she would have had to tell him the truth about herself, and the hurt caused by him spurning her would have been even greater if she had allowed her hopes to grow.

Melissa was roused from her reverie by a loud knock on the door. She hurried across to open it. Douglas stood there.

'Delivery for Miss Dornay!' He gave a mock bow and then with one long arm he indicated several bolts of cloth, each covered in fine sacking, that he had propped up against the wall. The fabrics from Wilkinson's.

'Thank you,' Melissa said. 'Could you bring them in?'

'Thing is,' the footman said, 'there's more and there's only me to carry everything upstairs. It'll take two, maybe, three trips. So let's get this lot inside and then I'll go down for the rest.'

Melissa held the door open while Douglas brought everything in. 'Where do you want them?' he asked.

'Over there.' Melissa pointed to the shelves on the wall facing the door.

When he'd stacked everything he said, 'Prop the door open with a book or something, would you, and then I won't have to knock each time.'

In fact it took only two more trips, and on the last one Douglas brought the boxes containing the buttons, hooks and eyes, ribbons, gold and silver bugle beads and threads.

'Phew!' he said, mopping his brow with a clean white handkerchief and pretending to be exhausted. 'Do you mind if I sit down for a moment?'

'Well . . .' Melissa began, but he had already crossed the room and flopped down on a chair near the window. Dust motes danced in the sun streaming through the windows and he squinted as he turned sideways and gazed out on to the square.

'Nice view you've got here,' he said. Then he turned to face her and grinned. 'Why don't you put the kettle on,' he said, 'and give a poor chap a cup of tea?'

'Well, I don't think . . .'

'. . . you ought to?' Douglas finished the sentence for her. 'I don't see why you shouldn't. There's no harm in it, surely, allowing a fellow to take his ease for a minute or two and look out at the trees and the flowers.'

Melissa was used to Douglas's flirtatious ways. It seemed he couldn't help himself from trying to charm every female in the house. He even had a smile and a wink for Reenie now and then. But Melissa had realised long ago that he was harmless. And now, rather than seeking her company, he was hoping to escape his duties for a while just as Reenie did.

But much as she sympathised with him she did not want to offer him refuge in the sewing room. This was her province and the only other person she welcomed here was Reenie. She would have to be firm. But before she could say anything a figure appeared in the open doorway.

'Douglas! What are you doing here?' Gwendolyn Winterton's pretty but vapid face was marred by a scowl. She was wearing a mauve day dress with a deep lace collar. Melissa had tried to dissuade her from that colour, because in her opinion it emphasised the pallor of her skin, but Gwendolyn had insisted. Gwendolyn had the blue georgette evening gown she had worn to the theatre draped across one arm. 'Well?' she said. 'I'm waiting for an explanation.'

Douglas leaped to his feet. It was the first time Melissa had seen him lose his composure.

'Miss Gwendolyn . . .' He looked at Melissa as if hoping she could help him but when she remained silent he went on, 'I've just carried all those things up – the delivery from Wilkinson's.' He gestured towards the bales of cloth and the boxes on the shelves. 'Everything needed to make your bonny frocks.' He ventured a smile.

Melissa knew that he shouldn't be talking in such a familiar fashion to the daughter of the house and, when Gwendolyn didn't reprimand him, she began to think that what Reenie had hinted at was true.

Gwendolyn looked at the shelves and she seemed to relax a little. But she still seemed ill pleased when she asked, 'So why were you sitting down?'

By now Douglas seemed to have recovered from his initial discomfort. 'Well, I was a bit hot and bothered – you know – heaving all that upstairs – several trips – and Miss Dornay was kind enough to offer me a cup of tea. In all politeness, I couldn't refuse, now could I?'

Melissa was furious. How could he? And the lie had tripped off his tongue so easily. 'I didn't—'

She was about to deny that she had said any such thing but she heard Douglas's intake of breath and saw the way he was looking at her. There was anguish in his eyes but there was also a slight smile on his lips. It was as if he were both pleading with her not to give him away but at the same time acknowledging his perfidy and drawing her into the conspiracy.

'Yes?' Gwendolyn said. 'What were you about to say?'

'I was going to say that I didn't see any harm in it,' Melissa said, keeping her fingers crossed behind her back.

'Didn't you indeed? To ask Douglas to take tea with you is quite improper. Douglas is a servant and you are . . . you are . . .' She foundered.

'And I am?' Melissa asked quietly. 'What exactly is it that I am? I'd really like to know.' Try as she might she could not hide the frustration she felt every time she thought about her position in the Wintertons' home.

Gwendolyn's pale face flushed an angry mottled red. 'Don't be impertinent,' she said. 'Taking that tone of voice with me! We took you in and have clothed and fed you ever since your mother died. My mother even passes on some of her clothes to you, which should by rights go to Ena, who is her personal maid. Are you not at all grateful for all we've done for you?'

Melissa hid her clenched fists in the folds of her skirt. She didn't know how to answer Gwendolyn. Was she grateful? She supposed so. The Wintertons had given her a home, and a very comfortable one, but they had made her feel like something in between a poor relation and a servant.

She had worked hard ever since she had first come here. And, as she had progressed very quickly from simple mending and alterations to designing and making most of the garments worn by Mrs Winterton and her daughter, she must have saved them much more money than they had spent on her keep.

While she stood there, seething with mixed emotions, Douglas stepped forward. He coughed gently.

'Ahem,' he said. 'I feel this is my fault. I was wrong to accept Miss Dornay's invitation.' Melissa shot him a look of fury and he continued hastily, 'I'm sure she only meant to be kind. After all, she has you and her mother to set an example to her. Two of the kindest ladies I've ever come across.'

Melissa raised her eyes heavenwards and wondered how on earth Douglas expected Gwendolyn to accept this claptrap. But, incredibly, she did. She looked at the footman fondly.

'And *you* are very kind to try and take the blame,' she said.

Douglas nodded and smiled a trifle graciously as if acknowledging his own noble nature. Then, thank goodness, he remained silent, otherwise Melissa thought she would have exploded.

'I'm going to the library to – er – read a book,' Gwendolyn said. 'Perhaps you would bring me a tray of tea and biscuits?'

'Of course,' Douglas said. 'I'll go and see to that at once.'

Gwendolyn moved further into the room and Douglas made to exit hastily. But when he reached the doorway he turned and, seeing that Gwendolyn had her back to him, he grinned and winked at Melissa. Angry though she was she could not but admire his audacity.

'Now then,' Gwendolyn said. 'The reason for my visit here. I thought I told you to repair the little holes on the hem of this dress.'

Melissa knew that the older girl would never admit to them being cigarette burns. 'I did mend them,' she said.

'Well, you missed a few. Here,' she thrust the dress towards Melissa, 'do a proper job this time.'

Gwendolyn turned and flounced out of the room. That was the only way to describe the way she tossed her head and stuck her chin up. Melissa couldn't help smiling even though she knew that the older girl, who had never liked her, now seemed to be her enemy.

She supposed she had better mend the new burn marks, for that was what they were; she had definitely repaired all the previous ones. If she refused, Gwendolyn would surely find some way to cause trouble for her. She pulled the gown on to the body form, secured it by doing up all the fastenings at the back and then kneeled to examine the hem.

She sighed. It wouldn't be too difficult but it would be tedious. The sooner she started the sooner she would be able to get on with the more exciting projects: the gowns that mother and daughter would be taking to the country house.

Her concentration was such that she did not hear Reenie knock softly and enter the room.

'What are you doing down there?' Reenie said, and Melissa was so startled that she pricked her finger with the needle.

'Ah!' she gasped and she put her finger in her mouth and sucked it. It would not do to get blood on Gwendolyn's gown.

'Eeh, I'm sorry. But you looked so strange crouching down like that. And now I've made you hurt yourself.'

'Don't worry. It's my own fault. I should have been wearing a thimble.'

'Is that the same dress you mended before?'

'Yes.'

'Humph,' was Reenie's only comment, but she shook her head in disapproval. 'Well, don't mind me. I told Polly I'd see to your fire. I feel sorry for the little lass and, besides, it gives me the chance to get out of the kitchen for a minute or two.'

Fires were kept burning all year round in this large house;

even at the height of summer the rooms never got too warm. Reenie kneeled to rake the grate a little, place some fresh coals on top and then sweep up the ashes, which she tipped into the bucket she'd brought with her.

Then she stood up and, with the bucket over her arm, she went to the door. 'I'll see you at dinner time,' she said.

To Reenie the midday meal was dinner although the family called it luncheon. Often none of the Wintertons was at home for this meal but Mrs Barton saw to it that the servants were fed. And very well fed at that.

Melissa smiled and nodded and, when she judged that her finger had stopped bleeding, she put her thimble on and went back to work. And as she worked she thought of Reenie and how hard her life was. And yet the other girl told her she was grateful to have a job in a house where there was plenty of food on the table and a bed of her own up in the attics, rather than a truckle under the kitchen table, which was where the lower servants in some other houses had to sleep.

Her only complaints were that there was no gas lighting on the attic floor and no fireplaces in the small bedrooms either. So candles it was to light your way to bed and to dress by and, in the cold weather, it was better to sleep with most of your clothes on.

As well as being hungry all the time Reenie suffered dreadfully when it was cold. Melissa remembered the first time she had met her. Reenie had been sent to her bedroom to help her unpack her belongings and she had looked around in wonder, taking special delight in the fire.

The altercation with Gwendolyn had been unsettling and that night Melissa lay awake for some hours. It was probably after midnight that she fell into a restless sleep where memories became confused with dreams.

She was her young self again, wandering round the house on a snowy day in January. Then, suddenly the weather changed, as it can in dreams. She and someone – she couldn't quite see who – were walking in bright sunshine. They didn't say anything but they were happy. So happy that Melissa could not understand why, when she woke, her pillow was damp with tears.

Reenie slept uneasily too. She hoped she was doing the right thing in persuading Melissa to go back to the park but, really, she couldn't go on moping like this. Not that Melissa made a fuss like some girls did. She simply locked disappointment away and refused to talk about it.

Reenie had been convinced that telling James Pennington the truth wouldn't make the slightest difference. She had not foreseen that he would treat Melissa so callously; that in the end he would be so ungentlemanly and not even bother to come and explain things. Melissa had tried to pretend it didn't matter but Reenie knew she had been hurt.

In the morning Reenie got up before anyone else was stirring as usual. When her work was done, she went to the kitchen and filled a jug with hot water. She would take it up and have a wash in Melissa's room as she always did when they were going out. Then they would get ready together and set off for the park. It was a lovely day and a few hours away from this house would do them both the world of good.

Chapter Eleven

Summer

Melissa hardly noticed when the sunshine and showers of spring began to give way to the warmth of early summer. The days lengthened and she took advantage of the extra hours of daylight to work both early and late. Once the fabrics had been delivered from Wilkinson's she had started making the new day dresses and evening gowns that Mrs Winterton and Gwendolyn wanted to take with them to the country house.

Mrs Winterton ordered that the usual day-to-day mending should be done by Ena, her personal maid, who was experienced enough, having done this kind of thing before Melissa came to the Wintertons' house. Ena resented what she thought of as an inferior position and she sat at the table in the sewing room, a disgruntled and discontented presence, until her work was done.

At least she didn't seek conversation, and Melissa soon learned to ignore her sulky face and get on with her work. At tea time Melissa would go down to have tea with the others and then she would go for a walk, just to get some fresh air before starting work again. However, she found the city streets dry and dusty, and she would slip into the cool freshness of the garden in the square if the gates were open.

One evening when she had almost finished work on the new gowns, she went out a little later than usual and the garden was empty, the gates padlocked. It was too late for the children and their nursemaids and too early for the gentlemen who strolled there with their cigars in the late evening.

Melissa stood still for a moment and breathed in the fragrance of the flowering shrubs. She looked longingly through the bars at the cool shadows gathering beneath the trees when she was startled by the sound of footsteps behind her. She spun round to find Douglas standing there.

'What a shock you gave me,' she said.

'I'm sorry, I didn't mean to. Do you want to go into the garden? I can let you in. It's my job to keep the keys.'

'And when I leave the garden how would I lock up again?'

'Ah, well, you couldn't. I would have to stay with you. We could take a stroll together or sit and talk for a while. I'm free until it's time for the family to have their evening meal.'

Melissa looked up at him. He was smiling in what he probably imagined was a winsome manner. He just can't help himself, she thought. He likes to think he's utterly charming and that women will be impressed by his looks and his manner.

She didn't want to go back in the house yet and she was tempted to accept his offer, although she would rather have walked in the garden by herself for a while. But then, looking up at him, she caught a movement on the balcony of the library window. Gwendolyn stood there. She was gripping the iron balustrade and staring down at them.

'Well?' Douglas asked. Then, alerted by her stillness he said, 'What are you looking at?'

Melissa didn't answer and the footman looked up and followed her gaze. He and Gwendolyn stared at each other for a moment and then Gwendolyn backed into the shadows of the unlit library behind her. Douglas's smile drained away.

He tried to sound casual when he said, 'Come to think of it, I'd better go in now. Better see if Joan has set the table properly. Can't trust these girls, you know.' He was unnerved but he didn't forget his studied charm. 'Do you mind if I leave you?' he asked. 'Perhaps we'll have our little stroll another time?'

He barely gave her time to respond before he turned and walked back to the house.

Melissa felt uneasy. She realised what it must have looked like to Gwendolyn. The two of them chatting so informally in the mellow light of early evening. She wondered about Douglas. Was he in love with Gwendolyn and she with him? If so, she did not see how there could be a happy ending. Gwendolyn must know that her parents would never countenance her marrying a servant and Douglas risked dismissal without references if their flirtation was ever discovered.

After a moment or two she looked up at the house and thought she saw two figures standing just a little way from the open window of the library. Suddenly one of them moved forward on to the balcony; it was Gwendolyn. The other figure, surely Douglas, stepped up behind her. Melissa thought she saw him place a hand on Gwendolyn's shoulder. Gwendolyn shook him off and made an angry gesture with one arm, pointing towards Melissa. Then she moved out of view suddenly, as though she had been pulled backwards.

She's suspicious of me, Melissa thought, although she has no reason to be. But how difficult it must be for them to have to keep their love for one another secret. And no wonder Gwendolyn suffers pangs of jealousy when she sees the way Douglas behaves, for she cannot legitimately bring him to heel.

As she could not enter the garden Melissa decided to

walk instead around the square. A bluey-grey dusk was seeping down over the chimneypots and, as she walked, Melissa saw the lamplighter approach with his pole balanced over his shoulder. One by one he stopped at the ornate streetlamps and manipulated his pole to turn the gas taps on before inserting the flame of his torch into the light.

Other men such as he would be performing the same task throughout the city and, with a pang, Melissa remembered how, as a small girl, she used to watch from the window of her childhood home as the lamps were lit, knowing that any moment her mother would say that it was time for bed.

The memory was poignant, and it was in a subdued mood that she continued to walk around the square a little ahead of the lamplighter. And then, in the lavender dusk ahead of her, she thought she saw the shadows move. She stopped and caught her breath. She didn't believe in ghosts but was as cautious as most would be when they came across something unexplained.

She stood perfectly still. She heard voices – children's voices – and she began to walk forward again. Had some children sneaked out from one of these grand houses? Escaped from their nursemaid, intent on adventure?

But just as she was about to walk on and greet them with a smile and urge them to go back to the safety of their home, a tall burly figure came up the steps from the semi-basement of the house nearest to them. He crossed the road and grabbed two of the little shadows by the scruff of the neck.

'Hop it!' he told them. 'This is no place for you. If I see you here again I'll call the constable.'

He released them and they darted away, followed by a slightly larger shadow who had been cowering by the railings. The man stood with his arms akimbo and watched them go. He must have heard Melissa's intake of breath because he turned, frowning, and then, seeing her more clearly, smiled.

'Good evening, miss. You're from the Winterton house, aren't you?'

'Yes, I am.' Now that she was close she could see that he was wearing the uniform of a footman. 'But who were they?'

'Street urchins,' he replied. 'Looking for somewhere to sleep, I'll be bound.'

'Somewhere to sleep? I don't understand.'

'They climb over the railings and make beds for themselves amongst the shrubs.' As he spoke Melissa heard a rustling sound. She stopped herself from glancing round but backed up to the railings making it difficult for the footman to see immediately behind her.

'Poor things,' she said.

'Aye, I feel sorry for the little beggars, but they know how to fend for themselves and I'd rather chase them away than hand them over to the workhouse or an orphanage.'

'But why chase them at all?'

'Well, apart from the fact that this is a private garden, they make a right mess of the place. Trampling on the flowers and relieving themselves behind the bushes. Sorry to speak so plain, miss, but you did ask.'

Melissa was dumbfounded. 'I've never seen them before,' she said.

'No, you wouldn't. Crafty little varmints, they are. You have to be sharp to catch them.'

As they talked the lamplighter passed them and began to light the way ahead.

'Well, miss, it's been a pleasure to talk to a bonny lass like you,' the footman said, 'but I have to get back to my duties.'

Melissa watched as he returned to the house where he worked. She remained quite still until the lamplighter finished lighting the lamps and left the square.

She was not surprised by the voice that whispered from behind her, 'Thank you, lady.'

She turned at last to face the railings, but at first she couldn't see anyone. Then the leaves of a bush parted and she found herself staring down into the grubby face of a small boy.

'Why do you thank me?'

'Whisht! Not so loud!'

'Sorry.' She found herself whispering.

'Thank you for not letting on. You knew I was here.'

'Yes. Are you going to stay here?'

'No.'

'I . . . I wouldn't say anything.'

'It's not that. I'll hev to catch up with me brothers and me little sister. Me big brother's a bit slow in the head and he can't look after them properly. I would hev climbed out when that feller catched them but I didn't want to be hauled over the spikes again.'

'Again?'

'Aye. The last time he caught us he pulled me out so rough that the spikes tore me coat and cut right into me skin. I'd be little use to them if I was hurt bad.'

'Do you really have nowhere to sleep?'

'We usually find somewhere warm and dry, but the streets are not safe at the minute. There's people – grown men – who would harm us. Especially me little sister. So we get into one of the gardens if we can. I hop over first and then me big brother lifts the little 'uns over to me. Tonight he was just too slow.'

'You must let me help you!'

'And how could you do that? Could you take us into your house?'

'No, I couldn't. I only work there.'

'Well, could you find someone with their own home who would take us in? There's four of us and we won't be parted.'

'No . . . I couldn't.' Melissa stared at him helplessly and was overwhelmed when he grinned.

'Divven't fret,' he said. 'It's not your problem.'

'Would the workhouse or an orphanage be so terrible?' she asked.

'Oh, they'd feed us and clothe us and learn us to read and write but they'd separate us. The boys from the girls and the big 'uns from the little 'uns. I might never see me little sister or me brothers again and I promised me mam I'd look after them. Well, I've got to go. You can help us over, if you like.'

Melissa watched as a small, ragged child, who couldn't have been much more than ten years old, emerged from the bushes and climbed to the top of the railings. The light from the nearest gas lamp shone on an untidy thatch of red hair.

'Catch us!' he whispered, and he launched himself towards her.

She caught him easily and was shocked by how light he was. It felt as though she was holding a small bag of bones. She set him down.

'Ta,' he said. 'I'll be off.'

She caught at his sleeve. 'But how do you know where your sisters and brothers will be?'

'They won't hev gone far. They know I'd come after them as soon as I could.'

'Wait – what's your name?' Melissa asked.

He grinned. 'They call me Ginger.'

Melissa smiled. 'Of course. Well, Ginger, take this.' She took a handful of coins from her pocket. 'I'm afraid that's all I have with me. But I can give you more if I see you again.'

'You won't see me again. Not for a while, at least.'

He took the coins and dropped them in his pocket, then turned and fled. Melissa was subdued as she walked back to the Wintertons' house. The Winterton House – that's how she thought of it. 'House'. It had never been her home.

Often when she worked late into the night Reenie would edge into the sewing room in her usual diffident fashion; for even though she and Melissa had been friends for more than four years she was still hesitant about putting herself forward.

Reenie was happy to sit without talking, just watching Melissa at work. But this evening Melissa wanted to talk. She told Reenie what had just happened, about the children being chased away from the square.

Her friend shrugged. 'I can understand why the lad doesn't want them to gan to the workhouse,' she said. 'But they'd be more likely to be taken to an orphanage and that would be just as bad.'

'Why?'

'Because he's right. They'd be parted. The girls from the boys, and the big ones from the little ones, just like he said.'

'But that's dreadful.'

'Most of them are not cruel places, you know. At least they don't intend to be cruel. It's just that even some charitable folk seem to think it's your own fault that you're poor. They train little bairns, right from the start, how to work for a living and they find you places when you're old enough.' Reenie suddenly grinned. 'Look what they did for me!'

'I wish there was some way I could help.'

'If you mean that, there is,' Reenie said surprisingly.

'Tell me how.'

'There's a woman who gives the bairns warm food and clothes – most of them cast-offs from decent families.'

'Clothes!'

'Aye.'

'But I could make clothes for her. Look at all the remnants of material I have left. I can't always use them up for you and me.'

'Aye,' Reenie said again.

'How do I find this woman?'

'There's an old almshouse down by the Central Station. They use it for a soup kitchen now. Good folk gan there and cook hot meals for the folk that hev no home to go to. The wife who gives the clothes away helps there. I've heard you can find her there most nights.'

'Then I shall go there. But first you must help me.'

'Me? Help you? How?'

'If I teach you to pin and tack we'll get some clothes made in half the time. Would you like that?'

'Aye, I would.'

'Good. But first I must finish the gowns Mrs Winterton and Gwendolyn are taking to the country.'

'I'll make us a cup of tea,' Reenie said. 'And then can I look at your drawings again? I've washed me hands.'

Some time before, Reenie had discovered the sketches Melissa made before she started work on a new gown.

'Eeh, Melissa,' she'd said, 'what bonny fine drawings these are. You're a proper artist!'

Melissa had smiled. 'Thank you. But I'm not a real artist. I do them to show Mrs Winterton and get her approval.'

'Well, no matter what you say they are, I think they're good enough to be hung up in the art gallery – or put in a magazine!'

Ever since she'd first found the costume sketches Reenie had loved looking at them, but now Melissa told her, 'No, not tonight.'

'Why ever not?' Reenie was both surprised and hurt.

'Because I'm going to give you a piece of cloth, a needle and thread and a box full of pins. You can have your first sewing lesson straight away.'

From then on Melissa worked harder than ever. One night, when everyone was sleeping, she put the finishing touches to a particularly elegant gown. She stood back from the body form on which the evening dress of creamy *mousseline de soie* was displayed and studied it. She'd had to use all her powers of persuasion to get Mrs Winterton to agree to the straight, clean lines and now, looking at it, she knew she'd been right.

Instinctively she knew that as Mrs Winterton grew older, even though she was more slender than her daughter, she should be discouraged from wearing dresses with the frills and fussy details that she so adored. The only decoration on this gown was some passementerie, a delicate pattern of beadwork that covered the bodice from the low-cut neckline to the tiny waist.

As she gazed at the shining fabric glowing in the light of the small fire, she was reminded of another moment: a cold winter's night when her mother had been sleeping and she had secretly finished the decoration on a dress for Gwendolyn. A soft sigh behind her made her catch her breath. Slowly she turned to face the fireplace and she saw, not her mother – how could it have been? – but Reenie, who had fallen asleep in the armchair.

Reenie must have sensed that she was being watched, for she opened her eyes. She gave Melissa a sleepy smile and then she looked up at the clock on the mantel. 'Eeh, Melissa,' she said, 'it's nearly midnight. Are you still working?'

'I've just finished the last gown. What do you think?'

Reenie got up and walked over to have a better look. 'It's beautiful,' she said. 'Every gown you make seems to get better and better. But how I wish that you could be wearing it instead of the mistress.'

'It wouldn't fit. I'm taller than Mrs Winterton.'

'But seriously, do you never wish you were making all them bonny frocks for yourself ?'

'I do make clothes for myself.'

'You know what I mean! I mean dresses like this one – ball gowns and the like.'

'But I don't go to any parties or balls, do I? And, besides, I'm allowed to order the fabric I need and make my own everyday clothes whenever I need to.'

'Aye, and a good job you make of them too. You look more like a lady than Miss Gwendolyn does, any day.'

'Yes . . . well . . . shouldn't you go to bed now? You have to be up so early in the morning.'

'I know, but can't we sit here by the fire and talk just a bit longer? Look – I brought a jug of milk up. I'll heat it in this little pan and we'll hev some cocoa.'

Reenie made the cocoa and then she insisted that Melissa have the chair while she sat on the hearthrug. They were both tired but Reenie wanted to talk. Everyone in the house was excited about going to the country. Mrs Barton felt important because she had been asked to instruct the cook the Wintertons had taken on for the country house.

The new cook was a plain country woman, Mrs Winterton had told her, and although she had come with the highest recommendation from another large establishment, Mrs Winterton wasn't sure if she would be able to provide the sort of sophisticated food that the Wintertons served their dinner guests in the town house. Likewise the maid-servants were to train the girls who would stay permanently in the country.

'Just think what an easy time they'll hev of it when the family aren't there,' Reenie said wistfully. 'Clothed and fed better than they've been used to, no doubt, and very little to do!'

Ena would still carry out the duties of lady's maid. No one would replace her, wherever Mrs Winterton was residing.

'She's really excited,' Reenie said. 'She's the only one of the servants who's been there before and she keeps going on about what a grand place it is. And she puts on such airs – I think the others are quite sick of her.' Reenie sipped her cocoa and gazed into the fire for a moment.

Melissa said, 'And they've never taken you there before, have they?'

'No, and I didn't expect them to. After all, there must be plenty of village lasses fit to peel the tatties. But this time they're shutting this house up and we're all going!' Her eyes were shining. 'I don't mind admitting that I'm excited too. I've never been to the country, you know. Hev you?'

Melissa shook her head. 'I don't think so.' She frowned, then she said, 'I may have been.'

'Surely you'd remember if you had?'

'No. You see it was a long time ago. When my father came home from the sea he would take my mother and me for trips. I remember a day at the seaside. He built sandcastles for me. And there was another day we went for a trip up the river.' Melissa frowned as she tried to retrieve the memory. 'My father held me on his lap. The sun was sparkling on the water like little bits of gold floating there. The air was fresh, not like the smoky air in town. I think the rocking of the boat must have sent me to sleep. The next thing I remember is sitting between my parents on a blanket on the grass. My mother made me a daisy chain . . . that's all . . . but, yes, it must have been a trip to the country.'

Reenie gave a muffled sob.

'What is it?' Melissa asked. 'Are you crying?'

'I suppose I am.'

'But why?'

'Because you painted such a lovely picture there. I could almost see it. Your da and your ma and you sitting amongst the flowers. You're lucky to hev memories like that.'

'I know I am. But if you really insist on staying here a while longer you can help me with the woollen smocks I've started on.'

Reenie tried to stifle a yawn. 'Right oh,' she said, and the two of them worked on until Melissa saw that her friend could barely keep her eyes open.

'Go to bed,' she said as she took the skirt Reenie had been tacking from her hands. She helped Reenie to her feet and walked with her to the door.

They whispered good night and then Reenie suddenly turned and hugged her. 'I thank the Lord every day that you came here,' she said. 'I don't think I was ever truly happy until I met you.'

The smell of good food cooking seemed to draw the silent crowd of shabby people across the well-trodden stones of the courtyard of the old Keelmen's Almshouse. The keelmen were the skilled boatmen who worked with the boatloads of coal on the river; and more than a hundred years ago they had built this almshouse for themselves on the site of a much older building. Now it was used as a soup kitchen for the city's poor and homeless who came every evening for at least one good meal before the end of another wretched day.

Melissa had no wish to push past the orderly queue so she took her place at the back and advanced silently towards the open door. She noticed that most of the people in front of her were either very young or very old. All were dressed in worn, shabby clothing and some did not have shoes. But although they seemed subdued they were reasonably cheerful, no doubt at the thought of the warming meal that awaited them.

The tantalising odour of nourishing broth grew stronger as Melissa approached the doorway. A neatly dressed elderly gentleman stood there smiling greetings and ushering the ragged crowd to the tables as if they were honoured guests. At first he was surprised at Melissa's appearance but then he saw the large brown paper parcel she carried and he beamed in approval.

'You've come to help,' he said.

Melissa nodded.

'If that parcel contains what I think it does then you must see my wife, Mrs Simmons – look, she's over there in the far corner with some of the children.'

Mrs Simmons was in the act of directing the small group of children to the end of one of the long trestle tables. She looked up distractedly as Melissa approached and then, her small charges settled with bowls of soup and chunks of fresh-baked bread, she turned and smiled.

'You've come to help,' she said, repeating her husband's words. 'Would you like to make sure the little ones drink up their milk?'

'Well, I'd like to but I can't stay long. I'm not supposed to be out too late.'

'Ah, I see. You're in service?'

'Yes.'

Mrs Simmons appraised her anew. 'Well, my dear, I took you for a young lady who had time on her hands and wished to do something useful with her life.'

Melissa smiled. 'I may not be a "lady" but I can do something to help your work. I've brought these.' She handed Mrs Simmons the parcel.

'What's this?' The elderly lady took it over to a table beneath one of the windows and began to untie the string. 'Cast-off clothes from your mistress's household? I hope I'm not going to disappoint you, my dear, but I have to tell the truth. We often get that sort of thing and I'm afraid to say not many of the clothes are much use. Too fancy for wear on the cold streets, even after I've done my poor best to alter them.'

'No, they're not cast-offs,' Melissa said.

And she watched as Mrs Simmons opened up the parcel and took out the first garment, which happened to be a warm woollen smock that would fit a small girl of about eight or nine.

'But this is wonderful,' Mrs Simmons said. 'And here's another one – and a jacket and waistcoat for a boy. Are they new?'

'Newly made.'

'Your mistress made them? How kind of her. She has obviously taken great care. You must thank her very much.'

Melissa was amused at the idea of Lilian Winterton sitting with scissors, needle and thread. She laughed softly.

Mrs Simmons looked at her questioningly.

'No,' Melissa assured her, 'Mrs Winterton may have provided the materials but I made them. And I'll make more if you want me to.'

'But this work is first rate,' Mrs Simmons said. 'So well cut and so neatly finished. Of course I would like you to make some more little garments – and perhaps a dress or two that I could give to the old ladies most in need.' She halted abruptly and looked abashed. 'But I shouldn't ask for too much, should I? I'm afraid that's a fault of mine. Please just make whatever clothes you can and remember to thank your mistress very much for providing the cloth.'

'Yes . . . I will. But now I must go.'

'Of course, my dear. I do not want you to be reprimanded.' Mrs Simmons walked with her to the door. 'But you haven't told me your name,' she said, just as Melissa was about to step outside.

Melissa turned and smiled. 'Melissa,' she said. 'Melissa Dornay.'

'Very well, Miss Dornay, I look forward to seeing you again.'

The kindly woman hurried back to her duties and Melissa crossed the sunken courtyard to the stone steps that led up to the pavement. Just as she reached them a small group of children hurtled down towards her.

'Have a care!' one of them shouted. 'Divven't knock the lady over – oh, it's you.'

Melissa stared at the young boy who had stopped in front of her. She recognised the thatch of red hair. 'Ginger,' she said.

'Aye, it's me.' He grinned at her; obviously pleased to see her.

His little family had gone ahead and suddenly they stopped and turned. 'Hawway, our kid,' the older lad shouted. 'Divven't tarry or there'll be nowt left.'

'I'm coming,' Ginger shouted back. 'Ta-ra then,' he said to Melissa, and he raced after his brothers and sister.

Melissa walked to the tram stop. The mood of the city was changing. Clerks and shop assistants were beginning the journey home. They worked long hours and, although some of them looked tired, their mood was that of prisoners or caged birds who had suddenly been set free. She heard three young women laughing at some joke as they hurried for the tram that would take them to their homes on the outskirts of the city.

It was a fine evening and other people were coming in to town. Marginally better dressed, they were arriving for a visit to one of the theatres or perhaps a meal at a good restaurant such as Alvini's. Melissa could sense their anticipation and excitement.

It would be hours before the other, less fortunate people would appear like shadows from the alleyways to find a sheltered doorway or the entrance of an arcade in which to spend the night.

Melissa was pleased that she had been able to do something to help, but she was not altogether at ease. Mrs Simmons had asked her to thank her mistress for providing the cloth.

Ought she to have told Mrs Winterton what she was doing? Should she have asked if it was all right to use the remnants in such a way? Mrs Winterton had told her long ago that she could use whatever cloth was left over for her own clothes. She could not have imagined that Melissa would do anything like this.

Melissa worried about it all the way home on the tram. Surely Mrs Winterton won't object, she thought. She subscribes to many charities and is forever getting involved with fundraising events. And she will probably be pleased if it becomes known that she is helping to provide clothes for some of the city's poorest children. But I ought to have told her . . . to have asked her permission, I know that now. And I must put things right before I start making any more garments.

She left the tram and walked towards the square. She was overtaken by an elegant carriage heading in the same direction. And then another. She remembered that the Wintertons were having a dinner party that evening. She had been asked to change the bead and ribbon trimmings on Gwendolyn's favourite green taffeta gown, and Mrs Winterton had insisted that she add a deep row of extra frills above the hem of a gown she herself had worn only once because she had found it too plain.

Melissa arrived at the house as the guests were descending from the second of the carriages. They were an elderly couple and Douglas had hurried down the steps to give the lady an arm. He was wearing his dress uniform. He looked like a pantomime prince, Melissa thought, with his knee breeches and his silk stockings clinging to his shapely calves. At least the Wintertons did not expect him to wear one of those powdered wigs like the footman in the house next door. She and Reenie had often giggled about that.

Douglas offered his arm to the elderly lady and as they

turned round he saw Melissa and he smiled over the head of his charge. She smiled in return and when the old gentleman had followed them and the pavement was clear, she made towards the steps that led down into the semi-basement. But before she descended she stopped. She had the feeling that she was being watched.

The sensation was so strong that she put one hand out and grasped a bar of the iron railings. Then she looked up just in time to see a flicker of movement at the open window of the library; a shimmer of silky green and then it was gone. A sense of unease took hold of her and remained with her long into the night.

As she lay awake she decided that she would ask to see Mrs Winterton the very next morning and tell her what she had done and ask her permission to go on making clothes for the children as an act of charity.

Lilian Winterton and her daughter were taking coffee in the morning room when Melissa knocked and entered. Lilian looked up in surprise. As far as she knew there was no unfinished sewing business to be discussed. She considered reproving the girl for not waiting for her to call 'enter' but decided against it. She had had enough unpleasantness for one morning.

Gwendolyn, who had been increasingly moody of late, had complained bitterly about being forced to attend the dinner party the night before, saying that the guests were boring and old. It was pointless trying to tell her daughter that the guests in question were people her father needed to cultivate for business purposes and, in any case, whenever they did invite a younger crowd Gwendolyn refused even to consider any of the eligible gentlemen as prospective husbands.

The discussion over the coffee cups had very nearly

become an argument so perhaps Melissa's arrival would be a welcome distraction. But to Lilian's surprise, her daughter's expression became sulkier than ever. The glance she directed towards Melissa was filled with hostility. Lilian could not understand what on earth was the matter with the girl. She decided to ignore her.

'Well, Melissa,' she said, and she tried to smile pleasantly. 'What is it that you want?' She did not ask her to sit down.

'There's something I must ask you,' Melissa replied.

'What is it?'

Melissa looked so hesitant that Lilian immediately supposed that the girl was going to ask for an increase in her allowance. She tried to recall what exactly she was paying her and realised that it probably wasn't enough. Lilian had decided that she could afford to be gracious but when Melissa responded to her question she surprised her.

Looking ill at ease Melissa confessed to what she had done and asked if it was all right to continue.

'Let me understand this,' Lilian said. 'You have been making clothes from remnants of cloth and giving them to some woman at the soup kitchen to distribute to the poor?'

'To the children, yes.'

'And how long have you been doing this?'

'I've only just started.'

'And why didn't you ask me before you did?'

'Because I assumed it would be all right. You have always told me that I may use the remnants how I please.'

'To make clothes for yourself, yes. I hadn't considered any other use.'

'I'm sorry.'

'We-ell, you should have asked, but I suppose it's all right.'

'No it isn't!' The outburst came from Gwendolyn. 'Melissa assumes too much, as far as I am concerned. She acts as if she is one of the family and she's not. She's simply your dressmaker.'

'Well . . .' Lilian felt uneasy. 'Perhaps not quite just my dressmaker. I mean, her mother was a friend . . .'

'No she wasn't!' Gwendolyn exclaimed. 'Mrs Dornay was also your dressmaker and you gave her your custom almost constantly. For which she must have been very grateful. After all, other women at our level of society patronise grand salons, they don't go to little corner dressmaking shops.'

'No, my dear, Emmeline Dornay's work was as good if not better than anything to be found in salons in Newcastle – or even London. That's why I went to her.'

'Exactly. It was a business arrangement. And I'm sure you paid her very well.'

'Well . . . I . . .'

For a moment Lilian felt true remorse when she remembered how she had avoided settling her account and how Emmeline – kind and gentle Emmeline Dornay – even with Christmas drawing near, had not pressed for payment. All she had requested was that Lilian should look after her daughter.

She looked at Melissa, not a child any longer but a tall and beautiful young woman. And when she saw her slender figure, her fine-drawn features and her cascade of dark curls she could not stop the black worm of jealousy from entering her heart. How lovely she is, Lilian thought. How graceful and how much more she looks like a lady than my own daughter.

And in that moment Lilian convinced herself that she had indeed done everything she could have done for Emmeline Dornay's child. She had given her shelter, fed and clothed her and encouraged her skills as a dressmaker. And perhaps Gwendolyn was right. Melissa was too independent. She had worked assiduously and given no trouble but neither had she ever properly expressed her gratitude.

Nevertheless, she did not want to stop Melissa from making clothes for the street children. But she must tell the people concerned that she, Lilian Winterton, had encouraged her to do so. Austin would be pleased that she was associated with such a good cause. Especially as – and none of his business associates must ever know this – he was responsible for making ever more poor folk homeless by his relentless buying of old property in order to pull it down and build more profitable houses for the growing middle classes and flats for the working people.

'Very well,' she said. 'I give you permission to carry on but you must make sure that you tell people that I, Mrs Winterton, have approved and encouraged you. Now you had better go.'

'Wait a moment,' Gwendolyn said. 'How can you be sure that she is telling the truth?'

'I don't understand?' Lilian said.

'She says she is making the clothes for charity cases but how do we know she isn't selling them?'

'Selling them?' Lilian was bewildered.

'Yes, selling them. Many a dealer would be pleased to give her a good price for garments of such quality. I think she's taking advantage of your generosity and making a tidy profit for herself.'

'I wouldn't do that!' Melissa, who had remained silent until now, could bear it no longer. 'Something like that would never occur to me! It's wicked of you to suggest such a thing!'

'Don't you speak to me like that!' Gwendolyn replied. 'You should remember your place in this house.'

Lilian stared at the two young women in dismay. She could almost feel the hostility that crackled in the air between them. But much as she loved her daughter, she knew that her suggestion could not be true. Melissa was surely as principled as her mother had been, wasn't she?

'No, Gwendolyn,' Lilian said, 'I don't think Melissa would do that.'

'Don't you? Then you have no idea what she's really like. Oh, she looks as good as gold, doesn't she? And acts as nice as ninepence. But you've no idea what she can get up to behind people's backs.'

Lilian was perplexed. 'I think you'd better explain,' she said.

Suddenly her daughter looked ill at ease. Lilian had no idea why.

'No, I'm not going to explain anything,' Gwendolyn said. 'Not in front of her.'

Gwendolyn rose to her feet, clumsily knocking the small table by her chair, and her coffee cup slid to the floor. So did the jug of cream and the basin of sugar. Lilian stared at the resulting mess on the fine Persian carpet with dismay but Gwendolyn flounced out of the room without a backward glance.

The door slammed behind her and Lilian looked up to see that Melissa, white-faced, was clenching her fists and trembling with some kind of emotion.

'You'd better go, now,' Lilian said. 'We'll talk again in the morning.'

Melissa was still half asleep when she heard the sobbing. She had been dreaming and it was a dream of loss and sorrow. She had been sitting by the fire with her mother and they had been playing the game of trying to find pictures in the burning coals.

'Look! There's a sailing ship,' Melissa cried. 'He's coming home. My father is sailing home!'

But as she said the words the precarious structure of coals collapsed and the ship plunged to the bottom of a fiery sea.

'No . . .' her mother breathed softly and then, as Melissa

turned to look at her, her beloved face seemed to tremble and become paler – then melt into the shadows.

Melissa's dream-self sobbed and looked around frantically but she was alone. Then the outlines of the room itself grew fainter and the comforting warmth died away. Melissa found herself in a cold dark place. But there was a light ahead and she was drawn towards it. Soon she found herself walking in the bright sunshine of the park. Reenie was with her but Melissa ran ahead. Someone was calling her. The voice came from the direction of the shady trees.

'Look,' he cried. 'See what I have drawn for you.'

In her dream she knew that James was waiting for her. She ran towards his voice but all she could see was his sketchpad lying on the ground. She picked it up but the page was blank, the voice had stopped calling and the dream began to fade. The park, the sunshine and the trembling leaves on the trees dissolved and vanished, the sobbing died away.

Melissa opened her eyes and sat up. She felt her cheeks and they were wet with tears. She rubbed the tears away and saw that Reenie was kneeling by the hearth, seeing to the fire as she did every morning. Reenie had told Polly long ago that this was one fire she need not worry about.

Reenie turned and smiled at her. 'There you are,' she said. 'I didn't want to wake you up in case I gave you a fright. Bad dream?'

'Yes,' Melissa said. But she said nothing further.

Reenie scrutinised her for a moment and then shrugged. 'Well, I suppose you'll tell me if you want to, but meanwhile shall I make a pot of tea? Look, I've put the kettle on. I'm earlier than usual so we can sit and drink it together.'

Melissa pulled on her robe and soon they were sitting each side of the hearth in companionable silence, enjoying the peaceful atmosphere before the big house came awake for the day.

'But why are you up so early?' Melissa asked at last.

'Couldn't sleep, I'm that excited. I can't stop thinking about how grand it will be in the country. Oh, I know it won't be a holiday – at least not for me, I'll probably hev to work just as hard as ever – but just think, when I've time to spare we'll be able to walk in the fields and by the river.'

'How do you know there's a river?'

'I heard Douglas telling Mrs Barton that the master has taken a fancy to fishing and he's bought some fishing rights or something along with the land. So I reckon there's bound to be a river. Hey, do you think we'll be allowed to go swimming?'

'I've no idea.' Melissa smiled. Reenie's excitement and enthusiasm had revived her spirits.

'Eeh, wouldn't that be marvellous!' Then Reenie's expression changed abruptly to one of concern.

'What is it?' Melissa asked.

'I can't swim. Can you?'

'No, I can't.'

They stared at each other for a moment and then burst out laughing.

'A right pair we'll make, won't we?' Reenie said. 'We'll sink or swim together!'

For some reason this made them laugh even more and the resulting good mood carried Melissa through breakfast. She was no longer quite so anxious about her appointment with Mrs Winterton. She was sure everything would be all right. As long as Gwendolyn was not there.

In fact Gwendolyn swept out of the morning room just as Melissa was about to enter. Surprisingly she was smiling. But it was a hard, tight, thin-lipped smile and when she turned her gaze on Melissa there was an unmistakable hint of triumph.

'Ah, come in, Melissa. And shut the door, will you?'

Lilian Winterton was standing by the window. She had been looking out into the square and, when she turned to face Melissa, the light was behind her, shining prettily through the strands of her fair hair but making it impossible to read the expression on her face.

'I've had a word with Mr Winterton,' she said, 'and he thinks it is a fine thing for you to make clothes for the poor children. But he agrees with me that you should have asked my permission first. I don't suppose you meant any harm but it does seem a rather underhand thing to have done.'

Mrs Winterton remained standing by the window and, once more, she did not ask Melissa to sit down.

'But you don't believe I am selling them, do you?' Melissa knew that she had spoken abruptly but she was still shocked by Gwendolyn's accusation.

'Erm . . . no, I don't.'

The way she said this, emphasising the 'I', made Melissa suspect that Gwendolyn had not changed her mind, no matter what her mother thought.

'Thank you,' Melissa said. 'May I go now?'

'No. There is something else I have to say.' She paused. 'As you know, we are taking the household to the country house very soon.'

This time the pause was longer and Melissa felt there was a need for some sort of response. 'Yes, I know,' she said. 'I'm looking forward to it.'

'Oh dear.' Lilian Winterton sounded genuinely upset. 'Are you?'

'Yes.'

'Well, then, I'm sorry to have to tell you that you will not be coming with us.'

'Not going to the country? But why?'

'Well . . . I'm not sure what you would do. I mean, you

have completed all the frocks that Gwendolyn and I will need while we're there – and a very good job you have made of them too – and if there are any repairs to do Ena is more than capable. I have decided it would be better for you to stay here and get on with the clothes we have planned for autumn.'

Melissa remained silent and Lilian Winterton hurried on nervously, 'Of course, you will not be alone in the house. As you know, Mr Beckett is growing frail and my husband believes that the upheaval will be too much for him. Gwendolyn pointed out that Douglas is quite capable of taking on the duties of a valet so Mr Winterton asked Mr Beckett if he would mind staying here to be in charge of the house. He seemed pleased to agree. So you will have him for company. We will engage a plain cook to come in daily to prepare simple meals for you. And the kitchen maid will do any housework that is necessary. There shouldn't be much to do in an empty house.'

'Reenie!'

'I beg your pardon?'

'The kitchen maid. You mean Reenie?'

'Yes. Gwendolyn suggested it out of kindness. She believes you two have become friendly.'

Only Douglas could have told Gwendolyn that, Melissa thought, and maybe his intention was kind but Gwendolyn had been prompted by pure spite.

'Mrs Winterton, may I ask you something?' Melissa said.

'Of course.' She sounded ill at ease.

'When did you decide that I would not be coming to the country?'

'Oh . . . I'm not sure exactly. I have been thinking about it for some time.'

But Melissa knew that was a lie. She believed that Lilian Winterton had only made the decision that very morning and that Gwendolyn had much to do with it.

Mrs Winterton dismissed her and she left the room without a word. She was disappointed, of course, but she was more concerned about Reenie, who was so excited at the prospect of going to the country. She could not bear to think of how disappointed her friend would be.

Chapter Twelve

Reenie was washing her hands at the sink in the scullery. She called over her shoulder to Melissa who was in the kitchen, 'There's no need for you to make the breakfast, you know.'

'I want to.'

'Don't you like my cooking?'

'Of course I do, but you have to admit you like your bacon a little more . . . erm . . . crispy than I do.'

'Are you suggesting that I can't cook owt without spoiling it?'

'Well, now that you mention it . . .'

Melissa smiled at her friend who, still drying her hands on a clean towel, had come to stand next to her.

Reenie pretended to be offended. 'It's a good job you and me is pals,' she said, 'or I'd probably clout you one.'

They looked at each other and burst out laughing.

Then Reenie said, 'Mr Beckett wants me to take his breakfast along to his room. He likes to read his newspaper in peace.'

When Mr Winterton's valet had been settled with his bacon and eggs, toast and a pot of tea, the two girls sat at the table and enjoyed a similar feast. Melissa had never stopped being amazed at the amount of food Reenie could consume and still stay so slim. It was probably because she worked so hard, Melissa thought.

'This is just the job,' her friend said as she wiped her plate with a thick-cut slice of bread. 'Shall I make us a few slices of toast now?'

Melissa agreed although she knew Reenie's 'few slices' would use up the rest of yesterday's loaf. But that didn't matter because Mrs Fearon would bring two loaves with her when she arrived to prepare lunch. It had been decided that Reenie should see to the breakfasts and that Mrs Fearon would come in to cook a midday meal and then leave a pan of broth and something cold for tea and supper.

'This is fun, isn't it?' Reenie said as she spread butter and honey on her toast. 'Just you and me in this big house.'

'Don't forget Mr Beckett.'

'Well, he's no bother, is he? I mean, so long as he gets his meals on time and his newspaper to read, he just sits in his room and dozes off by the fire.'

'He doesn't do much these days even when the family is here, does he?' Melissa said.

'No, he has an easy life compared to some.'

'Why do you think Mr Winterton keeps him on?'

'Because he's training up Douglas to take over. As soon as Mr Winterton thinks Douglas will do he's going to pension the old boy off. And I reckon that will be as soon as they get back from the country – that is, if Douglas has proved satisfactory.' Reenie wiped the crumbs from her mouth and reached for her third piece of toast.

'You ought to be a newspaper reporter,' Melissa said.

'And why's that?'

'Because you always know the latest news and all the gossip.'

'Are you being cheeky?'

'Not at all. I just wonder how you do it.' Melissa smiled at her friend fondly.

Reenie licked honey off her fingers and grinned. 'I keep telling you, while you sit in your room like that lass in the fairy tale, I keeps me eyes and ears open. Of course, being stuck in the kitchen for hours on end I divven't see much of the family but the other maids are always gossiping and they talk to each other as if I'm not there. I might as well be invisible as far as they're concerned.'

When they had finished their breakfast Reenie went along the passage to collect Mr Beckett's tray.

Melissa helped her wash the dishes before going upstairs. But she did not go straight to the sewing room. There was something she needed from the cupboard in her bedroom.

Soon she was intent on her work and she looked up startled when Reenie came into the room and said, 'Aren't you too old to be playing with your doll?'

Melissa smiled. 'I'm not just playing. I'm making clothes for her.'

'Same thing.'

'No, it isn't. You know how I make sketches of the clothes I'm going to make for Mrs Winterton and Gwendolyn? Well, sometimes I can't draw well enough to show them exactly what I intend. So . . .'

'I'm with you. You're going to make an identical outfit for the doll and they'll see exactly what you mean!'

'That's right.'

'Eeh, Melissa, you are clever. You ought to have your own place – your own business – and not just be here working for Mrs Winterton and her crosspatch daughter.'

Melissa frowned.

'What's the matter? What have I said?'

'It's all right.'

'You don't look all right.'

Melissa did her best to smile. 'That's what my mother

wanted for me. Her dream was that I should have my own salon one day.'

'Well, then, you'll have to make her dream come true, won't you?'

'If I can.'

But Melissa knew how difficult that would be. She had done her best to save money from her allowance but it might take years before she had enough to rent rooms and buy everything that was needed. Her mother had planned for her to have the money from the sale of the contents of her own salon but Mrs Winterton had agreed to let Aunt Janet keep it.

Her mother had believed that Lilian Winterton would help Melissa achieve her ambition but Melissa doubted very much if that would happen. She was too useful here. Mrs Winterton had told her often enough that her wealthy friends were envious of her fashionable wardrobe and how they had tried to find out the name of her dressmaker.

'I didn't tell them, of course,' she would say. 'They might try to entice you away from me and your dear mother would not have wanted you to go to some stranger's house where you would not feel at home.'

I wonder if she imagines that I feel at home here, Melissa had wondered. She could leave, she supposed. If she could save up enough to buy her own sewing machine, she might be able to rent a room in a respectable house in Heaton and take in alterations and mending. But the sort of customers who would come to her would not be able to afford the kind of fashionable clothes she had been working on for the Wintertons.

And the sort of work she would be doing was so poorly paid that she would probably have to toil around the clock just to pay the rent and keep herself. She would have precious little time to work on anything more ambitious and, in any case, customers such as Mrs Winterton would not come to a corner shop dressmaker.

'Come back,' Reenie said.

'Come back?'

'I divven't know where you went just then – some kind of brown study – but wherever it was it was making you miserable! Now, can you put your work aside for a while and come down for coffee?'

'Why can't we drink it here?'

'Melissa Dornay, will you just do as you're told for once! Now put that doll back in her box and follow me.'

'Melissa followed as Reenie led the way to Mrs Winterton's morning room on the first floor. Melissa stared round in astonishment. A pretty embroidered fire screen hid the empty grate and one of the occasional tables had been set up with coffee and a plate of biscuits. And because the skies outside were dark with rain clouds Reenie had lit the decorative oil lamps that stood on the occasional tables.

'There you are,' she said. 'Sit down and take your ease.'

'We can't stay in here,' Melissa said.

'Why not?'

'Well . . . it's . . . I mean, we're not supposed to.'

'Who's to know? And if you're thinking Mr Beckett might find out, he won't. He won't stir from his room until dinner's on the table.'

'Yes, but—'

Even though Melissa sounded hesitant Reenie took that for an answer. 'Right, sit down,' she said, 'I'll pour the coffee.'

A burst of rain spattered the windows and the world outside grew darker. Inside, the lustrous fabrics of the upholstery and the curtains glowed softly in the lamplight. Reenie looked round and gave a sigh of satisfaction.

'Isn't this grand?' she said as she glanced around the luxuriously appointed room. 'Sitting here like two proper ladies with nowt to do but enjoy themselves. It almost makes up for things, doesn't it?'

'You mean not going to the country?'

'Aye.' She sighed. 'I was looking forward to that but I wouldn't have been happy there without you, would I?'

'Wouldn't you?'

'Of course not. All the time I would have been thinking of you left here on your own.'

'Me and Mr Beckett.'

'And a barrel of fun he is! But you know what I mean, and I think it's a damn shame that the mistress listened to that spiteful daughter of hers!'

'What are you talking about?'

'I heard Ena telling Mrs Barton that Miss Gwendolyn had the most dreadful fit of the sulks. A right paddy she got into. She telt her mother that if you went to the country house then she wouldn't. And that would mean Mrs Winterton couldn't go either as there was no way they could leave her alone here. So her mother caved in. Miss Gwendolyn got her own way as usual.'

Everything Reenie had said confirmed what Melissa already believed. Gwendolyn didn't like her and there was nothing she could do about it.

'But divven't look so glum,' Reenie said. 'You and me is going to make the best of this and enjoy ourselves.'

'And how will we do that?'

'By treating it like a holiday. All right, so you've got your sewing to do and I've got washing-up and looking after the range, but there's no one here to chivvy me about, and when we've done our day's work we can take our ease. I'll be able to go out every day instead of just me day off and, I've decided, we're going to sit in this very room and take our coffee every day like proper ladies!'

Melissa could see that Reenie was determined, and she

was reluctant to spoil her friend's fun. 'All right,' she said, 'but now you'd better go back downstairs before Mrs Fearon arrives.'

It rained heavily for the next few days, and, spurred on by Reenie, they explored the house and marvelled at the beautiful things they found there.

'Look at all those books!' Reenie exclaimed when they ventured into the library. 'The shelves gan right up to the ceiling and there's even a sort of ladder thing so you can reach the ones on the top shelves. How many books do you think there are?'

'A few hundred?' Melissa guessed.

'Do you think Mr Winterton has read them all?'

'No, I don't think he's read any of them. I think he's simply bought them by the yard.'

'Books by the yard? Whatever do you mean?'

'Well, look at them. They're all leather-bound with gold lettering, and the blues or the reds or the greens are arranged on the shelves to make a sort of pattern.'

'But by the yard?'

'I've seen advertisements in magazines. You can send for books that will suit your house rather than your reading taste. They're there for decoration. I believe all the Wintertons are concerned about is the look of the room.'

'Maybe, but Miss Gwendolyn is always coming in here to read. At least that's what she says she's doing.' Reenie gave a wink and grinned mischievously.

Then they left the library to do some more exploring. They didn't go into any of the bedrooms. Instinctively both of them knew that it would be wrong to enter such a personal space. So they went down to the ground floor where the formal reception rooms were situated.

'Why don't we have our supper in here?' Reenie said when they had wandered into the large dining room.

Melissa stood at the head of the long polished table and looked around at the mahogany sideboard and the serving table, the dark oil paintings on the walls and the heavy crimson velvet drapes at the tall windows.

'No, too gloomy,' she said.

'Not when the lamps are lit and there are candles in them silver candelabras and the table is set with the best crystal and china,' Reenie responded.

'And what if we broke a piece of the crystal or china? Or dripped candle wax on the polished table?'

'There'd be hell to pay! I'd be sacked without a reference and then what would I do?'

'So we won't be eating in here,' Melissa said.

They left the room and crossed the entrance hall to the recently refurbished drawing room. Mrs Winterton had employed an impoverished titled lady who made a living advising people how to furnish and decorate their homes in the most tasteful manner.

The titled lady had done her best to rein in Mrs Winterton's exuberantly extravagant taste but she had not entirely succeeded. In Melissa's eyes the room was overcrowded, and instead of one or two tasteful ornaments there was a profusion of porcelain figures, jugs and vases and bright and brassy-looking ormolu.

'We could receive our important guests in here,' Reenie said.

'And who exactly would they be?'

'Oh, Melissa, divven't spoil my fun. I'm only pretending.'

'Yes, I know. I'm sorry. I like pretending too. It makes life less dreary and I reckon we both need a little fun.'

Nearly every day after that they played games of make-believe. Sometimes they pretended to be the daughters of the house, sometimes Reenie insisted that Melissa was the mistress and she, Reenie, was the lady's maid. Reenie would endeavour to copy Ena's attempts at talking 'posh' and she was so wickedly funny that Melissa told her she ought to be on the stage.

'Have you ever been to the theatre?' Reenie asked her.

'Yes, when I was a child. My mother loved the theatre. We went when we could afford to and I remember my aunt Janet telling my mother that the theatre was a sinful place and no innocent child should be exposed to such wickedness.'

'Your aunt?'

'My mother's sister.'

'She sounds a bit of a wet blanket.'

'She was. She didn't approve of anything my mother did, not even marrying my father.'

'You've never talked about her.'

'No, and I haven't even thought about her for years, thank goodness.'

They were quiet for a moment and then Reenie said, 'Do you realise it hasn't rained since yesterday morning? Why don't we go to the park this afternoon?'

Reenie knew that Melissa still had reservations about going to Leazes Park but in her own view it was better to face up to things and try to banish unhappy memories.

Melissa crossed to the window of the morning room and looked out. The sun was slanting across the rooftops into the garden. Some children from one of the big houses were playing there and their happy laughter echoed round the square. The girls were dressed in pretty pastel shades of muslin and the little boys wore sailor suits. Their nursemaids were sitting on the benches light-heartedly chattering amongst themselves.

For a moment Melissa remembered those other children, Ginger and his sister and brothers, who had tried to take shelter in the garden. She had wanted to help them and children like them and, thanks to her gift with the needle, she'd discovered there was something she could do. She couldn't find homes for them but at least she could ensure that some of the children were well and warmly dressed.

'Yes, we'll go to the park,' she agreed, and Reenie smiled her approval. 'We need some fresh air after all these days of staying indoors. But we won't stay too long. Tonight you can help me with some sewing.'

Mrs Fearon, a large friendly woman, looked at them askance when they went into the kitchen for their midday meal. 'You two seem pleased with yourselves,' she said.

'That's because we're looking forward to our dinner,' Reenie said. 'Mm, by the smell of it, it's Irish stew. There's no one can make stew like you, Mrs Fearon.'

'Get away with you! You're just saying that because you want second helpings.'

But Mrs Fearon looked pleased. She liked Reenie and approved of Melissa. She had worked in many houses on a casual basis. Some jobs had been easy and some had been difficult, depending on what was required of her. This job was one of the best yet, with two young lasses and one elderly gent to cook for. And no one to complain if she took the leftovers home with her. Not that she thought that was wrong. Many a cook helped herself to more than just the leftovers – especially if she was in charge of the ordering.

Mrs Fearon dished up four generous plates of stew. 'You'd better go and get Mr Beckett,' she told Reenie. 'He ought to have been along here by now.'

Reenie pulled a face. 'He'll be dozing off. And he gets so grumpy if I wake him up.'

Mrs Fearon smiled. 'He'll be even grumpier if his dinner gets cold. Now go and get him.'

But Reenie was spared the unpleasant task for at that moment the kitchen door opened and the elderly valet walked in. The four of them sat at the table together and consumed the delicious stew, followed by jam roly-poly and custard. Mr Beckett didn't speak until he had finished and then he thanked Mrs Fearon politely and asked Reenie if she would bring a cup of tea to his room.

'Well, that's that,' Mrs Fearon said as she took off her pinafore. 'There's a pan of broth as usual, and you'll find cold cuts and tomatoes in the larder. I'll trust you to wash up properly, Reenie, and I'll be off.'

The park was full of people enjoying the sunshine. They were mostly young mothers with children or elderly folk for, at this time of day, most of the population would be at work.

Reenie, dressed in a muslin frock that had once been Melissa's, and a straw hat trimmed with artificial daisies she had bought at the milliner's in the Grainger Market, looked like a little bird that had been set free from its cage.

'Isn't this grand?' she said. 'The sunshine and the flowers, and you and me out together. And dressed so smart, me in pale green and you in your favourite ivory – and with our daft bit hats on. If only we had a couple of them parasols we would look like proper ladies.'

'We are ladies, remember?' Melissa said.

'Oh, aye, I forgot. You're the daughter of the house and I'm your paid companion.'

'Why don't you be the daughter of the house for a change?'

'All right. But I'll have to keep me mouth shut!'

So when they found a table at the little open-air café it was Melissa who went to buy the lemonade and Reenie who sat and waited, like 'Lady Muck', as she put it. As Melissa carried the drinks back to the table she remembered Reenie's accident with the tray, which had led to their meeting with James.

'You look thoughtful,' Reenie said when Melissa got back to the table.

'Do I?'

'Yes, you do. And I can guess what you're thinking about. And I wish you wouldn't.'

Melissa knew that Reenie intended to be kind so she did her best to smile. They sipped their lemonade and, when the band began to play, they wandered over to listen. The grassy bank where they used to sit was too wet after the prolonged days of rain so they took their places amongst the crowd on the seats arranged in a circle around the bandstand. Reenie was soon tapping her feet in time to the music and mouthing the words of the songs that she knew. Melissa was free to think about James.

She hadn't known him for very long but they had got on so well together. Sometimes when they talked about painting or music or an exhibition at the museum they almost forgot that Reenie was there. But her friend had never seemed to mind. One day Reenie had said she felt a bit femmer – her way of saying she felt poorly – and that she didn't feel like going out. Melissa, not really believing her, but grateful all the same, set off for the park alone.

When James had taken her to the art gallery, she had been overwhelmed by the beauty of some of the paintings and puzzled by some of the others. She had listened enraptured as James explained them to her; told her about the lives of the artists who had painted them; told her that he hoped that his paintings would be exhibited one day. So far Melissa had only seen the sketches he had done in the park but she believed without question that his dreams would come true.

A stirring march came to an end and the audience around the bandstand clapped and cheered. Melissa roused herself enough to join in the applause but once the music started again her thoughts returned to James. Brief though their acquaintance had been, their friendship was beginning to mean much more to her. And she had believed he felt the same way. It would have been wrong to go on deceiving him even though the deception had started out innocently, so she had written him that note and left it in his satchel.

Had she really hoped that when James read the note he would smile and come along to tell her that it didn't matter, that he loved her whatever the truth of it was? It had been a forlorn hope. She remembered how she had sat at the table under the trees, her disappointment growing as the hours passed. She remembered how hurt she had been. And then Reenie had taken her back to the Winterton house, neither of them speaking much. They had never seen James again.

The concert was over and the audience began to leave.

'Hawway, then,' Reenie said. 'Let's have a walk to the pond and watch the bairns sail their toy boats.' Then suddenly she leaned close and gripped Melissa's arm. 'Divven't look now,' she said, 'but them two lads have been eyeing us up.'

'Which two lads?' Instinctively Melissa turned her head to look around her.

'I told you not to look! Two right bonny lads, they are, and they look respectable. They were sitting a few rows back. They're standing up but they've made no attempt to leave. Their heads are together and if I'm not mistaken, they've been talking about us.'

'We'd better go.'

'Aye, we had. And let's just see if they follow us. Now get up looking all unconcerned, like, and keep your eyes ahead!'

They walked together to the small boating lake and the temptation to glance behind was overpowering. Reenie suddenly reached for Melissa's arm and clung on to it. Melissa could feel that her friend was shaking and she glanced sideways. Reenie was almost bursting with the effort not to laugh and suddenly, her heart lifting, Melissa wanted to laugh too. Reenie looked round and they caught each other's eye. By the time they reached the water they were both shaking with laughter.

They stood at the water's edge and Reenie turned to look at Melissa full face. 'That's better,' she said approvingly. 'You looked right miserable before. Now you're my bonny lass again.'

Melissa turned to look back the way they had come. There was no one following them. 'Did you make that up?' she asked. 'Were there really two young men looking at us?'

'Oh, aye, and I meant it when I said they were right bonny. And well-dressed too. They look like proper young gentlemen.'

'Reenie, you're incorrigible.'

'Are you being rude?'

'No, I mean you could never be cured of your sense of fun – and I wouldn't want you to be. With you as my friend I could never stay gloomy for long.'

Reenie grinned. 'That's right. So what shall we do now?' She looked across the water. 'Are you any good at rowing?'

'I don't know; I've never tried.'

'Neither have I but there's always a first time.'

'No, Reenie, we couldn't . . .'

But her friend was already hurrying towards the wooden jetty where the rowing boats were tied. Melissa picked up her skirts and hurried after her.

Fergus Thorburn and his younger brother, Malcolm, stood half concealed by low-hanging branches of a leafy tree and watched the two young women as they made their laughing, oar-splashing progress across the lake.

'You're taken with her, aren't you?' Malcolm said. 'The dark-haired one.'

'Who wouldn't be?' Fergus replied. 'She's lovely.'

'The little one knew we were watching. I think she wanted us to follow and maybe catch up with them.'

'Perhaps. But that would not have been proper.'

'Always the gentleman, aren't you?'

'And you, little brother, are always the rascal. But if we're lucky enough to see these two young ladies again, and I intend that we should, then you really must behave yourself. The smaller of the two may be a madcap but I sense they are both quite innocent.'

'And you think Mother would approve?'

'I've no doubt of it. Mother would be delighted to meet them.'

Melissa and Reenie, their cheeks flushed with their recent exertion, hurried back to the Winterton house barely in time to awaken Mr Beckett for tea. Reenie changed into her work dress and a clean pinafore, and hurried down to set the table in the kitchen, although she knew that Mr Beckett would almost certainly ask her to bring him a tray. She had to knock several times before his sleepy voice called, 'Come in.'

'Honestly, Melissa,' she said later when they were eating large slices of bread and jam, and drinking their tea at the kitchen table, 'honestly, I think the poor old chap just sleeps for most of the time – and that's just as well, isn't it?' She grinned.

'Why?'

'Well, he might tell me not to go out so often. After all, the family may be away but I'm still supposed to be working, aren't I?'

'I don't think he'd mind,' Melissa said. 'After all, we're doing no harm.'

'No, we're not, are we? So what shall we do tomorrow?'

The next day Melissa needed to go into town to buy some buttons for the dresses she was making for the children. The young woman who usually attended to her in Wilkinson's looked askance at the cards of plain buttons Melissa had chosen. They were not like anything Miss Dornay had bought previously.

'Shall I put them on the account?' she asked.

'No, that's all right, I'll pay for them.'

Mrs Winterton had given her permission to use any remnants of fabric but she had not suggested that she would buy anything else that Melissa might need.

The packet was small enough to fit in the beaded handbag that Melissa had made for herself, and she and Reenie left the cool cavern of the shop and walked out into the baking sunshine of the streets.

'Pooh!' Reenie said. 'The stink gets worse, doesn't it?' She was referring to the horse droppings.

'It's because it's hot,' Melissa said.

'I suppose so. And there's more and more traffic in the streets. Tell you what, Melissa, let's gan to the park after all.' They had been intending to go to Tilley's for a pot of tea and toasted teacakes.

Melissa agreed and they set off to walk through the dusty crowded streets. Then a little way ahead of them they saw a small crowd of people. They seemed to be encircling something, and every now and then they laughed and clapped. To Melissa's embarrassment, when they reached the crowd Reenie pushed her way to the front and pulled Melissa after her.

What they saw was two flamboyantly dressed people: a young man and woman. They were acting out a scene from a play. It seemed the young man was courting the young woman but she had a witty refusal to his every plea. Not long after the two friends had started watching he asked her yet another question. The object of his desire opened her mouth as if she were about to answer him and then she shook her head and turned to the watching crowd.

She smiled impishly and said, 'And if you want to know the answer to that, ladies and gentlemen, you'll have to come along to the Palace tonight!'

The crowd groaned and laughed and complained good-humouredly, and the two young actors began to hand out playbills. Reenie grabbed one excitedly and all the way to the park she tried to persuade Melissa that they should go to see the play.

'Look,' she said, thrusting the playbill in front of Melissa. 'It says it's a musical entertainment. "A Happy Sad Story of Young Love Triumphing Over Heartbreak."'

'It could be sentimental twaddle,' Melissa said, but she was smiling.

'Divven't be a wet blanket! You know how fond I am of a good love story – like the ones in them penny papers the other maids read. And this one will have singing and dancing and bonny frocks! You know you'd love it just as much as me!'

Melissa remained unconvinced, and as they strolled along the walks between the flowered borders towards the lake Reenie got more and more impatient. 'Are we going to have a quarrel about this?' she asked.

Her voice suddenly cracked and, disconcerted, Melissa stopped walking and turned to find that Reenie's eyes were glistening with tears.

'You really want to go to the theatre, don't you?'

'Yes, I do.' Her lip trembled. 'It's all right for you. You've been to the theatre with your ma. I've never been once in my whole life.'

Suddenly she screwed up the playbill and flung it away from her, and her tears began to flow in earnest. Melissa instinctively reached out and took hold of Reenie's shoulders.

'Look at me,' she said but Reenie sniffed and shook her head rebelliously.

Melissa went on calmly and was pleased when her friend stopped gulping back her sobs and raised her head to listen.

'It's not that I don't want to go to the theatre,' Melissa said. 'It's just that I don't know how we'd manage it. Mr Beckett locks up every night at eight o'clock. How would we get in?'

'I don't suppose we could just tell him we were going, could we?' Reenie asked. She wiped her wet cheeks with the back of a hand. 'I mean, you've always come and gone as you've liked, haven't you?'

Melissa gave her a clean handkerchief. 'Well, not quite,' she said. 'Mrs Winterton approved of my going to church, my French lessons and my walks in the park but she made it quite clear that I should keep reasonable hours.'

'We'll just hev to go without telling Mr Beckett, then. And divven't fret, we won't be locked out. I know how we'll get in again.'

It was obvious that Reenie had made up her mind, and Melissa was loath to disappoint her. Her friend had had little enough pleasure in her life.

'That's that, then,' Melissa said. 'We'll go tonight.'

'Tonight!' Reenie's eyes now shone with happiness.

'Yes, tonight. Why wait? And if we're going to the theatre then we'll have to make sure that we're dressed up in our very best gowns.'

Once she had made up her mind, Melissa was aware of a growing exhilaration. She realised how much she needed to relax, to have some fun like other girls of her age. And she remembered how much she had loved the theatre.

The sounds of the park, the children playing, the ducks on the lake quacking as they hustled to reach the bread an old woman was throwing to them seemed to die away and Melissa was taking her seat in the plush red warmth of the theatre with her mother.

She remembered the sense of anticipation while you waited for the curtain to go up; the musicians in the orchestra pit tuning their instruments; then the moment when the conductor raised his baton and musicians and audience alike gave him their full attention.

After the overture the curtain would rise to reveal another world. A world more vivid than the real one. The light was brighter, the dark was darker, the people were more virtuous, more evil and much funnier. This was a world that drew you in across the footlights and carried you along towards the happy ending that you craved, and yet all the while you were on tenterhooks that it would not be achieved.

And then the present day world returned as Reenie took hold of her arm and shook her. 'Melissa, did you hear what I said?' She was frowning.

Behind her the old lady had thrown the last of the bread into the water and as she walked along the perimeter of the lake the ducks followed her quacking mournfully.

'Melissa!'

'Sorry. I'm listening.'

'About time. What can we do about Mr Beckett's supper? We'll hev to leave almost immediately. He'll be suspicious if I'm not in my maid's uniform.'

'I'll put one of Cook's large pinafores on and take his tray along myself. I'll tell him that you're not feeling well,' Melissa said.

'But that would be a lie.' Reenie's frown began to turn into a smile.

'Yes, it would.' Melissa pretended to look shocked with herself, then she said, 'I know, I'll tell him that you're not feeling quite yourself, that you are a little agitated. That would be nearer the truth, wouldn't it?'

Reenie's smile widened. 'Absolutely – but not in the way Mr Beckett would take it. Let's go back now.'

'Now? But we've only been here five minutes.'

'I know but I want to get everything ready for tonight. I'll have to build up the fire in the range to make sure that there's enough hot water for us both to have a bath. And we'll hev to hev a little fashion parade, won't we?' She put on her 'posh' voice, 'To decide which of our many lovely gowns we're going to wear.'

Reenie twirled round as if she was wearing a ball gown and then curtsied to Melissa. When she rose from the curtsey she laughed and resumed her normal way of speaking. 'Hawway, lass,' she said. 'Let's not waste any more time looking at those dratted ducks.'

Neither of them had noticed the two young men who had been watching from the shade under the leafy branches of a tree. Fergus Thorburn smiled as he watched them go. The one called Melissa really was stunningly beautiful.

'Go and pick that up,' he said to his brother.

'What?'

'That piece of paper the little madcap threw away.'

Malcolm sighed comically and did as he was bid.

'Give it to me.'

Fergus opened up the playbill and smiled. 'The Palace,' he said. 'That's where they're going. Little brother, I think I'll treat you to the theatre tonight.'

Chapter Thirteen

The servants' entrance of the Winterton house was in the semi-basement. At pavement level ornate iron railings prevented passers-by from falling into the narrow yard below. A gate gave access to a set of steep steps. The servants' door was in the dark passage under an archway formed by the grand stone stairway leading to the front door above.

At one side of the door was the window of Mr Beckett's room and, unfortunately for Reenie's plan, this window looked directly on to the steps that led up to the street. At the other side of the door was the window of Mrs Barton's room. And this would have to do.

Reenie explained her plan to Melissa.

'But he'll see us going up the steps,' Melissa said.

'No he won't, because we're not going to *leave* the house that way. We're going out of the front door, dressed to the nines, like two proper ladies going to the theatre. But as Mr Beckett will have locked the front door by the time we return, we'll have to get back in through Mrs Barton's window.'

'Which you will leave open before we go?'

'I won't actually leave the window open. I'll leave the catch off so's we can open it when we get back.'

'But what if Mr Beckett finds the catch is open and closes it again?'

'I divven't think he'll gan in there – he wouldn't think to. But just in case he does I'll leave a knife in the yard.'

'A knife? I don't understand.'

'You can slip the blade up between the top and the bottom frame and push the catch aside.'

'Where did you learn that?'

'It's surprising what tricks some of the workhouse brats pick up – those that've been living on the streets before they were caught.'

Reenie grinned. Melissa frowned.

'What is it?' Reenie asked.

'We'll still have to go down the steps past Mr Beckett's window,' she said.

'He'll be in the land of Nod by then and we'll hev to take care not to wake him. Honestly, Melissa, it'll be all right.'

Mr Beckett surprised and disconcerted them by appearing at the tea table rather than requesting a tray in his room.

'I feel I've been neglecting you,' he said.

'Not at all,' Melissa replied.

'That's right, we really divven't mind,' Reenie added, and Melissa shot her a warning glance.

'Nevertheless, I have been left in charge here and I apologise for shutting myself away so much. I am supposed to be here to help and guide you. Solve any little problems.'

'Mr Beckett, please don't feel guilty,' Melissa said. 'We know that if there was a problem we could come to you and we would.'

'Good.' Mr Beckett sat down and allowed Reenie to place two slices of boiled ham, a large helping of pease pudding, a hard-boiled egg and a tomato on his plate. Melissa passed him the bread and butter. 'You have been very kind to me, Reenie, waiting on me and never complaining,' he said.

'It's not my place to complain, Mr Beckett. I work here and I do as I'm told.'

'I know. They work you very hard, my dear, and yet you always remain cheerful. I want you to know that I do not mind your going out in the afternoons with Miss Dornay. I trust her judgement and so long as you do not overstep the mark and take advantage of the situation I shall certainly not say anything to Mr and Mrs Winterton when they return.'

Melissa and Reenie looked at each other across the table. The rest of the meal was eaten in silence, and when Mr Beckett rose to leave he smiled at them and said, 'I believe my sitting here with you has put a constraint on your usual cheerful chatter.'

'Oh, no,' Melissa said. 'I – I'm glad you joined us.'

The old valet bowed his head. His scalp, pink like that of a baby, shone through his thinning white hair. 'It's kind of you to say so,' he said. 'Now, Reenie, my dear. If you don't mind I'll trouble you to bring a supper tray to my room as usual.'

Melissa could see how hard it was for Reenie to conceal her relief. 'Of course, Mr Beckett,' she said. 'I'll be pleased to.'

Mr Beckett closed the door behind him and neither Melissa nor Reenie knew what to say.

Eventually Reenie said very quietly, 'Do you think he knows something's up?'

Melissa considered the question seriously and said, 'No, I don't think so.'

'That's all right, then.'

'What do you mean?'

'He's given us his blessing, hasn't he?'

'How have you come to that conclusion?'

'He said he didn't mind us going out, didn't he?'

'Yes.'

'Well, we're all right for tonight.'

'I'm not sure. He also said that we mustn't overstep the mark.'

Reenie gave a strangled sob. 'You're not going to change your mind about going to the theatre, are you? After I've got meself all excited. Oh, Melissa, I just couldn't bear that!'

Melissa was troubled. She couldn't see any harm in them going to the theatre but she wondered whether Mr Beckett would trust her judgement in this case.

As if she had read her mind Reenie said, 'We're not doing anything really wicked by going to the theatre. We'll hev a night out, we'll enjoy ourselves and we'll work all the harder tomorrow. Oh, do say we'll go!'

Melissa heard the passionate yearning in Reenie's voice and felt a rush of compassionate affection for her friend. And she realised that she was looking forward to this escapade as much as Reenie. 'Of course we will,' she said. 'Now let's wash these dishes and go up and get ready.'

Some time later, after they had bathed, they tried on various frocks, skirts and blouses. Amidst much laughter and posturing in front of the cheval glass in the sewing room they made their final decisions.

Reenie stepped back and stared at Melissa. 'You look so beautiful,' she said. She shrugged, turned and looked critically at herself in the looking-glass, 'But as for me . . .'

'You look lovely.'

'You're just saying that.'

'No, I wouldn't lie.'

They were wearing simple gored pale grey grosgrain skirts and high-necked muslin blouses. Reenie's skirt had once been Melissa's and when she had outgrown it she still had to cut it down to fit Reenie's small frame. Likewise with the blouses. Reenie's was pale pink and Melissa's was azure. Their dark grey jackets were in the 'Russian' style with nipped-in waists and high stand-up collars. Reenie was already wearing hers but Melissa would put her jacket on after she had taken Mr Beckett's supper tray to his room.

Melissa's faux tortoiseshell combs, with their crystal beading, shone in her luxuriant dark hair. She had helped Reenie to put her hair up in the same style as her own, using some pretty tawny celluloid combs they had bought at a stall in the Grainger Market, but Reenie gazed at herself critically.

'My hair . . . it's not the same as yours,' she said.

'It's exactly the same style.'

'But thin mousy brown doesn't look anything near as good as shiny black.'

'Yes, it does, and anyway, your hair isn't thin, it's fine. And it isn't mousy, it's light blonde.'

Reenie looked at Melissa and then grinned wryly. 'If you say so,' she said. 'Now I suppose you'd better take Mr Beckett his supper tray.'

They went down to the kitchen where Reenie had left the pan of broth simmering on the range. Melissa put Mrs Fearon's outsize pinafore on over her finery and carried the tray, set up with broth, a slice of bread and some cheese and water biscuits, to Mr Beckett's room. Luckily he had told them at the very start not to bother with bringing him a cup of cocoa later as his preferred drink at supper time was a glass of stout. And he kept his bottles of Murphy's in a cupboard in his room.

'She looked all right at tea time,' he said when Melissa told him that Reenie was not 'quite herself'. 'Do you think we should call the doctor?'

'Oh, no, I'm sure she will be better tomorrow.'

'Well, if you say so.'

Melissa placed the tray on the table by the fireplace. A small fire burned in the grate. These rooms below street level could be damp and cold, even at the height of summer. As she left the room she looked back and saw that Mr Beckett looked perfectly content and she thought that he was probably enjoying this time without the family as much as she and Reenie were.

Fergus Thorburn and his younger brother, Malcolm, alighted from their cab at the terminus in the Haymarket and looked across to the Palace Theatre where the queue for the second performance was already stretching up St Thomas's Street towards the top of the hill and Leazes Park – where they had first seen the two young women who had attracted Fergus's attention.

A ragged boy was entertaining the crew with a juggling act while a smaller waif went round with a cap. Fergus gazed across at them and smiled. 'There they are, as usual,' he said.

'Yes,' Malcolm said and grinned. Then, 'What now?' he asked. 'Are we going to buy our tickets?'

'Not yet. I want to make sure the two young women are coming – and where they will sit.'

'Are we going to try and get seats near them?'

'Only near enough to observe without being noticed.'

'What do you propose we should do while we wait?'

'Alvini's for a coffee and a glass of cognac, I think.'

'Good.' Malcolm started to cross the street.

'No, not you,' Fergus said. '*I'm* going to Alvini's and *you* are going to stay here and watch out for them. As soon as you see them you will come and tell me. Look . . . position yourself at the other side of this fruit stall.'

Malcolm, good-natured and biddable as ever, went to stand behind the stall, which was piled high with oranges and apples. The fruit glowed in the lingering sunlight and the sharp tang of the oranges and lemons lent a welcome fragrance to the dusty city air. The stallholder shouted his wares and filled brown-paper bags with fruit and vegetables for his customers. He pocketed the coin Malcolm dropped in his hand and asked no questions.

Fergus's younger brother grinned good-naturedly. 'I feel ridiculous, standing here like a costermonger,' he said.

'Well, you don't look ridiculous,' Fergus assured him. 'You look like an eager young gentleman who is hoping to see the young lady he is attracted to.'

'But it's *you* who is attracted,' Malcolm protested.

'I can't deny it. The dark-haired girl is both enchanting and elegant. And she interests me intensely. But what about you? Could you not find a corner in your heart for the little companion?'

'The madcap?' Malcolm laughed. 'She's a pretty little thing, that's for sure, but I don't think our blessed mother would consider her a lady.'

'Does it matter? In this case?'

'No, I suppose it doesn't. I'll be pleasant to the little maid so that you can be charming to the mistress.'

They smiled fondly at each other before Fergus turned and negotiated his way through the ranked hansom cabs and then across the tramlines to the coffee house and restaurant that was next door to the Palace Theatre.

On the pavement outside the theatre the juggling act went on and the cap that the smaller boy carried round was filling up with small coins. The queue, in a good mood, was generous. Fergus stopped and watched the lads. Co-ordination and dexterity, that's what was needed, and the young juggler possessed both those qualities.

After a moment he threw a coin and deliberately missed the cap. It made a clinking noise on the pavement and then began to roll towards the gutter. The smaller boy dodged between legs and caught it before it dropped into a drain. The older lad, his act interrupted, looked first at his companion returning with the coin and then at Fergus. His eyes widened and he grinned. Fergus turned so that no one in the queue could see his face and he winked.

'Your cap is full. If you pocket your takings now and go across to that fruit stall my brother will buy you each an orange,' he said.

The lad looked doubtful.

'Don't worry, he's expecting you.'

Seemingly something in Fergus's expression persuaded the lad to agree. A moment later, his pocket jingling with the evening's takings, he led his brother across the tramlines towards the fruit stall.

Already there were well-dressed people arriving to take their tables in Alvini's. The restaurant on the first floor was a much grander place than the coffee shop and ice-cream parlour on the ground floor. Fergus strolled into the coffee shop. The tables at the window were all taken. He raised his hat politely to an elderly woman sitting alone.

'Do you mind if I share your table?' he asked.

She looked up startled, stared at him through narrowed eyes and then smiled faintly. 'There are empty tables at the back,' she said.

'I know, but I like to sit by the window and watch the world go by, don't you?'

'That's why I'm sitting here,' she said drily. 'But, by all means, share my table if you wish.'

Fergus guessed that she had observed him keenly and made her mind up that he was harmless; that he was not a pickpocket. But nevertheless she moved her shopping bag to the other side of her chair. She's thinking, rather safe than sorry, he thought.

Despite the warmth of the day the elderly lady was dressed almost entirely in black. Even the chiffon scarf tucked into the neckline of her coat was black. Fergus saw that the cut of her clothes was good and the material expensive. She wore a surprisingly fashionable hat and the large bead on the end of her hatpin was made from carved

Whitby jet. Fergus recognised it as a mourning pin. He had bought an almost identical one for his mother.

She's in mourning, Fergus thought. She won't welcome conversation. Nevertheless when the waiter came to the table Fergus asked her politely if she would like another cup of coffee. She declined just as politely and said that she must go.

'I'll need a cab now,' she said to the waiter.

'Certainly Miss Surtees.'

Miss Surtees gathered up her shopping, and the waiter, showing all the deference owing to valued customers, preceded her to the door and gestured for the next cab in line to come over. When it arrived he helped her in. When he bowed his head in acknowledgement of the tip she gave him Fergus, who had been watching keenly, saw the man's satisfied smile.

Surtees, Fergus thought. She's obviously more than comfortably off. I wonder if my mother knows her. He tucked the name away in his memory for future reference. As the cab drew away Fergus noticed his brother coming across the street towards the café. He was smiling.

Reenie looked at the long queue with dismay. 'Eeh, Melissa,' she said. 'I never thought. We should hev come early to get a ticket.'

'It's all right,' Melissa assured her. 'I believe this queue is for the gods.'

'What are you talking about? What's the gods?'

'That's what they call the upper circle because it's so high up. The seats are the cheapest in the house – the theatre,' she explained when she saw Reenie frowning. 'So there's always a queue for them.'

'Well, we'd better tag on to the queue before it gets any longer.'

'No. Keep walking.'

When they reached the entrance to the theatre Reenie looked at the prices displayed in gold letters on the glass front of the ticket office. She looked dismayed.

'I divven't think I can afford any of the other seats – the circle or the stalls, even the back stalls.'

'Never mind the back stalls, we are going to have a seat in the front stalls. And it's my treat.'

'No, I can't let you pay.'

'Yes, you can. And you can buy us each an ice cream in the interval.'

Reenie screwed her face up for a moment as she thought about this, and then smiled widely and said, 'Right oh!'

They bought their tickets and a programme to share, and then followed a small crowd through a door into the warmth and dimness of the auditorium where a young woman examined their tickets and pointed the way to their seats. Melissa had secured seats near the front at the end of the row on the centre aisle. She explained to Reenie that this was to ensure they could leave promptly in the interval to get their ice creams.

But it also meant that they had to stand up each time someone else arrived, and Reenie had a fit of giggles when a very stout couple huffed and puffed as they squeezed past them. Then, as the house lights went down and the orchestra struck up a cheerful tune, Reenie, who was sitting in the aisle seat, dropped the programme and inadvertently kicked it under the seat in front of her.

She kneeled down to get it at the same moment a flustered late arrival tried to get past her to find his seat. He tripped over her and fell face forward across Melissa's lap. He yelped in surprise; the lady sitting next to Melissa, finding his face buried in the handbag on her lap, shrieked in fright, and from all around them came angry shushing sounds.

When the poor man had picked himself up, gone on to

find his seat and everyone had settled amidst a rustling of programmes, Melissa and Reenie had to hold each other's hand tightly as they tried to suppress their laughter.

'You ought to be on the stage rather than in the audience,' Melissa whispered.

And before Reenie could answer her, the gentleman sitting in front of Melissa turned and said, 'For goodness' sake!'

'Sorry,' Melissa mouthed.

Fortunately, before he could complain further, the curtains rose with a flourish and a line of pretty chorus girls, in spangled full-skirted costumes, swirled on to the stage in a graceful promenade and began to sing. The show had begun.

The Thorburn brothers had watched it all from their box with growing delight.

'Two innocents abroad,' Fergus murmured to his brother, 'and I'm sure what I think is true.'

'You're usually right.'

'Of course I am. That's why Mother thinks so highly of me. Now, we may as well enjoy the show while we're here.'

After the final curtain the audience began to leave the theatre reluctantly. They had called 'encore' again and again, but finally the curtain rose no more.

'That was wonderful!' Reenie told Melissa as they joined the throng.

'Yes, it was.' Melissa felt that she had been lifted on to a different plane of happiness and enjoyment during the performance and, realising how ephemeral the moment was, she tried to hang on to it for as long as possible.

While they had been in the theatre the skies had darkened and the Haymarket had become a different place. The streetlamps shone hazily through the encroaching shadows, the coach lights were lit on the hansom cabs and the market stalls, still busy, had spluttering kerosene lamps hanging from the overhead frames.

The good-natured mood of the theatre audience spilling out on to the pavements took on a harder edge as they began to jostle one another at the tram stop or fight for the hansom cabs. Reenie was shaken out of her trance when she was elbowed aside by the same young man she had caused to fall over when he arrived at the theatre.

'Manners!' she cried out, but he didn't even look over his shoulder as he leaped on a departing tram.

Reenie had stumbled backwards. She righted herself and looked round as if she had suddenly become aware of where they were. Her eyes rounded.

'What's the matter?' Melissa asked.

'Nothing. It's just – well – what time do you think it is?'

Melissa glanced back over her shoulder to the clock in the foyer. 'It's just after half-past ten.'

'I've never been out as late as this before. Have you?'

'No. When my mother and I used to go to the theatre we would go to the first house or the matinée.'

The crowd heaved and parted to make way for a boisterous bunch of young men who had just come out of a public house. Forceful without being belligerent, they were oblivious to the havoc they were causing as more respectable folk had to get out of the way as best they could. Melissa, fearful for her much smaller friend, grasped Reenie firmly by the shoulder and, as she did so, she felt her beaded handbag slip from her grasp.

Having made sure that Reenie was all right, she looked down expecting to see her handbag at her feet. But it had gone. Everything happened quickly after that. She heard a deep voice calling, 'Stop that lad!' and the crowds parted once more as a tall, well-made, gentlemanly figure hurried past.

At the same time a smaller and slighter version of the

gentleman who had rushed past came from nowhere, it seemed, to stand beside them. He shepherded them gently back into the foyer, which had now emptied of theatregoers.

'Are you all right?' he asked.

'Yes, thank you. But my handbag . . .'

'Don't worry. My brother should be able to catch the lad.'

'Lad?' Melissa queried.

'Yes,' the young man said. 'We were just behind you and we saw everything. Two ragged boys were hanging about. They must have been waiting their moment. As soon as that crowd of merry drunkards came by one of them dashed forward and grabbed your bag. Malcolm Thorburn, at your service, by the way, and my brother's name is Fergus.'

Malcolm Thorburn was expensively and tastefully dressed and he had the well-modulated tones of a gentleman. His eyes were blue and his hair was blond. There was no doubt that he could be called handsome.

Melissa became aware that, uncharacteristically, Reenie had remained silent. She glanced at her friend and saw that she was staring at their rescuer in a bemused fashion. She nudged her and, leaning towards her, whispered, 'Don't stare.'

'Sorry,' Reenie whispered back. 'Couldn't help meself. Tell you why later.'

And then the other man, Fergus, returned. He had the same blue eyes and blond hair as his brother but he was even more good-looking. In one hand he held Melissa's handbag and with the other he held a ragged boy by the scruff of the neck – or rather a fistful of his very grubby shirt.

'Your handbag, I believe,' he said to Melissa, smiling gravely.

'Thank you.' She took the bag.

'Would you like to look inside and check the contents?'

'Oh . . . yes.' Melissa opened the bag. In truth it didn't contain very much. A clean handkerchief, a comb, the stubs from the theatre tickets and a few coins. 'There's nothing missing,' she said.

'He wouldn't have had time to take anything,' Malcolm said. 'My brother caught up with him too soon for that.'

Fergus smiled at his brother pleasantly and then asked Melissa, 'And what exactly would you like me to do with this young scoundrel?'

Melissa stared at Fergus Thorburn in perplexity and then down at the boy. 'Do with him?'

'Yes. Would you like me to march him along to the police station?'

At this the lad began to squirm and attempt to get away. Melissa caught her breath when his captor cuffed him sharply round the head.

'Mr Thorburn—' Melissa began.

But the lad glared up at Fergus Thorburn and said, 'You didn't hev to do that!'

'Yes I did.'

The young thief scowled. 'I divven't understand you,' he said sulkily.

Fergus shot him a warning glance and then switched his attention to Melissa. 'Have you decided? What shall I do? Perhaps your – er – friend can suggest something?'

Reenie shook her head.

'What will happen to him if you take him to the police station?' Melissa asked.

'They'll toss him in a cell. Bread and water and then up before the beak. Sentenced to a birching, probably. And he's lucky – not so very long ago he'd have been hanged or transported for merely pinching a handkerchief, never mind a purse.'

Melissa looked at the boy. He looked just like anyone of the children she had seen at the soup kitchen. 'Why did you do it?' she asked him.

'That's obvious,' Malcolm Thorburn said. 'He's a thief.'

'I don't want you to take him to the police station,' she said.

'Very well.' Fergus loosened his grip on the boy's shirt. He felt in his pocket with his other hand. 'Here take this,' he said. He dropped some coins into the lad's grubby hand. 'Get yourself and your pal something to eat. Where is he, by the way?'

'I dunno. He ran off.'

'Well, no doubt he's skulking in some doorway or alley. He'll find you if he thinks you've got money.'

The lad grinned. 'Thanks, mister.'

Now that he was free he turned and fled.

'That was kind of you,' Melissa said.

'I sensed that you had a kind heart,' Fergus replied. 'I wanted to please you and, to tell the truth, I feel sorry for these little urchins.'

By now they were the only people standing in the foyer of the theatre. The commissionaire was locking up the ticket office and a cleaning woman with wrinkled stockings had started mopping the tiled floor.

'Well, now, what are we going to do with you?' Fergus said. 'I feel somewhat responsible.'

'Oh, no, that's all right,' Melissa told him. 'We must go home.'

'Shall I get you a cab?'

'Thank you but it isn't too far. We'll walk.'

'Very well then, my brother and I will escort you.'

'No, please . . . it's not necessary.'

'Oh, but it is. Just look outside.'

Melissa and Reenie both peered out into the darkness. In the time they had been talking night had taken over in the Haymarket. Light shone from the high set windows and open doorway of the cabman's shelter and the market stalls were like oases of light. They were still busy but the respectable theatregoers and coffee-shop customers had gone home and a more raffish crowd strolled along the pavements looking for a different sort of entertainment.

'By the way,' Fergus said, 'I do not believe we have been introduced. I am Fergus Thorburn and this is my young brother, Malcolm.'

'Yes, we know, he telt – told – us,' Reenie said.

'Good. And your names?'

Before Melissa could stop her Reenie began, 'This is Miss Melo—'

'*Melissa,*' Melissa said before Reenie could finish saying 'Melody Fotheringham'. 'Melissa Dornay. And this is my friend—'

'She calls me her friend but I'm really her maid,' Reenie interrupted. 'My name is—'

'Miss Reenie Jackson,' again Melissa spoke quickly before Reenie could come out with, 'Clarabelle Potts'.

'Well, then, Miss Dornay and Miss Jackson, now that we have been properly introduced, I insist that you allow my brother and I to see you safely home.'

Melissa realised that there was little use in protesting further. She didn't know quite how it happened but she found herself walking with Fergus while Reenie and Malcolm followed on behind. Nervous at first, she soon relaxed as Fergus and his brother began to talk about nothing in particular: the warm weather, the new tram routes, how pretty the parks and public gardens were this year.

When the parks and gardens were mentioned Reenie walked closer and nudged Melissa surreptitiously in the back as if she were trying to tell her something. But Melissa didn't understand.

Then Fergus disconcerted her by asking, 'Do you go to the theatre often? Just the two of you?'

Melissa hesitated and Reenie spoke from behind. 'What do you mean, just the two of us?'

'Alone. Without Miss Dornay's family?'

Melissa chose not to answer the question directly. 'This is the first time I've been since I was a child,' she said.

'So what made you decide to go tonight?'

Reenie spoke up. 'We saw two of the performers in the street. They were handing out playbills. We felt like a night out.'

'I see,' Fergus said. But Melissa wasn't quite sure what it was that he saw. He had had his head turned as he listened to Reenie, but now he directed his gaze at Melissa. 'And your family agreed that you could go alone? Accompanied by your companion, of course.'

Melissa was not sure how to answer him. Fergus and his brother were under the impression that she was a 'lady' and that Reenie was her servant. Perhaps now was the time to admit that she was a servant too. But before she could say anything Reenie answered the question.

'The family has gone to their country house,' she said, 'but I'm sure they wouldn't mind Miss Melissa enjoying herself.'

Fergus raised his eyebrows and Melissa imagined that he thought the situation odd. But he was obviously too much of a gentleman to pursue the matter further. She was still wondering whether to bring the game to an end when Malcolm changed the subject entirely.

'Well, I thought it was a jolly good show. Cheerful songs, lively dancing and lots of pretty girls. And quite harmless.'

'Harmless?' Melissa said.

'You know, the sort of entertainment a man could take his wife and family to. Suitable for two young ladies such as yourselves, in fact.'

At this point Reenie stopped suddenly and said, 'Well, we're just about home now. There's no need to trouble yourselves any further.'

'It's no trouble,' Fergus said. 'And even though these streets look eminently respectable, I think we ought to see you to your front door.'

'No, really,' Melissa said.

She knew what had prompted Reenie to say that. Once they got to the Winterton house in the square their little charade would be over. Instead of the 'mistress and her personal maid' going up the grand entrance steps and having the door opened by a footman, they would have to descend into the yard of the semi-basement and, furthermore, climb through a window to get into the house. How undignified! She couldn't help smiling as she imagined Fergus and Malcolm's astounded expressions.

Melissa felt a bubble of amused hysteria rise within her. She knew it wouldn't take much to set her off laughing. But then she glimpsed Reenie's agonised expression. The games they played meant so much to her. Melissa supposed the make-believe world compensated for the sheer drudgery of her existence. And, if she were honest with herself, she enjoyed them too.

When she had been a child her mother had encouraged her to play imaginative games. She had not thought it vain and silly, as Aunt Janet did. Melissa remembered one day when her aunt had called. Mrs Sibbet had opened the front door and then shown her in to their room just as Melissa and her mother, both draped in silks and satins, were pretending to be grand ladies at a ball.

'What is going on here?' Aunt Janet said disapprovingly.

Melissa's mother had smiled. 'We're playing games of pretend.'

'Pretend? What use is that? I don't understand.'

Emmeline Dornay sighed. 'No, I don't suppose you do. Even as a child you never had any fun.'

Aunt Janet's lips thinned. 'Fun? Life's not about fun. It's about hard work.'

'I know,' Emmeline Dornay replied. 'And I work very hard. That's why we need some fun.'

Melissa remembered that her aunt had shaken her head and murmured something about this being no way to bring up a child and that no good would come of it. She said she felt sorry for both of them. But later that night Melissa's mother had told her that it was Aunt Janet who was to be pitied. Lost in this reverie, Melissa failed to notice that they had turned into the square. Reenie was now very agitated indeed.

'Well, that's it, then. Here we are, aren't we, Melissa?' she said loudly.

Melissa looked up to see that Reenie had led them to within a few doors of the Winterton house. 'You can go now,' she said to Fergus and Malcolm. 'Good night – and thank you. We're very grateful but we don't want to keep you any longer, do we, Miss Dornay?'

'Oh, no, indeed we don't,' Melissa said. 'Good night, Mr Thorburn, and thank you.'

'Good night, ladies,' Fergus and his brother said in unison. But they made no move to go.

'Please, don't think me forward,' Fergus said, 'but I hope we'll have the pleasure of meeting up with you again?'

'That would be nice,' Reenie said.

Fergus turned to Melissa. 'Miss Dornay, shall we call tomorrow and leave our cards?'

'Oh . . . er . . . if you wish.'

'Then we had better see you to the door. We don't want to make a mistake and leave our calling cards at the wrong house, do we?'

Melissa heard Reenie sigh. 'All right, then,' her friend said. She led them to the Winterton house. 'Gan up – I mean, go up the steps, Miss Melissa. You've got your key, haven't you?'

'Key?' Melissa looked at Reenie wildly. Had she lost her mind? Had the game become real to her?

Reenie stared hard back at her. It was almost too dark to see her expression but the light falling across her face from the nearest streetlamp, incredibly, revealed that she was smiling.

'Yes, your key. It's in your bag. Go on, open it.'

Bemused, Melissa did as she was told and stared down into her bag helplessly.

'Oh dear, what's the matter?' Reenie asked, putting on a passable show of concern.

Once more it crossed Melissa's mind that her friend ought to be on the stage but the thought was fleeting. She had no idea what Reenie was going to say next.

'It . . . my key . . . isn't . . .' she stumbled.

'Don't say you've forgotten it again? You're always doing that, aren't you, miss?'

'Er – yes – I've forgotten it. What shall we do?'

The last was a genuine question. Melissa felt like laughing again but Reenie must have sensed her amusement because she took hold of her arm quickly and held it with unnecessary force.

'Well, don't worry,' she said. 'You wait here; I'll go down and enter through the servants' entrance. Then I'll let you in.'

'Why can't I come with you?' Melissa asked.

'That wouldn't be proper. Would it? It would be absolutely unheard of.'

Melissa thought she detected exasperation in Reenie's tone.

'Wait a moment,' Fergus said. 'Why don't you simply ring

the front doorbell? Surely the footman will let you in? That's his job, isn't it?'

'Oh, aye – I mean, yes, that's his job but he's off to the country with everybody else and there's only old Mr Beckett here. The poor old thing will be asleep now. It would be unkind to disturb him.' Reenie had almost gabbled her explanation. She paused only long enough to say, 'You wait here with Mr Thorburn and his brother, Miss Melissa. I'll have the door open in a jiffy.'

Reenie opened the gate in the railings and was about to descend the steps to the basement yard when Malcolm Thorburn stopped her. 'Wait, do you think I ought to come with you?' he asked.

'Certainly not,' Reenie said, and she shut the gate with a clang just in time to prevent him from following her. 'It wouldn't be proper.' She vanished into the shadows.

'Erm – I'm sure she won't be long,' Melissa said. 'You really don't have to wait any longer.'

'I wouldn't dream of leaving you standing here alone, even for one moment,' Fergus said. 'The streets are not safe at night. Even streets such as these. I imagine your staff have to be ever vigilant.'

'Yes, I suppose they do. The footman from one of the houses across the square is constantly on the lookout for the homeless children who attempt to make a bed for the night in the garden.'

Melissa was aware that she had spoken sharply but when she looked up at Fergus Thorburn's face she thought the lamplight revealed a wry smile.

'You care about the children,' he said.

'I do.'

While they had been speaking Malcolm had been leaning against the railings. Suddenly he moved towards them and said, 'You shouldn't have much longer to wait.' He smiled at his brother as if he was amused at something.

A moment later they heard the heavy bolts being drawn back at the other side of the front door.

'Oh, good,' Melissa said. 'Thank you so much for waiting with me. Good night.' She began to ascend the steps but was aware that Fergus and his brother had not moved. She turned and gave a constrained smile. 'Good night, then,' she repeated.

'Good night, Miss Dornay.' Fergus bowed slightly.

She heard the front door open and she looked round to see Reenie standing there. The hall was dark, the lamps unlit and Reenie was a small shadow hovering anxiously in the dimness.

At last Melissa heard footsteps receding behind her and she hurried up the rest of the steps in a most unladylike manner. Reenie almost pulled her inside and, after closing the door, the pair of them sank back against it, weak with laughter.

'Reenie . . .' Melissa said when she had caught her breath, 'what have you got us into?'

'Whisht!' her friend whispered. 'We divven't want to wake old Beckett up. Let's gan up to the sewing room; I've left a tray there to make cocoa.' She turned to go. 'Hawway,' she said over her shoulder, forgetting her own admonition to be quiet, 'and we're not going up the back stairs. Not two young ladies like us!'

They raised their chins and, holding their skirts daintily, they swept up the grand staircase as if to the manner born.

A little later, sitting cosily in their robes by the small fire and sipping cocoa, they laughed as they went over and over the night's events. And it was only then that Reenie surprised Melissa by telling her that their two gallant rescuers were the same young men who had been looking at them in the park.

'Are you sure?' Melissa asked.

'Positive.'

'What a coincidence.'

'I divven't think so.' Reenie nodded wisely over her cocoa.

'Are you going to explain?'

'Well, I divven't know how they managed it, but I reckon they knew we were going to the theatre tonight.'

Melissa looked doubtful. 'You can't be sure of that.'

'No, I can't, but it's just as well they were there, wasn't it?'

'Why?'

'Fergus got your handbag back for you, didn't he? And they saw us safely home.'

'To the very door!' Melissa found herself laughing again. 'Oh, Reenie, I didn't know what we were going to do. Our game of pretend would have been well and truly over if they'd seen us climbing in through Mrs Barton's window!'

Reenie grinned. 'Well, they didn't. And you came in through the front door like a proper lady.'

Melissa stopped laughing. 'Have you thought what we're going to do if they call with their cards, as Fergus suggested? I mean, we can hardly invite them in.'

'I'll just hev to keep a lookout,' Reenie said. 'I'll answer the door in one of me nice frocks and take the cards – there's a little silver tray on the hall table – and tell them that you are out visiting. That should do the trick.'

'I suppose so.'

'Divven't fret. I'll see to everything. They won't get in the house but I can drop a hint that we're going to the next band concert in the park. Would you like that?'

'I'm not sure.'

'Well, sleep on it. Tell me in the morning. Good night, Melissa. Thanks to you I've had one of the most enjoyable days in me little life.'

Fergus Thorburn and his younger brother made their way home to an entirely different part of the city. They talked quietly.

'Well, what do you think, now?' Malcolm asked.

'The same as I thought before. She's enchanting.'

'You know what I mean.'

'Yes, I do. That was a funny business at the door. Did you hear the bolts being withdrawn?'

'I did.'

'So even if Miss Dornay had her door key they couldn't have got in that way.'

'And as for her little companion,' Malcolm said, 'it was too dark to see exactly what was happening down there but I could swear she climbed in a window rather than open a door.'

'Really?' Fergus smiled.

Malcolm smiled and nodded. 'So, what do you think we should do?' he asked.

'I think we should tell Mother.'

Chapter Fourteen

The next morning they slept late. When Reenie hurried yawning into the kitchen she found Mr Beckett sitting at the table. He had made himself a pot of tea.

'Eeh, I'm sorry,' Reenie said.

'That's all right, Reenie, but you'd better see to the fire in the range before you make breakfast.'

Reenie turned and regarded the range with resignation. She hated the job. It had been hers when she first came to work in this house and she had never found it any easier. She felt sorry for poor little Polly, whose job it was now. While she was cleaning out the grate and raking the cinders, Melissa entered the kitchen. She took in what was happening and immediately started to make the breakfast. Mr Beckett raised his eyebrows but didn't comment. He reached for the pot and poured himself another cup of tea.

Not long afterwards the three of them sat in cheerful silence, enjoying plates of scrambled egg and bacon, followed by toast and marmalade and a fresh pot of tea.

Mr Beckett surprised them by saying, 'This is very pleasant, isn't it?'

'You mean because Melissa cooked the breakfast instead of me?' Reenie asked.

Mr Beckett laughed. 'Not at all. I mean it's agreeable

sitting here, just the three of us with no one to chivvy us about.'

'Surely no one chivvies *you*, Mr Beckett?' Reenie said.

'You'd be surprised. I may be the senior servant in this house but it's Mrs Barton who rules the servants' quarters.'

'Yes, I suppose it is,' Reenie agreed.

'And now here we are. Left in peace to get on with our lives as we please. And you two have looked after me very well.'

The old valet finished his cup of tea and stood up. 'And now, my dear,' he said to Reenie, 'I wonder if you'd be so good as to go and fetch my newspaper, and I won't trouble you again until lunch time?'

He placed the coins required on the table and left the room.

'Go on,' Melissa said. 'Go and buy his paper and I'll wash the dishes. You'd better change clothes when you get back in case we have guests this morning.'

'Right oh,' Reenie said.

She stuffed her mobcap in the pocket of her apron before taking it off and tossing it across a chair. Mrs Barton had drilled into the maidservants that they must never go out in their pinafores – even if they were only going along the backstreet to the paper boy who stood on the corner.

Melissa viewed the prospect of the Thorburn brothers coming to call with a certain amount of dread. She was sure that Reenie would be able to fend them off but she had not yet made up her mind whether she wanted to meet them in the park again. They were pleasant and amusing, that was true, but she sensed that Fergus had some interest in her that she couldn't quite explain.

Did he want to come courting? That would never do, for she had misled him by letting him believe she was someone she was not. The next time they met should she confess that it had all been a game? Would he be disappointed? Would he lose interest? And if he did, would she mind?

When she had dried all the dishes and placed them back on the dresser she hurried up to the sewing room and tried to concentrate on finishing one of the little woollen smocks she was going to take to Mrs Simmons at the soup kitchen.

Reenie had changed her clothes before she came to join her. Instead of her plain uniform dress she wore one of the summer dresses that Melissa had handed on and altered for her. She had managed to put up her own hair and she was pleased with the result.

'Now what am I going to do about me hands?' she asked. 'Last night I had gloves on, but if Mr Thorburn catches sight of these,' she held her work-worn hands out in front of her, 'he'll realise at once that I'm no lady's maid.'

Melissa looked at her critically. 'Pull those cuff frills down – here, let me. There, they cover most of your hands. Just try to keep them in the folds of your skirt – but try not to be too obvious. And now that you mention it, I wish you'd use the hand cream I bought you,' Melissa added.

'I do! Morning, noon and night. But no amount of cream is going to help, considering the work I do.'

Reenie moved restlessly to the window and looked down into the square. 'Do you think they'll come?' she asked.

'I don't know. I hope not.'

'Divven't you want to see him again?'

'Him?'

'Fergus. He was the one who was paying you all the attention.'

'I'm not sure.'

'Well, hev you decided? Shall I drop a hint about the park, or not?'

'Yes – I mean, no – oh, Reenie, I just can't make up my mind.'

'Well, be quick about it. Look! There's a cab just turning the corner into the square. It must be them. Come and see.'

Melissa joined her at the window and they both looked down nervously as the cab slowed down and pulled to a stop outside the house.

'Do you think I should try and open the door before they ring the bell?' Reenie asked. 'Mr Beckett might hear it and then he'll ask who's called.'

'Just say it was two gentlemen to leave calling cards. That much is true.'

Reenie left the window and hurried towards the door.

'No – it's all right. Come and look,' Melissa said.

'What do you mean?'

'It isn't them.'

Reenie rejoined her at the window and they watched as a well-dressed lady descended from the cab. Melissa didn't know whether she was pleased or sorry that it wasn't Fergus and his brother.

'Is she coming here? Or to the house next door?' Reenie asked.

At that moment the cab began to pull away to complete the journey round the central garden and out again. The woman turned and looked up at the house. Instinctively Melissa and Reenie backed away from the window a little. They didn't think she had seen them.

'Isn't she beautiful!' Reenie exclaimed.

'She's very elegant – and she is definitely coming here.' Melissa said this as the woman began to ascend the grand entrance steps.

She was dressed in clear cerulean blue and as they gazed down they found themselves looking at a nonsensical hat trimmed with tiny blue flowers. The hat was perched precariously on an elaborate coiffure of golden hair.

'Who do you think she is?' Reenie asked.

'I expect she's one of Mrs Winterton's friends who doesn't know that the family is away. You'd better go down and answer the door. And I suppose you'd better invite her in and offer her a cup of tea and then go along to the cab rank and get a cab for her.'

'Divven't you think you should come and offer her the tea? I'm just the kitchen maid.'

'She won't think so when she sees how smartly you are dressed.'

'No?'

'No.'

Reenie considered the suggestion for a moment and then said, 'It's no good, Melissa. As soon as I open me mouth I'll put me foot in it. You'd better come down and explain things to her.'

'Very well.'

The sound of the doorbell echoed through the house.

Reenie hurried away and Melissa followed more slowly. By the time she had reached the bottom of the grand staircase Reenie was coming out of the drawing room. She closed the door behind her and, turning, saw Melissa. She hurried towards her with rounded eyes.

'It's you she wants to see,' she whispered.

'That can't be so.'

'She asked for Miss Dornay. That's you.'

Melissa frowned. 'It's a mystery,' she said.

'Well, you won't solve it if you just stand there. She said a cup of tea would be *just too divine*.' Reenie put on an exaggeratedly posh voice, 'and that I was an *absolute angel*. So gan on in and find out what this is all about.'

Reenie vanished through the door that led to the backstairs and Melissa crossed the hall to the drawing room. She paused for a moment to gather her thoughts and then opened the door and went in.

The unexpected guest was standing by the ornate fireplace. She had taken down the bijou ormolu mantel clock and was examining it so intently that she had not heard Melissa come in. She was reflected in the gilt-framed mirror that hung above the mantel shelf and Melissa could see her rapt expression. The clock face was set between two plump gilt cherubs and framed with a pattern of foliage and sheaves of corn.

Something must have told the visitor that she was being observed but if she was embarrassed to be caught this way she did not betray it.

'Lovely, isn't it?' she said without even looking up. 'French and in the romantic style.'

She replaced the clock on the mantel shelf and only then did she look into the mirror at Melissa's reflection. She turned round and gave a brilliant smile. 'I see you have the candlesticks to match,' she said. 'And so many pretty ornaments. All so . . . so tasteful,' she said.

Melissa could have sworn that her visitor was suppressing a bubble of laughter and the sparkle in her eyes was almost conspiratorial. She thinks that most of this is as vulgar as I do, Melissa thought. She's being tactful but she's also inviting me to share the joke.

Her visitor's blue skirt and jacket were cut to show her trim hourglass figure. A frothy white collar peeped out above the high-buttoned jacket and Melissa's dressmaker's eye realised that this was a clever way of concealing her neck.

How old was she? Melissa could not tell. Perhaps the same age as Lilian Winterton, perhaps even older. But her hair colour was either natural or very skilfully tinted and her glowingly fresh complexion just might owe something to the clever use of cosmetics.

But there was a puzzle. Melissa was sure she had not seen this woman before and yet there was something familiar about her: the startlingly blue eyes and hair the colour of a ripe cornfield.

'Miss Dornay, I take it,' she said.

'Yes. And you are . . . ?'

Even before she answered Melissa had made the connection and it was no surprise to hear her saying, 'Clarice Thorburn.'

Of course. This attractive woman was the mother of Fergus and Malcolm, who had asked if they could call.

As if Mrs Thorburn had read her thoughts she said, 'I told my sons it would not be proper for them to call while your family is away from home. But Fergus was anxious to know whether you are all right after your adventures last night so I promised him that I would come instead.' Her smile was frank and engaging.

'Thank you,' Melissa said. 'But there's no need for concern. Reenie and I are quite unharmed and unperturbed by the incident.'

The last was not entirely true, Melissa thought. I am perturbed but for a different reason. This charming and amiable woman, like her sons, believes me to be the daughter of the house. She was reminded of a quotation from a novel Miss Robson had lent her, a novel by Sir Walter Scott: 'Oh what a tangled web we weave, when first we practise to deceive.'

'Reenie?' Mrs Thorburn said.

'My – er – my companion.'

'You mean the little maid who has gone to make a cup of tea, don't you?'

'Yes.'

'It's very good of you to treat her as you do. Fergus told me that you behaved quite like old friends. But I imagine you must be lonely here when your – when the family is away.'

Melissa was saved from answering when Reenie returned with a tray.

'Where shall I put this?' she asked. She eyed the ornate tripod tables positioned here and there about the large room.

Melissa looked at the highly polished surface of the tables. 'Oh – I'm not sure.'

'Miss Dornay, may I make a suggestion?' Clarice Thorburn said.

'Please do, Mrs Thorburn.'

The tray rattled in Reenie's hands and Melissa heard her gasp, but didn't look at her.

'Why don't we go somewhere less formal? A morning room perhaps?'

'Of course.' Melissa smiled. 'Reenie, I'm sorry, but would you bring the tray upstairs to the morning room?'

'Certainly, Miss Dornay. Go ahead and I'll follow you up.'

Reenie was talking her idea of 'posh' again, and Melissa had to work hard to restrain her laughter.

When they entered the morning room a cheerful fire was already burning in the grate. She looked at Reenie questioningly and her friend grinned.

'I was going to bring our – I mean your – coffee here later.'

Melissa shook out the small embroidered tablecloth that was kept in a little cabinet and spread it on the low table. It was Melissa's own tablecloth but they had thought it wise to use it rather than one of Mrs Winterton's.

Reenie placed the tray there and when she straightened up she said, 'Is there anything else, Miss Dornay?'

'No, thank you, Reenie.'

Reenie bobbed a curtsey and Melissa glared at her. She would have words with her friend and co-conspirator later!

For a moment she busied herself with pouring the tea and when she looked up she saw that Mrs Thorburn had taken off her gloves, which now lay in her lap, and had picked up one of the teaspoons. She was staring at it with pleasure.

'My dear,' she said, when she saw that Melissa was looking at her, 'an apostle spoon. How delightful. Do you have the full set? All thirteen of them?'

'I'm not sure.'

In fact Melissa did not know that the Wintertons had any apostle spoons. She had never seen them before. But obviously Reenie had known and she had rooted them out along with the Minton teacups, which her visitor now turned her attention to.

'Exquisite,' she said as she raised her cup. Then she smiled ruefully. 'You must think I am vulgar to talk like this. But I do so like fine things. Maybe it's because I grew up in genteel poverty but I have never truly got used to the fact that my life is so much easier now. Quite luxurious, in fact. Thanks to my dear late husband.'

'Your late husband?'

Normally Melissa would not have asked such a personal question but she sensed that Mrs Thorburn wanted to tell her.

'Yes, my dear,' Clarice Thorburn sighed. 'With very little discernible talent and relying simply on my looks, I joined a theatrical troupe. I was dreadful!' Here she laughed self-deprecatingly. 'But fortunately I attracted the attention of a wealthy man.'

She sipped daintily from her cup and then looked up in alarm as though something unpleasant had just occurred to her. 'But I should hate it if you thought I had married the darling man simply for his money. It was a love match. Sadly we didn't have many years together but he left me well provided for. And I was determined that my sons should marry as happily as I did.'

So that was it, Melissa thought. She has come here to see

what sort of person I am. She is sounding me out. Melissa didn't know how she should react to this situation. After all, she had only just met Fergus. Nothing had happened between them and she wasn't even sure whether she wanted his attention. But perhaps his mother, wisely, wanted to judge whether she was suitable before allowing Fergus to come calling. Reenie, Melissa thought. What have we got ourselves in to?

But if she was uneasy her visitor did not seem to have noticed.

'How clever,' Clarice Thorburn said, 'to have a little tablecloth embroidered to match the oriental pattern on the teacups. The pink, blue and turquoise of the porcelain are matched exactly in the sprays of blossoms on the cloth. Do tell me – where did you buy it?'

'The cloth?'

Clarice Thorburn nodded.

'Oh, no, I – we didn't buy it. I made it.'

'And embroidered it yourself ?'

'Yes.'

'But it's wonderful. Is embroidery a pastime of yours?'

'Yes, I suppose it is.'

'And who taught you to sew so skilfully?'

'My mother.'

Melissa had responded without thinking and now she saw her visitor looking at her quizzically. They were on dangerous ground. She could not have Mrs Thorburn asking personal questions about the family or where exactly they were and why Melissa was not with them.

The next question when it came was worse than that.

'When will your family be back in town?' Clarice Thorburn asked. 'I should like to make your mother's acquaintance. Perhaps I should leave a card?'

'Oh . . . yes, do.'

Melissa was fairly certain that Lilian Winterton, not recognising the name, would deduce that the person in question was not important and therefore she would simply ignore the card. But in any case, Melissa realised with relief, the card might never be seen by Mrs Winterton, for she could simply tear it up the moment her visitor had gone.

It was time to change the subject. 'Your tea must be cold,' Melissa said. 'Shall I ring for Reenie to bring a fresh pot?'

'Oh, no, that's all right, my dear. I really must be going.'

Clarice Thorburn put on her fine kid gloves and rose gracefully. Taking up a position before the mirror above the mantelpiece, she adjusted her hat. She took out her hatpin and put it in again. Melissa could not see that she had made much difference to the angle of the hat but then, by chance, she saw that Clarice Thorburn was not looking at her own reflection at all. She was using the mirror to observe Melissa herself.

When she saw Melissa looking at her she was not at all abashed. She simply smiled and said, 'I have enjoyed our little chat. I shall tell Fergus that you seem quite unaffected by your adventures last night. No doubt you will be hearing from him. Now, would you be good enough to ring for your maid to see me out?'

'I'll see you out myself.'

Clarice looked at her quizzically.

'I don't like to bother Reenie – she has so much to do.'

'Even with the family away?'

'Yes – well, this is a big house to keep dusted.'

'And you have no other help?' Clarice Thorburn opened her beautiful blue eyes wide, expressing astonishment.

Melissa was flustered. 'Yes – we have. A cook comes in daily, and then of course there's Mr Beckett.'

'Ah, yes, my son mentioned something about an elderly

servant and your not wanting to disturb him last night. Is he quite frail?'

'Not frail – just old and a little tired.'

'And when is the family returning?'

'At the end of this month.'

'Not long then. You must be looking forward to their return.'

'Mm.'

In order to bring this conversation to an end Melissa moved quickly to the door. On the way downstairs and on the landings Mrs Thorburn kept stopping to admire a picture here and a marble bust there.

'How grand,' she exclaimed. 'Melissa, my dear, you live in considerable style.'

Melissa did not reply and Mrs Thorburn said hurriedly, 'You are thinking I have no manners to speak of.'

'No, really . . .'

'Yes, you are and I don't blame you. Those in polite society are not supposed to mention possessions and how much they might be worth. But as I told you, I am quite spontaneous about such things. So please don't take offence.'

'I won't.'

They had reached the bottom of the staircase and Melissa started to lead the way across the expanse of marble tiles towards the front door when Clarice Thorburn suddenly darted towards a set of double oak doors.

'The dining room?' she asked.

Melissa nodded.

'Oh, I must have a peek.' She opened the doors and went in. 'My, I can just imagine the lavish dinner parties you have in here. Such affluence? Or do I mean opulence? My education was sadly lacking, you know. Not like my sons, who went to the best schools I could afford. But, in any case, whatever the word should be, the Wintertons are obviously very prosperous.'

Suddenly Mrs Thorburn's manner changed completely. From gazing round raptly she walked swiftly towards the door and out into the hall.

'I must go,' she said. 'I've taken up enough of your time. And Fergus will be waiting eagerly to see how well we got on.'

Melissa had made up her mind. 'Mrs Thorburn,' she said, 'there is something I must tell—'

'Whatever it is must wait, my dear, for I really must go.'

She had been waiting for Melissa to open the front door but now she opened it herself and stepped out into the sunshine.

'But—'

'Don't worry about sending your maid for a cab,' Mrs Thorburn called over her shoulder as she went down the steps. 'The cab rank isn't far.' And with a graceful wave of her white-gloved hand she hurried away.

Clarice Thorburn's exit had been so sudden that it left Melissa feeling confused. Mrs Fearon would be here by now preparing the lunch and Reenie would be helping so she would not be able to talk to her friend until later. Reenie would be eager to hear what had been said and Melissa needed to talk things over with her.

Despite Mrs Thorburn's free and easy manner Melissa felt she had been subjected to the sort of scrutiny that had left her feeling uncomfortable. She had decided to bring the childish charade to an end and had been about to confess that she was simply a seamstress rather than a member of the family but Mrs Thorburn had not given her the chance.

A short while later Clarice Thorburn reached home. She sat down, placed her feet up on the footstool that Malcolm placed before her chair, took off her gloves and accepted the glass of Madeira proffered by Fergus.

'Well?' her elder son said.

'Perfect,' Clarice replied. 'What a clever boy you are.'

Fergus smiled. 'And when do you think we should call?'

'As soon as possible.'

Both Fergus and Malcolm took up their own glasses and raised them to their mother, who raised her own glass in their direction and then sat back in her chair smiling with anticipation.

Reenie had found time to change into her usual working uniform, and she and Melissa kept glancing at each other over the table while they ate the cottage pie and broad beans that Mrs Fearon served up for lunch. It was delicious and so was the mixed fruit tart and custard that followed. Frustratingly, both Mr Beckett and Mrs Fearon seemed to want to linger over their cups of coffee. Mr Beckett opined how lucky they were to have such a repast when the poor people of Russia had suffered famine for two years.

Eventually Mr Beckett got up, which meant the others could also leave the table. Reenie got up straight away and began to clear the dishes. Mrs Fearon said she would leave the washing-up to Reenie as usual and told them what she had prepared for tea.

Mr Beckett left the womenfolk to it and made his escape to his room to reflect on his imminent retirement. He had a tidy sum saved and had a mind to rent a nice little flat in one of Austin Winterton's new developments in Heaton. What with his savings and the annuity he had been promised for his long and faithful service he would be very comfortable. He would even be able to afford a maid of all work to come in daily and look after him.

These pleasant thoughts were never far from his head, and perhaps that is why he had forgotten to ask Reenie and Miss Dornay about the visitor who had called that morning. He had heard the doorbell, and women's voices when Reenie answered the door. Whoever it was who had called was invited in and seemed to stay for some time.

Most likely the lady, not knowing that the family were away had called to see Mrs Winterton, and Miss Dornay had received her out of politeness. He was pretty sure that everything was above board but all the same he should have asked. Well, he wasn't going back along to the kitchen now. He would mention it some time later.

Once they were alone Melissa told Reenie what had happened during Mrs Thorburn's visit.

'It sounds as though you didn't like her,' Reenie said when she had done.

'I wouldn't put it as strongly as that. I mean, she was friendly and charming at first . . .' Melissa paused and tried to think how she could express her misgivings.

'But?' Reenie said.

'Well, she did go on about the china and the silver and all the lovely things that are in the house. It seemed a bit . . .'

'Vulgar?'

'I suppose so. And yet she was quite open about it. She actually told me that she thought it was because she grew up in poverty that she loved "fine things" as she put it.'

'But she's not poor now?'

'No, she said she had married a wealthy man.'

'She's a bit like Mrs Winterton, isn't she?'

'In what way?'

'Well, gossip has it that Mrs W's parents were quite poor and now she does her very best to spend all her husband's money and let people know there's plenty of it!'

Melissa smiled at this but something nagged at the fringes of her mind; some worry but she couldn't quite pin it down.

'Did you believe her?' Reenie asked.

'Believe what, exactly?'

'About the rich husband? I mean, maybe he didn't leave

her so well off and she's looking for a wealthy heiress for Fergus to marry?'

'Maybe.'

'So she'll be disappointed when she finds out you are not the daughter of the house.'

'I tried to tell her but quite suddenly something made her hurry away.'

There it was again, that troublesome thought that refused to surface.

'Poor Fergus will be disappointed.'

'If his interest in me is genuine.'

'You don't think it is?'

'I'm just not sure.'

'Do you like him?'

'I hardly know him, and now I really don't think we should go on with this.'

'But what if he has fallen in love with you and when he discovers you are not a rich heiress he will defy his mother and beg you to elope with him!'

Melissa laughed. 'You read too many of those penny romances.'

'I know – I love them. Beautiful virtuous maidens and handsome noble heroes who just happen to be rich. There's nothing like a good story to make you forget the cares and the worries of the day.'

'Well, I certainly don't want to elope with Fergus Thorburn, and if he and his brother do come calling in the morning you're not to drop any hints about meeting them in the park – or anywhere else.'

Reenie sighed. 'Right oh. Now, I'd better go and set the table for tea.'

'And afterwards we can get on with some sewing.'

Mr Beckett stayed in his room for tea and when Reenie went to collect the tray he was dozing gently in the armchair by the fire, which was almost out. Reenie kneeled down to make it up a little and then she put the cinder guard in place and rose to go.

'Thank you, my dear,' Mr Beckett said.

Reenie jumped in fright. 'Goodness, Mr Beckett, you frightened the life out of me.'

'I'm sorry.'

'I thought you were sleeping.'

'I was, and I'm glad you awakened me. If I'd stayed there much longer my poor old pegs would have grown stiff and painful. But now I think I'll read for just a little while longer and then have an early night. So you needn't bother to bring a supper tray.'

A wind sprang up that evening and rattled the windowpanes of the sewing room. Both Melissa and Reenie were quieter than usual. Reenie was fretting in case Melissa blamed her for the muddle they had got themselves into, and Melissa, as she cut and pinned and sewed, was trying to tease the knot of worry in her mind and unravel it.

When they said good night and went to bed they both lay awake for a while. Reenie was reluctant to give up her idea of a romance for Melissa, who was so beautiful and so kind and who deserved better than the sort of life she was living with the Wintertons. It was Reenie's dream that one day Melissa would have her own home and, if not a rich husband, then maybe the dressmaking salon she so desired, and that she, Reenie, would go and work for her. That was all she wanted for herself. Just to be able to help the only friend she had ever had.

Melissa lay in bed and listened to the rising wind soughing through the branches of the trees in the square. A memory floated up . . . her father had once said that wind blowing through leaves reminded him of the sound of the sea when it was in a restless mood.

Other sounds grew louder and then faded as the wind began to gust. A church clock striking midnight, a barking dog, a cat yowling and then, puzzlingly, the whinny of a horse followed by a muffled oath.

Melissa fell into an uneasy sleep but all the while her unconscious mind must have been worrying away at the thing that was bothering her. For early the next morning she sat bolt upright as the answer came to her. It was to do with what Clarice Thorburn had said just before her mood had changed and she took her leave. '*. . . the Wintertons are obviously very prosperous.*'

No wonder Fergus's mother had gone so hurriedly. She had made a mistake. She had revealed that she knew who lived in this house. Melissa could not understand it yet but now she feared that Clarice Thorburn's visit might be a more sinister charade than her own.

Chapter Fifteen

'Melissa, wake up!'

Melissa roused herself from her half-sleeping state and raised her head from the pillow. She pushed back her hair and tried to focus on the figure standing in the doorway. It was Reenie, her face pale and wan and showing every sign of agitation.

Thoroughly alarmed, Melissa struggled to sit up. 'What is it?'

Reenie groaned and clasped her hands in front of her, wringing them nervously.

'Are you ill?' Melissa pushed back the bedclothes and swung her legs over the side of the bed.

'No, I'm not ill. It's worse than that.'

What could be worse than that? Melissa wondered. Then caught her breath. 'Mr Beckett? Is he . . . ?'

'No, as far as I know there's nowt wrong with Mr Beckett but he'll hev a blue-faced fit when we tell him.'

'Tell him what?'

Reenie whimpered. She was so obviously distressed that Melissa began to get up to go and comfort her but her friend stopped her.

'Divven't stand up until I've telt you what's happened.'

'For goodness' sake, tell me, then.'

Even though there was no one else to hear her, her voice sank to a hoarse whisper. 'We've been burgled – ransacked. They've been right through the house.'

At first Melissa couldn't take it in. 'Are you sure?' she asked.

'Do you think I'm making it up?' Her friend sounded angry. 'This isn't a joke to scare you. Put your clothes on and come and see for yourself.'

'I'm sorry, I didn't doubt you. I was shocked, that's all.'

'Me too, and I'm sorry I snapped at you. It's no use us falling out, is it? But be quick. I want you to see everything before we tell Mr Beckett.'

They started in the morning room, where Reenie had first discovered that someone had been in.

'I came in to see to the fire so that it would be drawing nicely before we hev our coffee and – look – just look around you.'

Melissa did so and saw that all Mrs Winterton's pretty little ornaments, even the writing set from the desk near the window, had disappeared. There were marks on the wall where the pictures had been hanging.

It was the same story downstairs in the drawing room; the mantel clock, the candlesticks, the Dresden figures, everything gilt and gilded, valuable or simply decorative, was no longer in place. Even the mahogany sofa table and the little Sheraton tripod tables had gone. And here also, the walls were bare of paintings.

So were the walls in the dining room. The felt-lined drawers where the silver was kept were open and empty. Every last knife, fork and spoon had gone, as had the silver salvers from the sideboard. Hideous scratches in the polished surface of the dining table revealed that rough-edged boxes of some sort had stood there while they were filled.

'They hevn't missed much, hev they?'

Melissa felt her heart sink. 'Fergus and Malcolm Thorburn. I should have realised yesterday.'

Reenie frowned. 'What do you mean? We didn't see them yesterday.'

'No, but we saw their mother.'

'So?'

'Just before Mrs Thorburn left she let slip that she knew this was the Winterton house. I was so flustered that I didn't realise straight away what she had said.' Melissa groaned. 'If only I had we could have been prepared.'

Reenie stared at her helplessly. 'I divven't see how,' she said. 'I'm not sure what we could hev done.'

'We could have told Mr Beckett and he would have told the police.'

'And then we would hev been in hot water for playing such a foolish prank.'

'Of course. But not as hot as it's going to be now.'

Reenie folded her arms across her skinny frame and hugged herself. When she spoke it was hardly above a whisper.

'It's my fault. I was carried away with me daft romantic fancies. You the young lady and me your companion. I thought they were watching us because they were smitten by our charms – well, your charms, anyways, and all the time they must hev suspected we were playacting so they decided to get to know us and see what was up.'

'I'm as much to blame as you are,' Melissa said as the truth dawned.

'No, you're not.'

Their evening at the theatre and what had happened afterwards sprang vividly to life in her mind. 'Yes I am. I should have guessed that they arranged for that boy to steal my handbag so that they had a respectable excuse to get to know us. And I should have insisted that you and I took a cab home – alone – so they had no reason to see us to the door.'

'And what a fiasco that was!' Reenie smiled bleakly. 'That business of you not having your key and me going down to let you in. I shouldn't wonder if Malcolm hung over the rail and watched me climbing through Mrs Barton's window!'

Suddenly she turned round and made for the door.

'Where are you going?' Melissa asked.

'Come with me – but be as quiet as you can. Let Mr Beckett sleep just a little while longer.'

Reenie led the way down the backstairs and along the passage to the cook-housekeeper's room. When they were inside she shut the door behind them.

'Look,' she said. She hurried across to the window, the lower half of which was open. 'He's come in the same way I did with a knife to the sneck. And the cheeky beggar hasn't even bothered to close the window behind him.'

Melissa frowned. 'But they couldn't have taken everything they'd stolen out this way.'

'Of course they didn't. One of them got in through the window – Malcolm, I'd guess: he's smaller and thinner than his brother – and crept through to the back door and let the others in.'

'Others?'

'Aye, there'd hev to be more that the two of them. They must be part of a gang. And do you know who I think the gang boss is?'

'Who?'

'Their mother.'

'Of course.'

Melissa remembered the way Clarice Thorburn had lovingly handled the drawing-room clock, the apostle spoons, the Minton teacups – the teacups!

'Have they taken the best tea and dinner services?' she asked.

'No,' Reenie replied. 'It would hev taken too long to wrap every piece. If the house had been completely empty they would hev taken them for sure and they would hev known the best way to do it. Some of these villains started out as genuine removal men.'

'So they knew how to pack the Dresden figures and the crystal vases,' Melissa said.

'Aye, and how to get everything out quickly to the stable yard where a horse and van would be waiting.'

Melissa frowned as a memory surfaced. 'I thought I heard a horse whinnying in the early hours.'

'No doubt you did. They can muffle the poor beast's hoofs with sacking but they can't stop it having its say.'

'Oh, Reenie, what fools we've been.'

They stared at each other unhappily for a moment and then Reenie said, 'We'll hev to tell Mr Beckett what's happened, but let's at least hev a cup of tea first. Hawway along to the kitchen.'

Reenie had already seen to the range before she'd made her dreadful discovery, and now she filled the kettle and warmed the pot. Melissa sat dejectedly at the table wondering what on earth she was going to say to Mr Beckett. For of course she would have to be the one to tell him. She couldn't let Reenie take on that task.

No matter what Reenie said, Melissa felt that she was the one who was responsible for letting the Thorburn brothers gain access to the house. She knew very well that if she had objected strongly enough to them offering to see her and Reenie home they would not have been able to insist. Although, she thought, they might have followed them . . .

Nevertheless she had been irresponsible. They had carried their game of make-believe too far. How Aunt Janet would gloat if she knew about this. She had always said no good would come of it and had tried to discourage Melissa's mother from playing those games. Well, it seemed that in this instance Aunt Janet had been proved right.

'Shall we let him have his breakfast first?' Reenie asked. 'Let the poor man enjoy one last meal?'

'You make it sound as if Mr Beckett will be going to the gallows.' Melissa gave a faint smile but really there was no humour in the situation in which they found themselves. The situation they had brought about by their own actions, Melissa meticulously corrected her thoughts.

'No,' Reenie said. 'It's not him that'll be going to the gallows – it will be us!'

'You're exaggerating.'

'Only just. If Mr and Mrs Winterton think we had anything to do with it it'll mean prison for both of us.'

'Apart from being gullible, how could we have anything to do with it?' Melissa asked.

'They could argue that we knew the thieves and let them in.'

'But if that were true we would hardly be here now, would we? We'd have gone off to share the booty.'

'I suppose so,' Reenie said unhappily. And then her eyes lit up and with a little more animation she said, 'That's a good idea!'

'What is?'

'Why don't we run away? Mebbes gan to London?'

Melissa shook her head. 'If we do that they really will think we were in with the thieves, and if they ever found us – and they would – we wouldn't be able to prove them wrong.'

They stared at each other over the table. The tea in their cups had grown cold. Reenie sighed and stood up. 'I think we'd better get it over with and tell Mr Beckett straight away. Goodness!'

'What is it?'

'Look at the time.' Reenie was looking at the clock on the wall by the dresser.

'Nine o'clock,' Melissa said.

'Aye. So why hasn't Mr Beckett been along to see if breakfast is ready?'

'I think we'd better go and find out,' Melissa said. 'He's probably just overslept.'

'I've never known him do that all the years he's been working here.'

'I know, but he's getting older, and you've said yourself he sleeps a lot lately.'

'Perhaps he's ill?' Reenie ventured.

'Perhaps.'

They looked at each other in alarm, each jumping to her own conclusion. Melissa tried to suppress her darker thoughts but she found herself holding Reenie's hand as they made their way along the stone-flagged passage to Mr Beckett's room. Reenie knocked hesitantly but there was no response.

'He might not have heard that,' Melissa said. She stepped forward and knocked more firmly and after a slight pause she called, 'Mr Beckett?'

Still no response.

'What shall we do?' Reenie asked.

'Ssh,' Melissa said. 'Did you hear that?'

'What?'

They stood close to the door and leaned forward. This time they both heard a muffled groan.

'He *is* ill,' Reenie said. 'Shall we go in?'

Melissa knocked again and called out, 'Mr Beckett, may we come in?'

Not waiting for an answer she opened the door. They had expected to find him lying in bed but the bed was empty. Mr

Beckett, dressed in his nightshirt, was gagged, bound and tied to a hard wooden chair. His face was paper white and his usually neat and pomaded hair was hanging down in long untidy wisps over his face. When he saw Melissa and Reenie he groaned more loudly and they hurried over to free him.

When at last he could stand he began to shake violently. Melissa led him to the bed and urged him to lie, propped up amongst his pillows, which he refused to do until Reenie found his dressing gown. He put it on, tying the cord tightly and then submitted himself to the girls' anxious administrations.

'Eeh, Mr Beckett, what hev they done to you?' Reenie said. Tears were streaming down her face.

He was too distressed to answer but he gripped Melissa's hand.

'Go and get him a cup of tea,' Melissa said. 'Make sure it's hot and sweet.'

Melissa took hold of the chair that had recently been his prison and put it by the bed. She sat and held his hand until Reenie came back with the tea and then watched him drink it.

'Thank you,' he said when he had recovered sufficiently to talk. 'I've been so worried about you.'

'Worried about us?' Reenie said.

'Yes. I didn't know . . . I mean I thought they might have harmed you.'

Reenie shook her head but Melissa saw that she was having difficulty in stemming the tears.

'No, we've not been harmed,' Melissa told him. 'We didn't know anyone had been in the house until we woke up this morning.'

'Have they taken much? I'm assuming we've been burgled.'

Melissa hesitated. She knew how much distress her answer would cause him.

'I can see from your expression that they have. I didn't even hear them enter the house, you know.' He shook his head. 'They must have been in for quite a while when I heard something heavy being dropped along the passage. I opened my door and immediately felt a draught that told me the door to the stable yard was open. Then, I didn't see him coming, but one of them came at me and dragged me back in here. You saw what he did to me.'

'Did you see who it was?'

'A well-set-up young ruffian. I couldn't see his face properly but his hair shone bright gold in the moonlight coming through my window.'

Fergus . . . Melissa thought.

'Did he hit you?' Reenie asked fearfully.

'No. I don't think murder was his intent. Just larceny. Well, I suppose I'd better get up and see exactly what they have taken.'

'But first you must have some breakfast,' Melissa told him. 'Reenie and I will see to it and then come back for you.'

Mr Beckett's smile was gentle. 'No need for that. I believe now that I have recovered a little I will be able to come along to the kitchen under my own steam. And just a hot sweet cup of tea, please, and perhaps a slice of toast. We mustn't delay too long before the police are informed.'

No one could eat even a bit of toast, although all had second cups of tea. It seemed they were all reluctant to leave the table and go to inspect the burgled rooms. When they did the old manservant's face grew paler and paler as they surveyed the extent of the theft.

When they reached the morning room he said, 'It's almost as though the thieves knew exactly where to go and what to take – as if they had been in the house and had a thorough look around.'

At this Reenie gave a strangled sob and fled from the room.

Mr Beckett may have been old and tired but he still had his wits about him. 'What do you suppose Reenie knows about this matter?' he asked Melissa.

'Nothing! Reenie knows nothing! It wasn't her fault.' Melissa stopped. She had already made up her mind about what she was going to say.

Mr Beckett looked at her shrewdly. 'I think you and I should sit down and have a talk before we summon the constabulary,' he said.

Melissa knew that she must do everything possible to help catch the thieves but she did not know where to begin. Mr Beckett did not need to know about the countless games of make-believe she and Reenie had played. And in any case she wanted to absolve Reenie of any blame. Eventually she made it seem that it was all her own idea to pretend she was a daughter of the house.

'But why on earth do that?' Mr Beckett asked.

She looked down at her hands clasped tightly in her lap and remained silent.

'Foolish pride, I suppose,' her interlocutor said. 'It does not behove us to pretend we are something that we are not in order to make ourselves seem more important. I must admit that I had thought better of you, Miss Dornay.'

Melissa felt herself flushing. It had never been like that. Their games of make-believe had been light-hearted fun to amuse only themselves – never to impress others – but she could not tell the kindly old man that for fear of involving Reenie.

'Go on, then,' Mr Beckett said. 'I must hear all of it.'

She went on with her story and, without telling actual untruths she hoped she had managed to imply that she had led an unwilling Reenie into the foolish and dangerous escapade.

When she had done Mr Beckett rang the bell. When Reenie answered, her tear-streaked face a picture of misery, he said, 'Miss Dornay tells me that she has been very foolish, but she insists that you had nothing to do with it. I am going to write a letter, which you will take to the police station in Pilgrim Street. Is Mrs Fearon here yet?'

'She's just arrived.'

'Very well. I shall come down and have a word with her and then I am going to try and make some sort of inventory – a list of all we think has been stolen. I shall give this to the police and answer any questions they might care to ask. Then I will set off for the country house. Although the police will no doubt offer to inform him, I do not want Mr Winterton to hear about this from anyone but me. After all, I am responsible.'

'No!' Melissa and Reenie cried in unison.

'You are not responsible,' Melissa said. 'I am.'

'You may think so, but I was left in charge of this house and of you. I must answer for what has happened here.'

Both girls stared at him glumly.

'But whatever has happened,' he added, 'we will better be able to cope with things if we eat whatever Mrs Fearon sets before us at lunch time.'

Mr Beckett wrote the letter for Reenie to take to the police station and, when she had gone, he asked Melissa to help him make the list of missing valuables. They went from room to room with him dictating and Melissa writing everything down. As the list grew to several pages, she became more and more aghast at what she had been responsible for. When Mr Beckett observed her condition he made her sit down. They were in the dining room and she stared at the scratches on the dining table.

Seeing the direction of her glance he said, 'A good French polisher will be able to repair that. And as for all these valuable objects,' he pointed to the papers she had placed before her, 'they will be insured. The Wintertons will not suffer financially.'

'All those beautiful and expensive things . . .' Melissa said.

'Most of them expensive but not all of them beautiful.' He gave a wan smile. 'None of them were heirlooms, you know. The Wintertons are not an old family so nothing has been handed down over the generations. There is no sentiment attached to any of them. Everything that the thieves have taken is replaceable.' He paused and Melissa thought she glimpsed that smile again. 'And after her initial shock and rage, Mrs Winterton will thoroughly enjoy herself buying new things.'

'Why are you being so kind to me? I don't deserve it.'

'No, you don't. But you are not a wicked girl, you are a foolish one and, as I have been negligent of my duties, I do not feel it is my place to chide you. That is for others to do.'

He shook his head and Melissa felt a chill of foreboding.

'Ah, I think that is the constabulary arriving.' Loud voices echoed up through the house. 'I will receive them in Mrs Barton's sitting room and show them the window. After I have spoken to them no doubt they will want to question you.'

He led the way downstairs and Melissa followed. Her thoughts were in turmoil. She would answer the questions as truthfully as she could but first she must contrive a moment alone with Reenie. And she would have to be firm.

Reenie had returned, along with a police sergeant and a constable. Mr Beckett took them to the housekeeper's room and Mrs Fearon, bursting with curiosity, tried to find out as much as possible from Melissa and Reenie. They were not very forthcoming and, obviously cross with them, the cook made a point of clashing the pans and making much more fuss than usual.

When it was time to eat she served up large plates of Irish stew, for the two policemen as well, and intimated that if all plates were not cleared the culprits would have her to answer to.

When the policemen were ready to go Mr Beckett packed an overnight bag and sent Reenie along to the cab stand to fetch him a hansom.

'Do you really have to go?' Mrs Fearon asked. 'The police sergeant offered to telegraph the local constabulary and ask someone to inform Mr Winterton.'

'No. That wouldn't do. I must face the master myself.'

'Well then, couldn't you wait until morning? I don't like to think of you setting out on such a journey as late in the day as this.'

'It's only three o'clock and, depending on the trains, I should be at Brampton in not much more than an hour. The stationmaster will find a hire carriage to take me the rest of the way to Fernbeck.'

'I can see you're determined.'

'I am. And now I must ask you to come in tomorrow as usual and continue to do so until Mrs Barton returns.'

'Very well, Mr Beckett. And I wish you luck.'

After the old manservant had gone Mrs Fearon didn't linger. She took off her pinafore, put on her coat and hat, and hurried away. Melissa guessed she was eager to tell her family all about the robbery.

Reenie was silent while she scrubbed out the pans. Then, wordlessly, she made a pot of tea and put it on the kitchen table along with the milk and sugar. Melissa got the cups and saucers from the dresser.

Then Reenie burst out, 'Why wouldn't you let me tell them what really happened?'

'I couldn't do that. Not after I'd told them that you were only a maidservant and had had to do just as you were told. If you had contradicted that it would have made me a liar.'

'Why do you want to take all the blame?'

'Because I do feel that it's mostly my fault. I should have known better.'

Reenie flushed. 'Are you suggesting that I couldn't have known better because I'm somehow inferior?'

'Oh, Reenie, you'll never be inferior to me or anyone. You're priceless.'

'Hmm.' Reenie looked only slightly mollified. 'I still feel that I ought to say something.'

'Please don't. I don't want Mrs Winterton to dismiss you.'

'Why ever not? I can find another job.'

'What sort of job would that be if Mrs Winterton refuses to give you a reference?'

'The same goes for you.'

'Not quite. I'm not supposed to be a servant here. Remember? I was taken in as the daughter of a friend of Mrs Winterton's.'

'But she treats you like a servant. It's a disgrace!'

Melissa remained silent.

'Do you think she'll ask you to leave?'

'Not if she remembers her promise to my mother.'

'Huh!'

'But if she does ask you to leave, what will you do? Where will you go?'

'I'm a dressmaker – and a good one. I'll be able to find work.'

'But will I ever see you again?'

'I hope so.'

Reenie started snivelling again. Melissa passed a clean handkerchief across the table. 'Do you want to know what the police sergeant told me?'

Reenie dabbed at her eyes and looked up.

'He said that they had a pretty good idea who had robbed the house.'

'We know who it was. It was the Thorburn brothers.'

'Ah, but that is not their real name. The sergeant asked me to describe them – and their mother. He knew straight away who they were.'

'And what is their name?'

'Nobody knows. They keep changing it. But it's them, all right. Or so the sergeant said. Two good-looking young men and their handsome mother. The police know all about them but they've never been able to catch them in the act – or prove anything.'

'But if they catch them this time you and I will be able to identify them.'

'We'll be able to say that we knew them. But we didn't see them while they were actually in the house stealing things, did we?'

'No, I suppose not.' Reenie sighed and looked dejected. But then she perked up again. 'But they'll have to sell the things they stole, won't they? And Mr Beckett gave the police inspector a detailed list.'

'Yes, they'll sell them. But not in this city. In fact, the police think they will have vanished by now.'

'But what about all the things they've stolen?'

'Loaded into an innocent-looking removal compartment and sent by train early this morning, in all likelihood. They'll probably stay away and out of trouble until the money runs out. And then they might come back to Newcastle or go to another town. The police sergeant told me that Fergus and Malcolm, whatever their real names, have been criminals all their lives. Taught well by both mother and father.'

'But their father is dead, isn't he?'

'No one knows for sure. He vanished for good after he

had murdered an old gentleman whose house he was burgling.'

'A murderer!'

'Yes, and his sons are to be feared too. The sergeant said that if we really are innocent we've been extremely lucky.'

'And Mr Beckett too.' Reenie shivered. 'Do you think they'll come back and finish us off ?'

'I don't think so. They'll be well away from here by now. But even if they do come back you needn't worry. There's a policeman at the front door and another at the back.'

'To guard us?'

'Maybe,' Melissa said. 'Or maybe they are watching us to make sure that we don't run away.'

Chapter Sixteen

The family came home. The following morning Melissa was summoned to Mr Winterton's study. He did not ask her to sit but kept her standing all the while he questioned her. His manner was abrupt and his glance piercing. When he had no more questions to ask he stared at her coldly for several minutes before speaking.

'I am inclined to believe you,' he said. 'My daughter believes that you have somehow connived with the gang of thieves in order to rob us, but I have come to the conclusion that your foolish pride made you vulnerable and open to exploitation.'

Melissa held her head high and tried to return his gaze without flinching. At least she could take some comfort from the fact that he did not believe she was a criminal.

'Now, before I send for my wife and we decide what to do with you,' he continued, 'I will ask you once more. What part did the dim-witted little maid play in this?'

Angered by his description of Reenie, Melissa felt herself flushing but, nevertheless, kept her voice steady when she replied, 'Reenie is not to blame. She always does as I tell her.'

Mr Winterton narrowed his eyes. 'I'm not sure if that is a completely satisfactory answer but it's true she is a servant and would therefore not be able to refuse to do as you told her.'

Melissa remained silent.

'I shall not punish the girl,' Mr Winterton said. 'It is enough that she has had an appalling shock. But now would you bring Douglas in. He is waiting outside the door.'

Melissa opened the door and the young footman entered straight away. He brushed past her and went straight to the desk. Mr Winterton told him to go and ask Mrs Winterton to attend and Douglas left without once glancing at Melissa.

I am a pariah, she thought. No one here will admit to being my friend. But then even those who were prepared to pass the time of day with me were never truly my friends. Only Reenie . . .

Mr Winterton remained silent but pointed to the place before his desk where she had been standing just before. Melissa understood this to be a command that she return there.

When Douglas returned, not only was Mrs Winterton with him but also Gwendolyn. Her father looked surprised at her presence but he did not object.

'Douglas, will you arrange some chairs for my wife and daughter?' he requested. 'Here – one at each side of me.'

The footman did as he was told. When he had gone and Mrs Winterton and Gwendolyn had taken their seats, Melissa stood facing them across the desk. Three pairs of basilisk eyes regarded her coldly.

I feel as if I am one of the accused before the Spanish Inquisition or in the French Revolution, Melissa thought.

Then Mr Winterton spoke to his wife as though Melissa was not there. 'In all probability the girl is telling the truth,' he said. 'Mr Beckett believes her story and so do I. She is not a criminal.'

'Don't you think it's criminal to pretend you are someone

you are not?' Gwendolyn burst out. 'How dare she go about pretending that she is a daughter of this house? How mortifying if anyone were to believe she was my sister!'

'I didn't—' Melissa exclaimed, and as all three pairs of eyes swivelled in her direction she faltered.

She had never pretended to be the Wintertons' daughter. The games she and Reenie had played had not been as specific as that – not until the night the Thorburn brothers had insisted on seeing them home. But how could she explain that without involving Reenie?

'What were you about to say?' Gwendolyn demanded haughtily.

'Nothing.'

'Just as well, for there is nothing you can say. My mother took you in when your mother died and we have been more than good to you. You ought to be eternally grateful and instead you have been thoroughly dishonourable. If my father doesn't think you are dishonest then I do!'

'Gwendolyn . . .' her mother said. Until now Lilian Winterton had remained silent but now she seemed to rouse herself. 'You must not contradict your father, my dear, although I can understand why you are angry.'

'What about you, Mama? Aren't you angry?'

'Yes, I am. And I am very disappointed in Melissa. But now we must allow your father to decide what is to be done.'

The stare Gwendolyn directed at Melissa was entirely hostile. Lilian avoided looking at her completely.

Austin Winterton cleared his throat. 'I was going to ask you what should be done, my dear,' he said to his wife. 'After all, you were responsible for bringing her in to this house.'

'You want me to decide?'

'It is your place to do so. You counted her mother as a friend and no doubt you will want to honour that friendship. But you should also consider your loyalty to your husband

and your daughter. I trust you to make the right decision.'

He's pretending she has a choice, Melissa thought. But he's also made it clear that she hasn't.

Lilian Winterton looked down at the shining expanse of the desk in front of her. Eventually she raised her head and looked at Melissa. 'What my daughter says is quite true,' she said. 'I promised your mother I would give you a home if the need arose, and I did. You have been fed and clothed and wanted for no material comfort.'

'That is true. But I think I have earned my keep.'

'And so you should have done!' Gwendolyn interjected.

'Gwendolyn, let your mother speak,' her father said.

'Yes, you have worked hard,' Lilian continued. 'But you cannot deny that I have fostered your talent; given you every opportunity to learn and to gain experience.'

'Only so that I could make you and Gwendolyn the very latest fashions.'

'Be quiet!' Mrs Winterton said. Now she was angry. Melissa saw any lingering doubt she might have was fast disappearing. 'It ill behoves you to talk like this. Not after what you have done.'

Melissa knew that this was true but she had been angered by Mrs Winterton's suggestion that everything had been for her welfare rather than a means for the Winterton women to have the latest fashions at very little cost. But even so, she knew the family had every right to be angry.

'I'm sorry,' she said. 'Truly I am.' To her dismay she felt hot tears begin to run down her cheeks. Hastily she raised a hand and brushed them away.

'Huh!' Gwendolyn said. 'Crocodile tears.'

'Hush, my dear,' her mother said. 'Your father has asked me what must be done.' She paused. 'And I have decided Melissa must go.'

*

Melissa went straight to her room. She did not go to the kitchen for the midday meal. She had not gone down for tea either as she could imagine only too clearly what would be said by the household staff. And she knew she deserved it.

Reenie sought her out early in the afternoon and found her taking her clothes from the chest and the wardrobe and putting them on the bed. Melissa had pulled her trunk out from beneath the bed and opened the lid. Reenie stared at her in dismay.

'So she's putting you out?' she said.

'I suppose you can hardly blame her.'

'Do you have to leave straight away? That's cruel!' She could hardly speak for sobbing.

'I've been given a week to find somewhere to live.'

'Then why are you doing this now?' she asked as she watched Melissa emptying the chest of drawers.

'I want to be ready. There's no point in wasting time.'

'But where does she expect you to go? A young woman alone in the world.'

'Mrs Winterton reminded me that I had an aunt.'

'Your Aunt Janet?'

'Yes.'

'The wet blanket?'

'That's the one.'

Melissa smiled when she remembered the conversation they had had the first time she had told Reenie about her mother's sister and the way she had disapproved of them.

'But you wouldn't want to go to her, would you?'

'No.' And in any case I couldn't, Melissa thought.

She paused in her task and held a bundle of folded underwear to her chest as her mind returned to the day of her mother's funeral. She had stood in the open door of the front parlour, her mother's sewing room, and listened to Mrs

Winterton arguing with her aunt. Her aunt was angry and, reluctantly accepting that she was not going to get her own way, she had screeched, '... *I warn you, if things ever go wrong for Melissa – if you should tire of keeping her – that's just too bad. Tell her not to come to me!'*

Then Melissa, revealing her presence, had called out, *'I wouldn't want to!'*

And she still felt that way. She had too much pride to go to that hateful woman and ask for shelter. But in any case, even if she did, there was no doubt that her aunt would turn her away, though not before gloating over the misfortune that she had predicted.

Suddenly Melissa threw the neatly folded bundle of underwear down into the trunk and took her coat from the wardrobe.

'Where are you going?' Reenie wailed.

'I'm going to look for somewhere to live so that I can leave here as soon as possible.'

'Are you coming back?'

Melissa, seeing the panic in her friend's face, took hold of Reenie's hands. 'I'm coming back tonight if that's what you mean. We'll say goodbye properly, I promise you.'

After he had seen Melissa, Austin Winterton sent for Charles Beckett.

'You know you have to go, don't you?' he said.

'Yes, sir.'

'Well ...' Austin Winterton paused, 'I believe Douglas is quite capable of taking over from you as my valet. You've trained him well.'

'Thank you, sir.'

'And because of that I am not going to withdraw my offer of an annuity. You will be looked after.' He paused again. 'One of the new flats in Sandyford will be made ready for you, but before you go there are certain matters I want you to discuss with Douglas. Things he should know.'

'I understand, sir.'

'And you must impress upon him that an important part of being a good valet is to be discreet about his master's – erm – affairs, at all times.'

'Of course, Mr Winterton.' He bowed his head.

They understood each other perfectly.

Meanwhile Lilian Winterton was showing Lady Paule around the house and asking her advice on how she should redecorate and furnish the plundered rooms. Charlotte Paule was the same impoverished aristocrat who had advised her before and whose scheme for the drawing room had delighted her.

Austin had been very understanding. He had just about given her *carte blanche* to order whatever she would – so long as her plans remained within the boundaries of good taste. He had climbed further in society of late and, just as much as Lilian herself, he needed his home to be both elegant and impressive.

When Charlotte had gone, Lilian, exhausted, retired to her bedroom for an afternoon nap. But she found her thoughts whirling. To Lilian's delight the impoverished Lady Paule had said, 'Oh, do call me Charlotte, Mrs Winterton, and I will call you Lilian if it pleases you.'

Pleases me! Lilian was overjoyed to be on such intimate terms with someone from such an exalted position in society, even if she was as poor as a church mouse.

Eventually she found herself relaxing into a much-needed sleep, only to be awoken again with the unwelcome thought that she would have to find another dressmaker.

Melissa stood outside the house where she had grown up and wondered who lived there now. The house and its neighbours were not quite as she remembered them. Somehow they looked smaller and even a little shabby. But the gardens were tidy and the doorsteps were soapstoned, and each brass doorknob and letter box gleamed with the effects of daily polishing.

Of course, Miss Bullock no longer lived here. Melissa remembered that their former landlady had announced her intentions of going to live with a niece by the sea. And Martha Sibbet, where was she? Miss Bullock had promised to give the kindly woman a good reference so Melissa was sure she would be all right.

She looked lingeringly at the house where she had been so happy. Even if the new owner of the house did let rooms, Melissa knew that she would not be able to afford one. Reluctantly she took the tram to Scotswood; she would be able to rent a room more cheaply there. Here, to the west of the city, the streets lurched precipitously down towards the river. Instead of small gardens with half-walls and railings, the front doors opened straight on to the pavements.

The day had been warm and the pavements were hot and dusty. There was a slight wind blowing from the direction of the bone yard. But the homes were respectable enough and the children playing in the street looked reasonably clean. Melissa knew that many of the housewives in streets such as this let rooms to supplement their husbands' wages. Eventually she found what she was looking for: a corner shop. She went in.

The tinkle of the bell above the door brought the shopkeeper from the back room to stand behind the counter. He was an Asian gentleman wearing a sand-coloured overall over what looked like a smart suit.

'Can I help you, madam?' he asked.

Melissa thought she had better buy something and chose a quarter of a pound of pear drops to take back for Reenie.

After the shopkeeper, Mr Ali, as Reenie was to learn later, had shaken the pear drops into the scales and tipped them into a cone of paper, Melissa paid for them and then she told him what she really wanted.

That night Reenie helped Melissa to pack her clothes and belongings. They were very careful not to pack anything that Mrs Winterton might say was her property. The last to go in was the doll, Ninette.

'How are you going to carry all this lot?' Reenie asked.

'I shall have to get a cab.'

'I'll go and fetch one for you in the morning.'

'Before breakfast. I don't want to have to say goodbye to anyone. None of them has ever made me welcome here and now they are positively gloating.'

'Mrs Barton's not so bad.'

'No, but that can't be helped. I'm determined to leave as early as possible.'

Neither of them slept and when Reenie crept down from the attic floor even before the milk or the ice had been delivered, Melissa was dressed and ready to go.

'The cab's waiting,' Reenie said.

To Melissa's surprise Douglas was waiting by the door of the backstairs in order to help them down with the trunk and the bag.

'I hope you don't mind,' Reenie said. 'I told him last night because I knew we wouldn't manage on our own.'

Once they had reached the ground floor Melissa stopped Douglas from going down another flight to the kitchen.

'When I arrived at this house I entered by the front door,' she said. 'And I've already told Reenie that is how I intend to leave it.'

Douglas grinned as he and Reenie carried the trunk across the wide expanse of marble. He withdrew the bolts as quietly as he could and then helped them stow Melissa's belongings in the cab.

For one heart-wrenching moment Reenie clung to her as if she would never let her go and Melissa had to signal Douglas with her eyes. He came forward, took hold of Reenie and led her gently back to the steps. Then they both stood there as Melissa climbed up into the cab, and with a crack of the whip the cabman started their journey round the square towards the main street.

Melissa waved once and then turned her head and looked forward determinedly. She was leaving the Wintertons' house under a cloud. She did not have a reference, nor did she have sufficient money saved to set up a proper dressmaking business of her own.

And yet as they turned out of the square and the large houses started to recede into the distance, Melissa felt her heart lifting. Half-forgotten dreams began to stir into life under the threshold of her conscious mind. She was on her own but she was her mother's daughter. She would make those dreams come true.

Part Three

A Dream to Share

Chapter Seventeen

November 1893

Melissa pulled the curtains back as far as she could. There was only a half-net at the window but the room was still dark. And on days like this, with a sea fret creeping up the cobbled streets from the river, it was bitterly cold. Damp sooty air entered the house like a thief through the badly fitting window frames to seep into her very bones and steal all the warmth from her body. Nevertheless she pulled her shawl tightly around her shoulders and sat close to the cold windowpanes in order to catch what light there was.

Behind her a small fire crackled and the glowing embers were inviting; but if she sat by the fire to warm her toes she would not be able to see what she was doing. She could light her lamps but she had to be sparing with the lamp oil and her landlady, Mrs Bruce, controlled what time of day the gas lamps were lit.

Mary Bruce was careful with her money but she was a good landlady. As long as Melissa paid her rent on time she did not interfere and made no objection to the comings and goings of Melissa's customers. Although she reminded

Melissa constantly that they must wipe their feet well before entering her spotless hall.

Mary's husband, Tom, worked in the shipyards as a riveter. He worked long hours standing on wooden staging sixty or seventy feet above the shipyard floor with his workmate Geordie. Tom was right-handed and Geordie left-handed, and they hammered in the rivets with alternate strokes, their ears ringing with the sound. Tom Bruce brought good money home, but Mary saw no reason why the back bedroom and the front parlour, which they hardly ever used, should not bring in a little more. Mary did most of her grocery shopping at Mr Ali's corner shop and she never asked for 'tick'.

Tom and Mary had no children – it just hadn't happened – but nevertheless Tom didn't want Mary to go out to work. So she had thrown all her energy into keeping a comfortable home for him. The money she earned from lodgers helped her to buy 'nice' things and even put a bit away for rainy days.

Until recently all her lodgers had been men. Not what Mary called real working men like her Tom, but humble clerks with soft ink-stained hands, and storekeepers or shop workers. When the previous lodger left to get married she was just about to advertise for a new lodger.

Mary had often remarked to Mr Ali that she longed for a bit of female company – a female of the respectable sort, of course – so she was delighted when one day a smartly dressed young woman knocked at her door and said that Mr Ali had told her about the vacancy and had recommended Mrs Bruce as a landlady.

Both Mary Bruce and Melissa had been happy with the resulting arrangement, Mrs Bruce because Melissa was respectable-looking and even what Mary considered to be genteel. Melissa was pleased because the house was clean and the meals Mrs Bruce provided, although plain, were nourishing. Her landlady preferred to do all the cooking as she didn't want folk in her orderly kitchen. This meant that she charged a little more but Melissa accepted the arrangement gratefully. It would give her more time to get on with her dressmaking.

Melissa spent a large proportion of her savings on a second-hand sewing machine and made a visit to Wilkinson's to set herself up with the basic: needles, pins, threads and some ribbons. She had not taken anything from the Winterton house and had to start afresh.

Eileen Briggs, the assistant who usually served her, had looked askance at Melissa; this was not the usual sort of order for the Winterton household.

'I'm setting up on my own,' Melissa said. 'I . . . I've always wanted to.'

'Have you got a business card?' Eileen asked.

'No, not yet.'

'You'll have to have a trade card,' the friendly assistant said. 'Any little print shop would do some for you. Your name and address and a nice picture. One or two dressmakers leave their cards here. Look, I'll show you some.'

Some of the cards simply gave the name and the address of the dressmakers, but others had tiny drawings of graceful young women sitting at a sewing machine or sitting on a chair doing some hand sewing on a gown displayed on a body form. Melissa thought the cards delightful and decided to have some made as soon as she could afford it.

'I'd be happy to hand your cards to prospective customers and I would certainly recommend you,' Eileen said.

'Thank you. I'll consider it,' Melissa told her, 'but I've only just started out and I can't afford any cards at the moment.'

Eileen smiled. 'I'm sure you'll be able to afford some soon, but meanwhile write your address in this little book I keep on the counter.'

Melissa did so but when the older girl picked up the book to examine the address she frowned.

'What is it?' Melissa asked.

'Well, I don't wish to offend, Miss Dornay, but some folk might not wish to come to that locality.'

'It's perfectly respectable.'

'I know it is, but people have silly misconceptions. And they don't want to tell their friends that they've found a dressmaker in what they consider to be the wrong part of town.'

This is what Melissa had been afraid of, but she simply could not afford rooms in the 'right' part of town.

'Perhaps you should move to somewhere such as West Jesmond when your business starts to prosper,' Eileen suggested. 'Meanwhile, I will recommend you without fear. I know how good you are.'

Mr Ali allowed her to put a home-made card in his window and was happy to send clients her way. Most of the work had been mending and altering; taking seams in or letting them out, letting hems down or adding a band of material on to the bottom of a dress for a growing child. There was also tedious work such as turning collars and cuffs but this kind of thing told Melissa much about her customers. They might be hard up but they wished to appear clean and decent.

There had been plenty to keep her occupied but she could charge no more than a few pence for work like this. However, she had to pay her rent and she could not afford to turn customers away. She began to worry about her diminishing savings.

Then one day an attractive young woman arrived clutching the latest fashion magazine and a brown paper parcel, which Melissa guessed contained some fabric. She invited her in and the young woman entered with a waft of musky perfume. Melissa saw that although she was dressed fashionably someone should have guided her to a more elegant look. She was a little 'showy'. Her visitor introduced herself as Cora Willis and opened the magazine to show Melissa an illustration of a modish evening gown. She asked her if she could copy it.

'I can copy the style easily,' Melissa had told her, 'but this fabric is very expensive.'

'Oh, that's all right,' the young woman said. She opened up the parcel to reveal a shining bundle of burgundy silk and some lace trimming in a darker shade. 'My cousin Eileen works at Wilkinson's and she can find me remnants intended for the sales – perfectly good fabrics but not enough left to put on the shelves. It was Eileen who recommended you, you know.'

Melissa was overjoyed. This was exactly the sort of thing she wanted to do. She pulled the screen forward across the window and Cora stripped down to her silk underwear so that Melissa could take her measurements. She soon discovered that her first proper customer, although seemingly easy-going, had some very definite ideas of what she wanted. And some of those ideas were not in the strictest of good taste.

So, just as Melissa's mother had had to advise Lilian Winterton to be more restrained, Melissa endeavoured to persuade Cora that sometimes understatement was more attractive than extravagant frills and flounces. After a brief exchange of opinion Cora suddenly shrugged and smiled.

'Well, I dare say you know best,' she said, and after extracting a promise from Melissa to have the gown ready as soon as possible, she got dressed and left.

Melissa found it no hardship to work long hours. She was thoroughly enjoying herself. She hoped that this was the beginning of her new life. She hoped that it would not be long before word got round and other such customers started flocking to her door. She was confident that once Cora's friends saw the gown they would want to know who made it and then, perhaps, as well as copying the latest modes illustrated in the magazines, some of them would let her draw her own designs.

But all the while she worked on Cora's evening gown Melissa did not neglect her regular customers. They had brought her their simple mending and alterations and had come to rely on her. She could not let them down now.

When the dress was finished Cora was delighted.

'It's marvellous,' she said, 'just marvellous! I think I have found a perfect treasure in you, Melissa my dear. Now,' she produced a clipping from a magazine from her handbag, 'what do you think? Would this one be easy to copy?' Cora handed the clipping to Melissa. The dress was similar to the first one except that it had a more daring décolletage. 'Emerald-green taffeta, I think, for this one. And I suppose you had better adjust the neckline a little – you know, make it a little more modest; fill it in with some lace frills. I take your point about not being obvious.'

Cora laughed a deep throaty laugh and Melissa was puzzled. Nicely spoken though the young woman was, there was a certain brash air about her. Melissa could not imagine where exactly she was going to wear these gowns.

But how wonderful to have more interesting work to do. Cora had promised to pay five shillings and sixpence for each gown and she said that if Melissa could finish the second dress as quickly as possible she would be prepared to pay twelve shillings for the two and that she would collect them together when they were both finished.

'I shall tell Eileen to see that everything you need is delivered; I don't want you to have to waste time going into town.'

Melissa finished all the mending work she had in hand so that she was ready to start work on Cora's second dress. But there was something she did not wish to put aside. Not long after she had moved in to Mrs Bruce's house she had gone to the old almshouse to tell Mrs Simmons that she had left her place of employment. She didn't think it necessary to explain further but she said she was no longer in a position to make clothes for the street children.

'If it's just a matter of finding bits of cloth,' the kindly woman said, 'then there is no problem. As I told you when we first met, many of the ladies who help here are willing to pass on the clothes they have finished with. Would you be able to utilise them?'

'Of course I would,' Melissa told her.

Not long after she had moved in to her lodgings she had written to Reenie asking her to visit. Her friend had done so on her first day off after receiving the letter. She had walked all the way and her cheeks were glowing when she arrived. She entered the house and wiped her feet without being told. She looked around, her eyes shining.

'Your own place at last!' she said. 'And you've got it so nice. I like the way you've looped the curtains up and draped that piece of silk across the dressmaker's dummy. Oh, Melissa, isn't this exciting?'

'I suppose so.' Melissa smiled. She had not wanted to spoil her friend's joy by sharing her doubts about her new home's location.

Reenie visited Melissa every week after that and on the same day in November that Cora's emerald-green silk and black lace trim was delivered from Wilkinson's, she arrived in a state of high excitement. It was a cold day with a light coating of frost on the rooftops and on the pavements, and Reenie, whose fingers were numb, took time to take off her coat and hat.

'Where are your gloves?' Melissa asked.

'They've got so many holes that it's not worth wearing them,' Reenie replied.

'It's a good job I've got a spare pair, then, isn't it?'

The two old friends smiled at each other and Reenie sat on a little stool by the fire to warm herself through.

'I've got something to tell you,' she said.

'What is it?'

'In a minute. I'm not warmed through yet and I could do with a cup of tea.'

Melissa was torn. She wanted to start cutting out Cora's dress but she didn't want to work while Reenie was here. It wouldn't be fair to her to be distracted in the time they had together. So Melissa decided she could catch up with her work later.

'All right,' she said. She took the pot holder from its hook on the mantel shelf and reached for the kettle.

'No, you sit down in that comfy chair,' Reenie said. 'You look as though you need a little rest. Let me spoil you.'

Melissa could see there was no use arguing. Reenie took the kettle. Mrs Bruce allowed Melissa to make tea and toast at the fire in her workroom but otherwise she had to take her meals in the dining room. Reenie made for the door.

'Remember to knock,' Melissa told her.

'I will.'

Soon they were sitting by the fire with cups of tea, the flickering light making the room look cosy and somehow enclosing them in a warm secure world of their own. Melissa remembered days like this with her mother and she was glad that she had Reenie as a friend.

'Well,' she said, 'you were going to tell me something.'

Reenie's eyes widened and sparkled in the firelight. 'I divven't know where to begin!'

'At the beginning,' Melissa said.

'That's just it. I don't suppose any of us knows when exactly it began but we should have seen it coming.'

'Reenie!'

'All right. She ran off.'

'Who ran off ? Mrs Winterton?'

'Of course not! That one knows where her bread is buttered. No, Gwendolyn. And who do you suppose she ran off with?'

'Douglas?'

'Well, I can see it's no surprise, but, aye, you're right. Our fine young footman ran off with her to Gretna Green.'

'A runaway wedding.'

'She left a letter for her parents telling them that the next time they saw her she would be Mrs Douglas Horton. Well, that was a mistake, leaving the letter instead of posting it later, because the master and mistress guessed straight away where they would be heading and he took after them.'

Now that she had started it was as if the dam had burst and Reenie hardly paused to take breath. 'He told Mrs Winterton not to upset herself and that he'd put a stop to it.'

'How do you know what was said?'

'Gan on, Melissa! You know fine well that in a house like that the servants know most things. Well, anyways, the master took himself all the way to Gretna and he found them in some cottage or other – he called it a hovel. They were renting it from a farmer's wife. It was so small he couldn't stand up properly, he said.'

'But Mr Winterton was too late?'

'In one way he wasn't and in one way he was – much too late!'

'What on earth do you mean?'

'They hadn't tied the knot; they hadn't had time, but . . .'

'They were living together as if they were already man and wife?'

'Aye, they were. And when Mr Winterton came back he telt his wife that he'd told Miss Gwendolyn that it didn't matter and that no one should know. And if she came straight home with him it wouldn't spoil her chances of marrying someone respectable. But that Douglas must clear off – as far away as possible and never darken their doors again!'

Reenie grinned when she said this; a line straight from one of the penny romances that she loved.

'So Gwendolyn came back with her father?'

'No, she didn't. As I said, it was much too late.'

'I don't understand.'

'She was . . . well, you know, it was better that she married Douglas after all.'

'She was with child?' Melissa's eyes were as round as Reenie's.

'Aye, she was. About four months gone, she telt her father, so there was no chance of marrying her off quickly to some unsuspecting gent and bamboozling him into thinking the bairn was his.'

'Would the Wintertons have done that?' Melissa was shocked.

Reenie laughed. 'I'm sure of it. But they couldn't. Mr Winterton came home alone and said he'd washed his hands of her. He told Mrs Winterton that if Gwendolyn hoped that one day they would forgive her she had another think coming. But he couldn't let his flesh and blood starve so he would make her an allowance. However, he never wanted to see her or her husband or the child, and he was going to cut her out of his will.'

'That's dreadful!'

'Why should you care? She was never very nice to you.'

'No, she wasn't, but Douglas, for all his annoying ways, never ignored me like the others did. I think he was basically decent – and he must love Gwendolyn to do such a thing.'

'Eeh, Melissa, for all your brains you sometimes sound as if you were born yesterday. Douglas is pleasant to folk because it suits him to be. And in my opinion as soon as he saw Gwendolyn was taken with him he decided to go after her.'

'No, I think you're wrong. I think he really loves her. But he could never have believed her parents would allow such a match.'

'Mebbes that's why he made sure that they had to. And mebbes he's still hoping that Mr Winterton will come round one day and welcome him into the family.'

'Poor Douglas.'

'For goodness' sake, why do you feel sorry for him?'

'Because whether he really loves her not he will have to be a good husband to Gwendolyn for years to come. He'll have to dance to her tune for as long as it takes to persuade her father to forgive her.'

'And that might never happen.'

'No, it might not.'

They both shook their heads as they sipped their tea, then Melissa heaped a few more coals on the fire.

Mrs Bruce had taken a fancy to Reenie and said that if ever she could afford a daily maid she would try to tempt her away from the Winterton house. Reenie laughed and assured Mary Bruce that it wouldn't take much tempting – except that she would have nowhere to live. That was a problem, Mrs Bruce said, because although they had a tiny spare room, little more than a cupboard, she didn't think Tom would countenance a live-in maid. He didn't want any more women under his feet.

The landlady was happy to invite Reenie to the table and have what she called 'high tea' with Melissa. Tom would have a proper man's dinner when he came home and she would eat with him. But she sat with the girls in the small dining room and drank tea while they ate kidneys on toast and home-made raisin cake. Afterwards Reenie helped her to clear the table and wash the dishes, and then Melissa said she would walk Reenie as far as the tram stop. They had agreed it was better that she didn't walk all the way home now that it was dark.

When they reached the first tram stop they were still talking happily so they agreed to walk on to the next. The rows of small shops they passed were brightly lit and the windows attractive. With December almost upon them there was a queue of folk at the butcher's. Mr Pearce's reputation brought customers from surrounding districts so it was best to get Christmas orders in nice and early.

It was cold and the two friends' breath frosted on the air as they talked. They stamped their feet to keep their toes warm when they stopped at the next tram stop. Melissa waited with Reenie and it was not too long before a horse tram drew up and Reenie got on. Melissa waved until she could no longer see Reenie at the window. Then she turned to walk home.

She had not seen the hostile figure standing watching her from a narrow alley between two rows of shops and it was only when she was about to turn a corner that the figure emerged from the shadows and began to follow her. Once home, Melissa used her own key to open the door and slipped into the house.

The person who had followed her watched from the other side of the street. When Janet Cook had emerged from the butcher's she had been intrigued to see the daughter of the sister she had resented ever since they were children, in this part of town. Why was her niece living here? For live here she must. She had her own door key. Had that stuck-up Winterton woman kicked her out?

But it would not do to knock at the door and ask Melissa

directly. The girl would probably tell a pack of lies. No, it would be better to get it from the horse's mouth, as they said. Janet smiled to herself, pleased at the idea of comparing Lilian Winterton, with her braying upper-class voice, to a horse.

She turned and started to walk home, hugely pleased with the notion that the arrangement poor silly Emmeline had made had come to grief just as she, Janet, had predicted that it would.

When Cora arrived for a fitting of the second dress, she was delighted. 'Darling Melissa,' she said, 'you were so right. You have managed to make my waist look tiny without resorting to bones.'

'Your waist is tiny,' Melissa said. 'It was just a matter of emphasising it.'

Cora was pleased with the compliment, but she smiled in a way that suggested she was simply acknowledging a truth.

'When do you think it will be finished?' Cora asked. 'I'll need the gowns quite soon.'

'Can you wait a week?'

'A week today? That would be marvellous. And if this gown is as good as the first one I shall recommend you to all my friends.'

After Cora had taken her leave Melissa realised that she hardly knew anything about her. She did not have an address for her so she certainly didn't know who the young woman's friends could be. Perhaps Eileen would tell her something about her cousin next time she went to Wilkinson's.

The next morning brought a letter from France. It was from Miss Robson, her old schoolteacher. Melissa hurried her breakfast and took a second cup of tea along to the front parlour, which Reenie called her 'salon'. Mrs Bruce had already seen to the fire – a task she insisted on taking upon herself – and Melissa sat down to enjoy her old friend's letter.

My dear Melissa,

I was delighted to receive your letter telling me that you have moved out of the Winterton household at last. But I wish you had written sooner. Not hearing from you for all those weeks was very worrying. However, I won't scold you. We are not in the classroom now. And, in a way, I suppose I understand. I believe you wanted to get settled in to your new way of life before informing me of such an important step.

I am so pleased that we have corresponded over the years, for quite apart from my fondness for you, your letters have in a small way been a link with the city that I shall always call my home. But I doubt if I shall ever return to Newcastle now, my dear. I am very happy here in les Hautes-Pyrénées with my dear old school friend Amelia.

Melissa, my dear, have you ever thought that you could have your own salon here in Pau? I would be able to help you find the right premises and Amelia and her daughters would recommend you to all their friends. And apart from that, there is a large English community here. They are attracted to the mild climate but you would think they were still living in England with their golf and fox-hunting and steeple-chasing. The locals often refer to Pau as *la ville Anglaise*.

But why am I telling you about the English community as if to reassure you? You are half-French and the last time I saw you, you spoke the language perfectly. Oh, Melissa, I believe you would be happy here. So know that I wish you well from the bottom of my heart and I will pray that your brave venture succeeds. But please remember, if you ever have need of a home, there is one waiting for you here with me.

God bless you.

Your affectionate friend,

Harriet Robson

Melissa returned the letter to the envelope and sat for a moment gazing into the fire. What would it be like to live in her father's country? She had never been to France and did not even know if she had any living relatives there, and in any case if she had she doubted that she would ever be able to find them.

Not that she was close to her mother's family. Indeed, the opposite was true, and when she remembered the way her aunt Janet had behaved towards her mother and to herself on the day of the funeral she vowed anew that she never wanted to see her again.

Reenie was her true friend and she loved her as she would have loved a sister. She would never want to leave Reenie behind. No, much as she loved her old schoolteacher she did not want to leave Newcastle. She would do her best and make a success of her dressmaking business. She already had one fashionable client and Eileen had promised to send more. Melissa was determined that she would make her mother's dreams for her come true.

She rose and tucked Miss Robson's letter into the letter rack on the mantel shelf. Then, opening the curtains as far as they would go, she moved the body form into the best place to catch the light and continued work on Cora's dress.

'There's a woman to see you, Mrs Winterton.'

Lilian, seated at her writing desk in the morning room, looked up from the latest Army and Navy Stores catalogue and, irritated to be disturbed, she spoke more sharply than usual.

'Not a "woman", Ena, you must say a "lady".'

'No, Mrs Winterton, this person isn't a lady.'

Lilian Winterton frowned. 'Then why does she want to see me? Isn't this something that Mrs Barton or you could deal with?'

'She says she will speak to no one but you.'

'For goodness' sake, send her away.'

Lilian returned to perusing the catalogue. Since Melissa had gone she had not found a dressmaker good enough to replace her and, although she would not have admitted this to anyone in her social circle, she had taken to buying readymade clothes now and then. She did not buy them in the shops in Newcastle, of course – that would never do. She sent for them from London.

At the moment she was looking at illustrations of ladies' silk blouses. They were advertised as being suitable for morning or afternoon and she could not make up her mind between the black uncrushable silk with the cream embroidered front or the pink and white hairline-striped silk trimmed with guipure lace.

She sighed. The pink and white was delightful but maybe a trifle girlish. Perhaps the black would be better for a woman of her age; after all, it was very sophisticated. She imagined that Melissa would have guided her towards the black. She decided to have them both. Then she looked up.

'Why are you still here, Ena?'

'The woman insists that you will want to see her.'

'How dare she!'

'That's what I said but she says it's about her niece – Melissa Dornay. Her name is Mrs Cook and she says you've met her before – on the day of the funeral. She says you'll no doubt remember her.'

Lilian remembered her, all right. Emmeline Dornay's sister had been a most disagreeable and probably dishonest woman, who had been determined that Melissa should live with her and go to work in the pickling factory. Lilian had been equally determined that the child would come home with her.

She endeavoured to convince herself that it was because she had promised Emmeline and also that it was for the child's own good. And that was partly true. But she had to admit that she had been swayed by the fact that in giving her a home she had ensured that she had her very own personal dressmaker and a very good one at that.

She remembered how obnoxious Melissa's aunt had been – the insinuations she had made – and how Lilian had as good as bought Melissa by allowing Mrs Cook to keep everything Emmeline had intended should be given to Melissa.

And now what did she want? Did she want to see her niece? Would she stay at the door until she was allowed to do so?

Lilian sighed. 'All right, Ena,' she said resignedly. 'Show her up.'

Lilian went to sit by the fire. She guessed this would be an uncomfortable interview. She would have to tell Mrs Cook that Melissa was no longer here and why. She prepared herself for all kinds of unpleasantness. She was still trying to choose her words carefully when Ena showed the woman in.

Mrs Cook barely waited until the door shut behind the lady's maid before she marched across the room and blurted out, 'What happened?'

Lilian shrank back a little. Really, the woman was standing over her in a most intimidating way. 'Do sit down, Mrs Cook,' she said, gesturing gracefully.

'Oh, la-di-da! Aren't we being polite?' her unwelcome visitor said, but nevertheless she settled herself in the chair at the other side of the fireplace that Lilian had indicated.

How incongruous she looks in my beautiful morning room, Lilian thought. Charlotte Paule had chosen eau-de-nil, turquoise and peacock blues for the wallpaper and fabrics when she had redecorated this room and the angular figure in rusty black looked totally out of place – but not at all intimidated.

'Well, Mrs Cook,' Lilian decided to be brave, 'I'm afraid I have some bad news for you.'

'You've thrown her out.'

Lilian was taken aback and paused before she answered. 'Has – has Melissa been to you?'

'Of course not. She knows very well I wouldn't give her the time of day.'

'Then how do you know that I've – erm – that she has gone?'

'I've seen her. That's why I came to find out what happened.'

'And what did she say?'

'I haven't spoken to her. I want to know what the situation is before I do. But she was obviously living in the house I saw her enter so I decided to come here and find out why.'

'Well . . . I'm not sure how to tell you but your niece . . .' She hesitated.

'Go on.'

Lilian thought the woman's features became sharper with anticipation. When she had first been shown in, Lilian had thought Mrs Cook meant to cause trouble for her. But now she was not so sure. She obviously hated her niece as she had hated the girl's mother, Emmeline.

'Will you take a cup of tea?' Lilian said, and without waiting for an answer she rose and reached for the bell pull.

Janet Cook was taken aback. 'All right, if you say so,' she said, and looked round uneasily.

Lilian was relieved to see that her visitor's aggressive mood had subsided a little. She had resolved to tell her why Melissa had gone in a way that would no doubt give the mean-minded woman a great deal of satisfaction – and in a way that would absolve Lilian herself of any opprobrium whatsoever.

The second gown was almost ready and Cora was delighted with it.

'You really are talented, Melissa,' she said. 'I'm sure it won't be long before you will be the mistress of a flourishing salon.

'Now, to business: we'll be going on a family visit in a week or two's time. That's why I want you to make me a dress and coat suitable for travelling. I'll bring the fabric when I come to collect these two gowns.'

As usual Cora's visit passed in a whirl of cheerful gossip that told Melissa nothing of any substance. When she had gone Melissa still did not know anything about Cora's life. She had been brought up far too well to ask personal questions. Cora didn't wear a wedding ring and yet she had said, 'we'll be going on a family visit'. Who did she mean by 'we'? Her mother or a sister? And where exactly was she going?

Melissa was disappointed with the fabric that Cora brought for her travelling clothes. An unimaginative grey fabric known as 'shoddy': cloth made from torn up and unravelled rags with some new wool added. She was surprised that Cora had chosen this but maybe it was all she could afford after spending so much on two evening gowns.

Cora had not brought an illustration this time but she described in great detail what she wanted, which was quite straightforward. 'A skirt and a three-quarter-length coat,' she said. 'I will leave you to decide on the exact style. I have every faith in your judgement.'

Melissa knew that the cut would have to be expert in order to make something of the second-rate material. However, she determined to do her very best. Cora had brought a portmanteau in which to place the evening gowns and Melissa packed them carefully, covering them with tissue paper.

'How will you carry this?' she asked.

'Don't worry, I have a cab waiting. Perhaps you would help me out with it?'

Melissa was surprised that Cora had kept the hansom waiting. It would have been cheaper to dismiss it and then run up to the nearest cab stand to get another one when she was ready to leave. But it was not her place to say so.

With the portmanteau safely stowed, Cora hesitated before climbing in to the hansom. 'My dear,' she said, 'I haven't paid you for the gowns!' She opened her purse, looked inside and frowned. 'Oh dear, I have barely enough for the cab fare.' Then she looked up and smiled. 'I shall just have to pay you when I come back for my fitting. Or better still, leave it until my travelling clothes are ready and pay for everything at the same time. Is that all right?'

Cora barely waited for Melissa's nod of acquiescence; she climbed into the cab and gave a perfunctory wave as they pulled away. Very soon the hansom was merely a dark shape in the encroaching mist. The sound of the horse's hoofs striking the cobbles echoed eerily as Melissa hurried back into the house and shut the door against the winter night.

Cora did not come for her fitting. When she still had not appeared a week later Melissa decided to go to Wilkinson's to ask Eileen if her cousin was ill.

'My cousin?' Eileen said. 'I don't have any cousins. At least none that live here in Newcastle. The only cousin I have has gone to live in Canada.'

'But Cora . . . Cora Willis . . . you sent her to me.'

Eileen frowned as if racking her memory and then she smiled. 'Cora . . . oh, that young woman. She's an actress. She told me she needed two new gowns for an entertainment she is to appear in. The poor things often have to supply their own costumes, you know. She asked me to recommend someone who would do a first-rate job in record time. Naturally I thought of you.'

'But she's not your cousin?'

'No – I've told you.'

'Why would she say that?'

'Well, I don't know. Perhaps she thought you would do a better job for her if you thought we were related.'

'I would do my best for any customer!'

'Of course you would. But I assure you I'd never seen her before she walked in and asked if we had any nice remnants. But you asked if she was ill, didn't you? I'm afraid I can't tell you. I haven't seen her since she bought the emerald-green silk taffeta for a second gown. Remember, I had it delivered to you.'

'But what about the grey shoddy?'

'Shoddy?'

'Yes, for her travelling clothes.'

'She didn't buy it here.' Eileen looked offended. 'She must have gone to that fellow who has a stall in the Bigg Market.'

'Where can she be?' Melissa asked.

Suddenly Eileen's eyes widened. 'Oh, no, if Cora Willis was with the company at the Palace, they've moved on.'

'Moved on? What are you talking about?'

'They left at the end of last week. The posters are already up advertising the new company coming in to do the pantomime.'

Melissa did not realise that she had leaned forward to grip the counter.

'What is it?' Eileen asked. 'Oh, no. Didn't you take payment for the two gowns?'

'No . . . she said she would pay when both were finished. Then on the day she came to collect them she didn't have enough to pay the hansom – or that's what she said. But although I could have done with the money I thought it would be all right – after all, she gave me the material for her travelling clothes. I thought she would be coming back. It seems she may never have intended to.'

'Because she never planned to pay you.'

'But what about the material she left with me?'

'That was a trick to make you trust her. It's been done before. She'll have got it at the market, like I said. It won't have cost her much and it would be a small price to pay compared to what she should have paid you for making the two gowns.'

The two girls stared at each other across the polished counter, then Eileen lifted the hinged flap and said, 'Come with me. I'll take you to our rest room and make you a cup of tea.'

Chapter Eighteen

Eileen led the way up to a crowded little room on the top floor where the female assistants could take their short rest breaks. The gentlemen sales assistants' room was down in the basement.

As they climbed the stairs with the worn linoleum treads, Eileen said, 'Mr Wilkinson thinks it would be most improper for us to share a room even if it's only to have a cup of tea and a gossip.' She laughed.

Melissa understood that the kindly older girl was trying to cheer her up.

There were already two young women in the rest room and, although they looked surprised, both recognised Melissa as a regular customer and they smiled a welcome. Eileen asked one of them to go down and cover for her and girl said of course she would.

'They are a nice crowd here,' Eileen said. 'We try to be friends and oblige each other when we can.'

The remaining girl, who looked no more than fourteen years old, pointed to the teapot on an oilcloth-covered table and said, 'That'll be cold. Shall I make a fresh pot for you, Miss Briggs?'

'Yes, Louisa, that would be kind of you. And wash the cups as well, dear.'

The girl put the teapot and the used cups and saucers on a tray and left the room.

'There's a tiny kitchen along the corridor,' Eileen explained. 'Now why don't you sit down? Take the armchair by the fire.'

The gas fire popped and spluttered, and the armchair was old with stuffing escaping through holes in the armrests. Melissa sat down thankfully and looked around. The room was also used to store old boxes of buttons and cards of lace. There was a screen propped up against one wall and two dressmaker's dummies were draped in swathes of faded cloth. Light filtered in through one small window and Melissa could see smoke from the nearby chimneypots rising into the leaden sky.

She stared down at her gloved hands clutched in her lap. How could she have been so naïve? Had Cora meant to deceive her from the start, or had she just forgotten to come back and pay what she owed? No, she must have planned it. Why else leave the material for the travelling clothes she probably had no intention of ever coming back for?

Eileen had taken one of several rickety old dining chairs near the table. 'Is it very bad?' she asked. 'I mean, has this left you in difficulties financially?'

'It won't be easy but I should be able to manage,' Melissa said.

In fact she knew that it was going to be a struggle. She would be able to pay her rent for perhaps another two weeks if she did not get any more work.

'Ah, thank you Louisa,' Eileen said.

The girl had returned with the fresh pot of tea and clean cups. She smiled shyly and slipped away. It was time for her to get back to work. Eileen busied herself with the milk and sugar.

'Here, take your gloves off and drink this,' she said. 'I

don't know whether you take sugar but I've put a spoonful in. It's good for shock.'

'I feel such a fool. So . . . so stupid.'

'You mustn't feel too bad about it. I'm sure you won't be the only person that young woman has deceived. Why, she could so easily have bamboozled me. She asked if she could open an account here and I almost agreed, but I was saved by the fact that she only wanted remnants. You can't open an account if your first purchase is sale goods. I wouldn't be surprised if she's left a trail of debts all over town.'

'She seemed so genuine,' Melissa said.

'She's an actress, remember.'

'I didn't know that.'

'Did you not ask her anything about herself ?'

'No, I thought that would be impolite.'

'Melissa, dear, in future you're going to have to be impolite but in a very tactful way. You'll have to learn how to ask the right questions so that you will know whether you can trust your clients. If you have any suspicions whatever you must demand for payment in advance – of at least half the sum. Meanwhile, I promise I'll do my best to send more business your way. And I'll warn you if there's any chance that the person concerned might be a slippery customer. And if I do, you must hold on to the goods until you are paid.'

'I will.'

'I'm sad to say that many a so-called lady can be as bad about settling her account as an out-and-out criminal. People like that think only of themselves. They don't care that there are other folks working hard to try and make an honest living.'

'Yes . . . I should have remembered,' Melissa said softly. 'My mother sometimes had clients like that.' Including Mrs Winterton, she thought, who had promised much and then fallen short of her poor mother's expectations.

What had happened with Cora had been a bad blow but Melissa felt cheered by Eileen's sympathy, and on the way home her spirits lifted. Eileen had promised to send her more clients and meanwhile Melissa would have to take in more mending and alterations. With Christmas coming up there might even be some little party dresses required.

She remembered that even some of her mother's poorer clients wanted their daughters to look special for the Sunday school parties. Emmeline Dornay had always done her best for them, making fairytale frocks from second-hand fabrics. Melissa remembered how much pleasure that had given her mother and she resolved that she would not let this initial setback destroy her dreams.

She walked all the way back to her lodgings and she cheered herself further by thinking about the arrangements she and Reenie had made for Christmas. Melissa had been invited to join Tom and Mary Bruce on Christmas Day. On Boxing Day she had promised Mrs Simmons that she would go to the old almshouse and help with the free Christmas treats being provided for the homeless.

'What's your little friend Reenie doing over Christmas?' Mary Bruce had asked Melissa.

'She's working. She won't have any time off until the day after Boxing Day.'

'Then tell her to come along and help pick over whatever is left of the roast goose and the mince pies. It'll be nice for Tom and me,' Mary had said, 'not having any young folk of our own. We'll make quite a party of it.'

Melissa thought back over the Christmases in the Winterton household. She had never been invited to the family table, and the household servants had never made her truly welcome in their celebrations in the kitchen, although she and Reenie had always managed to cheer each other up with a few mince pies and a cup of tea by the fire in the sewing room. But this Christmas, thanks to kindly Mrs Bruce, Melissa was looking forward to perhaps the happiest Christmas since before her mother had died.

Although it was only early evening the sky was dark and in the neat rows of houses she passed on the way home the curtains were already drawn against the chill night air. Behind some of them friendly lights glowed and in houses where the curtains had not yet been drawn Melissa glimpsed a passing show of comfortable domestic scenes.

When she reached the house where she lived she was puzzled to see that the curtains of the front parlour – her own room – were closed. They were of heavy material but they had not been drawn properly and light showed in the gap. Melissa paused before she inserted her key in the lock. Could Mrs Bruce have entered her room, perhaps to clean it, even though Melissa had told her that she would do the necessary work herself ?

As soon as she entered the house she heard the sound of conversation. The voices were low and she could not make out what they were talking about. But then she heard her own name. She closed the front door quietly behind her and held her breath as she listened.

One voice belonged to her landlady, Mrs Bruce, and the other to someone she had hoped she would never see again. Melissa clenched her fists and then took the few short steps to the door of her room and opened it abruptly.

Two people sat by the fire and they had obviously been engaged in deep conversation. At the sound of the door opening two faces looked up in her direction and both were hostile.

'Well, Melissa,' her aunt Janet said. 'I never expected to see you again.'

'Nor I you. Why have you come here?'

'I thought it my duty.'

'Duty?' Melissa was astonished. How could her aunt have known she was living here? And why did she think it her duty to visit her?

Janet Cook answered the first question without being asked. 'I saw you in the street,' she said. 'You and another young lass. I followed you home.'

'Why would you do that?'

'I was curious. The last time I saw you was on the day we buried your poor foolish mother. If you remember, you spurned the offer of a good home with me to go and live with that hoity-toity Mrs Winterton.'

'My mother was neither poor nor foolish, and she did not want me to live with you. She knew you would have sent me to work in a factory.'

'There's nothing wrong with good honest work.'

'I'm not saying there is but she wanted me to carry on with her work; she wanted me to be a dressmaker. That's why she asked Mrs Winterton to take me.'

Aunt Janet shook her head in a false gesture of sorrow. 'And now Mrs Winterton rues the day she allowed you into her home.'

'How do you know that?'

'I've been to see her.'

Melissa was filled with foreboding. She glanced at Mary Bruce, whose kindly features had taken on a look of shock and disbelief.

'Mrs Winterton told me why she had to ask you to leave. How, after all the years of kindness, you had repaid her with ingratitude. How you let criminals into her house to rob her blind. I actually felt sorry for her.'

'I'm sure you didn't,' Melissa said angrily and she saw her landlady purse her lips with surprise and disapproval.

'Oh, I admit I didn't take to her. I thought she was wrong to encourage you to be something you weren't intended to be, but she told me how she had helped you, bought everything you needed and how you had broken her heart when you did what you did.'

'Broke her heart? She hasn't got one!' Melissa laughed, and regretted it immediately when Mary Bruce's expression changed to one of condemnation.

Mrs Bruce stood up. 'I'll leave you with your aunt, Melissa, and when she's gone I want to speak to you.'

Melissa stepped aside to let her landlady by. Mary Bruce avoided her eyes and Melissa felt the chill as she swept past her and along the draughty passage. She heard the kitchen door close and then she turned to face her aunt.

'I suppose you told her your version of what happened.'

'I told her the truth.'

'The truth according to whom?'

'To Mrs Winterton, of course.'

'And what exactly was that truth?'

'That you conspired with a vicious bunch of thieves and allowed them into the house.'

'I didn't conspire with them and I didn't allow them into the house. If I had I wouldn't be here, I would either have fled with them or be in prison.'

'Mebbes. But mebbes you're not in prison because Mrs Winterton felt sorry for you.'

'Is that what she said?'

'She didn't have to say it in so many words. I put two and two together.'

'And made up your mind that I was guilty.'

Her aunt rose and smiled in a self-satisfied way. 'Well, I must say, it's nothing more than I expected.'

'What do you mean by that?'

'Your mother always had ideas above her station and she brought you up to be like her. If you'd lived with me I'd have made sure that you worked hard and knew your place.'

'Get out.'

'Don't worry, I'm going. And I've said this before and I'll say it again: don't ever think you can come to me for help.'

Melissa didn't demean herself by responding. She held the door open wide until her aunt had passed, and waited until the street door closed before she gripped the door with both hands and slumped against it. Mrs Bruce wanted to see her and Melissa could guess only too well why.

'You'll have to go, you know that, don't you?' her landlady said coldly.

Melissa knew it would be useless to protest. Her aunt had no doubt poured out her poisonous version of events and it was no wonder that Mary Bruce looked so shocked and angry. But Melissa's silence threw her off balance.

'Look,' she said, 'I don't know the truth of it but I can't believe you're an out-and-out criminal.'

'I'm not.'

'But you can't deny you kept bad company.'

'I can't.'

'Well, at least you're being honest at last. But whatever the truth of the matter, Tom would be very angry if I let you stay.' She paused again as if waiting for Melissa to say something and then continued, 'So, don't bother about giving notice. Your rent's paid up until the end of the week and then you'll have to go.'

'But that's only three days away!'

This time it was Mary Bruce's turn to remain silent. Melissa stared at her obdurate face, nodded her head and left the room.

Melissa spent the next few hours sorting and packing her belongings. Then, despite the lateness of the hour, she pulled on a warm cloak and slipped out into the wintry weather. She hurried up to the shop on the corner. Mr Ali stayed open until nearly midnight. The shop was full of people making last-minute purchases and Melissa waited quietly at the back of the queue until all the customers had gone.

'Now, Miss Dornay,' the shopkeeper said. He lifted the flap in the counter and crossed to the door. He turned over the card that was hanging there to show the closed sign. 'I am about to lock up and return to the bosom of my family. It would not be proper to lower the blind while you are in here, so I would be obliged if you would tell me what it is that you want.'

Melissa had had time to think what she would say and decided to tell the whole story. Mr Ali listened gravely and then shook his head in sorrow.

'I am very sorry for you, Miss Dornay,' he said. 'I believe that you are an honest young woman but I can understand why Mrs Bruce wants you to leave. And now you are asking me to help you find somewhere else to live.' He leaned back against the counter and folded his arms across his brown overall. 'I have a customer who would be glad to let you have a room. She is in desperate need of the money. But even so, I will have to tell her something of what you have told me.'

'Of course.'

'The trouble is that although the house will be clean, it is at the bottom of the hill nearer to the river.'

'I don't mind. I must find somewhere before the end of the week.'

'Could you pay a week's rent in advance?'

'Yes.' Melissa knew how very little that would leave her but she was confident that she would soon be able to start earning again.

'Well, then, Miss Dornay, it is too late to send you to Mrs Thompson tonight but I will get my wife to write a letter to her. My wife is English, you know, and will make a better job of it than I will, for all people say I speak the language more correctly than some of the natives!' He smiled. 'Good night, then, Miss Dornay. You can call at the shop and collect the letter as soon as I open up in the morning.'

'That's very kind of you. Good night, Mr Ali.'

Melissa hardly slept. Before she left the house in the morning all her belongings were packed and she was ready to go. Mr Ali had only just opened the shop and he handed her the promised letter.

'Oh, and you can give this to Mrs Thompson,' he said. He handed her a biscuit tin. 'Broken biscuits for her children,' he explained. 'No payment required.'

She hardly had time to thank him properly for the letter before the shop filled with early morning customers.

It was a cold bright morning and the pavements were slippery with frost. Melissa had to take care as she made her way down the steep streets towards the river. Even at this time in the morning the air rang with the clanging and the hammering from the shipyards and the hooting of tugboats on the river. And even without a wind, the smell from the bone yard grew stronger the further downhill she ventured.

When she reached the street where Mrs Thompson lived she was filled with misgiving. There were few newly soap-stoned steps and few shining doorknobs here. Every house had a tired and shabby look, although there was no outright dirt and neglect. She found Mrs Thompson's house and stared with consternation at the frayed faded curtains hanging at the window. Nevertheless she pulled the doorbell. She had no choice.

Mrs Thompson looked surprised. It was a moment or two before she seemed to understand what Melissa was saying.

'Mr Ali sent you? You want to rent my front room? A young lady like you?'

'Yes – yes to all those questions.' Melissa was aware of

curtains twitching in a window across the street. 'Please would you read this letter?'

'All right. I better had. And you'd better come in before old Bella across the way pushes her nose right through her dirty window!'

Mrs Thompson's kitchen was warm enough, with a fire burning in the range, and the deal table top was scrubbed clean, as were the wooden floorboards. There were no rugs. And apart from an old dresser and four wooden chairs there was no other furniture.

'Sit down, will you?' Mrs Thompson said. 'I can't hev you standing like that as if you're about to take off any minute, although I wouldn't blame you. What's that you're holding, by the way?'

'Oh,' Melissa said, 'it's a tin of broken biscuits from Mr Ali.'

'God bless the canny old heathen. That'll do for the bairns' tea when they get back from school.'

Melissa sat at the table while Mrs Thompson read the letter. When she had finished she folded it and put it back in the envelope. She looked across at Melissa with raised eyebrows. 'Well, you've been through the wars,' she said at last. 'But if I can believe everything Sally Ali says, then I don't see why I shouldn't risk it. For sure, there's nowt for your thieving pals to pinch in this house.'

'They're not my pals!' Melissa said.

'Eeh, divven't fret, hinny. I was just kidding. The way Sally explains it they made a right fool of you.'

'Yes, they did.' Melissa felt the heat rising and staining her neck. Was she never going to be free of it? She felt hot tears of anger pricking at the back of her eyes.

'I think you need a cup of tea,' Mrs Thompson said.

Without saying anything further she rose and busied herself making tea in an old brown teapot. Melissa noticed how thin she was and how, despite her smiles, her eyes remained sad. Her hair was pulled back tidily from her face and her all-enveloping pinafore was clean, although patched several times.

'There you are, pet,' she said a moment or two later as she placed a cup of tea on the table before Melissa. 'No milk and sugar, I'm afraid, but drink it while it's hot.'

'Thank you.'

'Now I understand you'll need the front room to yourself to do your sewing?'

'That's right.'

'Well, you can hev it. But I'm afraid that's all you can hev. There's no spare bedroom. Me and the two little lasses sleep in one, and the three lads in the other. Two bedrooms – that's all there is upstairs. So you'll hev to sleep in the front room along with your things. There's a single bed in there. Me old mother slept there until she died.'

Melissa stared down into her cup. Steam rose from the pale brown liquid.

'What's the matter? Are you afeared of ghosts? Me ma wouldn't have hurt a soul when she was alive so I doubt she would do it now that she's dead.'

'No, it's not that.'

'Is it the fact she died in there – on that very bed? I can assure you everything was washed down thoroughly after the funeral. The mattress was sponged and beaten and put out in the yard to air, and the very bed springs scrubbed clean with carbolic. You'll not catch owt nasty in my house.'

Melissa heard Mrs Thompson's voice harden and she looked up quickly.

'No, it's nothing like that,' she said. 'It's just that I'll have to see my clients – customers – in there and the bed . . .'

'I understand. You'll want to look tidy. Well, that's no problem. I've got a lovely oriental bedspread – all bonny colours. You can cover your bed up with that every day and mebbes put a cushion or two on top. Will that do? Hawway, I'll show it to you. It's already in there.' Mrs Thompson led the way to the front parlour and opened the door. She stepped in first and looked around with some pride. 'I keep it nice, you'll hev to admit.'

Melissa looked around and her heart sank. There was an old table, the top scratched and faded, two chairs by the window, and the bed Mrs Thompson had mentioned against one wall. The pattern on the wallpaper was barely discernible but, again, everything was very clean.

'I'll hev to charge you extra for the coal,' Mrs Thompson said, 'and mind you don't let any sparks spoil me rug.'

Melissa looked at the rug. 'But it's lovely,' she said involuntarily.

'Aye, it is. Me husband brought it home from Arabia or some such place. Like the bedspread I telt you about. Look, here it is, folded up on the bed here.'

Mrs Thompson shook the material out and the colours glowed in the dim corner of the featureless room. Melissa began to feel as though she could make something of this place after all.

'Billy was a sailor, you know. Deep sea. He earned good money and life was comfortable enough, even though I sometimes didn't see him for over a year. But each time he came home he made sure there would be another bairn to keep me company. But, hawway, let's gan back in the kitchen and I'll see if there's owt left in the teapot while we settle how much rent I'm going to charge.'

While they were talking Maud Thompson told Melissa that she was a widow – or rather, she thought she might be, for Billy simply hadn't come home from his last voyage. Either he'd jumped ship somewhere or had gone overboard. One day when she'd gone to the shipping office as usual to collect her pay there wasn't anything for her. The clerk told her that Billy Thompson was no longer in their employ.

'I was in a dreadful state,' she said. 'There I was with five bairns to feed and no money coming in. I divven't know how I would have managed without Sally Ali's man. He gave me as much tick as he could and slipped me little bits of leftover cheese and sliced meats and that from the shop. Like me he didn't believe Billy would jump ship and never come back to his wife and bairns. The ship had sailed round the Cape, you see, and it gets a bit rough down there with two oceans meeting. Sally's husband used to be a seafaring man himself and he knew how easy it was to lose a man overboard.'

'Mr Ali, a sailor?'

'Aye. Until he met Sally, who was serving tea and buns at the Seaman's Mission.' Mrs Thompson grinned. 'Then he didn't want to go to sea ever again. He put all his savings into that nice little shop and he's become a real leader of the community. At least that's what my old school friend Sally calls him.'

Before Melissa left Mrs Thompson asked her if she needed a hand to shift her stuff and they arranged that she would send up her two oldest lads, Billy Junior and Sam, as soon as they came home from school. 'Then mebbes you'll hev time to get settled in before I gans to work.'

'To work?' Melissa was surprised.

'Aye. How else do you think I pay the rent and clothe and feed five bairns? I do cleaning jobs in the shipping offices and I help out in the Keelman's Arms on the quayside most nights. None of that pays much but it's all I can find. I'm glad Mr Ali sent you down here, and that's a fact.'

A little later Mary Bruce watched while Maud Thompson's two elder lads started emptying Melissa's belongings from her room and stacking them on the pavement.

'Are you going to trust them with that sewing machine?' she asked.

'Of course I trust them.' Melissa was indignant.

Mrs Bruce flushed. 'I think you misunderstood. I didn't mean that they would run off with it.' She gave a wry smile. 'They wouldn't be able to. The pavement's like a skating rink. No, I meant they look over little to be carrying that down the street. What if they slip and fall?'

'I'll carry it,' Melissa said.

'Same goes. It's not the night for doing a flit, is it?'

'I'm not doing a flit! You've given me notice and I've found somewhere else. And I believe my rent is paid up to date.'

'Eeh, Melissa, lass, it was only a way of talking. Lissen, we've got a handcart in the backyard. You can borrow it if you like, and that way it should only take you a couple of trips to shift everything. Only one if the pavements weren't so treacherous. As it is, it'll take the three of you to control it on the way downhill.'

Mary Bruce took the Thompson lads through the house to the yard and then let them out into the lane with the handcart. A little later they appeared at the front door. Their eyes were shining and their cheeks were rosy. Melissa realised they were enjoying themselves.

Melissa saw no point in lingering. She wanted to get away as soon as possible so, against her own better judgement, she piled everything she owned on to the handcart and tied it down with the rope the landlady supplied. Sam and Billy Junior were in a state of high excitement and Melissa had to restrain them from setting off straight away. She still had to return her house key.

Mary Bruce had been hovering in the passage. 'Do you want to check the room?' Melissa asked her. 'To make sure I haven't helped myself to anything that belongs to you?'

'There's no need to take that attitude. I don't for one moment think you are a thief and I wish your aunt had never come here and told me what she did. But once she had I was duty-bound to tell Tom. I would never keep secrets from him. And he said you must go.'

'Of course. Here is your key.'

Mrs Bruce took the key and slipped it into the pocket of her pinafore. 'And here is something for you,' she said. She handed Melissa a florin. 'That's your change from the five and sixpence weekly rent.'

'Why are you giving me this?' Melissa asked.

'Well, you're not staying the full week, are you?'

'But what about giving notice?'

'You didn't have to. I asked you to leave. Although you needn't have cleared out so quickly you know.'

'I thought it best.'

Melissa stared at the coin in her hand. She didn't like accepting something she thought was not due to her but she couldn't deny that she needed the money. Maud Thompson was asking two shillings for one room, without coals or food. In her hand she held her first week's rent.

'Go on – put it in your pocket. It will make me feel better.'

'Thank you,' Melissa said, and she did as she was told.

They said goodbye quickly after that and Melissa and the Thompson boys set off down the road on their treacherous journey. The handcart was not very wide so Melissa's belongings were piled precariously high. There was no way that Sam or Billy could see over the top of the load so Melissa had to direct them. It was not a matter of pushing the cart, for if they had let it go it would have run downhill powered by its own momentum. Both lads hung on grimly to slow it down and every now and then they steered it into the kerb, which acted as a brake.

Melissa walked at the side with one hand hanging on to

the rope that was securing her belongings. Somewhere along the way they acquired a following. She heard pattering footsteps and shrill laughter. The lamplight revealed children of all shapes and sizes in shabby or even ragged clothes. With Melissa and her handcart leading the way the little troupe looked like a circus cavalcade.

The gleeful noise rose in a crescendo as, at last, they managed to stop the cart at the door of Melissa's new lodgings. And then, suddenly, a door across the street opened and a fierce old woman appeared with a broomstick and yelled at the children to go away. They scattered immediately.

At the same time Maud Thompson opened her door and yelled, 'For goodness' sake, Bella, heven't you anything better to do than shout at harmless little bairns!'

The old woman retreated and slammed her door.

'Nebby old thing,' Maud Thompson grumbled. 'That one minds anybody's business but her own.'

At that point Melissa found herself thinking of Reenie and how much she would have enjoyed the chaotic journey down the bank. And how they would both have been laughing by now.

Now that they had stopped, the Thompson boys had started shivering with the cold. 'Now, lads,' their mother said, 'put a couple of bricks under the wheels and help Miss Dornay get her things inside.'

The Thompson boys worked quickly and when everything was unloaded Melissa asked them to take the cart straight back to Mrs Bruce. When they returned she gave them three pence each, but noticed that they handed the money straight over to their mother. Then she was left alone in her room.

She was warm because of the physical exertion needed to unpack and arrange her belongings. When she stopped because she could do no more that night she sat down on the bed to rest and very soon realised how cold the room was. She looked towards the hearth. The grate was empty; the bars clean with not even a speck of old ash on the hearth. Perhaps there hadn't been a fire in this room since Mrs Thompson's mother had died. Well, she knew how to lay and light a fire – when she'd been a child she'd helped her mother often enough – but there was no coal in the scuttle.

She remembered that Mrs Thompson had told her that she would have to buy her coal from her and she picked up the scuttle and went along the passage to the kitchen. She knocked but there was no reply so, eventually, she opened the door and entered. There was no one there except the oldest boy, Billy. He was sitting at the table with his arms outspread and his head down. He had been asleep but the cold draught caused when Melissa opened the door must have wakened him because he raised his head and looked over his shoulder. He smiled sleepily.

'I'd like to speak to your mother,' Melissa said.

'She's gone to work – down to the Keelman's Arms on the quayside. The bairns are all in bed and I'm in charge.'

Billy appeared to be no more than ten years old but looks could be deceiving. Melissa had learned from her visits to the old almshouse that many of the city's children were so ill fed that they did not develop properly and could look years younger than they were.

'What do you want, Miss Dornay?' he asked. 'Me mam said I was to help you if you needed anything.'

'I want to light a fire in my room, Billy. I need some coal.' She saw a worried look cross his face and she added, 'It's all right. I'll be paying your mother for the coal. You can tell her how much I've taken.'

His grin was rueful. 'Well, that won't be possible because there's nowt left to take.'

'No coal?'

'No, the coal house is empty. You can gan out and hev a look if you don't believe me.'

'No . . . of course I believe you.'

'You can sit by the fire in here if you like. There's enough coal to keep it going until me mam comes back. She'll bring a bucketful up from the pub as usual. If she remembers she might bring another bucket for you.'

'Is that how you get your coal? I mean, does your mother always bring it back from work?'

'Aye, if the gaffer's in a good mood. And I helps out by gannin' over the wall of Dobson's coal yard and stuffing a sack.'

'You steal it?'

Billy looked offended. 'I only take the rubbish; the little bits that are lying about the yard. No one else would want it. At least that's what me mam says. Tell you what!' His face lit up. 'If you mind the bairns I'll gan and get some right now. It's not far. I could be back before the hour's up.'

'No, it doesn't matter.'

'Is it the bairns you're worrying about? They won't give you no bother. They're all fast asleep.'

'It's not that. You've worked hard today and I can see you're weary. I don't want to send you out when you should be resting.'

Melissa went back to her room. She was cold and hungry. She undressed as quickly as she could, pulled on her night-dress and got into bed. The sheets were clean but worn, and the blankets rough. After lying shivering for a while Melissa got up and placed her cloak on top of the bedclothes.

It was a while before she slept. She wondered about the morality of sending a small boy to steal coal, even if it was only the sweepings from the yard. She suspected that if she had five children to keep warm and no man to bring in a decent wage she might do the same.

Tomorrow she would have to go to the coalman and buy a small sack of coal. She would also have to go to Mr Ali's shop and buy whatever provisions she could afford to keep her going.

The curtains were thin and did nothing to prevent the winter moon from shining through to reveal the poverty of her surroundings. A feeling of intense loneliness almost overwhelmed her. Then bittersweet memories came flooding in. She remembered another winter's night when she had been little more than a child. She had woken up and gone to the window to gaze out on a world made beautiful by clean fresh snow. But the beauty had not lasted more than a few hours. By morning the snow was melting and the pavements were awash with soot-stained slush.

But her home had been warm and filled with love. Her mother, whose life had not been easy since Melissa's father had been lost at sea, had worked hard to provide for her. And Emmeline Dornay had had dreams of an even better future for her daughter. Melissa wondered if her mother was looking down from heaven at her now and if her heart was breaking.

A cold tear trickled down her cheek and she wiped it away angrily. She knew it was wrong to give way to self-pity like this. She thought of Ginger, the small boy who had no mother and no home save the streets. He looked after his brothers and sister as best he could with no advantages except his quick wits and his will to survive.

I have so much more, Melissa thought. I have a roof over my head and the skills my mother taught me. And I also have the dreams she dreamed for me. I must not betray her. I must make those dreams come true.

Chapter Nineteen

The cold air almost took Reenie's breath away and the skin of her face was tingling. Despite her sturdy winter boots she could no longer feel her toes. She stopped, moved the handle of the basket further along her arm and reached into her pocket for Melissa's letter. Not wishing to take off her gloves, she fumbled with the envelope, extracted the letter and examined it for about the third time since she had got off the tram.

Melissa's instructions and the map she had drawn were clear enough but, glancing around at the mean little houses and the cobbled streets that fell away so steeply down to the river, she still found it hard to believe that she had come the right way. She stuffed the letter back in her coat pocket and set off once more for Melissa's new lodgings.

The staff at the Winterton house had been given no time off since the middle of December as they prepared for the grand receptions and dinner parties that Mrs Winterton had planned. Christmas Day, a time for families, had been a strange affair. The only guests had been an elderly spinster sister of Mr Winterton, and Mr and Mrs Frost, who were Mrs Winterton's parents.

As well as having peeled, scraped and chopped mounds of vegetables, when the time came to serve, Reenie had been instructed to put on her best grey dress and a fancy white pinafore and help to carry the steaming hot serving dishes to the table. She observed the guests with curiosity and interest.

Miss Winterton, tall and ungainly, had been quiet and overawed by her brother's lavish surroundings, but the Frosts were a cheery little couple who moved and spoke with a sort of heightened reality. They reminded Reenie of actors on a stage. No one could remember any one of the three of them having visited the house before, although Ena told the assembled servants round the table in the kitchen that Mrs Winterton visited her parents now and then; usually in response to a letter from her mother.

'Probably asking for money,' the lady's maid had added unpleasantly.

Gwendolyn and her husband, Douglas, had not been invited and it was clear how unhappy Mrs Winterton was about that. And that was the probable reason for inviting Mr Winterton's sister and Mrs Winterton's parents. It would be to try to give some semblance of a happy family occasion. That was the general opinion.

However, the family members had been banished, like Cinderella, well before midnight on Christmas Day because on Boxing Day the Wintertons had been 'at home' to an endless round of fashionable visitors. The upstairs staff had been kept busy 'waiting on' to the point of exhaustion and, in the kitchen, Mrs Barton had not sat down all day. In the scullery Reenie had stood at the sink helping Polly to wash dishes until their hands were sore and their legs were aching.

Reenie had been promised the next day off but there was so much clearing-up still to do that the promise was broken. But now, one day later than planned, she was free until supper time and she was going to see Melissa. Finally she found the right street and the right door. Before she had time to knock the door was opened.

'I saw you coming,' Melissa said. 'I've been keeping watch at the window this past half-hour!'

'Am I late?'

'No, but I've been so looking forward to seeing you! But don't let's stand here in the cold. Come in.'

Reenie followed Melissa into the front room and her first impression, despite the fire crackling in the hearth, was that it wasn't much warmer inside than out. She tried not to betray her feelings but Melissa must have read her mind.

'Don't worry, I'll build the fire up. I've been trying to be economical with the coal.'

Reenie was filled with consternation. While Melissa busied herself with the coal tongs she looked round and saw that the wallpaper was faded and had stains here and there, which spoke of damp. And what furniture there was looked as if it had come from a back lane junk shop. But, surprisingly, there was a beautiful brightly coloured spread on the bed and a rug with similar patterns by the hearth.

She realised that Melissa had straightened up and was looking at her.

'My landlady's sailor husband brought the bedspread and the rug home from Arabia. It's good of her to let me use them.'

'They're real bonny.'

'Mr Thompson didn't come home from his last voyage.'

Reenie didn't know what to say. She guessed that Melissa was thinking of her own father.

'Well, don't just stand there,' Melissa said. 'Take your hat and coat off and I'll make a cup of tea.'

Reenie remembered the basket she was carrying. She put it on the table and, like a stage magician revealing some piece of magic, whipped off the checked cloth that was covering the contents.

'Look,' she said. 'Old Ma Barton has a heart after all. She

guessed I would be coming to visit you and just see what she's sent for us to eat.'

Reenie began to empty the basket, placing the contents on the table. There was almost a whole fruit loaf, a dozen sausage rolls and about half a pound of cheese. There was also a large loaf of bread. Reenie gazed at it doubtfully.

'It's a little stale but I suppose we could always toast it.'

'Of course we could. We'll have a veritable feast. But first you must come and warm yourself by the fire.'

While Reenie warmed her toes and fingers Melissa told her everything that had happened.

'I can't believe that Cora woman would do such a thing!' Reenie exclaimed. 'What a crafty cat she must be.'

'Eileen – she works at Wilkinson's – says I'm partly to blame. I should have found out more about her and kept the frocks until they were paid for.'

'Aye, you were too trusting there. I hope you've learned your lesson.'

Reenie was already indignant on Melissa's behalf but when Melissa told her why she had had to move, her indignation turned to fury.

'So that was it. When you wrote to me to tell me you'd changed lodgings I thought it might be to save a little on the rent. I would never hev believed that nice Mrs Bruce would sling you out, and all because that wicked aunt of yours couldn't mind her own business!'

'Well, let's not talk of it now,' Melissa said. 'I bought a quarter-pound of sliced ham from Mr Ali's shop and he threw in a half-pound of pease pudding. With everything you've brought this will be a proper Christmas celebration.'

For the rest of the day they did no more than eat and talk. Over lunch Reenie asked Melissa how she had spent Christmas Day. 'Were you all alone?'

'No, I had the children to look after.'

'What children?'

'My landlady's children. Mrs Thompson was working all day at a pub on the quayside.'

'What would she have done if you hadn't been here?'

'Billy would have coped.'

'The eldest?'

'That's right. Although I don't think he's much more than ten years old. He looks after his brothers and his sisters at weekends when his mother's at work. And during the week he often has to bring them home from school and get them their tea.'

'Poor bairns,' Reenie said. 'But at least their ma's got a job.'

'She has more than one. As well as working at the public house – that's where she is today – she goes cleaning in some of the shipping offices. Honestly, Reenie, she looks exhausted most of the time. It makes me realise how lucky I am.'

Reenie looked at Melissa and saw that she meant it.

Once more Melissa interpreted her friend's expression. 'I'm young and strong. I have a skill my mother taught me and in next to no time I'll be moving up the hill again.' She smiled.

'Well, anyways, what did you and these bairns have for your Christmas dinner?'

'Mrs Thompson left a big pan of broth. She made it with a ham bone she brought home from work at the pub. It was delicious.'

'And that was all?'

'Sally Ali brought a whole box of oranges.'

'Sally Ali? What sort of name is that when it's at home?' Reenie grinned.

'Her name is Sarah and she's married to Mr Ali, who keeps the corner shop. Mrs Ali was at school with Mrs Thompson; she's very kind.'

'And what about Boxing Day?' Reenie asked.

'I went to help at the soup kitchen, as promised. I was there all day. I probably washed as many dishes as you did.'

'Aye, well, I divven't hev to wash quite so many these days; not now there's another little lass in the scullery doing the work I used to do. But, like I said, you mustn't do that sort of thing too often. You've got to look after those ladylike hands of yours.'

They smiled at each other companionably and continued their lunch. Afterwards Melissa blew out her cheeks and placed her hands on her stomach with fingers spread as if she was bursting.

'That was good,' she said.

'Aye, and all the better because of the good company.'

'But, seriously, I think I've eaten too much. Perhaps we should go for a walk.'

'Where on earth would we go?' Reenie glanced out of the window at the heavy grey sky.

'Down to the river,' Melissa replied. 'Remember we used to walk there? There's always something to see. The ships, the people; it's interesting.'

'Interesting it may be but on a day like this it will be perishing!' Reenie said. 'Let's stay here by the fire.'

So they did. But later Reenie wondered if Melissa had been trying to save on the coal. If they'd gone out she could have banked the fire down so that it would burn less. While they talked Melissa put a cheerful face on and told her not to worry; that she would be getting plenty of work in. In fact, Mrs Ali, the shopkeeper's wife, had already called with a bundle of mending and she'd promised to put a card in the shop window free of charge and recommend Melissa to all her friends.

When it was time to go Reenie looked at the table. 'What about those dishes?' she asked. 'Here, pass that tray. I'll gan along to the kitchen and wash them for you.'

'No, just put the tray on top of that little cupboard under the window. I'll wash them later. You have enough dishes to wash every day. I have very few. Now don't argue with me!'

Reenie smiled. 'Well, at least let me help you clear the table.'

'All right, you can cover up the food that's left and put it inside the cupboard. It's so cold under that window that it's like a proper pantry.'

When the table was clear Melissa folded the cloth and lifted up the sewing machine from where it had been stowed in a corner. She took a pile of folded clothes from one of the chairs and got out her sewing basket.

'Are you going to work tonight?' Reenie asked.

'Yes. Why not?'

'Oh, no reason. I just thought you might give yourself a holiday today.' Melissa closed the curtains and concentrated on lighting the oil lamp, which stood on top of the cupboard. 'I must catch up with this mending,' she said. 'My customers are waiting for these things. And, besides, I have had a holiday. Today has been wonderful.'

'Well, aren't you at least going to light the gas? You'll ruin your eyesight if you work in this poor light.'

'Well . . . perhaps later,' Melissa said.

'Oh, for goodness' sake!' Reenie's concern made her sound brusque. 'Where's the meter?' She took her purse from her pocket.

'No, it's all right – don't . . .'

But Reenie had already opened the door and gone out to the passage. The light from the streetlamp just outside shone through the fanlight above the door. She found the meter where most meters were in small houses such as this, on the wall in the tiny porch. She fed in three pennies, satisfied that would keep Melissa going for a day or two, and went back to find Melissa looking upset.

'You didn't have to do that,' she said.

'Now, divven't gan on at me. I've sat by your fire all day and drunk your tea and eaten your ham so the least I can do is put a few pence in the meter. I can afford it, you know. I've nowt else to spend me wages on.'

She put her coat and hat on and took her leave reluctantly. 'I wish I could stay here with you,' she said. 'One day, mebbes.'

'Yes, one day.'

'Now wrap yourself up in that shawl if you're going to see me to the door. It's bitter cold out there.'

When Reenie opened the front door she jumped back in fright, startling Melissa, who was right behind her.

'Divven't you dare hit me, you ruffian!' she said.

Melissa looked over Reenie's shoulder to see the bulky figure of a man. He had his hand raised as if he were about to strike Reenie but the light from the lamp fell across his face and revealed that he was almost as startled as she was. He recovered himself quickly. 'I wasn't going to hit you, you stupid little lass. I was just about to knock on the door.'

'Divven't call me stupid. It's you that's stupid, creeping up and frightening a body like that.'

The man sighed. 'I wasn't creeping up. I was simply trying to make a call on Mrs Thompson. Now will you tell her I'm here?'

'Why? Who are you?'

'That's none of your business. Now do as you're told, there's a good lass, and go and get Mrs Thompson.'

'Divven't talk to me like that. I'm not a servant here.'

The man laughed. 'I didn't think you were. Maud Thompson could never afford a servant. Now are you going to get her?'

'No, I'm not, because she's not in.'

'Pull the other one.'

'I beg your pardon? Are you suggesting I'm telling lies?'

Melissa decided this had gone on long enough and she put her hands on Reenie's shoulders and drew her aside. 'My friend told you the truth,' she said. 'Mrs Thompson has not come back from work yet.'

The man's eyes widened as he looked at Melissa. Reenie could see how surprised he was.

'And may I ask who you are and what you're doing here?' he said.

'I rent a room from Mrs Thompson,' Melissa told him.

'Do you indeed? She's subletting, is she? Well, she never told me, but that's good news in a way because now she might be able to start paying off the arrears in her rent.'

'Is that why you're here?' Melissa asked. 'Are you the rent collector?'

'Yes, young lady, I am.'

'Then what are you doing here today?' Reenie interrupted. 'Most folk don't pay their rent until Friday.'

Melissa gripped Reenie's arms, willing her not to anger the man. That would only cause trouble for Mrs Thompson.

But, far from being angry, he laughed. 'That's precisely why I've come along today. I'll be back tomorrow and I don't want any of the bairns coming to the door to say their ma's out and that she's forgotten to leave the rent.'

He looked at Melissa as if hoping for a more reasonable response. 'I didn't have to come tonight but I thought it only fair to warn Mrs Thompson that the new landlord is not so understanding as the old one and he won't put up with it much longer. Now will you tell her that?'

Melissa nodded. 'I will.'

'I'll bid you good night, then.' He turned to go but stopped and looked at Melissa long and hard. 'I don't know what has brought you here, miss, a lady like you, but I feel I should advise you to try and find somewhere better. Things are going to change around here.'

Reenie worried all the way home and long into the night. She had been shocked to find Melissa living in such a poor area. No matter that Mrs Thompson's house was reasonably clean, she suspected that the sort of customers Melissa wanted would not venture that far away from the more respectable streets further up the hill.

Melissa had assured her that she had plenty of mending and altering jobs, but what sort of work was that for a dressmaker as talented as she was? It was all the more frustrating because Reenie could think of no way that she could help her friend.

And what was all that about Mrs Thompson being behind with the rent? The rent collector, for all his cheek, didn't seem to be a bad sort. After all, he had come to warn Mrs Thompson about the new landlord. Reenie could only hope that now Melissa was lodging there and paying her rent for her room, Mrs Thompson would be able to pay off the arrears.

Meanwhile, all she, Reenie, could do was go to visit Melissa every week and try to cadge a few little luxuries from Mrs Barton to take along and make life a little more enjoyable.

Melissa stayed up until after midnight, catching up with her work. When she heard Mrs Thompson come home she went along to the kitchen. She knocked and entered just as her landlady was lighting the oil lamp that stood on the bare scrubbed table.

'Hello, pet,' Mrs Thompson said. 'You're up late. Hev you been working?'

'Yes. But I wanted to give you these.' Melissa placed half

of the loaf that Reenie had brought on the table, and the rest of the sausage rolls. 'I'll never be able to eat all this myself and it would be a shame to waste them.'

'That's very kind of you, hinny. The bread'll be grand toasted in the morning for the bairns' breakfast.'

'There's something else.' Melissa hesitated for a moment and then she gave Mrs Thompson the message from the rent collector.

Mrs Thompson sighed. 'It was good of him to warn me, I suppose. I'll try and give a little extra every week until I've caught up.' She took off her coat and hung it on a hook on the door. She turned to face Melissa and smiled.

'Would you like a drink?' she asked. 'I'm going to have one; I'm fair parched.'

'Shall I make us a pot of tea?' Melissa asked.

'No, not tea, hinny. I mean a proper drink!'

She drew a bottle from her coat pocket and put it on the table. Then she went into the scullery and came back with two clean cups. She placed them on the table next to the bottle and then sank down on to the nearest chair with a heartfelt sigh.

'Sit down, lass, and we'll hev ourselves a nice little sip of Old Tom.' She began to unscrew the cap of the bottle.

Melissa sat down but she looked at the bottle doubtfully. 'What's Old Tom? A cordial?'

Maud Thompson laughed. 'Bless you, Melissa, hinny, Old Tom's cordial enough if it's pleasant you mean, but no, pet, this isn't a fruit drink, it's good hard liquor and just what I need at the end of a working day.' She held the bottle near to the oil lamp so that the clear liquid inside caught the light. 'It's gin,' she said. 'And at half a crown a bottle, it's worth every penny.' She poured a measure into one cup and then paused with the bottle held over the other. 'Now are you going to have some?'

'No, thank you,' Melissa said.

'Divven't say you've signed the pledge?'

'Joined the Temperance League? No, I haven't.'

'I was joking, pet. But don't you ever take a drink?'

'I've never had the opportunity.'

'Well, how about it? Go on – keep me company – I hate drinking alone. Just a little taste to see if you like it.'

Without waiting for an answer Mrs Thompson poured a drop into the other cup and pushed it across to table to Melissa, then she raised her own cup and said, 'Bottoms up!'

Melissa sipped the drink hesitantly and knew at once that she didn't like it. It had a strange sharp yet sweet taste that caught in the back of her throat. Maud Thompson laughed.

'You don't have to tell me,' she said. 'From the look on your face you won't be asking for a fill-up.'

She had already emptied her own cup and was in the act of pouring herself some more. She raised the cup in Melissa's direction again and nodded towards the bottle. 'Best half a crown I've spent this week,' she said. 'Mother's ruin, they call it, but in my opinion it ought to be called Mother's comfort!'

She took another drink, this time more slowly, and her eyes closed as she savoured it. 'By God, that was good,' she said as she put the empty cup down on the table. She picked up the bottle, looked at it longingly but then shook her head and screwed the cap back on. 'No more or I'll not hev a clear head when I gets up the morrow.'

Mrs Thompson stood up, knocking her chair over and looked down at it in surprise. 'Eeh, I'm getting that clumsy,' she said.

'Here, let me help you.' Melissa rose and hurried round to pick up the chair.

'Thanks, pet.'

'Well . . . good night, then.'

'That's another day over, eh?'

Mrs Thompson went to see to the fire. The coals flared momentarily when she disturbed them and illumined the sheer exhaustion outlined in her gaunt face. Melissa slipped quietly away.

Back in her own room she folded the clothes she had mended and put her sewing things away. This work would just bring in a few coppers. She could only hope that more mending and alterations would come in soon.

Lying in bed she wondered about Mrs Thompson and her bottle of gin. It had cost her half a crown. That was a lot of money; maybe half her day's wage. She wondered how often her landlady brought a bottle home. Could this be the reason she had fallen behind with her rent? Melissa had seen the results of drinking during her work at the soup kitchen: the poor souls who had spent all their money on alcohol and as a result had become workless and homeless.

Some of the good folk who helped at the soup kitchen could hardly hide their disapproval but Mrs Simmons could not find it in her heart to condemn them. 'Just think of the lives they lead,' she had said to Melissa. 'The sheer grinding poverty of their days. No wonder the poor souls needed something to comfort them.'

Mother's comfort . . . that's what Mrs Thompson had called her bottle of Old Tom. Melissa could only hope that the poor woman would not come to rely on it too heavily and make herself and her children homeless.

At tea time the next day there was a loud knocking at the door. Usually, if their mother was out, one of the children would run along to answer it. But the knocking went on and on so eventually Melissa put down the shirt she was altering and went to the door herself. The rent collector stood there. He smiled when he recognised her.

'Is Mrs Thompson home?' he asked.

'I'm not sure.'

'Well, I'd be obliged if you would find out.' Melissa was about to go when he added, 'And if she's not there one of the bairns will do. Billy, probably.'

Melissa looked over his shoulder and was aware of curtains twitching in the house opposite. 'Very well,' she said.

She knocked on the kitchen door but there was no response. She paused a moment and then entered. There was a flash of movement and she saw the door to the scullery closing. She heard children's voices and then someone – it sounded like Billy – saying, 'Whisht!'

Melissa crossed to the scullery door, opened it and saw all five children trying to hide under the bench. Billy looked up at her with pleading eyes.

'There's no one in,' he whispered. And seeing Melissa's puzzled frown, he added, 'Our mam said that if anyone called we had to pretend to be out.'

'I see.'

Useless to ask whether their mother had left the rent money with them. Melissa knew what the answer would be. She closed the door quietly and then the kitchen door, and went back to face the rent collector.

He spoke before she had a chance to say anything. 'I can see from the look on your face that you're going to tell me Mrs Thompson is not at home.'

'I'm afraid that's so.'

'And the children?'

'I'm sorry.'

'Well, that's not an answer but it doesn't matter because I can see that despite my warning she hasn't left the rent money.'

'It doesn't seem so.'

'You did give her my message, didn't you?'

'I did. But she was tired when she came home from work last night and maybe she didn't—'

The rent collector held up his hand. 'Don't make excuses for her. Just tell her again. This new landlord doesn't have the patience the old one had. He's got plans and he's looking for any excuse to turn people out. Mrs Thompson had better be careful.'

'I'll tell her. As soon as she comes home tonight.'

'You'd better. And when I come along next week I want there to be no excuses. Good day to you.'

Nearly a week later all save one of Melissa's customers had been to collect their mended clothes. But no one had given her any new work. She mentioned this to Mrs Ali when she came to collect her little daughter's school smock.

Melissa had let the hem down. She suspected that the shopkeeper's wife could have done this herself but she was being kind. Perhaps for Melissa's sake, or perhaps by helping Melissa, she was helping her old school friend Maud Thompson. At Melissa's invitation Mrs Ali sat down for a cup of tea.

'It's a hard time of the year,' Mrs Ali said. 'Many of the men are laid off when the weather is too bad for them to work. And although some of the builders' labourers get wet money that's less than half they would get for a proper day's work. I'm sure once the weather picks up you'll have plenty customers but until then have you thought of getting a job in the sewing room of a department store?'

'I've considered it,' Melissa replied. 'I've even talked it over with a friend who works at Wilkinson's. But to work in a department store you have to have served a recognised apprenticeship.'

'And haven't you?'

'No, everything I know I learned from my mother.'

'Pity. And I suppose an apprentice's pay wouldn't be enough to keep you.'

'Apprentices don't get paid at all.'

'And how long would that be for?'

'Two years.'

Mrs Ali shook her head. 'How do they get away with that?'

'It's because the girls are training. And at least they don't charge the apprentices a learning fee.'

'Can they do that?'

'My mother served an apprenticeship with a fully trained corner dressmaker and my grandfather had to pay a fee. But even if I had enough savings to keep myself for two years I'd only get a job paying about seven shillings and sixpence a week at the end of it.'

Mrs Ali's large blue eyes filled with concern. 'When I hear things like this I realise how lucky I am. I have no training of any kind. When I left school my mother kept me at home to look after the little ones. I've never had to bring home a pay packet. The only job I had was to help serve teas at the Seaman's Mission. And that was voluntary.

'That's where I met Ali and here I am married to a good man and comfortably off, with no worries about where the next meal's coming from, while my old school friend Maud can hardly manage to feed herself, never mind the bairns. And a beautiful, intelligent young woman like you can barely earn enough to pay her rent.

'The sooner the winter's over, the better,' Mrs Ali continued. 'When folk have a bit spare cash you might be asked to make some nice little dresses for Easter. But meanwhile, how will you manage?'

'Well, I might have found something,' Melissa said.

'And what's that?'

'My friend at Wilkinson's told me that the department stores might not employ me in their sewing rooms but that they would probably give me piecework – you know, blouses and shirts and the like to make at home. All I'll have to do is show them some of my work.'

'And have you got some nice things to show them?'

'There's a coat and a skirt that a certain customer didn't collect. The material is poor but I'm confident that the cut and the stitching will pass muster. And then I could always show them Ninette.'

'And who exactly is Ninette?'

Melissa smiled and she got up and went over to the bed where Ninette had been resting among the cushions.

'Let me introduce you.'

'A doll!' Mrs Ali said. 'And I don't think I've ever seen a doll like it. Is it French?'

'Yes, my father brought it home when I was a little girl.'

'May I hold her?'

Melissa handed her the doll.

'Her clothes! They're so beautiful. They look like something from a fashion magazine.'

'They are. And look – there are more.' Melissa brought the large shoe box over that contained all of Ninette's outfits. 'Go on, you can have a look at them.'

Mrs Ali took all the little garments out one by one and laid them on the table. 'You made these, didn't you?'

'Yes.'

'I wish I was still a little girl and I would ask you if I could borrow your doll and take her home and play with her!'

'She's not really a doll to be played with. That would hurt her feelings. Ninette is more of a fashion mannequin now.' Melissa was smiling.

'You should be designing gowns, not just making them.'

'I'd like to do that.'

'Well, maybe if you show the people at the department store all these things they'd let you do that.'

'I don't think so. They've never heard of me.'

'One day everyone will have heard of you and I'll be able to say that you once mended my little Lucy's school smock! But listen, Melissa, if you like I can give you another order straight away. I've bought a beautiful doll for Lucy's birthday. I've hidden it on top of the wardrobe. It has the sweetest little party dress but that's all. Do you think you could make some other dresses for it? And perhaps a little coat and a bonnet?'

'I'd love to do that.'

'I can buy whatever material you'd need if you just make a list.'

'Better than that, I'll see Eileen, my friend at Wilkinson's, and ask her for some remnants. You never know what she might throw in in the way of ribbons and scraps of lace if I tell her what it's for.'

'Wonderful! I'll go and get the doll straight away and I'll give you some money. You must tell me how much you think you'll need. Is that all right?'

Melissa would have liked to have said that it didn't matter and that Mrs Ali could pay her later but her savings were getting dangerously low and her recent earnings would only just pay next week's rent.

'Yes, that's fine,' she said.

Chapter Twenty

March 1894

A boisterous March wind was blowing up from the river when Melissa set off on her usual morning journey. It was very early, and dark figures, their heads and faces muffled by caps and scarves, marched like a silent army down the steep streets towards the shipyards, the studs of their steel-capped boots striking sparks from the cobbles. The slighter, more insubstantial figures of clerks and shopworkers, both male and female, hurried in the opposite direction. Like Melissa they were heading towards the town.

Soon she was standing with the other women in an orderly line stretching along the pavement from the locked doors of the shirt factory. She had pulled a long scarf over her head and was wearing her warmest gloves. She held her bundle of shirts close to her body to gain some extra warmth.

Her fellow home workers greeted each other quietly but cheerfully. When she considered the sheer drudgery of their lives Melissa marvelled at their stoicism. Most of them worked from seven in the morning until after midnight. Melissa often did this herself but she did not have children to look after, nor anyone to feed but herself.

After Christmas there had been very little dressmaking work. She had enjoyed making a complete wardrobe for Lucy Ali's new doll and Mrs Ali had insisted on paying her more than she had asked for. But since then she had only made coppers for a few mending jobs.

'You'll have to save up and find new lodgings nearer to the more fashionable areas of town,' Eileen, her friend at Wilkinson's, had told her.

'But how can I save if I'm not earning anything?' Melissa had replied.

'Well . . . there is some work I could tell you about but you might not like it.'

'What work? And why wouldn't I like it?'

'Because it's not very well paid. In fact, there are some society ladies who are trying to change things. I've read about them in the newspapers. They liken it to slave labour.'

'But if it's the only work I can get I must consider it.'

'Very well. I happen to know that the shirt factory is taking on stitchers. Stitchers work at home and that's slightly better than working in the factory itself, for at least you can work in comfort.'

'Tell me about it.'

'The shirts are cut out in the factory and bundled up in dozens. You take your bundles home, stitch them, sew the buttons on, and take them back to be laundered and packed.'

'That doesn't sound too difficult, simply making up ready-cut shirts.'

'Except that the pay is so little that you have to stitch an awful lot of shirts to make a living.'

'How much do they pay?'

'Usually seven pence a dozen.'

'A dozen?'

'I'm afraid so.'

They looked at each other solemnly for a moment and then Melissa said, 'I've no choice. If they'll take me on I'll have to do it.'

'And meanwhile I'll go on recommending you to anyone who wants a good dressmaker,' Eileen said. 'You never know, there might be someone with enough sense not to be put off by your address.'

Melissa called at the shirt factory and a brisk supervisor set her to work making a test garment.

'Very good,' she said when Melissa handed her the finished shirt. 'Have you got your own sewing machine?'

'Yes, I have.'

Melissa was surprised by the question but the supervisor explained that many of the stitchers did not have machines of their own, so the factory either let them hire one or buy one from them, paying the cost price in instalments. She also told her that her finished work would be examined by experienced employees and if it was not correctly done she would not be given any more. Also she would have to pay the cost of any alterations that were needed.

'You'll have to buy your own buttons and thread, but we can supply them to you cheaper than you would get them elsewhere; likewise your sewing machine oil. The finished shirts should be brought back the next morning,' she added. 'How many would you like to start with?' When Melissa hesitated the woman said, 'Some experienced stitchers manage two dozen.'

Two dozen shirts in one day, Melissa thought, and that would earn her one shilling and tuppence. This truly was slave labour. But she needed the money so she said that two dozen would be fine.

As the supervisor handed Melissa her first bundle of two dozen shirts she said, 'You need not count today. I'll start the reckoning from tomorrow. However, I must warn you that after that, if you are more than a day late returning the shirts, threepence will be deducted. Do you agree to our conditions?'

Melissa had had no course but to agree and she had taken her first day's work home in a linen bag – which was also her responsibility to keep clean. The first batch of shirts took her twelve hours to complete and she barely had time to stop for a bite to eat. Gradually, as she became more experienced, she had managed to cut the hours down but she soon realised that many of the other stitchers took much longer than she did.

She could see the exhaustion in their faces as they brought their work in very early in the morning and collected the next batch of shirts. This morning a group of stitchers was huddled around another woman, who was crying.

'What is it?' someone outside the group asked.

'She's fallen behind with her payments,' another said. 'If she doesn't give them what's owing today, they're going to take the machine back and she'll never be able to manage even half of what she usually does if she has to sew them by hand.'

'We can't hev that,' a third speaker said. 'Hawway, lasses, let's see what we can do.'

She gave her bundle to another woman to hold and began to go around the assembled stitchers holding out her pinafore. Melissa heard the clink of coins as the other women began to throw them in.

'A farthing's all I can spare,' someone said. 'I'm sorry.'

'Me too,' another added.

'Divven't fret, hinny,' the collector said. 'We'll all give what we can. There's enough of us here to make up the payment.'

'Eeh, I'm that sorry, Nell, I can't give nowt at all,' the next woman she stopped in front of said.

'That's all right. We all know the trouble you've had, having to pay a doctor for the bairn.'

Melissa felt humbled by the love and concern that was demonstrated by the women's generosity and when her turn came she gave sixpence, which was all she had with her.

'Thanks, pet,' Nell said. 'You never say much but I telt the other lasses you were all right.'

By the time the factory door was about to open enough money had been collected to cover the woman's instalment and she was now weeping with relief.

'How will I ever pay you all back?' she asked.

The woman called Nell told her, 'We don't expect you to. At least I don't. What about you other lasses?'

She looked around the group and Melissa thought no one would have the nerve to disagree with this cheerful raw-boned woman.

In the ensuing silence Nell said, 'There, you see? But for heaven's sake pull yourself together and don't fall behind again. And another thing – if anyone else gets into trouble I'm sure you'll be pleased to help out like the rest of us.'

The woman, too full of emotion to say more, nodded. She wiped her eyes on her pinafore and was ready with the rest of them when the doors opened.

And now all charitable thoughts were pushed aside. Those who could get in first and have their completed shirts inspected would get their new bundles first and would be able to hurry home to start work as soon as possible. They made sure that they kept their own place in the queue but, despite their anxiety, no one attempted to push in.

Melissa had got there early enough to be one of the first. It didn't take long before she had handed her shirts in, had them examined and received her pay. Then she set off to her lodgings with the new batch. She would have to start work straight away because she wanted to get as many done as possible before Reenie came.

Luckily Reenie was a little later than usual. When Melissa

heard the knock at the door she folded the finished shirts and put them in the bag, then she tidied the table before going to answer the door. Reenie would only worry if she thought Melissa had to work so hard. Melissa had no intention of telling her friend that after she would have to work until the early hours of the morning to make up the time she had taken off.

But despite her welcoming smile she could not disguise how tired she was.

'Look at you!' Reenie exclaimed. 'You look half asleep. Were you working late last night?'

Melissa told her that she had been. She didn't say that she had already put in a good few hours that very morning.

'Well, I think you need some fresh air to blow the cobwebs away. Put your coat on and we'll gan down to watch the ships on the river.'

'Don't you want a cup of tea first?'

'No, I'll treat you to breakfast at Olsen's.'

It didn't take long to walk down to the quayside, where they found the usual well-ordered turmoil as ships docked and were unloaded, and others were loaded before setting sail.

'Look at that, Melissa,' Reenie cried suddenly, and she took hold of Melissa's arm and pointed to a magnificent four-masted sailing ship nudging its way upriver, guided by two fussy little paddle tugs. 'I wonder where she's come from. You have to call a ship "she", you know.'

Melissa smiled at her friend's enthusiasm. 'Oh, I don't know,' she said. 'Somewhere far away – across many oceans – somewhere strange and exotic and extraordinary.'

They stood amidst the hustle and bustle on the quay and watched as the seamen balanced on the spars of the breathtakingly tall masts and furled the sails.

Then Reenie turned to Melissa and said, 'That's better.'

'What's better?'

'There's some colour in your cheeks and you divven't look so washed out. Hawway, let's gan and hev coffee and toast and a couple of them almond cakes.'

They sauntered along the quayside, walking upriver towards the bridges. Reenie had decided that Melissa not only needed fresh air but she also needed to have a break from the sheer drudgery of making up two dozen shirts a day. Oh, her friend had tried to convince her that it was easy but Reenie had seen her becoming pale and washed-out-looking.

She didn't know that much about sewing but she could guess what the hours hunched over the sewing machine were doing to Melissa and she had been racking her brains on the best way to help her. Melissa had assured her that as soon as she could afford better lodgings things would improve. Her friend at Wilkinson's would be able to find her some proper dressmaking work and she could leave the drudgery behind. And as if her life wasn't hard enough, Melissa was still making clothes for the homeless people. She took them, when she could, to Mrs Simmons at the soup kitchen.

Mrs Simmons . . .

Reenie almost stopped in her tracks. Why hadn't she thought of that before? She could lay odds that Melissa hadn't told Mrs Simmons of her problems. Reenie had never met the woman but from everything Melissa had told her she sounded like a very kind and decent old body. Reenie was sure Mrs Simmons would help Melissa if she could.

But the problem would be that Melissa might be too proud to ask for help. Well, there was only one thing for it. Reenie would have to persuade her to do it, and from the look of her it would have to be as quickly as possible.

Reenie had been staring into the mid-distance without really looking where she was going but now, having made her mind up to tell Melissa what she thought she should do, she looked about her again. And something she saw almost made her turn and run.

But instead she gripped Melissa's arm and said, 'I'm fair gasping. Let's gan into this café for a cup of tea.'

'In here?' Melissa looked at the café doubtfully. 'But I thought we were going to Olsen's?'

'We were – but I fancy a change, don't you?'

And holding on to Melissa's arm she almost dragged her into the small but reasonably respectable café. Melissa walked towards the nearest oilcloth-covered table but Reenie dragged her away.

'No, not here by the window,' she said. 'If we sit there it's like we're on show to all them cheeky sailor lads!'

Melissa refrained from pointing out that the table they were heading for was next to a group of foreign-looking sailors wearing jaunty uniforms. She sat at the table obediently while Reenie took the menu and gave the order to the waiter.

She knew why Reenie had dragged her in here because she had seen what Reenie had seen. Just a short distance ahead of them, seated on an upturned barrel, there was a young man with a sketch pad. He had been intent on the scene before him; no doubt capturing with a few skilful strokes the incongruity of the new steamship and the three-masted sailing ship moored alongside each other.

There was no mistaking his deft movements, his concentration, and the way a lock of his light brown hair fell forward over the page when he bent his head. Taken so utterly by surprise, Melissa's breath had caught in her throat and her heart had begun to beat painfully against her ribs. And Reenie, dear Reenie, must have guessed what pain the sight of the artist would cause her.

So her friend had pulled her into this café, not knowing

that it was already too late. Melissa knew that she must pretend that she had seen nothing. She would sit and drink and eat whatever Reenie ordered. For no one, not even Reenie, must ever know how much James Pennington had meant to her and how he so casually had broken her heart.

That night Melissa worked into the early hours in order to finish her shirts. Then, although she was bone weary, she could not sleep. She lay awake until it was almost time to get up and then slept just long enough for the old dream to return and torment her.

She was walking in the park on a sunny day. Someone was calling her from within a grove of graceful trees. It was James and he was telling her to come to him. Clusters of white and pink blossom hung from the branches and as she entered the grove the blossom fell on her hair. She began to run, following his voice, but she never found him.

Only his sketchbook lying on the ground. In her dream she picked it up to see what he had been drawing but the page was blank. And as she looked at it a tear fell from her eye and a damp mark spread across the page. The sky clouded over, the summer day became chill, and as the dream faded Melissa began to shiver. She woke up.

Melissa sat up quickly, wondering if she had slept too long. But when she glanced at the clock on the mantel shelf she realised that she had time at least to have a cup of tea before setting off for the shirt factory. After drinking her tea she made her bed and set the room to rights so that she would be able to start work as soon as she returned.

Before leaving she opened the large shoe box where she kept the clothes she had made for Ninette. The doll itself was sitting on the bed propped up against the cushions. Underneath the doll's clothes was her purse. She took what money she needed for more buttons and thread and put the purse back under the doll's clothes.

The air was damp; a fine drizzle, too slight to be called rain, formed tiny beads of moisture on her face. Melissa tucked the bag containing the shirts inside her coat. If they got wet Miss Bond, the supervisor, would scold and probably stop part of the payment. It would make little sense as the shirts were going to be laundered anyway but Melissa had learned that Miss Bond was always looking for excuses to hold back some of the money the stitchers had earned. No doubt she was following orders.

The drizzle turned into a light shower and then, without warning, into a downpour. Melissa ran the rest of the way and arrived at the factory door along with most of the other stitchers, some of them without coats and all of them worried that their precious bundles would not pass muster. At least Miss Bond had sufficient humanity to open the doors early and everyone crowded inside thankfully.

Then Melissa had to wait along with some of the others for the girl who sold the buttons and the thread. She took her time as usual, painfully adding up the quantities and the amounts in a large cashbook.

But at least the rain had stopped when Melissa set off for her lodgings. The drenched streets looked fresh and new. A watery sun struggled to shine through gaps in the clouds. A flower seller cheered up a dreary corner with a bright display of daffodils. A crowd of sparrows fussed and chattered, fighting for some scattered bread that someone had strewn across the cobbles. Even though the morning air already carried the sooty smell of hundreds of fires Melissa could not help but be cheered by the promise of spring.

She was young and she was strong, and although the work she was doing was backbreaking and tedious she had already started to put a little of her money by each week. Her only regret was that she had not been able to make as many clothes for the homeless who came to the soup kitchen as she would have liked. But she did her best to take at least one small simple garment every week and Mrs Simmons was always welcoming and grateful.

Her mood had become so buoyant that she was completely unprepared for the scene that greeted her outside her lodgings. The door of the house was open and two burly men were carrying out the furniture and household goods and dumping them on the pavement. Maud Thompson was running round like someone demented. But every time she got near her belongings one or other of the men pushed her none too gently away. A little way apart from the scene the Thompson children huddled together miserably, with Billy Junior watching over them like a faithful sheepdog.

Many of the neighbours had come out to watch, including the old lady, Bella, from across the way. She beckoned Melissa over. 'Come here, hinny. It's best you divven't get drawn into it.'

'But what's happening?'

'It's an eviction. Maud's been hoyed out. The landlord's not giving her any more chances to catch up with the rent she owes. The bailiffs are taking anything she has to sell, which will go towards paying off the debt.'

'The debt? But I thought she was paying extra every week. She said she would.'

'No doubt she did. And no doubt she meant to. But I reckon the gin got the better of her.'

'She's not a drunkard!'

'I never said she was. It's just that she doesn't think she should deny herself a treat now and then. And if you look at it one way, why shouldn't she? She works all the hours God sends. Then she has the children to care for. Who can blame her for making a friend of Old Tom? The trouble is, she can't afford to.

'So now the landlord has sent the bailiffs in. They'll take

her stuff away and sell it – if they don't manage to knock it to pieces the way they're chucking it out.'

Melissa grew agitated. 'But they're taking my belongings too!'

'Of course. They'll empty the house and then they'll change the locks. And look, here's the horse and cart coming down the street now. They'll load everything on to it and take it away to the sale rooms.'

And as soon as the cart stopped outside the house that was exactly what the men started to do. First of all the pitiful sticks of furniture and then the pots and pans and household linens.

'But they can't take my things. There's my sewing machine!'

She was about to cross the road and remonstrate with the men when Bella put a hand on her arm to restrain her. 'Can you prove it's yours?' she asked. 'A receipt or something?'

'I haven't got one.'

'Then they won't let you take it. The bailiffs will take everything they think belongs to Maud.'

'No! Not Ninette!'

The old woman frowned in puzzlement but Melissa was already hurtling across the road to try to retrieve her doll. Before she got there one of the men had placed the sewing machine on the cart and the other tossed the doll and her box full of clothes carelessly on top of a pile of household linen.

Then to her dismay her mother's needlework box followed and, as it landed, the lid fell open and bobbins of coloured cottons, packets of needles and pins, scissors and thimbles were scattered amongst Maud Thompson's sheets, blankets and tablecloths.

'No – stop – please be careful!'

Perhaps she had it in mind to snatch her things back and she moved towards the cart when she felt a hand on her shoulder.

'Leave that be,' a man said.

Melissa turned to find herself facing the rent collector. 'But the doll and the needlework box belong to me – and so does the sewing machine – and look – those are my clothes!'

'I can't help that. They were in the house and who's to say what belongs to you and what belongs to Mrs Thompson.'

'But you know I've been lodging here!'

'Maybe so. But that doesn't mean that I know what's yours and what's hers.'

'But I'm telling you.'

The man shook his head. 'And you could be lying,' he said. 'You should hear the stories I've been told by other folk in this situation. "That sideboard belongs to my sister." "I've borrowed the sofa from my dear old grandmother." If I believed any of that I'd be too daft to do this job.'

'I don't know how you can,' Melissa said bitterly. 'How can you put people out like this?'

'It's not up to me. I gave Mrs Thompson plenty warnings. You know that yourself.'

'What do you expect her to do? Where will she go with the children?'

'The workhouse, I expect.'

'No!'

'It's not so bad. They'll get shelter and regular meals.'

'But she might be separated from the older children.'

'She should have thought of that.'

'You're heartless!'

'Listen, miss, I'm doing my job. I don't make the decisions. And any landlord might have evicted her by now, not just Mr Winterton.'

'Winterton!'

'Aye, that's his name. And he's not interested in collecting rents from these old houses. He wants to pull them down and build new ones. I told you, he'll take any chance he can to evict the tenants.'

'But what about the other ones? The ones who don't fall behind with the rent.'

The rent collector gave her a strange look and Melissa sensed his reluctance when he said. 'Well, maybe he'll put the rent up until very few of them can afford it any more. And those who can . . . well, maybe he'll make life difficult for them.'

'That's wicked.'

'Perhaps so. But think of the nice new houses he'll build for respectable working people. They'll be infinitely better than these old slums.'

'They're not slums. They're people's homes.'

The rent collector's manner hardened. 'I can't stand here talking. I advise you to clear off and find new lodgings for yourself.'

'At least let me take my own belongings from the cart.'

'I can't do that – I've told you. Everything will have to be sold and the money will go to the landlord.'

'*Mr Winterton.*' Melissa realised she was shaking with rage.

Behind them the men had finished emptying the house and they began to board up the windows. A locksmith had arrived and he began to change the locks. Melissa watched in despair.

'I suppose that's to prevent anyone from seeking shelter there,' she said. Her tone was bitter.

'Exactly. We can't have the Thompsons sneaking back in and making a mess of the place.'

'I don't know how you can live with yourself,' Melissa said.

The rent collector finally lost patience with her and turned away. One of the men was securing the pile of furniture with ropes. Another stood by as if sensing that Melissa or Mrs Thompson might make a dash for it and try to pull something off the cart. Then to the sound of hammering, punctuated by Mrs Thompson's despairing shrieks, the cart pulled away.

Melissa stood and watched helplessly as everything she owned was carried away. All she had left was the clothes she was wearing and the bundle of cut out shirts she had just collected from the shirt factory. Not only was she homeless but she had probably lost her job as well. For how could she sew the shirts up now?

Now that the drama was over the neighbours crept away to their houses. No one stayed to comfort the weeping Maud Thompson or her shivering children. No one save the old woman, Bella.

'Hawway, in, hinny,' she said to the distraught woman. 'You can stop with me.'

Mrs Thompson looked at her uncomprehendingly.

'You and the bairns. I've the house to meself and to tell the truth I get lonely. You'll all hev to share one room and I'm not offering charity, mind. You can do a bit cleaning for me and you'll hev to pay rent. And perhaps the bairns can help out a bit – run errands and the like.'

'You mean it?'

'I wouldn't say it otherwise. But, mind you, there'll be no drinking in my house. The minute you bring a bottle home with you then out you go. The lot of you.'

Melissa watched as Maud Thompson gathered her children together and followed her old adversary into her house. The door closed behind them. The street was empty. Melissa was alone. And only then did she realise that not only had the bailiffs taken her sewing machine, her mother's precious workbox and her doll, Ninette, they had also taken all the money she had left in the world.

Chapter Twenty-One

Miss Bond was not pleased to be called from her office. She received Melissa in the entrance hall and listened to her request.

'You want me to give you back the money you paid for your buttons and thread?'

'Yes. Here they are.'

'And the shirts?'

'I won't be able to do them.'

The supervisor frowned. 'May I ask why?'

'My landlady has been evicted. I'm homeless.'

'But you could find new lodgings.'

'They took all my belongings – the bailiffs.'

'Ah, I see. But if you could find somewhere to live we would loan you a sewing machine – there'd be a hire fee of course – or you could buy and pay for it in weekly instalments.'

'My savings were in one of the boxes they took. I wouldn't be able to pay any rent.'

'What are you going to do?'

'I don't know.'

The supervisor was not known to be overly sympathetic but now her features softened. 'I'm sorry, Melissa. I know there are few landladies who would take you in without a week's rent in advance. Is there no one you can turn to?'

'No . . . at least there might be.'

Miss Bond looked relieved. 'Good. If you can find somewhere I'll willingly take you on again. You are one of my best stitchers.' Then she became businesslike again. 'Now give me the shirts.'

To Melissas astonishment the supervisor opened the bag, took out its contents, and counted the pieces. She saw Melissa's expression and, without embarrassment she said, 'I have to make sure everything is here. That's our policy. In fact I ought to ask you to pay a small fee for them.'

'A fee? Whatever for?'

'You've had our property for several hours. I could have given them to another stitcher. You've wasted our time and time is money.'

Melissa was speechless with dismay.

'It's all right. I'll let you off. But as for the buttons and the sewing thread, I'm sorry. I can't take them back. That isn't our policy.'

She turned and walked away briskly along the stone-floored passageway, her footsteps echoing down the brown-tiled corridor long after she had turned a corner and a door had slammed shut behind her.

Melissa stepped out into the street and the skirt of her coat was immediately caught by the wind and blown around her ankles. The scarf she had wrapped around her head slipped and blew against her face. She pulled it back and was about to set off when she realised that she did not know where she was to go.

When she had told Miss Bond that there might be somewhere she could go she had been torn between going back to the corner shop and confiding in Mrs Ali, and going to the old almshouse to ask help from Mrs Simmons, as Reenie had advised her to. She stood on the pavement, unmindful of the worrisome wind, and considered her choices.

Mrs Ali might be able to find her somewhere else to lodge but, even so, the landlady would want at least a week's rent in advance. And how would she pay any rent at all until she found a job of some sort?

So . . . Melissa considered Mrs Simmons. She was a kindly woman who devoted her life to what she and her kind called 'good works'. She was never judgemental about the folk who turned up at the soup kitchen but always concerned and compassionate about those she thought of as 'charity cases'.

Do I mind being thought of as a charity case? Melissa wondered. Will pride stop me from asking for help? She stood there for some time until she began to attract the attention of passers-by.

It was only when an old and shabbily dressed woman approached and asked, 'Are you all right, hinny?' that she roused herself, turned her back on the direction she had come from and began to walk towards the city centre. She knew she had no choice. She would have to go and ask help from Mrs Simmons.

Melissa decided to walk down through the covered Grainger Market where at least there would be shelter from the weather. It would be hours before anyone arrived at the old almshouse in order to start preparing the huge pans of soup. She had learned that Mrs Simmons was one of the first to arrive and she hoped to catch her before she got too busy, and to explain her predicament. But what was she hoping for? Mrs Simmons and her friends helped to feed and clothe the homeless. As far as Melissa knew they never found homes for them.

But perhaps Mrs Simmons might know of a well-off family who needed a seamstress. Her heart sank. A position like that would be little different from that she had occupied in the Winterton household, and the Winterton family, without knowing it, had made her already stressful situation worse.

She had reached the Grainger Market. Usually the sights and smells of this large indoor market were interesting and even exciting but, today, Melissa noticed only the wan faces of the poorer citizens hurrying from stall to stall to try to find bargains to feed their families: cheap cuts of meat, bruised vegetables, and yesterday's unsold bread.

Melissa saw a youth clutching what looked like a long shopping list. He handed it to the owner of a fruit and vegetable stall. The basket he carried awkwardly over one arm was large, like that to be found set out in a grocer's shop full of goods for sale. Melissa wondered how heavy it would be if he was going to fill it.

The smell of fresh coffee from the Italian coffee stall was enticing. Melissa was drawn towards a vacant stool but when she reached into her pocket instinctively she found only the packet containing the thread and the buttons she had bought from the shirt factory.

Walking on past the coffee stall she saw the window of the haberdashery that was situated under the mezzanine café at the Nunn Street end of the market. That gave her an idea and she went in. The shopkeeper, a thin, competent-looking woman, was serving a customer. She pulled out a length of black satin ribbon, measured it on the brass rule set into the counter, cut the ribbon, and put it in a small paper bag. Then she picked up a black veil, which was lying folded nearby, and put that into the bag also.

The customer, a middle-aged lady with a sad face, paid for her purchase, nodded her thanks, and left the shop without saying anything.

'Recently bereaved,' the shopkeeper told Melissa unnecessarily.

Now that there was no other customer Melissa took out the packet of shirt buttons and sewing thread and shook a few of the buttons onto the glass counter.

'Do you want to match them?' the shopkeeper asked.

'No. I have a gross here. They're very good quality. I was wondering if you would buy them.'

The woman gave her a keen glance before picking up one of the buttons, placing in her palm and examining it closely. 'I don't buy stolen goods,' she said.

'They're not stolen! I bought them this morning.'

'From the shirt factory?'

'Yes. How do you know that?'

The woman gave a thin smile. 'Because I recognise them. Every now and then some woman will come in and try to sell me some. She'll tell me that she has some left over or she bought too many, or some such tale when the truth is that she's stolen them.' She put the button back on the counter and folded her arms over her chest. 'Now off you go before I call the police.'

Melissa could feel the hot colour rising. 'Call the police if you like. I'm not a thief.'

'Then why are you selling them?'

'I . . . I bought too many.'

It seemed to Melissa that the woman had been inclined to believe her. She should have told her the truth. But instead the hesitation and the clumsy lie had hardened her heart again.

'Look, I get all kinds of stories told me but I've never heard of anyone buying a hundred and forty-four buttons too many. You're in some kind of trouble. I know what life is like for the stitchers and I feel sorry for you. But I know what you'll have paid for them at the shirt factory – if paid for them you have – and I can get them for half that price.'

'I would take that,' Melissa said in a voice barely above a whisper.

But the woman shook her head. 'It's no use. I'm not going to change my mind. If I took them and word got round there'd be no end to others like yourself coming in with buttons and thread.'

Melissa wanted to say that she wouldn't tell anyone. She wanted to try just once more to get the woman to change her mind. But something stopped her; the remnants of her pride. She swept the buttons back into the bag and left the shop, her head high and her face flaming with anger and embarrassment. When the door swung shut behind her she was swallowed up by the crowd and was carried forward in the throng without heed to where she was going.

When she emerged from the market into Grainger Street the bustle on the pavements was just as bad. She began to walk down towards the Central Station. Maybe she could go in and sit by the fire in one of the waiting rooms. She could pretend she was waiting for a train.

But from the moment she entered the station one of the railway staff began to watch her suspiciously. He was a tall, bearded, imposing man with a full set of brass buttons on his smart uniform. Melissa was just about to go through the door of the nearest waiting room when he strode forward and placed a hand on her shoulder.

'Travelling far, are you?' he asked.

'Er – no, not far.'

'And which train might you be waiting for?'

Melissa decided to tell the truth. 'Well, actually I'm not travelling anywhere. I just wanted to sit by the fire for a while.'

She moved instinctively towards the comforting crackling sound of the coals but his grip hardened.

'Oh, no, you don't. We can't have lasses like you bothering decent people.'

'What do you mean, lasses like me?'

'The sort of lass who plies her trade in our nice respectable station.'

Melissa stared up at him, eyes wide with shock. She knew full well what he meant. 'I'm not that kind of woman,' she said. 'I – I'm a dressmaker.'

He laughed. 'And we all know what dressmakers do to buy some jam for their bread, don't we? Now off you go.'

'How dare you!'

'Now, come along, bonny lass,' the man said. 'I have nothing against you personally but you can't stay here. Now would you rather walk out of your own free will or shall I march you out, which will cause you much embarrassment?'

Melissa realised that they were attracting attention so she walked away with as much dignity as she could muster. Her head was seething with unhappy questions. Why had the railway official thought she was a woman of the streets? She was respectably dressed, if a little untidy by now. But he had seemed to sense immediately that she was not a genuine traveller. She supposed that was his job, to observe the hundreds of people who came into the station every day and assess who might be up to no good, such as pickpockets and street women. Perhaps it was her air of desperation that had marked her out. That must be it.

The wind had sprung up again and people were clinging on to their hats as they hurried by. Melissa tightened her scarf and, with her head down, she set off in the direction of the old almshouse. She had not gone far when she nearly tripped over something that rolled with some force to stop just in front of her foot. She stared down and saw a potato. She looked round in surprise, expecting to see someone clinging on to an unruly shopping basket, but instead she saw a group of ragged children seemingly singing and dancing in a circle.

How strange, she thought. She frowned and peered

through the strands of hair that the wind had teased out from under her scarf. She soon realised that the children weren't singing, they were screeching taunts in singsong voices, and neither were they dancing. They were encircling something – or someone – and their attitude was far from friendly. Their cries came and went on the gusts of wind and above the children's shrill voices could be heard the hoarse cries of someone in distress.

Melissa hurried towards them. The children were small and she imagined that they were tormenting one of their number – some game that had got out of hand. The cries of their victim grew louder and she knew she must intervene.

Now she could see over their heads and, in the centre, she saw what she imagined to be an older boy half crouching as he clasped a large basket of fruit and vegetables within his arms, turning this way and that as the smaller children tried to tear it from his grasp. She recognised the basket before she recognised the youth she had seen in the market.

'Stop that!' Melissa cried, and a few heads turned towards her. She thought she would never forget their pinched, dirty faces. They were children and yet they had become savages and all for a basket of food. 'Stop!' she cried again. 'Leave him alone!'

For a moment the wild activity ceased and the children stared at her. Then one of them called out, 'What's it to you?'

'Aye,' another child shouted. 'It's none of your business. Haddaway!'

Now all the children had turned to face her and the leaders stepped forward menacingly. Melissa felt a thrill of fear and had to remind herself that these were children. But even so, she took a step backwards, stumbled, and fell down.

Her head hit the pavement and she closed her eyes. When she opened them she saw at once what had caused her fall. There, on the pavement beside her, was another potato. The children were silent now and they stared down at her, their faces revealing no emotion. Melissa sat up groggily. More of her hair had escaped from the confines of her scarf; she raised a hand to brush it back and winced when her hand touched her forehead.

Suddenly one of the children pushed himself forward through the throng. She stared up at him and recognised the shining thatch of red hair. She did not know whether he recognised her but he turned to face the gang of ragged children.

'Leave the lady alone,' he said. 'She's a good 'un. And leave Danny be as well. You know his ma's kind to us and you'll spoil things if you pinch all his shopping.'

Some of the children were bigger than the boy Melissa knew as Ginger but they moved away obediently.

'Hey!' he called after them. 'Afore ye gan you can help pick up the tatties.'

One or two of them scrabbled around after the fallen potatoes and an older lad, Melissa thought it was Ginger's brother, helped Danny to his feet.

'Do you want a hand?' Ginger said, turning back to look down at Melissa.

'No, thank you, I can manage.' She got to her feet and as she did so a sharp pain radiated from the sore place on her forehead.

By the time Melissa had risen and brushed the dust and dirt from her skirt, all the children save Ginger's brothers and little sister had vanished. Danny stood clasping his basket and looking round uncertainly as if he could hardly believe his ordeal was over.

'Thank you,' Melissa said to Ginger.

He grinned. 'It was nothing.'

'No, it wasn't. I don't know that I could have stopped them.'

Ginger suddenly looked sombre. 'They're hungry.'

'I know.'

They looked at each other for a moment and then Ginger said, 'I'll hev to go.'

'Wait . . . where . . . ?'

But Ginger and his little family sped away without a backward glance.

Melissa and the unfortunate youth Ginger had identified as Danny were left looking at each other.

'Ginger's a canny bairn,' Danny said.

His speech was slow and there was something about him that made Melissa look more closely. He was older than she had first thought. This was a young man in his twenties or even thirties. He was good-looking and had a trusting gaze.

'Yes,' she said, 'he's a good lad.'

'He helped me.'

'Yes, and me.'

'I must go home. My ma's waiting.'

'Of course.'

'Will you come with me?'

Melissa was perplexed but she was spared from answering when a stout woman wearing no coat and enveloped in a large cream-coloured linen apron hurried towards them and called, 'Danny, where hev you been?'

He turned to face her and his smile became almost angelic. 'I've been to the market,' he said. 'You sent me. Don't you remember?'

By now the woman had reached his side. She was much smaller than he was and she gazed up at him fondly. 'Of course I do. How silly of me. Thank you for reminding me.'

'You're getting forgetful, Ma,'

'I am. Aren't I lucky to hev you?'

Instead of answering he said. 'This lady helped me. Her and Ginger.'

Danny's mother turned to face Melissa. 'What happened?' she asked.

'Some children were teasing him,' Melissa told her. She did not know whether she ought to reveal the extent of Danny's distress.

'Little beggars,' the woman said. 'I've telt them to leave him alone – I even bribe them with bits to eat when I can – but they will pick on him.' She paused. 'My son is – well – he's not like other lads his age, you see. But he's a good lad and quite harmless,' she added.

'I can see that,' Melissa said. 'He could easily have lashed out at them but all he did was try to protect your shopping.'

'And Ginger was here, was he?'

'Yes. He made the others go away.'

Danny's mother smiled. 'He would. He has a hard life and he's probably a clever little thief, but there's no badness in him. Real badness, I mean. Well, now, I'd better get this bonny lad of mine home. Are you coming, Danny?'

'I want the lady to come. She fell down.'

'Did the bairns knock you over?' Danny's mother asked.

'No, I tripped.'

'She was trying to help me.'

'Well, you'd better come along with us then,' Danny's mother said, and she smiled. 'To tell the truth you look as if you could do with a cup of tea – and maybe a bite to eat as well.'

Melissa went with Danny and his mother although she had no idea where they were leading her. But surely it could not be far if Danny had done his mother's shopping in the Grainger Market. And his mother was wearing her pinafore, suggesting that she had just slipped out from somewhere nearby.

Very soon they turned into the tunnel formed by one of the railway arches. The gas lamps, needed even at this time of day, flared to reveal white-tiled walls that were cracked and grimy, and there were puddles in the gutter left from when the rain must have blown in earlier in the day.

As they walked through the tunnel a train rattled and thundered overhead, startling Melissa so that she stumbled and nearly fell. But Danny's mother steadied her and she looked into her face searchingly. Then she narrowed her eyes and peered more closely.

'Is that a dirty mark or a bruise on your forehead?' she asked. 'I can't see properly in this light.'

'I told you, the lady fell down,' Danny said.

Danny's mother squeezed Melissa's arm sympathetically. 'Come along, pet, it isn't far now,' she said.

When they emerged from the tunnel they turned right and just a little way along Melissa could see the lights from a large window spilling out and cheering a day that had lost its sparkle. The window proved to be that of a café. A half-net covered the lower part of the window and, above, the legend proclaimed, 'Ella Malone's'.

'That's me,' Danny's mother said proudly. 'Ella Malone. And this fine establishment belongs to me. And to my son Danny, of course. Now come along in and sit down, pet. You can hev anything you want from the menu and you're my guest.'

They entered the café and one of the customers, a postman in uniform, rose from his table. 'They've been as good as gold, Ella,' he said, his gesture taking in the other customers, some of them fellow postmen, who were quietly getting on with their meals.

'Thanks, Jack. Now if you could settle this young lady over there,' Ella pointed to the only vacant table, 'I'm going to get her a nice plate of something and a cup of tea.' She turned to smile at Melissa. 'Right, pet?'

Melissa stared back at Ella. The café was warm and bright

after the walk in the draughty streets. In the background she could hear the rattling and whistling of the trains. In the café there was only the quiet murmurings of the customers. But something was wrong. The sounds were becoming all mixed up and Ella's voice seemed to resonate from somewhere far away.

'Yes,' she said, 'thank you.' She took one step forward and then slipped unconscious to the floor.

Chapter Twenty-Two

When Melissa opened her eyes she found herself lying on a narrow bed in a small bedroom. Three people were looking down at her: Ella Malone, her son, Danny, and the postman, Jack.

'Here you are, then,' Ella said.

'Here she is,' Danny echoed his mother and gave the sweetest of smiles.

Melissa frowned and immediately winced when pain shot through her forehead.

'Do you think we should call a doctor?' Jack, the postman, asked.

'I'll go,' Danny said. 'I like Dr Forster.'

'Well, it is a nasty bump,' Ella said. 'What do you think, pet?' she asked Melissa.

'No . . . I'm all right.'

'If it's paying the doctor you're worried about, forget it. You helped my son and you're my guest. Dr Forster can send his bill to me. That's a nasty bump,' she added. 'Maybe it ought to be looked at. Yes, I've made my mind up,' she said, then turned to face the two men. 'Danny, you go and fetch Dr Forster and, Jack, would you mind going down and keeping an eye on things in the café? Take orders if there are any and tell them I won't be long.'

'I've given you a lot of trouble,' Melissa said when Danny and Jack had left the room.

Ella smiled at her. 'No trouble at all, dear. I'm pleased to be able to help you.'

'How did I get upstairs?'

'Danny carried you. He's strong as an ox.' Ella spoke with pride. 'He might be a bit slow – I mean he doesn't think as quickly as he should – but he's good-natured and willing, and I couldn't run this café without him. Now, I'm going to help you off with your coat and shoes and you're going to lie down and rest.'

In no time at all Melissa found herself settled amongst clean pillows and covered with a silky eiderdown. When Dr Forster arrived he examined Melissa gently and declared that in his opinion she would be fine; but that she should not attempt to leave before morning.

'Well, that's it, then,' Ella said. 'You'll have to stay the night.'

'No . . . really.'

'I insist.' Then she looked at Melissa keenly. 'Will anyone be waiting for you?'

Melissa's head was hurting and she found that she had to concentrate very hard. 'Waiting for me?'

'Will anyone be worrying when you don't come home?'

'Oh . . . no, there's no one waiting for me. In fact I don't have a home to go to.' Melissa was horrified when she realised what she had said.

Ella was silent for a moment and then she sat down on the bed. 'I don't know your story and you're too flustered to be telling me now. But in the morning, when you've had a good breakfast inside you, we'll have a little talk. Right, pet?'

Melissa nodded agreement. There was nothing else she could do.

Ella went back to her duties in the café but later she came

back with a cup of tea and a ham sandwich. And then later still she brought Melissa a clean towel and a large pink flannelette nightgown – obviously one of her own.

'The bathroom's along the passage,' she told Melissa. 'Do you think you can manage?'

'Yes – thank you.'

'Right, pet, I'll say good night. The postmen have gone home to bed long since, but there's a few railwayman wanting a bite to eat at the end of their shift. It's back to the kitchen for me.'

She drew the curtains before she left the room.

Melissa had no idea what she would do or where she would go after she'd eaten the promised breakfast the next morning, but she was almost too weary to care. Not long after she got into the clean comfortable bed she fell into a deep dreamless sleep.

A few days later Reenie stood outside old Bella's house shaking with anxiety.

'What do you mean, you don't know where she is?' she said. 'Do you mean you just left her on her own with no thought about what might happen to her?'

Reenie was frantic. She had come to see Melissa on her day off as usual and found Mrs Thompson's house boarded up and a big padlock on the door. Even though she could see very well that the house was empty she began to beat her fists against the door.

Curtains twitched and eventually a door across the street opened and an old woman came out into the street.

'For heaven's sake, stop that racket!' she called.

Reenie hurried across the road and asked the woman if she knew where Melissa was. The old lady shrugged and told her she had no idea.

So now they confronted each other.

'Why is the house boarded up?' Reenie asked.

'Bailiffs.' The word was loaded with contempt.

'But Mrs Thompson . . . her children . . . what happened to them?'

'I took them in.'

'But what about my friend?'

'I've already telt you. I don't know where she went.'

'For goodness' sake! At least tell me whether she walked up the street or down!'

The old lady frowned. 'The last time I saw her she wasn't walking anywhere. She was just standing there . . . in the road . . . watching the cart trundling off up the hill.' She opened her eyes wider as if she'd had an idea. 'Perhaps she went after it – to try and get her belongings. Not that they would hev let her have anything.'

Reenie felt like weeping with rage. 'So you took Mrs Thompson and her bairns into your house and not one of you gave a thought to Melissa!'

'Was that her name?'

'You didn't even know her name!' To Reenie this made things even worse. 'But what about Mrs Thompson? She was her landlady. Didn't she even wonder what had happened to her?'

'Maud Thompson was nearly out of her mind with worry about herself and her bairns. You couldn't expect her to be thinking about someone who was just a lodger, could you?'

'Why ever not? She was happy to take her money all those weeks!'

The old lady looked at her impassively. Reenie saw that she was wasting time so she turned and walked away. She had no idea how she was going to find her friend until she reached the corner shop and remembered that Melissa was on friendly terms with Mrs Ali. She might know something.

Mr Ali invited Reenie courteously to walk through into

the back shop where she was met by the smell of something cooking. Something sweet and yet spicy. She had never smelled anything quite like it before – although it was certainly appetising.

Mrs Ali, a pretty, plump Englishwoman, saw Reenie's puzzled expression and smiled. 'I'm cooking a dish from my husband's country,' she explained. 'It pleases him when I try.' Then she read the concern in Reenie's expression and hurried on, 'But what is it that you want?'

When Reenie explained that she was looking for Melissa and had hoped that Mrs Ali might know what had happened to her, the kindly woman looked upset.

'I don't know where she went,' she said. 'I'm sorry that she didn't come to me. I would have found some way of helping her.'

Reenie turned to go.

'Listen, pet,' Mrs Ali said. 'If you find your friend, please tell me. I'm as worried about her as you are.'

Reenie agreed although she didn't tell Mrs Ali that no one could possibly be as worried as she was because no one in the world could love Melissa as much as she did.

Out in the street again, Reenie stood still while she tried to imagine what Melissa would do. Mrs Simmons . . . she thought. I telt her to gan and see the woman about getting better lodgings . . . that's where she'll have gone.

But it was early in the morning and Reenie knew there would be no one at the soup kitchen yet. She was wondering what she could do to fill the time in when she saw a postman coming down the hill towards her. She thought it strange. Early as it was it was still late for a postal delivery. And, another thing, the postman wasn't carrying a bag.

The man walked past her, on down the hill and, to her surprise, he stopped outside the boarded-up house. And then she knew – although she had no idea why – that he was looking for her. She began to run down the hill and when she arrived with glowing cheeks and out of breath, he grinned at her.

'May I ask you your name?' he said.

'Reenie – Reenie Jackson.'

'Then you're the lass I'm looking for. This is for you.' The postman held an envelope towards her. She stared at it speechlessly. 'Go on – take it,' he said. 'It's not going to bite you.'

Suddenly Reenie snatched the envelope and opened it. She had already guessed who it was from but could not stop the tears of joy when she saw Melissa's handwriting. The note was short and all too soon she looked up, unaware of the tears streaming down her face.

'How did you know where to find me?' she asked.

'It's your day off, isn't it?'

'Yes.'

'Well, Melissa guessed you would come here round about now and that you would be worried, so she asked me to bring this letter along.'

'But how? I mean who . . . ?'

'Who am I and how do I know your pal?'

'Yes.'

'I'm a postman.'

'I can see that!' Reenie's composure was returning and with it her animated ways.

He grinned at her. 'When my shift's finished I go for a bite to eat in Ella's café. Ella Malone's. That's where your pal is now. Ella took her in. She would have written sooner but that bump on the head fair knocked her for six.'

'Bump!' Reenie's alarm returned. 'What happened?'

'Doesn't she tell you in the letter?'

'No. There's nothing about a bump.'

'Well, don't worry. She's fine now and no doubt she'll

explain everything when she sees you. What *does* she say in the letter, if I may ask?'

'Just that she's fine and I'm not to worry, and that Jack – that's you – will take me at once to see her.'

'So are you coming?'

'Of course I am.'

At the end of April pale sunlight streamed along the canyon formed by the railway viaduct on one side and the tall old buildings on the other and warmed the window tables in Ella Malone's café. Melissa, wrapped in one of Ella's outsize aprons, was wiping the tables down and filling up the salt and pepper pots and the sugar bowls. Most of the café's customers were postmen or railway workers, and at the moment there was a lull between late breakfasts and early lunches.

When she had finished the tables she began to polish the glass display case on the counter. She used a mixture of hot water and vinegar and crumpled up pages of a newspaper rather than a cloth, which Ella told her would leave smears. Mrs Malone would soon be filling the shelves of the display case with doyley-covered plates of sandwiches and home-made cakes and scones.

Behind the counter, in one corner, the hot-water boiler hissed quietly. Melissa had never managed to count how many pots of tea were filled each day. Ella believed in making fresh pots frequently, not like in some eating establishments where a dark brown stewed liquid was the order of the day.

The glass counter polished, Melissa began to put clean glasses and fresh jugs of water on every table. When she had done that she looked round as though seeking some other task.

'For goodness' sake, sit down, lass,' Ella said. 'I'll finish filling the shelves and we'll have ourselves a cup of tea.'

'Shall I make the tea?' Melissa asked.

'I said sit down!' Ella pretended to scold. 'You'll wear yourself out. You never stop.'

'Neither do you,' Melissa protested, but she sat down obediently.

Ella brought the tea to the table and persuaded Melissa to try one of the freshly baked currant scones.

'What do you think?' she asked when Melissa had taken one or two mouthfuls.

'As delicious as ever.'

'Don't you notice anything different about it?'

Melissa took another bite and concentrated for a moment. 'No, I don't think I do. Have you tried a new recipe?'

Ella shook her head and her smile broadened. 'Same recipe, different cook; Danny made them.'

'That's wonderful.'

'He didn't want me to tell you until you'd tasted one. He thought it would be a nice surprise.'

'Well, it is.'

Ella looked round. The tables were beginning to fill up. She sighed. 'I suppose I'd better get round and take the orders,' she said.

'No, I'll do that.' Melissa stood up and reached for the small notebook and pencil, which was waiting on the counter.

Ella watched as Melissa took the orders. She always smiled and chatted to the customers, and they obviously liked her. I don't know what I ever did without her, Ella thought. I just hope I can persuade her to stay.

She gathered up the cups and plates they had just used and put them on a tray. In the kitchen Danny was at the sink washing dishes. He looked round and smiled at his mother as if he hadn't seen her for days rather than just about ten minutes. Ella had to turn away quickly or he might have seen the tears.

She loved the lad so much and although she boasted about everything he could do she knew that he would never be able to manage on his own if – when – she passed away. If she couldn't find a solution to this problem soon the worry of it might send her to an early grave.

She put the dishes she was carrying on the bench and Danny asked her, 'Did Melissa like the scones?'

'She thought they were lovely.'

Danny smiled. 'So is she.'

And in that moment the ghost of an idea drifted across Ella's consciousness. There may be a way, she thought. It's a long shot but I'll have to try, for Danny's sake as well as my own peace of mind.

The next day was Melissa's day off. She had been up early and served breakfasts to the railwaymen who had come in when their nightshift in the repair sheds was over. Then Ella had insisted that Melissa go upstairs and wash and change before her friend arrived.

Melissa loved the luxury of hot water coming from a tap. She had stripped off and now she wet her flannel and used a cake of Ella's favourite carnation soap to wash herself all over. No matter how appetising the food that was served in Ella's café, she couldn't abide the lingering odours that clung to her hair and clothes.

When she was dressed she looked at herself critically in the mirror in her bedroom. She had arrived here with nothing more than the clothes she was wearing. Since then Ella had bought her a skirt, three blouses and some underwear. Ella had slipped out to the shops herself and chosen them, then handed them to Melissa as a *fait accompli*.

'I asked the lass in the shop what young lasses were wearing these days,' Ella had told her.

None of the garments was exactly what Melissa would have chosen herself but she had made a few discreet alterations and was pleased with the results. She still had her coat, and Ella had given her a surprisingly fashionable hat, which she had said she had bought for a wedding and never worn because the wedding was called off !

When she went down to the café Reenie had already arrived and she had brought Mrs Ali with her. Ella insisted that they stay long enough to have tea and toasted teacake, and they settled happily at a table by the window. Sally Ali had been to visit twice before. Reenie had kept her promise to let the shopkeeper's wife know of Melissa's whereabouts and the first time she had called at the café she had berated Melissa for not coming to her for help.

The second time she had just wanted to gossip but today there was an air of suppressed excitement about her. She had brought a large shopping bag with her and while they ate their teacakes and sipped their tea she had placed it under the table. When they had finished Reenie cleared the table and instead of suggesting they should go she sat down again.

'Go on,' she said to Mrs Ali.

They smiled at each other like conspirators. 'What's going on?' Melissa asked. 'What have you two been up to?'

'Just wait and see,' Reenie said.

'I went to Paddy's Market the other day,' Sally Ali said.

Melissa waited to hear what she would say next.

Mrs Ali reached down into her shopping bag and as she lifted something from it she said, 'And just guess what I found.'

'I have no idea,' Melissa said faintly, although she had the feeling that something important was about to happen. She felt a growing excitement.

Mrs Ali straightened up and placed a small bundle of old clothes on the table. At least that's what it appeared to be at first, but when Melissa looked more closely she saw that it was a baby's shawl. Once long ago someone had crocheted this with loving fingers but now it was old and yellowing, although quite clean.

'I washed it,' Sally Ali said. 'Go on – pick it up.'

Melissa picked up the bundle and dared not hope that what she suspected was true. She unwrapped the shawl carefully and saw that she had been right. A doll lay there. She looked bedraggled; one of her ringlets had unravelled and her porcelain face was cracked but it was unmistakably Ninette.

'I'm sorry she's damaged,' Sally Ali said. 'She was dirty too, but I cleaned her up a bit.'

Melissa stared with joy at the doll her sailor father had brought her so long ago. 'How much do I owe you?' she asked.

'Nothing at all.' Mrs Ali held up one hand when she saw Melissa was about to protest. 'I still feel bad that you didn't think to come to me when you were in trouble. This'll make it a bit better. But, look, there's this as well.'

She placed a large shoe box on the table; the box that had once held a pair of Emmeline Dornay's button-up boots. Melissa saw Sally and Reenie holding their breath and watching her closely as she lifted the lid.

'They're all here,' she said. 'The doll's clothes are all here. I can't understand it.'

'What can't you understand?' Reenie asked.

'Why Ninette should have been on a market stall all these weeks later. Surely someone should have bought her for a child – even if she is a little worse for wear.'

'Well . . .' Sally said.

'What is it?' Melissa asked.

'Actually someone had bought it. It wasn't on the stall. It was behind the stall.'

'I don't understand.'

'The daughter of the stall holder was playing with it.'

Suddenly Reenie burst out laughing. 'As she told it to me, Sally just about leaped over the stall and snatched the doll out of the poor little lass's hands!'

'You didn't!' Melissa stared at the shopkeeper's wife in astonishment.

Sally blushed. 'Not exactly. I saw the child playing with the doll and asked her mother how much she wanted for it. At first she said it wasn't for sale and then I . . . well . . . I told her I'd pay double what she'd paid for it.'

'Then the child's own mother snatched the doll out of her hands, bundled it up and handed it over!' Reenie took up the tale.

'She threw in the box of clothes at no extra cost, which made me think she hadn't told the truth about how much she'd paid for it,' Sally said. 'But it was worth every penny just to see the look on your face when you opened the shawl.'

Not daring to hope too much, Melissa took out the doll's clothes and she caught her breath when she saw her purse, still there, lying at the bottom. Her fingers trembled when she opened it but, of course, the money had gone.

'Is anything the matter?' Reenie asked.

'No,' Melissa said. 'Nothing at all.' She did not want to spoil her friends' obvious pleasure in being able to give her the doll back. 'I can't thank you enough.'

After that Sally Ali allowed herself to be persuaded to have another cup of tea, and then she said she would have to get back to cook her husband's midday meal. 'I wouldn't care, Ali is a better cook than I am, but he insists a woman's place is in the kitchen.' She smiled fondly and they all laughed. Then she waved goodbye.

Reenie insisted on clearing the table for a second time. 'It's your day off,' she said.

'But it's your day off too,' Melissa replied.

'Oh, go on, let me spoil you,' Reenie said, and she carried

the tray to the counter and then went straight through to the kitchen where Melissa heard her talking animatedly to Mrs Malone and Danny.

Melissa took Ninette and the box of clothes up to her room before they left the café. Then they walked up towards the city centre although they had not decided yet where exactly to go.

'Why don't we just do some window shopping?' Reenie suggested. 'We could look at the new summer fashions.'

Melissa agreed and for a while they went from shop to shop, looking at gowns of organdie, French grey cloths, and silk and cotton blends. There were gowns of lavender, cerulean blue, light greens, the softest pastels, cream and white. The sleeves were long and straight, and some had great puffballs of fabric at the top in the style known as 'leg-o'-mutton'. Most dresses were abundantly trimmed with flounces of lace.

'What do you think?' Reenie asked as she watched Melissa staring at the window of an exclusive gown shop in the arcade.

'Lovely. But you know me. I don't like anything to be too fussy.'

'Yes, I know you, and that's why I'm so disappointed.' Reenie was no longer smiling.

'What do you mean?'

Reenie sighed. 'Look, I didn't tell you but I have to go back early today. The Wintertons are having a dinner party tonight. There are going to be a lot of guests – city councillors and the like. Anyways, Mrs Barton's got everyone running around like scalded cats and she says if I come back early I can have an extra half-day some time soon.'

'Is that why you're disappointed? Because you'll have to go back soon?'

'Of course, but it's more than that.' She paused and then

said quickly as though she had been nerving herself to say this, 'It's you I'm disappointed with and if you let me treat you to a cream cake in Tilley's I'll tell you why.'

Reenie refused to say anything until they were seated at a table at the window in the upstairs room. The window looked out on the traffic surging round the huge Doric column that was Grey's Monument. In the past Melissa had enjoyed looking at the figure of Earl Grey standing proudly on the top and wondering how a Prime Minister had found time to encourage the development of blends of his favourite tea. Today she barely glanced at the passing show as she waited impatiently for Reenie to tell her why she was disappointed in her.

Only when the tea had been poured and the cream cakes chosen did her friend suddenly reach across the table and take both of Melissa's hands. She looked at them for a long while, turning them over to inspect the palms and back again and then she shook her head in undisguised disapproval.

'What is it?' Melissa asked.

'Just look at them. They're as bad as mine.'

Melissa withdrew her hands from the table top and put them on her lap so that Reenie could not scrutinise them any longer.

Her silence annoyed Reenie further. 'I'm a kitchen maid,' she said. 'No matter how much cucumber lotion I rub in every night I'm never going to have the hands of a lady. But you! You're not supposed to be up to your elbows in dish-water in some cheap café. You're a dressmaker, not a waitress and kitchen hand.'

'It's not a cheap café,' Melissa said with some heat. 'Ella Malone keeps a perfectly respectable establishment and serves good food to working men.'

'All right. I'm sorry if I sounded as though I was criticising Mrs Malone. As a matter of fact I like her very much. It's just that you should not be working there.'

'She took me in when I had no money and nowhere to go. She offered me a home if I would help out. How could I refuse?'

'And does she pay you well?'

'Of course she does!'

'And are you saving your money? Putting something by each week?'

Melissa nodded. She guessed what was coming.

'So are you looking for somewhere else to live?'

'Why should I?'

Reenie's eyes blazed. 'Have you forgotten your dreams? Have you given up all idea of opening your own salon?'

Melissa stared down at the tablecloth for a long while and then answered softly, 'No, I haven't forgotten my dreams.'

'Thank goodness for that!' Reenie topped up the tea in her cup and, tipping in two spoonfuls of sugar, she stirred it vigorously. 'So my next day off we'll start looking for lodgings for you.'

'It's not as easy as that.'

'Why not?'

'I lost my sewing machine and my workbox, remember. All I have left is a gross of shirt buttons and some sewing thread.'

Reenie was not to be put off. 'But you could do alterations by hand?'

'Yes.'

'And even make whole garments?'

'Yes. It would take longer, but of course I could do it.'

'And you might not have to do without a sewing machine for long.'

'What do you mean?'

'Well, a second-hand machine wouldn't cost too much,

would it? After all, the one the bailiffs took wasn't new, was it?'

'No, and it's true you can find quite good machines advertised in the newspapers. They're usually being sold by impoverished dressmakers who can't make ends meet,' Melissa smiled ruefully.

'Well, that's it. We'll get you one of those second-hand machines.'

'I can't afford one yet.'

'But together we could afford one. I've got quite a bit put by.'

'I couldn't take your savings.'

'You could have every penny I've got willingly, but you can pay me back if you like and, even better, when you've got a posh salon you can let me come and work for you.'

Melissa looked at her friend wonderingly. 'You mean it, don't you?'

'Of course I mean it. I'm not sitting here blethering just to hear the sound of my own voice.' She paused and sipped her tea. Then, as she replaced her cup in the saucer, she said, 'So that's settled then. Next week we'll start looking for a place for you to live.'

Melissa opened her mouth to say something and then closed it again. She knew that her friend was right. She ought to have been making plans herself rather than waiting to be reminded of her dreams. She would do as Reenie suggested: she would find somewhere to live and start all over again.

But this surge of hope and renewed ambition was accompanied by a feeling of discomfort. Ella Malone had taken her in, given her a home and paid her well for the work she did in the café. Ella had come to rely on her and she knew that she had grown fond of her, and so had Danny. How could she tell these good people that she was planning to leave?

Melissa and Reenie lingered, doing their best to ignore the impatient glances of the waitress who wished to clear their table and set it up for the next customer. The woman sighed loudly every time she had cause to pass their table and eventually Reenie whispered, 'Let her huff and puff as much as she likes. We've paid for our tea and cakes and we're entitled to sit here.'

'I know,' Melissa said. 'But it's not really fair, is it? We're stopping someone else having this window table.'

'We got here first.'

'But, even more important, the waitresses look forward to their tips. The more people they serve, the more tips they will get.'

Reenie frowned as she thought about this. Then she said, 'You're right. We'd better go.' She opened her purse and, taking out a penny, she slid it under her plate. 'I'd have left another halfpenny,' she said, 'if only the woman could hev brought herself to smile. You should always be pleasant to customers, it seems to me.'

Totally at ease with each other again, Melissa and Reenie left Tilley's and spent another twenty minutes looking in shop windows.

'You would look lovely in that,' Reenie said as they gazed at a sea-green muslin dress.

'It's lovely but it's not very practical,' Melissa replied.

'Well, what about that cream linen skirt and matching jacket?'

'A bit severe – but yes, it's elegant.'

'You'll have to have at least one fashionable dress when you receive your customers.'

'I know, but what can I do?'

'Well, how about going to see your friend at Wilkinson's? She may have some remnants. You could start making something for yourself right now.'

'But I thought we were saving up for a sewing machine?'

'A good dress is just as important.'

'You're right. I'll go to Wilkinson's.'

'Today?'

Melissa laughed. 'What a bully you are.'

'I know, but it's for your own good.'

They were laughing when they parted and Reenie was smiling all the way back to the Wintertons' house. She realised that it was to be expected that Melissa would be unsettled by what had happened to her. But when she saw the look in her friend's eyes when they gazed at the latest fashions she knew it was time to give her a nudge in the right direction.

It was going to be all right, she was sure of it. She allowed herself to daydream about the brilliant future that lay ahead for Melissa and how everyone would know that she, Reenie, had helped and encouraged her to fulfil her dream.

Chapter Twenty-Three

'Melissa! How wonderful that you've called today. But where have you been?' Eileen looked both surprised and delighted.

'It's a long story,' Melissa told her.

'Well, come and tell it to me during my tea break,' Eileen said.

She lifted the flap in the counter to allow Melissa to pass through and then she led the way to the shabby little room on the top floor.

Over tea and biscuits Melissa told Eileen what had happened to her since their last meeting.

'Well, I'm sorry to hear of your troubles,' Eileen said when Melissa lapsed into silence, 'but your friend Reenie is quite right. It's time you remembered what your plans were. And as a matter of fact I do have some suitable remnants that would do for the kind of two-piece costume you describe, and I can throw in a paper pattern if you like. Of course you can adapt it to suit your own ideas.'

'I'd like that.'

'Then why do you look so worried?'

'It's just that my room above the café is so small.'

'You're thinking it's going to be difficult to lay it out?'

Melissa nodded.

'Then you must do the cutting here. There's a room along

the corridor with a large table. The assistants are allowed to make things up for themselves. Come along, we'll get you started straight away!'

In little more than an hour Melissa found herself with all the pieces cut out and everything she needed bundled up in a brown-paper parcel.

'And now I'll tell why I was especially pleased to see you today. I have a client for you. She has just come out of mourning. She needs some alterations done to the clothes she hasn't worn for so long, but she also wants some new gowns and costumes too. In fact there will be enough work to keep you busy for months.'

'It's kind of you to think of me. But how can I do it? She could hardly come to my little room above the café.'

'She wouldn't have to. That's why it's such an opportunity for you. She asked me if I could find someone who would be willing to go to her home – she has a sewing machine – and I immediately thought of you. That was yesterday. And here you are. It must be fate!'

'But I work in the café all day. I would have to go in the evenings.'

'I'm sure that will be all right. Shall I give you her name and address?'

Melissa nodded.

'Here you are – she left a card. Her name is Miss Surtees and she lives in Jesmond. It would only take you about half an hour to walk there.'

As she walked back to the café Melissa felt that she had been blessed with good friends and she wasn't sure if she deserved them. Both Reenie and Eileen had urged her to try again. Why had she allowed herself to be so despondent?

She had received a great shock when she had lost her home and her belongings, and had become depressed. She had gone through the Slough of Despond like Christian in

The Pilgrim's Progress, and that made her feel guilty. She had thought of no one but herself. She had allowed Ella to comfort and cosset her. Adding to her guilt was the knowledge that she had been nowhere near the soup kitchen. She could have explained to Mrs Simmons what had happened and offered to help in whatever way she was able.

Well, she would remedy that as soon as she could. She would make herself the new skirt and jacket and go to see Miss Surtees. She wouldn't expect any time off from her duties in the café. She would work as hard as ever for as long as she was there. But, somehow, she was going to have to tell Ella that the time was approaching when she must leave.

Melissa knew how difficult that would be and she was already feeling uneasy when she approached the café. Then she stopped and stared ahead. Something was wrong. For a moment she did not understand what it was and then she saw that the street, always gloomy because of the tall buildings, was gloomier than ever. There was no cheerful light spilling out from the café window. Had Ella closed earlier than usual? Melissa had never known her to do that.

In the road outside the café there was a horse and trap. Had visitors come to call? And as she stood there wondering, the door of the café opened and a figure stepped out into the street. He was carrying a black bag. Dr Forster.

Melissa began to run. The doctor heard her coming and turned to face her.

'Ah, Miss Dornay,' he said. 'I'm so glad you've come home. Mrs Malone collapsed in the kitchen about an hour ago. Her son came to tell me.' He smiled faintly. 'When I arrived I found a postman waiting on table.'

'Jack.'

'That's his name, I believe. Anyway, I advised him to finish serving the customers as soon as possible and close the café. Mrs Malone was upstairs in bed. Apparently her son had carried her up by himself.' The doctor shook his head.

'Danny is very strong,' Melissa said. 'But please tell me, how is Mrs Malone?'

The doctor looked grave and Melissa experienced a chill of fear. 'She is not a well woman,' Dr Forster said. 'For all she looks robust her heart is not strong.'

Melissa gasped and the doctor spoke kindly. 'Please don't be alarmed. I do not believe she is going to die in the immediate future. But she must make life easier for herself. It was a blessing when you came to stay.'

'I shouldn't have gone out today!'

'Don't blame yourself. I don't believe it was only physical exertion that brought this on. It was worry.'

'Worry?'

'Mrs Malone confided in me that she frets constantly about what will happen to her son. Danny Malone is a good-hearted young man and a willing worker, and he is certainly not what some unkind people would call retarded. However, he will always need someone to look after him – or rather to guide him; to give him direction. There is no other family. His father died long ago. There's just the two of them, and unless Mrs Malone finds some solution to the problem soon I fear that she will worry herself to death. As I said, thank goodness you are here.'

'What can I do?'

Dr Forster smiled at her. 'You can do what a daughter would do. I suspect she regards you as such. Make her rest for a day or two. Don't let her go anywhere near the café. Take her meals up to her room and tell her that you and Danny can manage very well until she is feeling better. Well, good night, Miss Dornay.'

The doctor was just about to climb up into his trap when he turned and smiled. 'By the way, you will find the faithful postman guarding the gates, so to speak. Even though I suspect he must get up very early in the morning he refused to leave until you came home.'

Jack was sitting at the table in the kitchen. He was reading a newspaper by the light of an oil lamp. He looked so at home there that Melissa wondered, as she had before, exactly what his relationship with Ella was.

He raised his head and found her looking at him. It was as if he had read her mind.

'Ella and I are pals. Best pals. I'm married, you see,' he went on, surprising Melissa with his confidences. 'But my wife is in hospital – a special sort of hospital, God Bless her, and she'll never come out. But it's for better or worse, you know. I believe in keeping promises, especially those made before God. I visit her every week but she doesn't know me. Ella Malone has seen me through some bad times.'

The postman rose and folded his newspaper. 'Well, now that you're here I'll go home. Danny is sitting with her but she wants to see you. And if you decide to open for business tomorrow I'll come along and help as soon as my shift is over.'

Melissa put her parcel in her room and removed her coat and hat before going to Ella's room. She knocked and went in. Danny was sitting by his mother's bed and holding her hand. He looked round as Melissa entered and she didn't know which face showed the greatest relief, his or his mother's.

'Melissa, pet,' Ella said, 'would you persuade this lad to go down and have some supper? He must keep his strength up.'

'Shall I make something for him?' Melissa asked.

Danny nodded his head delightedly but his mother shook hers. 'No need. Danny is quite capable of heating up a pan of broth for himself and cutting a slice or two of bread and cheese.'

'Does Melissa want supper?' Danny asked. 'I can see to it.'

'Set a place for her at the table. She'll come down shortly. Now off you go.'

Danny left the room obediently and Ella indicated that Melissa should take the chair he had just vacated.

'He's a good lad,' Ella said, and there was something in her voice that warned Melissa not to challenge that statement. Not that she would have done.

'I know he is,' Melissa said.

'He works hard, he does as he's told, and he tries to please. Especially those people he likes. And he likes you.'

Melissa wondered where the conversation was leading but she sensed that she was only required to listen. Ella took her hand.

'Whoever marries my son will get a good man and a good business,' Ella said.

Melissa was taken aback.

'He'd be a good husband. And you've got to admit that he's a bonny lad.'

'Er – yes, he is.'

'Of course, although he works hard he hasn't got a head for business. His wife would have to be the brains to his brawn.'

Ella paused and looked away. Then she continued. 'If I die he'll be lonely and frightened. I can't let that happen.'

Melissa saw that tears were streaming down Ella's cheeks. 'Please don't cry,' she said. 'Dr Forster said that you mustn't get upset.'

'Let me finish what I have to say. If I could find a good woman to marry him, who would promise to look after him as I have done, then I would leave everything I own to that woman.' Suddenly Ella squeezed Melissa's hand. 'You know what I'm saying, don't you?'

Melissa nodded and stared at her mutely.

'But you don't have to answer me straight away. Just

promise me that you will think very seriously about it. Will you?'

'Yes. But—'

'No, don't say anything now. Go down and have a bite to eat with Danny. Don't bother to bring anything up for me. I want to sleep now.'

Melissa rose from the chair and left the room. She knew no more was required of her that night.

A week later Reenie breezed into the café and demanded to know whether Melissa had gone to Wilkinson's as she had promised to do.

'Go and sit down, I'm busy,' Melissa told her, but she managed a smile. 'I'll come and talk to you as soon as I've given those two men their bacon and eggs.'

'I'll bring you tea and a slice or two of toast, if you like,' Danny said.

Reenie smiled at him. 'That would be nice.'

After the breakfast rush was over Melissa managed to go and sit with Reenie and have some tea and toast herself.

'Did you go to Wilkinson's?' Reenie asked.

'Yes, I did and I bought some remnants to make myself a skirt and jacket.'

'Good. Have you made it up yet?'

'No.'

'Well, if you go and get ready you can explain why not when we go.'

'Reenie, I'm not coming out with you today.'

'Why not?'

'I can't.'

'I don't understand. Mrs Malone has never objected to you having a day off before. And, anyway, where is she?'

Melissa told Reenie everything that had happened since the last time they had seen each other. She told her how elated she had been when Eileen had told her she had found a client for her, but how everything had changed when she came home and found Dr Forster at the door.

'Well, I can see you had to help out.'

'Yes.'

'There's something you're not telling me.'

'Well . . . it's just that Mrs Malone has asked me – I mean, she wants me to stay here and help her run the café.' Melissa decided not to tell Reenie about the proposal Danny's mother had made. That was personal and she must deal with it herself.

'Haven't you told her about your plans for the future?'

'No, I haven't really had the chance.'

Reenie shook her head. 'The way I see it,' she said, 'is that you are just making things more difficult by delaying. If you don't tell her soon, Mrs Malone would have every right to think you are quite happy to stay here,' she said. 'But right now you've got to go and see this Miss Surtees and hope that she hasn't found another dressmaker.'

'That's impossible. I can't leave the café.'

'It's not impossible, and you can leave the café.'

'But how will Danny manage?'

'He'll manage because I'll be here to help him,' Reenie said.

'But this is your day off. You don't want to spend it cooking and washing dishes and waiting on table.'

'Don't I just! I'm a better cook than you give me credit for. I've learned a lot from old Ma Barton, you know. Although, as I see it, Danny can manage most of that as long as there's someone to watch him. As for washing dishes,' Reenie grinned, 'I can do that with my eyes closed. And when I'm waiting table the customers will get a smile and a bit chat to cheer their day. Now go on upstairs; make yourself look as smart as you can – put that daft hat on. Today is going to be the start of your new life!'

'But—'

'No buts. I'll break the news to Danny. I think he likes me so he won't mind.'

'I'll have to tell Ella,' Melissa said.

'Leave that to me. In a while I'll take her lunch up on a tray and I'll tell her that I've ordered you to have a day off. She surely won't object to that.'

'You . . . you won't upset her, will you?'

'Of course I won't! What do you think I am? An ogre?'

'No, just a bully!'

The two of them smiled at each other and Melissa already felt her spirits lifting.

When she was ready Reenie looked her over and said that she would do. 'But for heaven's sake,' she added, 'I wish you would buy yourself some hand lotion. How many times have I told you?'

'I have some. I smooth it in every night.'

'Well, you're not using enough.'

'Don't nag!'

'All right. Now off you go.'

When Melissa left the café and set off towards Miss Surtees' house in Jesmond she felt as though a burden had been lifted from her shoulders. Then immediately felt guilty. Ella's proposal that she should marry Danny had shocked her. She had promised to think about it but that was only because Ella was in no state to be upset further. The last week had been so busy that she had barely had time to think what she could do to make the situation easier.

She would have to tell Ella that she couldn't stay at the café and marry Danny because she had other plans for her life; but she had accepted that she must wait until Ella was on her feet. She could only hope that her refusal would not make Ella collapse again.

But today, her friend had come and somehow set her free

from her constant fretting, if only for a few hours. As she walked through the gloomy tunnel formed by the railway arch it was as though she was leaving some dark place behind and walking towards a more hopeful future.

Reenie had insisted that Melissa should walk only as far as the grand portico of the railway station and then take a cab. 'We can't have you arriving hot and bothered from a long walk or even a crushed ride on a tram.'

She had wanted to give her the cab fare but Melissa had refused. Ella paid her well. She could afford the cab fare. And that made her feel guilty again.

Miss Surtees' house was set back from the road. It was well guarded by a tall privet hedge. The gates were open and Melissa paused in the entrance to gaze at the small but elegant villa, well-tended lawn, and colourful herbaceous borders thriving in the May sunshine. She was completely unaware that she herself was being observed by someone standing under the shadow of a tree at the other side of the street.

She walked towards the rather grand front door and the well-proportioned stone porch. Everything about the house and grounds was tastefully understated, but definitely gave an air of affluence. All was so well ordered and peaceful that Melissa felt self-conscious when she heard the crunch of her own feet on the gravelled drive. She felt like an interloper.

The sound of the bell echoing through the house startled her, and Melissa thought how Reenie would laugh and compare the moment to something in one of the gothic novels she loved.

A polite young maidservant opened the door and when Melissa explained her presence she invited her in. As the door closed behind her the man who had been watching her smiled broadly. It was her, he was sure of it. He just couldn't believe his luck.

*

Melissa was shown into a pleasant drawing room where the exquisite paintings and ornaments, though not obviously expensive like those in the Winterton house, gave a discreet impression of great wealth.

'Welcome, Miss Dornay, I am so pleased you have found the time to come and see me.'

Miss Surtees, although elderly, rose as gracefully as a much younger woman from a chair at the table where she had been looking through some papers; from the glimpse Melissa was afforded they looked like drawings. 'The young lady at Wilkinson's recommended you very highly.'

'That was good of her.'

'She has told you what I require?'

'I think so. You wish to come out of mourning so you would like some of your clothes to be brought up to date?'

'And some new ones made.'

Miss Surtees spread her hands and looked down at her severe black day gown. 'I am sure if my dear sister is looking down from heaven she would think I have worn black for long enough. She loved bright fashionable clothes and would constantly send me pages torn from fashion magazines. I never pointed out to her that by the time she received the magazines in India and then sent them on to me the fashions depicted therein might already be months out of date.'

Miss Surtees smiled fondly at the memory although in her eyes there was a hint of lingering sadness.

'Your sister lived in India?' Melissa asked politely.

'Yes. Her husband worked for a London company that imported Indian craftwork and furniture. You know the sort of things I mean: cabinets and boxes of intricately carved sandalwood, oil lamps and table tops of Benares brass, cane chairs, the kind that grace hundreds of conservatories up and down this land. And, of course, ivory: fans, combs, jewellery, and carved figures – mostly depicting some god or goddess. My brother-in-law, Laurence, was the head buyer based in Bombay; he had an eye for all that was good and authentic. Disgracefully the salary they paid him in no way matched his value to the company. Our parents did not want my sister to marry him but she was the baby of the family and had always been indulged, so they gave in gracefully when she declared he was the only man she could ever love.'

Miss Surtees smiled in fond remembrance. Then she said, 'It is so good to have someone sympathetic to talk to, but I am afraid I am wasting your time.'

'No, what you tell me is fascinating.'

'That is kind of you to say so. Sadly both Laurence and my sister, Celia, were victims of an outbreak of cholera nearly two years ago. I shall have no more captivating letters – no window to another, more exotic world. And I shall never see my darling Celia again. At least until I join her in heaven. If you believe in such things,' she added drily.

'I'm sorry.'

Miss Surtees' eyes were sad but she smiled when she said, 'But at least I have their son, my nephew and only living relative. He came to school and to study in England and has been living with me while he tries to establish himself in his chosen career. I am as fond of him as only a doting maiden aunt can be.' She laughed self-deprecatingly. 'Now shall we go to my dressing room and discuss the contents of my wardrobe?'

While Melissa went through the contents of Miss Surtees' substantial wardrobe Reenie was thoroughly enjoying herself in the café. She had soon realised that Danny was a much better cook than she was; he seemed to have an instinctive flair. But she was good at washing the pots – hadn't she had enough experience? – and at clearing and setting up the tables, and very good indeed at taking orders and chatting to the customers. They liked her cheery ways and happily let themselves be talked into ordering more than they had intended to.

She was so busy and enjoying herself so much that she quite forgot to take up a tray for Mrs Malone. So when she was enjoying a quick sandwich during a lull she was surprised to see Ella, fully dressed, walk into the kitchen. Ella looked just as surprised. She walked to the swing door that led through to the café and, pushing it slightly, looked through. Then she turned to face Reenie and Danny, who was also sitting at the kitchen table.

'Where's Melissa?'

'Melissa has gone to see a lady,' Danny answered before Reenie had a chance to answer the question herself.

Mrs Malone looked puzzled.

Reenie got up quickly. 'Eeh, I'm sorry,' she said. 'I should hev brought you your tray. Sit down and hev some broth and I'll tell you all about it.'

Reenie decided that now was the time to get things straight. She would tread as carefully as she could, for she certainly did not want to be the cause of Ella having another bad turn, but the truth must be told. So while Danny's mother was enjoying her bowl of broth Reenie told her exactly who Melissa had gone to see and why. Ella didn't say anything, only listened. Reenie was expecting her to be upset but she was worried by the apparent degree of her distress.

'The lass should have said something,' Ella said, and her tone was faintly accusatory.

'She didn't want to upset you.'

Ella remained silent.

'She's very grateful that you took her in,' Reenie added.

'And is she good? At this dressmaking business, I mean.'

'She's more than good. She's the best. It would be a sin if

she gave it all up before she'd even properly started.'

Ella considered this for a moment and then she said, 'Well, I certainly won't object to her going off to this lady's house and making her clothes. But that means, I suppose, that one day she will be leaving us. I'll have to advertise for a good lass to take her place. Dr Forster said I must not contemplate continuing to run this café by myself as I did before Melissa came.'

'I'm sure Melissa will stay until you find someone.'

'But that someone won't be Melissa, will she?'

'What do you mean?'

'Danny and I have grown very fond of her.' She stared into her empty soup bowl for a while and then she said, 'And there's something else. Something Melissa has obviously not told you.'

'What's that?'

'Danny, go and fill up the sugar bowls,' his mother told him, and when he had left them Ella Malone told her what her hopes for the future had been. Reenie listened in astonishment. She realised that Danny's mother must have been desperate to make such a proposal to her friend, but she supposed that was mother love.

When Ella had finished talking Reenie saw that there were tears in her eyes. 'I love that girl like a daughter,' she said. The tears spilled over and Ella rummaged in her pocket for a large clean handkerchief.

'Ma – what's the matter?' Danny, coming back into the kitchen, saw her crying and he looked distressed.

Ella wiped her eyes. 'Nothing, pet. Don't you worry. It's just your ma being foolish.'

The bell on the door of the café rang to announce that someone had entered. Reenie rose quickly. 'I'll go and see to it,' she said. 'But I want you to go back to your bed and lie down and rest. I'll bring you a cup of tea as soon as I can and then you and me is going to hev a little talk.'

Instinctively Reenie went round the table and hugged Danny's mother. 'Don't cry any more,' she said. 'It's going to be all right.'

Melissa could not remember when she had enjoyed herself so much. Miss Surtees had good taste and obviously she also had the money to indulge it. The clothes the young maidservant took from the wardrobe were only a little out of date, and Melissa told Miss Surtees that in her opinion some of them needed very little or no alteration at all.

'That is very honest of you to tell me so,' Miss Surtees said.

'But why shouldn't I be honest?'

'Because you have done yourself out of some work. Now, tell me, what do you think of the way these clothes have been made?'

'I think whoever made them is very good indeed.'

'Yes, she was, and that is probably why I believed everything she said. But eventually I realised that she was not quite as honest as you are; she would charge me for work that was really not needed and I believe she sometimes ordered more fabric than was required, which she would make up and sell to other clients. Your friend in Wilkinson's has told me that there are many unscrupulous dressmakers like that,' Miss Surtees said, 'and that is why I asked her to find someone else for me. I believe she has done me an enormous favour in recommending you.'

'You haven't seen my work yet,' Melissa smiled.

'But I have listened to what you say and I am impressed by your knowledge. So I shall take the chance that your skills are as comprehensive as that knowledge. When can you start?'

Melissa was taken aback by the suddenness of the question. 'As soon as you like,' she said.

'Then let us go downstairs and discuss the arrangements. And perhaps you would stay and take luncheon with me?'

'Oh . . . thank you, I'd love to.'

'Good. My nephew is a dear, and he doesn't neglect his old aunt, but I miss female company.' She saw Melissa's surprised expression. 'Oh, I have friends and acquaintances,' she said. 'I have known one or two of them since I was a girl, but every one of them has married and all they wish to talk about, it seems, is the achievements of their children and their blessed grandchildren. Promise me, Melissa, when you marry, as you surely will, and if you have a family, take pity on poor old spinsters like me and spare them the details of nurseries and schoolrooms and budding careers in the professions or the city.'

'I promise you,' Melissa said. 'Although I have no plans to marry.'

'But you are so beautiful. Surely there is at least one hopeful young man paying court, if not more.'

'No, not even one.'

Even though Melissa turned her head away and tried to keep her tone level, Miss Surtees must have sensed her distress but all she said was, 'Well, I'm sure there will be.

'Bridget dear,' Miss Surtees addressed the young maidservant who had been putting the clothes away again, 'will you tell Cook that we have a guest for luncheon and then set another place at the table? And say we will not wait for my nephew. He can lunch in solitary splendour if he chooses to be late again.'

Although her words were censorious there was a smile in her voice and Melissa guessed that whatever kept Miss Surtees' nephew from the table did not anger his aunt too much.

They went back to the drawing room to wait there until luncheon was ready.

'Tell me what you think of these drawings,' Miss Surtees said. She led the way to the table where she had been sitting when Melissa arrived.

Melissa looked down at the sketches, which had been spread out on the table, and saw immediately how good they were. There were drawings of street scenes, buildings, countryside, animals and people. But they were not English scenes, neither were they English people. And lions and tigers and elephants were not to be found in English woods and fields.

'This is India,' Melissa said as she gazed at a group of monkeys playing in the dust before a small, beautiful temple.

'Yes.'

'Did your sister draw these?'

'No, her son is the artist.'

'But he is very good.'

'Yes, isn't he? That's why I am happy to support him until he can support himself. Ah,' she cocked her head as she heard the front door open and close, and quick footsteps in the hall. 'I believe that is my nephew arriving in time for lunch, for once. I am glad that you will meet him.'

The drawing-room door opened and Miss Surtees' nephew came into the room. Melissa turned to greet him and at first both he and she were speechless with shock.

Melissa felt that the air between them was filled with some kind of energy. And then he stepped forward and said, 'Miss Dornay!'

'James,' she whispered and then, suddenly galvanised, she fled the room.

Chapter Twenty-Four

'Melissa – wait!'

James caught up with her and placed himself between her and the front door.

Melissa clenched her hands. She could not look at him. Staring down at the black and white tiles of the floor she said softly, 'I must go.'

'No, please hear what I have to say.'

Before she could answer Miss Surtees joined them. 'Obviously you know each other,' she said. 'Do you care to explain?' She addressed this question to her nephew.

'This is Melissa Dornay,' James said.

'I already know that. She is my dressmaker.'

'She is the young lady I met in the park before I went away. I told you about her.'

'Ah, yes. You told me about a beautiful young woman and her jolly maid. But I don't believe you told me her name.'

'No . . . I didn't. But I was going to. I was going to ask you to go and see her parents.'

'Really? Then why didn't you?'

'Because he found my letter,' Melissa said. 'And then he didn't want to see me again.'

James and his aunt both turned to look at her.

'The letter is not the reason I went away,' James said.

'Went away?'

They stared at each other.

Miss Surtees tutted impatiently. 'This is all very cryptic,' she said. 'But I sense that I must give you some time alone to talk to each other. James, why don't you take Miss Dornay into the conservatory? It is very pleasant in there today. I shall tell Cook to delay luncheon for half an hour. I presume that will be sufficient time to get this muddle sorted out.'

Miss Surtees was about to leave them but she saw Melissa was still staring obdurately at the floor. 'Please go and talk to James, my dear. Whatever has occurred, I assure you he is an honourable young man. If he has angered you then give him a chance to explain.'

The conservatory was warm. Melissa noticed a green painted stove. It was quite unlike the conservatory in the Wintertons' house, which was large and formal, with potted plants arranged grandly in regimented rows. This conservatory was smaller and filled with strange and beautiful foliage. There were flowers the like of which Melissa had never seen before.

'My aunt loves anything that is beautiful, unusual and strange,' James said when he saw her looking in wonder at the many shades of green and gold and silver. 'The ubiquitous aspidistra is not allowed houseroom here. My aunt knows to within a day when something rare will flower. Sometimes the flower will die before nightfall and she will have spent the whole day sitting here and watching it bloom and fade.'

Melissa knew that James was trying to put her at ease but she had no wish to be swayed by his charm.

'Will you at least sit down?' he said with a hint of impatience. He gestured towards a bamboo sofa. 'Not the sofa?' he said when she shook her head. 'Are you so afraid that I will sit beside you? Well then, take this chair and I will take another one. I assure you the cushions are comfortable.'

Still unwilling. Melissa sat in the chair he indicated.

'My mother chose this furniture and my father had it shipped specially for my aunt.'

'From India?'

'Ah, so you have decided to speak to me,' James said, and he gave a rueful smile. And then, straight after, he said, 'I didn't leave because of your letter, you know. In fact, I only found it when I was packing and it made the situation even more distressing. I could not come and explain. I did not have an address for you so I could not even write to tell you that it did not matter at all that you were not a so-called "lady".'

'That didn't matter to you?'

'No, of course not.'

'We were only playing a game. Reenie and I did not intend to deceive you deliberately. Do you believe that?'

James smiled. 'I do. And I can guess who instigated the game: Reenie.'

'Oh, you mustn't blame Reenie. I enjoyed our games of pretence too.' Melissa had begun to smile but then she remembered why she had been so anguished. 'Then if it didn't matter to you that I was a servant just like Reenie, why did I never see you again?'

'I told you, I went away. I had to go to India. My father had succumbed to cholera. My mother wrote to me to come as soon as I could. She needed me. My father's company had booked my passage. I could not wait until the next week when I would have seen you again in the park.'

'You had to go to your mother – of course.'

He sighed. 'But by the time I got there my mother had succumbed to a second outbreak of the same disease.'

'Oh, James, I'm so sorry.'

'I had to close up the house and see to all the paperwork.' He was quiet for a moment and then he said, 'My mother would have loved you.' His eyes shone with unshed tears.

Melissa smiled and said gently, 'How can you be sure?'

'How could she not?'

The way he looked at her made her catch her breath.

'Your mother would not have minded that I am not from the same sort of family as you are?'

'My mother liked people for what she perceived them to be, not because of whatever place in society they occupied.' His voice lightened. 'Otherwise she wouldn't have married my father.'

'James, how can you say that?'

'Because it's true. My father was not what they call a "gentleman", although he was the most kind and gentle of men that you could ever wish to meet. He absolutely refused to accept money from my grandfather for he believed that he alone was responsible for his wife and family. Me.

'He was a clever trader with an eye for all that was true and beautiful. He did not draw or paint himself, but my mother was convinced that he had an artist's eye and that I inherited whatever talent I had from him.

'But now, thank God, I have found you. Do you know, I have been haunting that blessed park ever since I came back to England? Do you ever go there these days?'

'Hardly ever. My life has changed since I last saw you.'

He looked at her keenly. 'You have not been happy?'

'No.'

Suddenly he rose from his chair, took her hands, and pulled her to her feet. 'Melissa, do you care for me at all?' he asked.

She looked into his face and saw his grey eyes, anxious for her answer.

'Yes, I do,' she whispered.

His anxiety melted away and his smile was radiant as he drew her closer. Suddenly the conservatory became a place of enchantment. The perfume of the flowers enfolded them and her senses reeled.

'Melissa . . .' he whispered.

'Ahem.' The polite cough came from the doorway of the conservatory. They sprang apart. James's aunt was standing there.

'As I don't want my excellent cook to give her notice I would be glad if you would come to the table now,' she said. 'You can tell me anything I need to know or not, as you wish, over luncheon.'

'It sounds like a story in a romantic novel,' Reenie said. They were sitting at a window table in the café and Melissa had told her what had happened. 'Did he take your hand and declare his love for you?'

Melissa laughed. 'Sometimes I think you should be writing novels, not just reading them. But there was a moment when I did feel like a romantic heroine.'

'When was that?'

'At the first touch of his hand. You've said it yourself. My hands are a disgrace, but he didn't seem to notice.'

'Too carried away with passion, I should think.'

'Reenie!'

'So what happened after his aunt came into the conservatory?' Reenie asked.

'We had lunch and afterwards James had to go and start painting a portrait of some rich lady and I began work on Miss Surtees' gowns.'

'Why are you frowning?'

'What will Miss Surtees think when I tell her why the Wintertons dismissed me?'

Reenie looked grave. 'I suppose you have to tell her?'

'You know I must be honest.'

'What did James say about it?'

'I haven't told him either. I told you, we didn't have the chance to talk.'

'If he cares for you he will understand how it happened.'

'Do you think so?'

'I've met the lad, remember, and I do.'

Melissa looked hopeful for a moment but then she sighed. 'But that's not all, is it? What about my position here? Ella needs me.'

Reenie grinned. 'Divven't fret over that. Me and Mrs Malone hev got on famously today and we've had a good old chinwag. I'm going to come here every week on me day off and let you gan to Miss Surtees' house.'

'I can't let you do that.'

'Try stopping me. And by the way, I think Danny wants me to come too.'

Reenie glanced over to the counter where Danny was carefully filling up a pot of tea for the two railway men who had just come in. He sensed her gaze, looked over and smiled.

'In fact we get on so well,' Reenie continued, 'that I wouldn't be surprised if Mrs Malone is wondering whether she'd like *me* to be her daughter-in-law one day.'

Melissa was stunned. She didn't know what to say.

'You didn't tell me that part of the plan, did you?' Reenie asked.

'No . . . I thought it was up to me to sort it out.'

'Well, you should hev told me. I would have set your mind at rest straight away.'

'But you can't do this just for me.'

'It's not just for you. I've telt you, I love coming here. Oh, I know it's hard work but it's a damn sight more cheerful than the Wintertons' house. The mood there's been terrible since Mr Winterton apparently found some letters that Mrs Winterton had been hiding. Ena says he threw them on the fire and telt his wife she was a deceitful ingrate – whatever that means. And now she can't say anything to him – I think she's frightened of him – so she's taking it out on the rest of us. I'm not the only one who'd like to give notice. But, anyways, Melissa, don't you think I could make a good job of running this place?'

'I'm sure you could. But . . . but do you like Danny enough to marry him?'

'Well . . . I look forward to seeing him and we get on together and we hev a good laugh. Bless him, he's the nicest-natured fellow I've ever come across, and where would I meet a man like that if I stayed in the Wintertons' house?

'I'm not romantic like you, Melissa, neither am I beautiful.' She raised a hand. 'No, don't go on about my good bones and all that. Chances are I'll turn into a scrawny old woman. And this way, if things work out, I'll be a scrawny old woman with a bonny, fine set-up husband and a good business to run. Forget all about that part of your problem. It's solved.'

Melissa relaxed a little. As usual, Reenie's positive attitude had cheered her and allowed her to believe that everything would be all right. The café had filled while they were talking, and Melissa, Reenie and Danny had no time to talk until all the customers were served and happy with their meals.

Jack called in to see how Ella was. He had brought a bunch of flowers, a mixed bunch of stocks and sweet william. They were from his own garden, he explained. And the expression on his face told Melissa that this high-principled man, who would always keep the promise he had made before God, nevertheless was in love with Ella Malone.

When the café was closed Ella came down, and she and Danny sat in the kitchen for a bite of supper. Melissa walked with Reenie to the tram stop near the station. It was already dusk and they did not notice two figures detach themselves from the shadows and begin to follow them.

After saying goodbye to Reenie, Melissa went to the soup kitchen in the old almshouse. Mrs Simmons was pleased to see her.

'I've been so worried about you, my dear.'

'I'm sorry but I – well, I had to move and I lost my sewing machine.'

'I knew there must be some good reason; you're not the type of person to let people down.'

'But I'd still like to help. Until I buy another machine I'll do what I can by hand. It won't be as much as before.'

'Whatever you do, we'll be grateful. And, my dear, I don't know how to say this – I don't want to offend you – but if you have had troubles of some kind you should have come to me.'

On the way back to the café the streets were already filling with the sort of people who did not make themselves seen in daylight. Dark shapes huddled in the tunnel formed by the railway arch. Some of them were children. Melissa wondered, as she often had, what had become of Ginger and his little family. Perhaps one day she would be able to find them and help them. She hoped so.

Two, more substantial, figures walked some distance behind her and followed her all the way to the café where they drew back into the shadows.

'Well now, you will agree that she seems to be living here,' one said to the other.

'I do, and how fortunate that you were watching the Surtees house when she arrived there.'

'I missed my lunch and tea waiting for her to come out again,' the other said aggrievedly. 'I followed her here even though I knew you and Mama would be tucking in to a grand meal at Alvini's.'

'You did right, little brother. And you did right to come and get me. And I'm so pleased with you that I'll take you straight back to Alvini's and let you order anything on the menu – anything at all.'

When the brothers returned to the restaurant their mother was waiting for them in the private dining room they had hired.

'What a stroke of luck this might prove,' she said. 'We've been watching that house for weeks, trying to think of a way of getting in without resorting to crude breaking and entering – so risky, my dear boys. What a pity that wretched little seamstress overcharged Miss Surtees once too often. I almost had her persuaded to let me in to have a look at the wonderful flowers in the conservatory when Miss Surtees was visiting her reading circle.'

'But now it seems Miss Surtees has found another dressmaker, for as we discovered, that's what Miss Dornay's true function was at the Winterton house,' her elder son said. 'And furthermore, although I believe she did not know it, a dressmaker who once had some romantic connection with her nephew.' He turned to his brother. 'Remember the tender meetings we observed in the park?'

The Thorburn family ordered themselves a magnum of champagne.

Ella was back in the café the next day and she insisted she was fighting fit.

'She's a grand little lass, that pal of yours, a real gem,' she told Melissa.

'I know.'

'And, er – has she told you . . .' Ella suddenly looked awkward, 'has she told you that she might be getting engaged to Danny?'

'Something like that,' Melissa said.

'Look, I'm sorry, pet, I know you must be disappointed but I don't see how you could run the café along with your dressmaking business, do you?'

'No, you're right.'

'I hope this won't come between you and your pal. Her getting the man you might have married?'

'No, not at all. I want her – both of them – to be happy.'

'That's very generous of you,' Ella said. 'You're a real lady and I hope you'll find a good man for yourself one day.'

This was all spoken without irony, and as Melissa observed the way Ella looked at her son she realised that his mother would always believe that any girl who married him was lucky indeed.

Ella insisted on sending her away early to her dressmaking work in Jesmond and Melissa set off with mixed feelings. She was glad that James's aunt had come to find them in the conservatory because she knew that before things went any further with James, she must tell him exactly why the Wintertons had dismissed her.

Reenie had made her believe that James would understand, but she still felt uneasy about Miss Surtees' reaction. In her heart Melissa knew that the worst she had done was to have been naïve and unwary, but her foolishness had had serious consequences.

Miss Surtees, whose own house was filled with valuable objects, might prove to have more sympathy for the Wintertons than for Melissa. And that might cause trouble for James. But she was denied the chance of sorting anything out, for when she arrived Miss Surtees said that James had told her at lunch time that he would be late home. It wasn't just that he expected to work late but Mrs Winterton had invited him to stay for dinner.

'Mrs Winterton?' Melissa turned a gasp of surprise into a cough and covered her mouth with her handkerchief.

'Yes. That's the lady whose portrait he is painting. He says she is beautiful but makes herself look less so by trying to appear younger than she is. She wears clothes that would be more suitable for a young girl than a mature woman. But she confided in James that her husband likes her to dress that way.' Miss Surtees frowned.

'James says that he senses Mrs Winterton is, for some reason, desperate to please her husband. However, my nephew does not want to paint a flatteringly false portrait of the lady so he will have to be tactful. The Wintertons mix with all kinds of important people and this could further his career.'

Miss Surtees had gone on talking happily so she had not noticed Melissa's distress.

'Is that a summer cold you have?' she asked when she at last spotted the handkerchief.

'No, I don't think so. It's just that the town was dusty.'

'As usual,' Miss Surtees said. 'We could do with a shower of rain to settle it. Did you walk here?'

'Yes.'

'Do you know I have no idea where you live? I should have asked you that.'

'At the moment I am looking for new lodgings so I'm staying with a very kind woman who has a café near the Central Station.'

'Indeed?' Miss Surtees looked surprised but didn't question Melissa further. 'Well, the room next to my bedroom is now your sewing room. I believe everything you need is in there, but if not, you only have to ask and I will telephone Wilkinson's. Or rather I will ask you to do that. To tell you the truth I am nervous of the blessed contraption.'

Miss Surtees smiled and Melissa realised how much she liked her. This would make it all the more difficult if James's aunt disapproved of her.

She settled down to her work, but all the time, at the back of her mind, there was the worry of not having managed to tell James yesterday everything that had happened. Now it seemed the situation was worse than ever. James was painting a portrait of Mrs Winterton. He was working in the very house where she had spent so many unhappy years and where that stay had ended so disastrously.

She had just laid a gown out on the table and was about to unpick the side seams when she paused as another thought struck her. Was it at all possible that James would come across Reenie? Probably not, for Reenie was not an upstairs maid. But if chance should bring them together, what on earth would they say to each other?

While she worked she heard a slight rattling of the windowpanes and she looked up. It was raining. Had Miss Surtees the power to command the weather? She suppressed a somewhat hysterical laugh and decided to relay the incident to Reenie, who would find it as amusing as she did.

Two hours later Miss Surtees entered the room and said, 'Enough. You will strain your eyes if you continue without a break and, as it is getting late, I think you should go home now.'

'Oh . . . but . . .' Melissa began.

'I know you will be disappointed not to see James,' Miss Surtees went on kindly. 'I am not so old as to be unaware of your feelings for each other, but as he has not spoken to me, I assume there must be something that is unresolved between you.' She waited for Melissa to say something, but when she didn't Miss Surtees smiled. 'Very well, I will say no more. But I hope he will be home in time to talk to you tomorrow.'

Before Melissa left the house Miss Surtees asked if she should telephone for a cab.

'No, thank you,' Melissa said. 'The rain will have settled the dust and I need some fresh air. I would rather walk.'

They said good night and Melissa set off for the long walk back to the café. The streets in this part of town were pleasant. The houses were elegant and the gardens attractive. The recent rain had washed the pavements clean. Melissa, trying to escape from worrying thoughts, allowed her senses to be assuaged by the fragrance of many flowers and the soft rustling of the leaves.

Then, as she crossed over a lane that led to the mews blocks, a figure stepped out from behind a stone pillar to confront her. Startled, Melissa stepped back and caught her foot on the kerb. She began to fall when her arms were seized and she was pulled forward until she was resting against a man's body.

'Miss Dornay,' she heard him say.

She looked up to find herself staring into the face of Fergus Thorburn. She began to shake.

'Don't be frightened,' he said. 'I'm not going to harm you. At least I won't unless you would be so foolish as to scream and make a fuss. Now, stand up straight and put your arm through mine and we'll stroll along and talk just like any courting couple.'

'Courting – you!'

'Now I wonder how you managed to make that sound so insulting.' He laughed.

'Let go of me. I have nothing to say to you.'

'Maybe not, but I have plenty to say to you.'

'I don't want to listen.'

'I'm sure you don't, but if you care for that young man at all, I think you should.'

'Young man?'

'James. James Pennington.'

An icy fear flooded through her. 'You're not going to hurt him!'

'No, not physically.'

'What do you mean?'

'We've been watching that young man. It seems he is a talented artist. He could live a life of ease on the allowance given to him by his aunt, but he chooses to work hard and devote himself to furthering his career. But what if it became known that he was associating with a criminal?'

'I'm not a criminal!'

'There are people who think you are as good as one. The Wintertons, for instance. And I believe that he has just been commissioned by Mr Winterton to paint his wife's portrait. I wonder what Mrs Winterton would think if she discovered that James is – shall we say – very close to you.'

'But why would you tell her?'

A group of people passed them and walked towards a large house where all the lights were blazing. It looked as though there was some kind of party taking place.

'I won't if you do what I say.'

'No.'

He laughed. 'You don't even know what I'm going to ask yet.'

'Whatever it is it will be wrong.'

'In your eyes perhaps, but not in mine. What is wrong is that some people should own so many pretty but useless objects when those same things could be sold for good money and help other people.'

'Oh, so you liken yourself to Robin Hood!'

Fergus guffawed. 'I must say I admire your spirit. You have changed since the last time we met. But no, I'm no Robin Hood. I may rob the rich but I do not give to the poor. Unless you can count the Thorburn family among their number.'

'You want me to help you rob Miss Surtees.'

'I do. I shared a table with the lady in Alvini's coffee house last time we were here in Newcastle and I marked her as a likely target even then.'

'Why did you have to come back?'

'We keep moving on, but, as I say, we knew there were still rich pickings in this city. Your beloved James's aunt is not the only one.'

'Why shouldn't I tell the police about this?'

'Because if you do, everything will come out and you will lose for ever all chance of finding dressmaking clients in this city, and probably lose your sweetheart as well.'

Melissa could hear her heart pounding. She could feel it beating painfully against her ribs. She found herself gasping for air and the world began to spin. Her eyes closed, but as she began to fall Fergus grasped her arms roughly and hauled her upright.

'Don't faint on me,' he rasped.

The grip on her arms was painful and the shock brought her to her senses. She opened her eyes wide.

'That's better. Now take a deep breath and pay attention.'

'What do you want me to do?' Melissa asked weakly.

'I thought you'd see sense,' Fergus said, and she hated the smug confidence betrayed by his tone. 'You must leave one of the windows in the conservatory off the latch. Once one of us is in they'll open the door for the rest of us.'

Melissa flinched.

'Don't worry, we won't hurt anyone. They'll be asleep upstairs and we know what we're doing. They won't even know they've been burgled until they come down in the morning.'

'But what if someone notices the conservatory window is open?'

'There are plant pots on the windowsill. I know, I've been round and had a look late one night. Just make sure the opening is obscured.'

'And what excuse do I give for going into the conservatory?'

'Miss Surtees goes to her reading group tomorrow. All you have to do is make sure the little housemaid doesn't notice. Are you listening to me?'

'Yes.'

'If you do what you're told you will never see me or my kin again. If you don't I'll ruin the pleasant little life you hope will be yours one day. Do you understand?'

'Yes.'

'Good.'

Fergus Thorburn smiled and tipped his hat as if they were friends who had had a perfectly normal conversation, and then he half bowed and turned to go.

Afterwards Melissa was never quite sure which direction he had taken. He seemed to vanish as quickly as he had arrived. Sick and trembling, she leaned back against a stone pillar. Why had this happened now? Hadn't she suffered enough? Was one act of foolishness going to haunt her for the rest of her life?

Bleakly she considered the choice Fergus had offered. If she helped them gain entrance to Miss Surtees' house he had said that no one would be hurt. After the robbery he and his family would disappear. Nothing would be lost except what Fergus had called 'some pretty but useless objects'. But what about Melissa's integrity? How would she feel every time she entered Miss Surtees' home, knowing that she had betrayed her kindly trust?

And if she refused to help them would Fergus really carry out his threat and destroy her life, and James's too? Despairingly she decided that he would and it would not simply be a matter of revenge. Men like Fergus Thorburn had a reputation to live up to. In order to keep what power he had a successful criminal must not make empty threats.

Melissa fought a hollow feeling that was growing inside her, threatening to banish any remaining hope that she could find a way out of this predicament. If I go along with his plans, she thought, I would not be able to live with myself. But if I refuse to help, not only will I lose James but I may destroy his career too.

Hardly knowing where she was going Melissa began to walk. The respectable suburban streets were silent save for the echo of her footsteps. Bitterly she reflected that just a very short while ago she had been happy and her life full of renewed hope. But now the joy of meeting James would be forever tainted. And whatever decision she made her life would never be the same again.

But she could not simply leave things be. A decision, no matter how painful, must be made. With a sense of weary resignation she prepared herself for what she must do.

Chapter Twenty-Five

The next night, or rather, in the early hours of the morning, Fergus and Malcolm Thorburn, with one accomplice, left their horse-drawn van brazenly in the street outside Miss Surtees' house. They had muffled the horse's hoofs with sacking and they were blessed with an overcast and seemingly moonless sky.

They wouldn't be long, for they had bribed the dishonest seamstress well to tell them exactly where the finest pictures and *objets d'art* were to be found. Unlike the Wintertons, with their ostentatious display of wealth, Miss Surtees was known to be a collector of small but extremely valuable works of art. Fergus suspected that one picture alone would make this night's work worthwhile.

With caps covering their heads and mufflers half concealing their faces, they slipped through the gate into the front garden.

The gravel was a nuisance so they stepped over the herbaceous border and walked across the lawn until they got to the place where the paths diverged and the gravel ended. Fergus tested the conservatory window and smiled with satisfaction when he found it gave under the pressure of his hand. Their accomplice was small, slight and nimble.

'In you go and open the door for us,' Fergus said softly.

And then it seemed all hell broke loose. To the accompaniment of shrill whistles large figures materialised from the shadows and came running towards them. In no time at all they were overcome.

'The bitch!' Fergus pulled down his scarf and screamed to no one in particular. 'I'll see she pays for this.'

James, fully dressed, appeared at the conservatory door.

'It's all taken care of, sir,' the police inspector said. 'You can tell Miss Surtees to rest easy.'

'But how did you know they planned to rob us tonight?' James asked.

'As I told you earlier this evening, we were given information.'

'But by whom?'

'By your aunt's precious dressmaker!' Fergus bellowed.

'Now then . . .' the inspector began.

'What has Melissa to do with this?' James asked.

'She's helped us before,' Fergus said. 'Just ask Mrs Winterton, if you don't believe me. This time I should have offered her a bigger cut.'

'Blast you!' one of the policeman suddenly shouted. 'Look out, the little devil's got away!' The smallest of the three thieves had kicked his shins, squirmed out of his grasp and made a break for it.

'That's right – scarper!' Malcolm Thorburn, his cap knocked awry and his scarf unravelled, called after the departing figure.

Fergus laughed and shouted, 'Don't let the bastards get you!'

The policeman whose shins had been kicked so viciously was hopping up and down with pain and, for a moment, it looked as though the brothers' accomplice had escaped round the side of the house. Then a high-pitched scream of rage, followed by a string of curses, pierced the night air.

A burly policeman emerged from the shadows, pushing his captive before him. In the continuing struggle the small thief's cap fell off and a cascade of bright hair tumbled down.

'A woman,' her hefty captor said in astonishment.

The inspector stepped forward and unravelled the scarf that had been covering her face. 'Well, well,' he said. 'Mrs Thorburn, I believe?'

For an answer she stared at him defiantly.

'Well done, lads,' the inspector continued. 'We've not only caught this pair of rascals but we've snared the brains behind their criminal activities too.'

'Damn you!' Clarice Thorburn spat. 'Damn you to hell!'

The inspector made a signal and the three Thorburns were placed in handcuffs. 'No, madam,' he said. 'We're not going to hell. You are. For someone like you and your precious sons, prison will be hell on earth and I can guarantee you all will be staying there for a very long time.'

He paused and addressed the company in general. 'I think Miss Dornay has more than made up for the trouble she caused us once before.'

The thieves were led away and James was left trying to make sense of everything he'd heard.

'I'm afraid it is quite true,' Lilian Winterton said to James some hours later. 'That is why we dismissed her. I told her that I would make sure she never entered a decent house again and I would blame myself for this if it were not for the fact that your aunt ought to have asked her to provide references.'

'But Melissa told the police about the planned robbery herself,' James said. 'Why would she do that if she were part of the gang?'

'Probably, as the thief said, he didn't offer her a big enough inducement.'

James had to control a spurt of anger. He did not want to believe one word this dreadful woman had uttered. He let his thoughts return to the day before. Melissa had gone by the time he got home and, as his aunt had been out, she could not tell him the reason. Was it because Melissa did not want to see him any more? Had she only been interested in his aunt's wealth?

He remembered how Melissa and Reenie would play games of pretend. Were the games as innocent as Melissa had claimed or were they all part of some bigger game? Some criminal game?

'Mr Pennington, shall we get on with the sitting?' Mrs Winterton asked.

'No, I don't think so.'

'I beg your pardon?'

'I find that I no longer wish to paint your portrait. I'm sorry.'

James walked from the room, leaving Lilian Winterton astounded.

As he hurried away from the house he heard his name being called. He turned to find Reenie running after him.

'She said you'd be here and she said I had to tell you,' she said breathlessly.

'Reenie, I don't know what you're talking about.'

'I didn't know it was you who was painting Mrs Winterton's portrait, but Melissa told me you were and that I was to watch out for you today.'

'You've spoken to her?'

'Yes. She called here early this morning. She came to the kitchen door.'

'You know where she is?'

'She told me not to tell you but I had to say that she was sorry and she asked me to give you this letter.' Reenie handed him a thick envelope and, despite the circumstances, she grinned. 'I think she's written a whole book. You'd better go and sit somewhere quiet and read it. She says she's explained everything.'

After James had gone Reenie went back to the house to find Mrs Winterton standing in the open front doorway.

'What do you think you've been doing?' she asked.

'Giving a letter to Mr Pennington.'

'From Melissa Dornay, I presume?'

'Aye.'

'And who gave you permission to do so?'

'No one.'

'Insolent girl. Speak to me like that again and I will dismiss you. Now come here and tell me what you know about this business.'

'No I won't.'

'Then pack your bags and leave this house immediately.'

'Aye,' Reenie smiled broadly. 'I will.'

Lilian Winterton's rage carried her up the grand staircase and along the passage to her morning room on the first floor. The décor that she had once thought so tasteful now seemed to be a discordant *mélange* of sickly green and harsh blues. Her head aching and her stomach churning, she crossed to the fireplace and pulled the bell cord ferociously.

When Ena appeared she snapped, 'You took your time!'

'I came as quickly as I could, madam,' the lady's maid said.

'Bring me a pot of tea,' Lilian ordered. 'And take that smirk off your face!'

Her expression impassive, Ena replied, 'I wasn't smirking, madam. Why would I smirk at you?' Without waiting for a reply the maid left the room.

Lilian was left seething with impotent fury. The girl had seemed to be completely unperturbed by the accusation and, furthermore, she had given the impression of not caring what

Lilian said to her. She despises me, Lilian thought. They all do. They know that Austin thinks little of me and that he can barely bring himself to speak to me since he found the letters.

Austin Winterton, irate that Lilian had exceeded her allowance yet again, had searched her writing desk for unpaid bills. As well as the bills, he had found Dermot's letters. Lilian still trembled when she recalled his rage. She imagined that the whole household had heard his angry bellowing. But the chilling contempt that followed had been even worse. No wonder the servants didn't respect her when her husband treated her with such disdain.

Since then she had tried desperately to please him, to charm him, to win his admiration once more, but gradually she had come to realise that it was not just her deception that had caused the change in Austin's behaviour. He had troubles of his own.

Austin never came to her bed these days. But neither did he spend any nights away from home. In the past Lilian had often wondered whether her husband was really working late and sleeping at the apartment above his offices, or whether he was visiting some establishment where his ill-disguised taste for young flesh could be catered for.

But if this were the case, something must have happened to bring this behaviour to an end. One day, some weeks ago, Lilian had searched her husband's dressing room. The tablets she found there shocked her profoundly. It was common, though unspoken, knowledge that mercury was thought to be a cure for syphilis.

She had no one she could confide in. She could not even take comfort from the granddaughter Austin refused to allow in the house.

The tea Ena brought her grew cold as she sat and contemplated the miserable years that lay ahead.

*

James sat down in the humid warmth of his aunt's conservatory and tried not to think about the moment when he had been just about to take Melissa in his arms. The memory was bittersweet: sweet because of his remembered anticipation of joy, and yet painful because now he wondered if he would ever be given that chance again.

He opened the envelope and began to read her letter and as he read it his anger grew. He was angry with the Thorburns, mother and sons, who had tricked her so cruelly, and angry with the Wintertons who, it seemed, had taken advantage of her for years and had then dealt with her so harshly.

But he was also angry with himself. Angry because for a fleeting moment in Mrs Winterton's drawing room he had doubted Melissa's integrity. The thought had entered his mind that Melissa might indeed have aided and abetted the robbery and that she had only been interested in his aunt's wealth – not James himself. He had dismissed such treacherous thoughts instantly – but he didn't know if he could forgive himself for entertaining them in the first place.

At the end of the letter Melissa asked him to forgive her. He groaned aloud. There was nothing to forgive her for. He must find her and tell her so. And he hoped fervently that they would be able to put these dreadful events behind them.

Reenie finished putting the new menus on the tables, pushed up her sleeves in a gesture that had become characteristic, and stood with her hands on her hips as she looked round the café with pleasure and approval. She breathed in the aroma of mince and dumplings coming from the kitchen where Ella was busy, and she smiled when she imagined how satisfied the customers would be at lunch time.

Danny was behind the counter filling the glass display cases with the ham and pease pudding sandwiches he had just made, and several customers were finishing off their breakfasts of bacon and eggs, black pudding, and fried bread. Reenie thought she had never been so happy in her life.

Except . . . if only Melissa were here, she thought, and then smiled ruefully. Melissa had gone, and in Reenie's opinion it had been the right thing to do. But they would continue to write to each other, and one day, Reenie was sure of it, they would see each other again.

She collected the dirty plates from one of the tables and asked the two men sitting there if they wanted their teapot filled again.

'Aye, Reenie, pet, and tell Mrs Malone that was grand.'

'I will, Mr Simpson.'

Reenie had made friends with the regular customers – postmen and railway workers – and after a week or two she knew most of their names. There wasn't much passing trade at this side of the railway viaduct. So when the lone woman entered the café Reenie looked at her curiously.

The woman was plainly but respectably dressed and she was thin and sour-looking. As soon as the door had closed behind her, her eyes swept the room as though she was looking for someone. At first Reenie wondered if she was an angry wife looking for a husband who had misbehaved.

But obviously she did not find whoever it was she was looking for because, grumpily, she sat at one of the vacant tables and picked up the menu. Reenie decided to give her a moment or two but seeing that the woman wasn't really looking at the menu she approached the table.

'Can I help you?' she asked.

The woman looked Reenie up and down and said brusquely, 'Where's the other waitress?'

'There isn't one,' Reenie said. 'There's only me.'

The woman frowned. 'I was told Melissa Dornay worked here.'

Reenie looked at her more keenly. 'Who told you that?'

'A friend of hers. Mrs Ali. Such a nice woman.' The woman made an effort to smile but both words and sentiment sounded false.

Reenie was not fooled. 'Why did you go to Mrs Ali and who are you?'

'I'm Melissa's aunt,' the woman said.

'I thought so.'

The woman was surprised. 'What do you mean, you thought so?'

'You are exactly as Melissa described.'

They stared at each other and, for a moment, Reenie thought Melissa's aunt was going to drop her artificially friendly manner and retort in kind but, although Janet Cook's expression became more pinched than ever, she maintained her pretence.

'I told Mrs Ali how worried I was.'

Yes, and poor good-hearted Sally must have been taken in by her, Reenie thought. But I'm not. 'And why is that?' she asked.

For the first time Janet Cook looked flustered. 'Well . . . I mean . . . losing her job at the Wintertons', and then being turned out of her lodgings. Naturally I wondered what became of her.'

'She found other lodgings.' Reenie was struggling to control her temper.

'Yes, I know, but her landlady was evicted, wasn't she? I talked to the old woman across the street and she said Melissa lost everything.'

'My, you have been busy.'

'I beg your pardon?'

'Pushing your nose in where it's not wanted, no doubt trying to cause even more trouble for Melissa.'

'How dare you! I told you, I'm her aunt and I want to help her.'

'And how did you plan to do that? Were you going to come here and tell Mrs Malone the whole story? The story according to you, that is. Were you going to try and get Melissa turned out of here too?'

'What a wicked thing to suggest! Why would I do that?'

'Jealousy.'

'I beg your pardon?'

'You were jealous of your own sister – oh, yes, Melissa told me all about you – and when the poor woman died and you couldn't torment her any more you decided to take it out on her daughter. Well, you're too late.'

'What do you mean?'

'Mrs Malone already knows the truth of it.'

'Yes, I do.' Reenie turned to find Ella standing behind her. 'Melissa told me everything and there's nothing you could say that would make me think ill of her. And now I want you to leave my café.'

Trying to keep her dignity Janet Cook rose to her feet. 'But—' she began.

'And if you're not quick about it, that fine son of mine,' Ella turned her head towards Danny, 'will escort you out into the street in a most undignified manner.'

Melissa's aunt scowled. 'All right, I'll go, but where is she? I have a right to know.'

'No you don't,' Ella said. 'But I will tell you this much. She's gone somewhere where you'll never find her. Now get out.'

'Melissa, my dear, is the heat too much for you?'

'No, I'm fine. I think I'm getting used to it.'

'Well, you've been here for a month now, so perhaps you're becoming acclimatised.'

Miss Robson and Melissa were sitting in the shade of an umbrella at a little café in a square made elegant with lime trees. At the far side of the square a flower seller had a magnificent display of blooms so bright that they almost hurt the eye.

From the park came the sound of the band. They were playing a medley of tunes from the London stage. Melissa visualised the gay uniforms of the bandsmen and the fashionable summer gowns of the women in the largely English audience. As Harriet Robson had written, so many British people had settled here in Pau.

The waiter brought them the iced lemonade they had ordered and Melissa clasped the glass, glad to feel its cool surface through the fabric of her white lace gloves. She sipped the lemonade gratefully.

'I can't tell you how happy I am that you came here,' Miss Robson said.

'And I am grateful that you let me stay.'

'Tell me, my dear, now that you are here in your father's native land, does it make you feel at all . . . well . . . French?'

Melissa smiled. 'Yes, in a way.'

'Good.'

'But I must find work,' Melissa said. 'I cannot allow you to keep me in idleness like this.'

'Well, if you are ready, I can find plenty work for you, my dear. Amelia, her daughters and many of her friends are excited and impatient at the thought of having a good dressmaker here in Pau.'

'How do they know I'm good?'

'Because I've told them.'

Melissa laughed.

'And I've also shown them your doll, Ninette, and the

wonderful clothes you have designed for her. But now I must go. I must keep my appointment with some local children whose parents are anxious that I should teach them English.' Miss Robson rose from the table. 'What will you do, now? Go back to the house?'

'No, I may go for a walk.'

'I was about to suggest that. Why don't you stroll along the Boulevard des Pyrénées and gaze at the wonderful view?'

'I will.'

Melissa tried her best to smile but as Miss Robson watched her walk away she grieved to see how dejected the girl was. When she had first arrived Melissa had been completely honest with her and told her the whole sorry story of her life since her mother had died.

She had also told her how fortunate she was to have friends like Reenie and Mrs Malone.' And how they had helped her pack what little she had and given her money to add to her savings to make the journey to France possible. She had promised to repay them as soon as she could but they had insisted it was a gift.

Melissa had told her about James Pennington and how she had instructed Reenie not to tell him where to find her. Miss Robson sensed that Melissa regretted this, for now she would never know whether James would have wanted to come or whether he would have read her letter, thrown it away in disgust, and forgotten about her.

That's why Miss Robson had sent a letter to England.

As usual Melissa found the view from the boulevard breathtaking. The road snaked along the edge of the plateau so that you could look out over the river and the plain and on to the Pyrenean peaks. On the iron handrail there were little plaques that told you which mountain was directly in front of you and how high it was.

This was a favourite place for artists, both amateur and

professional, to sketch the dramatic view. They sat on their folding stools with their palettes and their easels or their sketch pads, some of them enjoying the daily social interaction with like-minded people as much as their own artistic endeavours.

Melissa would steal a glance at their work as she passed by. Today her attention was caught by a sketch pad lying on a stool. The top page was blank. For a moment the world shifted. Melissa dragged her gaze from the page and looked up at the mountains. Eagles were soaring over the craggy slopes.

She looked back at the sketch pad and this time she saw the satchel propped up against the stool.

Most canvas satchels looked like that, didn't they?

Then the sociable chatter of those nearby faded as Melissa remembered her dreams. The dreams of love and loss and longing. The dreams that had made her cry.

The bright sun reflecting on the blank white page made her eyes ache. She closed them but she could not banish the images from her mind.

The grove of trees . . . the sylvan grove, James had called it . . . the pink and white blossoms. Had they been real or had they only trembled on the branches in her dreams?

And then there had been the voice calling.

Melissa . . .

Her dream self had run towards that voice . . . run towards James, but she had never found him.

She became aware that people were moving past her. It was time to return to hotels and villas for afternoon tea. Soon the rustle of skirts and the footsteps receded along the boulevard and she knew she was alone.

Melissa . . .

The voice in her head was louder. And then a shadow passed in front of her.

'Melissa, open your eyes.'

She caught her breath.

'For God's sake, Melissa, speak to me!'

Melissa opened her eyes slowly, not daring to hope. Not wanting to be disappointed. She wasn't. This was no dream. James Pennington stood before her.

For a long time neither of them spoke. They simply stared at each other.

Then, 'What are you doing here?' Melissa asked.

'I came to find you.'

'How did you know where I was?'

'Reenie told me.'

'I told her not to.'

'I know. I was frantic. I had to find you but Reenie had left the Wintertons. Eventually I persuaded the cook, Mrs Barton, to tell me where she had gone. But Reenie refused to tell me where you were. Until she got instructions from a higher source.'

'Who was that?'

'Your old schoolteacher, Miss Robson. She wrote to Reenie telling her that, if she loved you, she was to disobey your order. So she did. I set off for France immediately but I didn't want to turn up on your friend's doorstep in case you refused to see me. So I walked about the town and waited and hoped.'

Then a look of great sadness passed across his face. 'Melissa, did you never intend to see me again?'

'I thought it best.'

'Best!' There was a hint of anger in his voice. 'For whom?'

'For you.'

'What on earth made you believe that?'

'You read my letter. You know what I did. I thought it would ruin your career if people knew about me.'

James looked incredulous. 'Ruin my career? Oh, Melissa,

of course it wouldn't. You have done nothing wrong – and everybody who is important knows that.'

'But your aunt?'

'She read the letter you left me.'

'And what does she think about it?'

'The same as I do. In fact she thinks you should put me out of my misery as soon as possible.'

'Misery?'

'Melissa, I've missed you so. We lost each other once and now it seemed that I was going to lose you again.' He took her hand. 'Don't you know how much I love you?'

Melissa looked up into his grey eyes; a lock of hair fell down across his brow as usual. She smiled at him and, as the shadows began to steal down the sides of the mountains, he took her hands and held them as if he would never let her go. In the valley far below she could hear the tumbling waters of the river.

'Please say that you feel the same,' James said.

'I do,' Melissa whispered.

'And will you marry me?'

He read the answer in her eyes and all the misery of the past months faded as he drew her into his arms. There, on the Boulevard des Pyrénées, they kissed and Melissa felt her spirit soaring like the eagles high above the mountains.

Later, sitting in a little street café, as the lights came on and the town prepared itself for the evening activities, James reached across the table and took her hand.

'Where shall we live?' he asked. 'France or England?' He frowned for a moment and then said, 'The answer I think is to live in both countries. Live in England all summer and come here for the winter. I could paint wherever we are and you could sew; have a salon of your own in each country. Would that please you?'

'Very much.'

'Then why are you crying?'

'Because I'm thinking of my mother and how happy she would be that her dreams are about to come true.'

'And your dreams, Melissa?'

'To be with you.'

Just for You

BENITA
BROWN

[© Norman Brown]

Just for You

Picture . . .
The fashions of the time

Discover . . .
The facts behind the fiction

Revealed . . .
The inspiration behind *The Dressmaker*

Find out . . .
How Benita started writing

Just for You

The fashions of the time . . .

In the 1880s the bustle was popular, although it is difficult to understand why. At one stage the rear appendages were so large and angular that it was said you could balance a tea tray there. In my novel, Emmeline Dornay tells her daughter, Melissa, that in her opinion such a bustle makes the wearer look like the back end of a pantomime horse.

Bustles were made from a variety of materials including hoop wire, springs and horsehair. They were uncomfortable and impractical; can you imagine trying to sit down? Furthermore many of the materials of the time were heavy upholstery-weight fabrics like silk damasks, brocades, failles, deep-pile velvet, satin and heavy wools trimmed with pleats, ruffles, tassels, beads and passementerie.

In the summer, dresses were made of lighter materials such as silk, muslin and colourful cottons. However, beads, braids, fringes and other fashionable trimmings added to the weight considerably.

Gowns were almost always made in two shades of material. Vivid colours such as deep red, peacock blue, bright apple green, royal blue, purple, mandarin and sea green were used alone, in combination, or in tartan fabrics. Some colour combinations were very strange! Evening dresses were in softer hues such as white, pink, soft green or mauve, but they might be extravagantly trimmed in contrast colours such as bright red. Red of all shades was a particular favourite of the time. During the day necklines were generally quite high, often with a stand-up collar. Evening dresses had low necklines and sometimes the décolletage was quite extreme.

But what went on underneath all this finery?

A tight-laced corset was essential. Corsets were usually made of cotton or silk and could be pale blue, pink, turquoise, peach or even red. They were often trimmed with ribbons, lace and embroidery. Even respectable women wore fancy underwear.

A chemise was worn next to the skin in order to keep the corset clean. Then, on top, there were the petticoats; the first one of red flannel, the rest of silk and taffeta. A taffeta petticoat trimmed with lots of frills gave an elegant rustle. Drawers were trimmed with tucks, insertions, lace, ribbons and embroidery. They were made from cotton, linen or silk for the summer and flannel for the winter. Stockings were either black or white.

Outdoors in the winter, well-off women wore little jackets of fur, fur and velvet, or sealskin, and full-length coats in broadcloth and moiré, or velvet trimmed with Russian sable. For the evening, a sweeping full-length cloak might be worn with a collar flaring up around the face.

Shoes and boots had small Louis heels and were often coloured to match the dress. The toe might be squared at the tip, rounded or pointed. Coloured satin or fine kid was used for formal slippers and boots and kid, sometimes combined with cloth uppers in white, black or bronze, was used for informal.

The hair was dressed high, with a small fringe over the forehead. By the end of the decade pompadours were worn. This was a style whereby the hair was swept up high from the forehead. Often, fake hair pieces were used to add height and depth. The 'Titus' hairstyle was also popular. This involved cutting the hair very close to the head. The hair was then curled with hot tongs, and styled with various ornaments including flowers.

Both bonnets and hats were worn in the 1880s. Toques, turbans and boater shapes were in style. But the shape was not so important as the trimming. Veils, wings, huge bows, feathers and flowers could be seen. Most hats and were relatively small and worn off the face to show the hairstyle.

All this glamour and luxury was the preserve of society ladies, the upper middle classes and the rich such as my character Lilian Winterton, who kept her own seamstress, Melissa Dornay, to design and run up the latest fashions for her.

Further down the scale respectable housewives bought ready-made clothes of sufficiently good quality to last. If necessary the garment would at some stage be cut down and passed on to the children. The poorer members of society would visit second-hand, even third- and fourth-hand shops for garments which still had some wear in them. At Paddy's Market on the quayside in Newcastle, cast-off clothes and shoes could be bought for a few coppers.

Victorian clothes were very much a symbol of who you were, what you did for a living and how much money was in your bank account. Maybe times haven't changed so much . . .

Just for You

The facts behind the fiction . . .

My stories are set in Victorian and Edwardian times. That period fascinates me and I love the reading and research I have to do in order to get the setting right. I scour second-hand bookshops and I've built up a fine collection of recipe books, books on household management and catalogues of the time such as those produced by the Army and Navy Stores. I want my characters to wear the right clothes, eat the right food and furnish their homes exactly as 'real' people would have done.

I've got a trade catalogue of household goods and I have a marvellous time choosing such things as dinner sets, pots and pans, coal scuttles, mantelpiece clocks, photograph albums, needlework boxes and even plants for the conservatory, just as if they were for me and not for the houses and the characters in my books.

I also have old recipe books so that, in the days when food was seasonal, my characters can serve the correct meals in any given month. My favourite book is a huge tome called *The Woman's Book, Contains Everything A Woman Ought To Know*. It has chapters entitled Household Management: Cookery, Children, Home Doctor, Business Dress, Society, Careers and Citizenship, and more.

I try to make my fictional world authentic and sometimes the characters themselves can prompt even more enjoyable research. I've had to find out about the lives of servants, music hall stars, artists, photographers, office workers, shop assistants and fish lasses. And for this book I researched the lives of dressmakers. As you can imagine, I had a marvellous time with the fabrics and fashions but when it came to the lives of the women who worked in the clothing trade I discovered some harsh realities.

Dressmaking was an honest and popular employment but there were many different types of dressmaker. There were the court dressmakers who made clothes for society ladies nd who could become rich and sought after. But in the little rooms beyond the luxurious mirrored salons, the young seamstresses who worked for them endured appalling conditions.

Those who worked in the workrooms of large department stores suffered from marginally poorer conditions and although they benefitted from the training offered, the apprentices were not paid anything at all. Once they had served their two years they were paid only a few shillings for a week's hard labour. Novels written at the time often featured a young seamstress who could barely make ends meet and turned to prostitution.

A girl might think she was lucky if she was taken on as a seamstress by a reasonably wealthy family. She would have been provided with a bed and board but she would be paid very little and was often exploited.

But the most unfortunate women were those who worked in the 'sweat shops' and the home workers. In the 1880s a woman called Mrs Lavinia Casey, a home worker, made shirts at seven pence a dozen, working from seven in the morning until eleven at night. In that time, as well as looking after her children, she normally made two dozen shirts. Her total daily wage amounted to one shilling and two pence and from her weekly earnings she had to pay two shillings and sixpence for the hire of her sewing machine, plus about one shilling and three pence for sewing machine oil and sewing thread. She could barely keep her family with what she earned but if she couldn't keep up the payments for the sewing machine it would be taken away and she would not be able to go on working.

Women who were fully trained dressmakers could always aspire to set up their own little business at home. They could make up the latest fashions for their customers at a competitive price. The customer would choose a style from a magazine and agree to pay maybe five shillings or a little more if the garment was special.

In this book I've tried to recreate the lives of some of these women and I hope you will appreciate how difficult it was for Melissa to fulfil her dreams.

Just for You

The inspiration behind The Dressmaker

I'm often asked where I get my ideas from and it's difficult to give a proper answer. People, places, overheard snatches of conversation, stories in newspapers; anything can set my imagination going.

Two old prints which my husband gave me were the starting point for this book. Both pictures are entitled 'The Milliner and The Dressmaker' and each shows the same two young women and a pretty little girl. The labels on the back of the pictures say 'circa 1856' but judging by the clothes the women and the child are wearing they may be of a slightly later date.

One woman has dark hair and the other woman and the child have fair hair and look like mother and daughter. All three are dressed fashionably. Their gowns look as if they are made of satin and they are frilled and flounced with ribbon and lace trimmings. The hairstyles are elaborate and the two grown-ups wear necklaces and earrings.

In one of the pictures they are posed in what looks like a grand room with lavish furnishings. We see a hint of a fluted pillar, a sweep of heavy drapes, a large potted plant in a huge urn and an elegant sofa. The three are grouped in front of this sofa. The dark-haired young woman holds a fan in one white-gloved hand and looks on as the fair-haired woman hands a single rose to the little girl. The rose has been taken from a pretty bouquet held in the young woman's other hand.

The second picture is less formal. The dark-haired woman stands with her back to us as she reads what might be a magazine. Her head is turned towards her friend who is reading it over her shoulder. Beyond them the little girl stands before an upright piano with a fat white cat tucked under one arm. She is holding the unfortunate creature's paws over the keys of the piano. Even from the back you can tell that the cat is an unwilling pianist.

This second picture is altogether more natural and yet what is unnatural about both pictures is that these two young women are supposed to be a milliner and a dressmaker. What kind of clients do they have that they can afford to live so well and wear such gorgeous clothes and jewellery? Why are they taking their ease and why is there not a hint of their workroom in sight?

I began to wonder about them. Are they perhaps court dressmakers with a salon in Bond Street and a host of rich clients? No, they look too young to have achieved such success. It's not surprising that their clothes are fashionable; after all, they could have made them themselves; but what about the jewellery and their obviously more-than-comfortable lifestyle?

Sadly, I decided that these pretty young women had turned to an older profession, as many pretty young dressmakers did in those times. I began to speculate about their lives and about the lives of other dressmakers. That's when another girl walked on to the stage: Melissa, a talented dressmaker who was determined to succeed honourably. I found Melissa and the world she inhabited utterly enthralling. I hope you have enjoyed her journey from difficult beginnings to the happy ending she deserved, as much as I have.

Just for You

How I started writing

The first time I saw my work in print was when I was eight years old and I had a poem in the school magazine. I've heard other authors say that they always wanted to be a writer. At the time I'm not sure I knew exactly what a writer was, but I knew that I wanted to write. I had other stories and poems published in the school magazine but after I left school there was a long gap – not that I gave up trying.

When my father asked me what I wanted for my twenty-first birthday I asked him for a typewriter. I still have it – a portable Olivetti Lettera that went everywhere with me, even on holiday. I wrote stories and plays without much success.

Then, when I was at home with my second baby, I used to listen to the BBC *Morning Story* and felt inspired to try and write one. My story was based on my teaching experience in London. I sent it off to the BBC but my husband, who worked in broadcasting, told me not to be too hopeful as he knew they received hundreds of scripts every week. Yet my submission was accepted and I was overjoyed.

But that wasn't the way to fame and fortune. *Morning Story* never took another of my stories, although some years later I did have two or three accepted by local radio.

By now I had four children. One day just before Christmas

I saw an advertisement in a magazine saying 'Writers make more money!' The text was set in a little box surrounded by pound note symbols. Well, I'm a writer, I thought, and I'm not making any money at all.

My husband thought it might be some writing school who were after taking my money rather than giving me any, but I followed it up nonetheless – along with a lot of other impecunious writers – and soon I found myself writing scripts for the girls' picture story papers – *Mandy, Judy, Debbie* and co. It was like storyboarding; I wrote them scene by scene and an artist drew the pictures. I really enjoyed writing these scripts but I probably went on for far too long – about fourteen years!

By the time our youngest was about to go off to university I decided that I had to grow up and write a novel. To begin with I thought I'd better try something that wasn't too long, so I did my research in the local library and found the *Rainbow Romances* published by Robert Hale. I was thrilled when they accepted my first attempt and I wrote three more, using the pseudonym Clare Benedict. Then doom – the publisher decided to pull the plug. *Rainbow Romances* were no more.

The next step was something bigger – contemporary romances for *Scarlet*. I was still writing as Clare Benedict. But after I'd written my third book for them, they too closed their doors. The *Scarlet* imprint was no more.

So I had to start again. I'd always wanted to write about the region I grew up in, and the turn of the last century is a period that has always fascinated me. Newcastle was one of the richest cities in Europe during the late 1800s, and yet there was dire poverty. There was so much going on in the region – so much to write about.

I decided to go to a writers' conference. It must have been fate. When I signed up I was sent the details of some competitions. One of them was to write the first chapter of a saga. I decided to have a go and sent it off. I still have my prize which was presented after the dinner on the first night of the conference. It's on my desk beside me now: a tartan-patterned ballpoint pen.

Winning the competition gave me the confidence to go on. I finished the book, was lucky enough to find an agent, and was thrilled when Headline accepted my first saga, *A Dream of Her Own*. I'm pleased to say Headline is still going strong!